A BOOK OF SHORT STORIES

A BOOK OF
SHORT STORIES

BY
MAXIM GORKI

Edited by
AVRAHM YARMOLINSKY
and
BARONESS MOURA BUDBERG

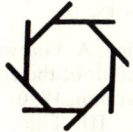

OCTAGON BOOKS
A DIVISION OF FARRAR, STRAUS AND GIROUX

New York   1973

Copyright 1939 by Holt, Rinehart and Winston, Inc.
Copyright © 1967 by Avrahm Yarmolinsky and Moura Budberg

Reprinted 1973
by arrangement with Holt, Rinehart and Winston, Inc.

OCTAGON BOOKS
A DIVISION OF FARRAR, STRAUS & GIROUX, INC.
19 Union Square West
New York, N.Y. 10003

Library of Congress Cataloging in Publication Data

Gor'kii, Maksim, 1868-1936.
   A book of short stories.

       CONTENTS: Huxley, A. Foreword.—Chelkash.—One autumn evening.—The affair of the clasps. [etc.]
      I. Yarmolinsky, Avrahm, 1890-   ed.
  II. Budberg, Moura, ed.   III. Title.
PZ3.G678Bo3 [PG3463.A15]   891.7'3'3   72-13528
ISBN 0-374-93216-6

Printed in U.S.A. by
NOBLE OFFSET PRINTERS, INC.
New York, N.Y. 10003

CONTENTS

	PAGE
FOREWORD, BY ALDOUS HUXLEY	vii
CHELKASH (1894)	1
ONE AUTUMN EVENING (1894)	43
THE AFFAIR OF THE CLASPS (1895)	53
CREATURES THAT ONCE WERE MEN (1897)	68
NOTCH (1897)	146
CHUMS (1898)	155
TWENTY-SIX MEN AND A GIRL (1899)	174
CAIN AND ARTYOM (1898)	192
RED (1900)	237
EVIL-DOERS (1901)	257
BIRTH OF A MAN (1912)	289
GOING HOME (1912)	303
LULLABY (1917)	307
THE HERMIT (1923)	327
KARAMORA (1924)	360
NOTE ON THE TRANSLATIONS	404

FOREWORD
by ALDOUS HUXLEY

WITH an author whom we have read only in translation we have no direct acquaintance; we have to infer him. Entities such as ultra-violet light and Hertzian waves are invisible and intangible; but they produce observable effects upon the world around them, and from these effects we are able to infer the nature of the forces which produce them. It is the same with literature which we cannot read in its original language. Such literature produces certain observable effects upon the translator and from the nature of these effects we are able to infer the nature of their cause. From a good translation it will be more easy to draw a reasonably correct inference than from a bad one. But even the best translation permits only of inferential knowledge, never of direct acquaintance with the spirit and essence of the original. In most cases the substitution of inferential knowledge for direct acquaintance results in a loss to the reader. Not always, however. From Mallarmé's exquisitely refined version of "The Raven," who could infer the cheapness and vulgarity of Poe's original? In English, the poem is a reciter's piece; in French, a kind of magic spell of wonderful solemnity and power.

From the translation of Gorki's writings, what are the inferences that we are able to draw concerning the nature of his art? The most significant fact that seems to emerge is that Gorki was a writer who relied for the production of his effects at least as much upon verbal texture as upon composition. There have been great writers who cared as little for verbal texture as such painters as David and the Lenains cared for the texture of their pigment. There have been others for whom, as for Chardin or Rembrandt, surface quality has seemed as significant, as profoundly expressive, as structural form. Gorki belongs to the second category. (This is why, no doubt, his work is so hard to translate, why so few translations are satisfactory.) Some of his most fundamental ideas seem to be expressed by means of variations in the surface texture of his writing. For example, the idea that, beneath all the squalor and misery and cruelty of human life, and in spite of these things, there exists an underlying reality that would reveal itself, if only men would take the trouble to uncover it, as beautiful and good—this idea is expressed almost entirely by means of variations in the verbal texture of the writing. It is not stated; it is implied by the arrangement of the words and phrases in which other matters are expressed. The device which Gorki most frequently employs for the rendering of this idea is a modulation, sudden and without transition, from the most brutal colloquialism into language of lyrical intensity and elevation. Such modulations are, of course, almost impossibly difficult to render in another language. But even from the most baldly literal of translations we can see what it is that Gorki is after, we can infer the expressive subtlety of the original.

Gorki is not content to imply the existence of beauty latent in squalor, of an underlying goodness substantial to the evils and stupidities of common life. He is also concerned, in his works of fiction, to describe virtuous characters. "The Hermit," for example, contains a subtly executed portrait of a good man, and one can find many other portraits of the same kind scattered through his writings.

Gorki's virtuous characters are interesting not only in themselves, but also because they illustrate very clearly the difficulties which imaginative writers have always had in portraying the good. Many writers have not even attempted the task. Thus, with the exception of the Duke in *Measure for Measure*, not one of Shakespeare's characters is an actively good person. (Incidentally, the Duke is not a person, but a symbol.) Of those who have attempted the task, practically all have chosen to portray good people who were, in some way or other, seriously defective. In this respect, Gorki's hermit is typical of his class. He is good—but on the verge of being dotty; good—but wholly uneducated; good—but childish to the point of having, in the innocence of his heart, deviated into incest; good—but utterly unaware of the larger problems of social life, accepting the existing social order unthinkingly, as a fish accepts the water in which it swims. We find some or all of these characteristics in the overwhelming majority of the virtuous characters in imaginative literature. Prince Myshkin is an epileptic; the Cheerybles and the later Pickwick are infantile old gentlemen, who have never grown up; Tolstoy's virtuous peasants are always peasants, hopelessly unaware of the world outside their village; Tennyson's Galahad chastely refrains from caressing the thighs of women, but can see no objection to "cleaving the casques of men"; Seraphita is a supernatural monster; Little Nell makes one feel sick; Uncle Toby never questions the rightness of Marlborough's campaigns and is an innocently charming figure of fun. There is something defective about them all. Not one of them is at once good and intelligent; good and grown-up; good without being absurd.

There are, I believe, several reasons for this curious state of things. First of all, very few imaginative writers have themselves been adult good men or women; consequently they find it extremely difficult to describe the nature of the experience of one who is both virtuous and grown-up. In the field of ethical and aesthetic values, knowledge is a function of being. We know as much or as little as our nature allows us to know. The same words carry entirely different meanings for people on different planes of being. "Charity," for example, connotes one thing to a saint, quite another thing to the average sensual man. Even if saints were accomplished imaginative writers, which they seldom are, they would probably be quite incapable of making the life of sanctity fully comprehensible, much less interesting and attractive, to the general public. They would be incapable for the simple reason that their vocabulary would not carry the same meanings as the vocabulary used by their readers. When writers attempt to portray a person who is both virtuous and grown-up, they generally succeed only in portraying a prig. Goodness combined with absurdity or mental defect is much easier to paint than goodness combined with intelligence. Not only do absurdity and mental defect facilitate the writer's task; they are also reassuring for the reader. An adequate portrait of a grown-up virtuous person would probably make the beholder feel rather uncomfortable. It would be a case of Hyperion to a satyr, with every reader in the rôle of the satyr. But if the good person is represented as being physically deformed, or silly, or uneducated, or an unthinking accepter of the existing order, no discomfort will be experienced. In some respects, at least, the reader will be able to feel himself superior to the virtuous character. Gorki's hermit does not put us to shame, because he is manifestly a half-wit. It is the same with Myshkin, the Cheerybles, Uncle Toby and the rest. Their failings permit us to retain our self-esteem. We are all shorn lambs and, unless the wind were tempered for us, should feel extremely chilly under the blast.

A. H.

A BOOK OF SHORT STORIES

CHELKASH

Darkened by the dust of the dock, the blue southern sky is murky; the burning sun looks duskily into the greenish sea, as though through a thin gray veil. It can find no reflection in the water, continually cut up by the strokes of oars, the screws of steamers, the deep, sharp keels of Turkish feluccas and other sailing vessels, that pass in all directions, plowing up the crowded harbor, where the free waves of the sea, pent up within granite walls, and crushed under the vast weights that glide over its crests, beat upon the sides of the ships and on the bank; beat and complain, churned up into foam and fouled with all sorts of refuse.

The jingle of the anchor chains, the rattle of the links of the railway trucks that bring down the cargoes, the metallic clank of sheets of iron falling on the stone pavement, the dull thud of wood, the creaking of the carts plying for hire, the whistles of the steamers, piercingly shrill and hoarsely roaring, the shouts of dock laborers, sailors, and customs officers—all these sounds melt into the deafening symphony of the working day, and hovering uncertainly hang over the harbor. And fresh waves of sound continually rise up from the earth to join them; deep, grumbling, sullen reverberations setting all around quaking; shrill, menacing notes that pierce the ear and the dusty, sultry air.

The granite, the iron, the wood, the harbor pavement, the ships and the men—all swelled the mighty strains of this frenzied, impassioned hymn to Mercury. But the voices of men, scarcely audible in it, were weak and ludicrous. And the men, too, themselves, the first source of all that uproar, were ludicrous and pitiable: their little figures, dusty, tattered, nimble, bent under the weight of goods that lay on their backs, under the weight of cares that drove them hither and thither, in the clouds of dust, in the sea of sweltering heat and din, were so trivial and small in comparison with the colossal iron monsters, the mountains of bales, the thundering railway trucks and all that they had created. Their own creation had enslaved them, and stolen away their individuality.

Heavy giant steamers, with their steam up, whistled, hissed, seemed to heave deep sighs, and in every sound that came from them could be heard the mocking note of ironical contempt for the gray, dusty shapes of men, crawling about their decks and filling their deep holds with the fruits of their slavish toil. Ludicrous and pitiable were the long strings of dock laborers bearing on their backs thousands of tons of bread, and casting it into the iron bellies of the ships to gain a few pounds of that same bread to fill their own bellies. The men, tattered, drenched with sweat, stupefied by weariness, and din and heat; and the mighty machines, created by those men, shining, well-fed, serene, in the sunshine; machines which in the last resort are, after all, not set in motion by steam, but by the muscles and blood of their creators—in this contrast was a whole poem of cruel irony.

The clamor oppressed the spirit, the dust fretted the nostrils and blinded the eyes, the sweltering heat baked and exhausted the body, and everything—buildings, men, pavement—seemed strained, ready to burst, losing patience, on the verge of exploding into some immense catastrophe, some outbreak, after which one would be able to breathe freely and easily in the air refreshed by it. On the earth there would be quietness; and that dusty uproar, deafening, fretting the nerves, driving one to melancholy frenzy, would vanish; and in town, and sea and sky, it would be still and clear and pleasant.

Twelve times there rang out the regular musical peal of the bell. When the last brazen clang had died away, the savage orchestra of toil had already lost some of its volume. A minute later it had passed into a dull, repining grumble. Now the voices of men and the splash of the sea could be heard more clearly. The dinner-hour had come.

When the dock laborers, knocking off work, had scattered about the dock in noisy groups, buying various edibles from the women hawking food, and were settling themselves to dinner in shady corners on the pavement, there walked into their midst Grishka Chelkash, an old hunted wolf, well known to all the dock population as a hardened drunkard and a bold and dexterous thief. He was barefoot and bareheaded, clad in old, threadbare, velveteen breeches, in a dirty print shirt, with a torn collar that displayed his dry, angular bones tightly covered with brown skin. From the ruffled state of his black, slightly grizzled hair and the dazed look on his keen, predatory face, it was evident that he had only just waked up. There was a straw sticking in one brown mustache, another straw clung to the scrubby bristles of his shaved left cheek, and behind his ear he had stuck a little, freshly-picked twig of lime. Long, bony, rather stooping, he paced slowly over the flags, and turning his hooked, rapacious-looking nose from side to side, he cast sharp glances about him, his cold, gray eyes glittering as he looked for someone among the dock laborers. His thick and long brown mustaches were continually twitching like a cat's whiskers, while he rubbed his hands behind his back, nervously clenching the long, crooked, clutching fingers. Even here, among hundreds of striking-looking, tattered tramps like himself, he attracted attention at once because of his resemblance to a vulture of the steppes, because of his lean, hungry look and because of that peculiar gait of his, as though pouncing down on his prey, so smooth and easy in appearance, but inwardly intent and alert, like the flight of the bird of prey that he resembled.

As he reached one of the groups of ragged dockers, reclining in the shade of a stack of coal baskets, there rose to meet him a thick-set young fellow, with purple blotches on his dull face and scratches on his neck, unmistakable traces of a recent thrashing. He got up and walked beside Chelkash, saying, in an undertone:

"The dock officers have got wind of the two cases of goods. They're on the look-out."

"Well?" queried Chelkash, coolly measuring him with his eyes.

"What do you mean, 'well'? They're on the look-out, I say. That's all."

"Did they ask for me to help them look?"

And with a smile Chelkash looked toward the storehouse of the Volunteer Fleet.

"You go to the devil!"

His companion turned away.

"Ha, wait a bit! Who's been decorating you like that? Why, what a sight they have made of your signboard! Have you seen Mishka here?"

"I've not seen him this long while!" the other shouted, and hastily went back to his companions.

Chelkash walked on, greeted by everyone as a familiar figure. But he, usually so lively and sarcastic, was unmistakably out of humor today, and made short and abrupt replies to all inquiries.

From behind a pile of goods emerged a customs-house guard, a dark green, dusty figure, of military erectness. He barred the way for Chelkash, standing before him in a

CHELKASH

challenging attitude, his left hand clutching the hilt of his dirk, while with his right he tried to seize Chelkash by the collar.

"Stop! Where are you going?"

Chelkash drew back a step, raised his eyes, looked at the guard, and smiled dryly.

The red, good-humoredly crafty face of the watchman, in its attempt to assume a menacing air, puffed and grew round and purple, while the brows scowled, the eyes rolled, and the effect was very comic.

"You've been told—don't you dare come into the dock, or I'll break your ribs! And you're here again!" the man roared threateningly.

"How d'ye do, Semyonich! It's a long while since we've seen each other," Chelkash greeted him calmly, holding out his hand.

"Thankful never to see you again! Get along, get along!"

But yet Semyonich took the outstretched hand.

"You tell me this," Chelkash went on, his gripping fingers still keeping their hold of Semyonich's hand, and shaking it with friendly familiarity, "have you seen Mishka?"

"Mishka, indeed, who's Mishka? I don't know any Mishka. Get along, mate! or the inspector'll see you, he'll—"

"The red-haired fellow that I worked with last time on the 'Kostroma'?" Chelkash persisted.

"That you steal with, you'd better say. He's been taken to the hospital, your Mishka; his foot was crushed by an iron bar. Go away, mate, while you're asked to civilly, go away, or I'll chuck you out by the scruff of your neck."

"A-ha, that's like you! And you say—you don't know Mishka! But you do. I say, why are you so cross, Semyonich?"

"I tell you, Grishka, don't give me any of your jaw. Go-o!"

The guard began to get angry and, looking from side to side, tried to pull his hand away from Chelkash's firm grip. Chelkash looked calmly at him from under his thick eyebrows, and not letting go of his hand, went on talking.

"Don't hurry me. I'll just have my chat out with you, and then I'll go. Come, tell us how you're getting on; wife and children quite well?" And with a spiteful gleam in his eyes, he added, showing his teeth in a mocking grin: "I've been meaning to pay you a call for ever so long, but I've not had the time, I'm always drinking, you see."

"Now—now then—you drop that! You—none of your jokes, you bony devil. I'm in earnest, my man. So you mean you've come down to stealing in the houses and on the streets?"

"What for? Why, there's goods enough here to last our time—for you and me. By God, there's enough, Semyonich! So you've been filching two cases of goods, eh? Mind, Semyonich, you'd better look out! You'll get caught one day!"

The enraged Semyonich trembled and struggled, spluttering and trying to say something. Chelkash let go of his hand, and with complete composure strode back to the dock gates. The customs-house guard followed him, swearing furiously. Chelkash grew more cheerful; he whistled shrilly through his teeth, and thrusting his hands in his breeches pockets, walked with the deliberate gait of a man of leisure, firing off to right and to left biting jeers and jests. He was paid back in the same coin.

"I say, Grishka, what good care the authorities do take of you!" shouted one out of a group of dockers, who had finished dinner and were lying on the ground, resting.

"I'm barefoot, so here's Semyonich watching that I shouldn't graze my foot on anything," answered Chelkash.

They reached the gates. Two soldiers felt Chelkash all over, and gave him a slight shove into the street.

Chelkash crossed the road and sat down on a stone post opposite the door of the inn. From the dock gates rolled rumbling an endless string of laden carts. To meet them, rattled empty carts, with their drivers jolting up and down in them. The dock vomited howling din and biting dust.

Chelkash, accustomed to this frenzied uproar, felt in excellent spirits. Before him lay the attractive prospect of a substantial haul, which would call for little exertion and a great deal of dexterity; Chelkash was confident that he had plenty of the latter, and, half-closing his eyes, dreamed of how he would go on a spree tomorrow morning when the business would be over and the notes would be rustling in his pocket. Then he thought of his comrade, Mishka, who would have been very useful that night, if he had not hurt his foot; Chelkash swore to himself, thinking that, all alone, without Mishka, maybe he'd hardly manage it all. What sort of night would it be? Chelkash looked at the sky, and along the street.

Half-a-dozen paces from him, on the flagged pavement, there sat, leaning against a stone post, a young fellow in a coarse blue linen shirt, and breeches of the same, in plaited bark shoes, and a torn, reddish cap. Near him lay a little bag, and a scythe without a handle, with a wisp of hay twisted round it and carefully tied with string. The youth was broad-shouldered, squarely built, flaxen-headed, with a sunburnt and weather-beaten face, and big blue eyes that stared with confident simplicity at Chelkash.

Chelkash grinned at him, put out his tongue, and making a fearful face, stared at him with bulging eyes.

The young fellow at first blinked in bewilderment, but then, suddenly bursting into a guffaw, shouted through his laughter: "Oh! you funny chap!" and half getting up from the ground, rolled clumsily from his post to Chelkash's, dragging his bag in the dust, and knocking the heel of his scythe on the stones.

"Eh, mate, you've been on the spree, one can see!" he said to Chelkash, pulling at one leg of his trousers.

"That's so, suckling, that's so indeed!" Chelkash admitted frankly; he took at once to this healthy, simple-hearted youth, with his childish clear eyes. "Been off mowing, eh?"

"To be sure! You've to mow a verst to earn a groat! It's a poor business! Folks—crowds of them! Men had come tramping from the famine parts. They've knocked down the prices so, it doesn't pay. Sixty kopecks they paid in Kuban. And in years gone by, they do say, it was three, and four, and five rubles."

"In years gone by! Why, in years gone by, for the mere sight of a Russian they paid three rubles out that way. Ten years ago I used to make a regular trade of it. One would go to a settlement—'I'm a Russian,' one said—and they'd come and gaze at you at once, feel you, wonder at you, and—you'd get three rubles. And they'd give you food and drink—stay as long as you like!"

As the youth listened to Chelkash, at first his mouth dropped open, his round face expressing bewildered rapture; then, grasping the fact that this tattered fellow was romancing, he smacked his lips and guffawed. Chelkash kept a serious face, hiding his smile in his mustache.

"You funny chap, you chaff away as though it were the truth, and I listen and believe you! No, upon my soul, in years gone by—"

"Why, and didn't I say so? To be sure, I'm telling you how in years gone by—"

"Go on!" the lad waved his hand. "A cobbler, eh? or a tailor? or what are you?"

"I?" Chelkash queried, and after a moment's thought he said: "I'm a fisherman."

"A fi-isherman! Really? You catch fish?"

"Why fish? Fishermen about here don't catch fish only. They fish more for drowned men, old anchors, sunk ships —everything! There are hooks on purpose for all that."

"Go on! That sort of fishermen, maybe, that sing of themselves:

> We cast our nets
> Over banks that are dry,
> Over storerooms and pantries!

"Why, have you seen any of that sort?" inquired Chelkash, looking at him with a sneer.

"No, seen them I haven't! I've heard tell."

"Do you like them?"

"Like them? Maybe. They're all right, fine bold chaps —free."

"And what's—freedom to you? Do you care for freedom?"

"Well, I should think so! Be your own master, go where you please, do as you like. To be sure! If you know how to behave yourself, and you've nothing weighing upon you—it's first rate. Enjoy yourself all you can, only be mindful of God."

Chelkash spat contemptuously, and turning away from the youth, dropped the conversation.

"Here's my case now," the latter began, with sudden animation. "As my father's dead, my bit of land's small, my mother's old, all the land's sucked dry, what am I to do? I must live. And how? There's no telling.

"Am I to marry into some well-to-do house? I'd be glad to, if only they'd let their daughter have her share apart.

"Not a bit of it, the devil of a father-in-law won't consent to that. And so I shall have to slave for him—for ever so long—for years. A nice state of things, you know!

"But if I could earn a hundred or a hundred and fifty rubles, I could stand on my own feet, and look askance at old Antip, and tell him straight out! Will you give Marfa her share apart? No? all right, then! Thank God, she's not the only girl in the village. And I should be, I mean, quite free and independent."

"Ah, yes!" the young man sighed. "But as 'tis, there's nothing for it, but to marry and live at my father-in-law's. I was thinking I'd go, d'ye see, to Kuban, and make some two hundred rubles—straight off! Be a gentleman! But there, it was no go! It didn't come off. Well, I suppose I'll have to be a hired man. For I'll never manage on my own bit—not anyhow. Heigh-ho!"

The lad extremely disliked the idea of bondage to his future father-in-law. His face positively darkened and looked gloomy. He shifted clumsily on the ground.

Chelkash asked him: "Where are you going now?"

"Why, where should I go? Home, to be sure."

"Well, mate, I couldn't be sure of that, you might be on your way to Turkey."

"To Tu-urkey!" drawled the youth. "Why, what good Christian ever goes there! Well, I never!"

"Oh, you fool!" sighed Chelkash, and again he turned away from his companion. This stalwart village lad roused some feeling in him. It was a vague feeling of annoyance, that grew instinctively, stirred deep down in his heart, and hindered him from concentrating himself on the consideration of all that he had to do that night.

The lad he had dismissed thus unceremoniously muttered something, casting occasionally a dubious glance at Chelkash. His cheeks were comically puffed out, his lips parted, and his eyes were screwed up and blinking with extreme rapidity. He had obviously not expected so rapid and insulting a termination to his conversation with this long-whiskered tramp. The tramp took no further notice

CHELKASH 11

of him. He whistled dreamily, sitting on the stone post, and beating time on it with his bare, dirty heel.

The young peasant wanted to be quits with him.

"Hi, you there, fisherman! Do you often get drunk like this?" he was beginning, but at the same instant the fisherman turned quickly towards him, and asked:

"I say, suckling! Would you like a job tonight with me? Eh? Tell me quickly!"

"What sort of a job?" the lad asked him, distrustfully.

"What! What I set you. We're going fishing. You'll row the boat."

"Well. Yes. All right. I don't mind a job. Only there's this. I don't want to get into a mess with you. You're so awfully deep. You're rather shady."

Chelkash felt a scalding sensation in his breast, and with cold anger he said in a low voice:

"And you'd better hold your tongue, whatever you think, or I'll give you a tap on your nut that will make things light enough."

He jumped up from his post, tugged at his mustache with his left hand, while his sinewy right hand was clenched into a fist, hard as iron, and his eyes gleamed.

The youth was frightened. He looked quickly round him, and blinking uneasily, he, too, jumped up from the ground. Measuring one another with their eyes, they were silent.

"Well?" Chelkash queried, sullenly. He was boiling inwardly, and trembling at the affront dealt him by this young calf, whom he had despised while he talked to him, but now hated all at once because he had such clear blue eyes, such a healthy sunburned face, and stubby, strong hands; because he had somewhere a village, a home in it, because a well-to-do peasant wanted him for a son-in-law, because of all his life, past and future, and most of all, because he—this babe compared with Chelkash—dared to love freedom, which he could not appreciate, nor need. It is always unpleasant to see that a man you regard as baser or lower than yourself likes or hates the same things, and so puts himself on a level with you.

The young peasant looked at Chelkash and saw in him an employer.

"Well," he began, "I don't mind. Why, it's work I'm looking for. I don't care whom I work for, you or any other man. I only meant that you don't look like a working man—a bit too—ragged. Oh, I know that may happen to anyone. Good Lord, as though I've never seen drunkards! Lots of them! and worse than you, too."

"All right, all right! Then you agree?" Chelkash said more amicably.

"I? Ye-es! With pleasure! Name your terms."

"That's according to the job. As the job turns out. According to our catch, that's to say. Five rubles you may get. Do you see?"

But now it was a question of money, and in that the peasant wished to be precise, and demanded the same exactness from his employer. His distrust and suspicion revived.

"That's not my way of doing business, mate!"

Chelkash threw himself into his part.

"Don't argue, wait a bit! Come into the tavern."

And they went down the street side by side, Chelkash with the dignified air of an employer, twisting his mustaches, the youth with an expression of absolute readiness to give way to him, but yet full of distrust and uneasiness.

"And what's your name?" asked Chelkash.

"Gavrila!" answered the youth.

When they had come into the dirty and smoky eating-house, and Chelkash, going up to the counter, in the familiar tone of an habitué, ordered a bottle of vodka, cabbage soup, a cut from the joint, and tea, and reckoning

CHELKASH 13

up his order, flung the waiter a brief "put it all down!" to which the waiter nodded in silence—Gavrila was at once filled with respect for his employer, who, in spite of looking like a crook, was so well known and trusted here.

"Well, now we'll have a bite and talk things over. You sit still, I'll be back in a minute."

He went out. Gavrila looked round. The restaurant was in a basement; it was damp and dark, and reeked with the stifling fumes of vodka, tobacco-smoke, tar, and some acrid odor. Facing Gavrila at another table sat a drunken man in the dress of a sailor, with a red beard, all over coal-dust and tar. Hiccuping every minute, he was droning a song all made up of broken and incoherent words, strangely sibilant and guttural sounds. He was unmistakably not a Russian.

Behind him sat two Moldavian women, tattered, black-haired, sunburned creatures, who were chanting some sort of song, too, with drunken voices.

And from the darkness beyond emerged other figures, all strangely disheveled, all half-drunk, noisy and restless.

Gavrila felt miserable here alone. He longed for his employer to come back quickly. And the din in the eating-house got louder and louder. Growing shriller every second, it all melted into one note, and it seemed like the roaring of some monstrous beast, with hundreds of different throats, vaguely enraged, trying to struggle out of this damp hole and unable to find a way out to freedom. Gavrila felt something intoxicating and oppressive creeping over him, over all his limbs, making his head reel, and his eyes grow dim, as they moved inquisitively about the eating-house.

Chelkash came in, and they began eating and drinking and talking. At the third glass Gavrila was drunk. He became lively and wanted to say something pleasant to his employer, who—the good fellow!—though he had done nothing for him yet, was entertaining him so agreeably. But the words which flowed in perfect waves to his throat, for some reason would not come from his tongue, which had suddenly grown heavy.

Chelkash looked at him and smiled sarcastically, saying:

"You're screwed! Ugh—milksop!—with five glasses! How will you work?"

"Friend!" Gavrila muttered. "Never fear! I'll do right by you! Let me kiss you! Eh?"

"Come, come! Here's another drop!"

Gavrila drank, and at last reached a condition when everything seemed waving up and down in regular undulations before his eyes. It was unpleasant and made him feel sick. His face wore an expression of foolish enthusiasm. Trying to say something, he smacked his lips absurdly and bellowed. Chelkash, watching him intently, twisted his mustaches, and kept on smiling morosely.

The eating-house roared with drunken clamor. The redheaded sailor was asleep, with his elbows on the table.

"Come, let's go then!" said Chelkash, getting up.

Gavrila tried to get up, but could not, and with a vigorous oath, he laughed a meaningless, drunken laugh.

"Quite screwed!" said Chelkash, sitting down again opposite him.

Gavrila still guffawed, staring with dull eyes at his new employer. And the latter gazed at him intently, vigilantly and thoughtfully. He saw before him a man whose life had fallen into his wolfish clutches. He, Chelkash, felt that he had the power to do with it as he pleased. He could rend it like a card, and he could help to set it on a firm footing in its peasant framework. Feeling himself master of another man, he thought that never would this peasant-lad drink of such a cup as destiny had given him, Chelkash, to drink. And he envied this young life and pitied it, sneered at it, and was even troubled over it, picturing

CHELKASH 15

to himself how it might again fall into such hands as his.

And all these feelings in the end melted in Chelkash into one—a fatherly sense of proprietorship in him. He felt sorry for the boy, and the boy was necessary to him. Then Chelkash took Gavrila under the arms, and giving him a slight shove behind with his knee, got him out into the yard of the eating-house, where he put him on the ground in the shade of a stack of wood, then he sat down beside him and lighted his pipe. Gavrila shifted about a little, muttered, and dropped asleep.

II

"Come, ready?" Chelkash asked in a low voice of Gavrila, who was busy tinkering with the oars.

"In a minute! The rowlock here's unsteady, can I just knock it in with the oar?"

"No—no! Not a sound! Push it down harder with your hand, it'll go in of itself."

They were both quietly getting out a boat, which was tied to the stern of one of a whole flotilla of barges laden with oaken pegs, and big Turkish feluccas, half unloaded, half still full of palm-oil, sandalwood, and thick trunks of cypress.

The night was dark, thick strata of ragged clouds were moving across the sky, and the sea was quiet, black, and thick as oil. It wafted a damp and salt aroma, and splashed caressingly on the sides of the vessels and the banks, gently rocking Chelkash's boat. At a long distance from the shore rose from the sea the dark outlines of vessels, thrusting up into the sky their pointed masts with lanterns of various colors at their tops. The sea reflected the lights, and was spotted with masses of yellow, quivering patches. They quivered beautifully on the velvety bosom of the soft, dull, black water. The sea slept the sound, healthy sleep of a workman, tired out by his day's toil.

"We're off!" said Gavrila, dropping the oars into the water.

"Yes!" With a vigorous turn of the rudder Chelkash drove the boat into a strip of water between two barges, and they darted rapidly over the smooth surface, that kindled into bluish phosphorescent light under the strokes of the oars. Behind the boat's stern lay a winding ribbon of this phosphorescence, broad and quivering.

"Well, how's your head, aching?" asked Chelkash, kindly.

"Awfully! Like iron ringing. I'll wet it with some water in a minute."

"Why? You'd better wet your inside, that may get rid of it." He held out a bottle to Gavrila.

"Eh? God's blessing on it!"

There was a faint gurgling sound.

"Aye! aye! like it? Enough!" Chelkash stopped him.

The boat darted on again, noiselessly and lightly threading its way among the vessels. All at once, they emerged from the labyrinth of ships, and the sea, boundless, powerful, lay open before them, stretching far into the distance, where there rose out of its waters masses of clouds, some lilac-blue with fluffy yellow edges, and some greenish like the color of the seawater, or those dismal, leaden-colored clouds that cast such heavy, dreary shadows. They crawled slowly after one another, one melting into another, one overtaking another, mingling their colors and shapes, dissolving and again arising in new forms, majestic and morose. There was something fateful in this slow procession of soulless masses. It seemed as though there, at the sea's rim, they were a countless multitude, that they would forever crawl thus sluggishly over the sky, striving with dull malignance to hinder it from peeping at the sleeping sea with its millions of golden eyes, the vari-colored, vivid stars, that shine so dreamily and stir high hopes in all who love their pure light.

"Beautiful, eh, the sea?" asked Chelkash.

"It's all right! Only I feel scared," answered Gavrila, striking the water with the oars vigorously and evenly. The water faintly gurgled and splashed under the strokes of the long oars, splashed glittering with the warm, bluish, phosphorescent light.

"Scared! What a fool!" Chelkash muttered, sarcastically.

He, the thief, loved the sea. His effervescent, nervous nature, greedy after impressions, was never weary of gazing at that dark expanse, boundless, free, and mighty. And it hurt him to hear such an answer to his question about the beauty of what he loved. Sitting in the stern, he cleft the water with his oar, and looked on ahead quietly, filled with desire to glide far on this velvety surface, not soon to quit it.

On the sea there always rose up in him a broad, warm feeling, that took possession of his whole soul, and somewhat purified it from the sordidness of daily life. He valued this, and loved to feel himself better out here in the midst of the water and the air, where the cares of life, and life itself, always lose, the former their keenness, the latter its value. At night the soft sound of its drowsy breathing hovers over the sea, and this boundless sound fills man's soul with quietude, and curbing his evil impulses, stirs in it potent dreams.

"But where's the tackle? Eh?" Gavrila asked all at once, peering uneasily into the boat.

Chelkash started.

"Tackle? I've got it in the stern."

"Why, what sort of tackle is it?" Gavrila inquired again.

But Chelkash felt ashamed to lie to this boy, and he was sorry to lose the thoughts and feelings which this peasant lad had destroyed by this question. He flew into a rage. That scalding bitterness he knew so well rose in his breast and his throat, and impressively and harshly he said to Gavrila:

"You're sitting here—and I tell you, you'd better sit quiet. And not poke your nose into what's not your business. You've been hired to row, and you'd better row. But if you can't keep your tongue from wagging, it will be a bad lookout for you. D'ye see?"

For a minute the boat quivered and stopped. The oars rested in the water, setting it foaming, and Gavrila moved uneasily on his seat.

"Row!"

A sharp oath rang out in the air. Gavrila swung the oars. The boat moved with rapid, irregular jerks, noisily cutting the water.

"Steady!"

Chelkash got up from the stern, still holding the oars in his hands, and peering with his cold eyes into the pale and twitching face of Gavrila. Crouching forward, Chelkash was like a cat on the point of springing. There was the sound of angry gnashing of teeth and of bones creaking.

"Who's calling?" rang out a surly shout from the sea.

"Now, you devil, row! Quietly! I'll kill you, you cur. Come, row! One, two! There! You only make a sound! I'll cut your throat!" hissed Chelkash.

"Mother of God—Holy Virgin—" muttered Gavrila, shaking and numb with terror and exertion.

The boat turned smoothly and went back toward the harbor, where the lights gathered more closely into a group of many colors and the straight stems of masts could be seen.

"Hi! Who's shouting?" floated across again. The voice was farther off this time. Chelkash grew calm again.

"It's yourself, friend, that's shouting!" he said in the

direction of the shouts, and then he turned to Gavrila, who was still muttering a prayer.

"Well, mate, you're in luck! If those devils had overtaken us, it would have been all over with you. D'you see? I'd have you over in a trice—to the fishes!"

Now, when Chelkash was speaking quietly and even good-humoredly, Gavrila, still shaking with terror, besought him:

"Listen, let me go! For Christ's sake, let me go! Put me on shore somewhere! Aïe-aïe-aïe! I'm done for entirely! Come, think of God, let me go! What am I to you? I can't do it! I'm not used to such things. It's the first time. Lord! Why, I shall be lost! How did you get round me, mate, eh? It's a sin! Why, you're ruining a man's soul! Such doings."

"What doings?" Chelkash asked grimly. "Eh? Well, what doings?"

He was amused by the youth's terror, and he enjoyed it and the sense that he, Chelkash, was a terrible person.

"Shady doings, mate. Let me go, for God's sake! What am I to you, eh? Friend—!"

"Hold your tongue, do! If you weren't wanted, I shouldn't have taken you. Do you understand? So, shut up!"

"Lord!" Gavrila sighed.

"Come, come! You'd better mind!" Chelkash cut him short.

But Gavrila by now could not restrain himself, and quietly sobbing, he wept, sniffed, and writhed in his seat, yet rowed vigorously, desperately. The boat shot on like an arrow. Again dark hulks of ships rose up on their way and the boat was again lost among them, winding like a top in the narrow lanes of water between them.

"Here, you listen! If anyone asks you anything—hold your tongue, if you want to get off alive! Do you see?"

"Oh—oh!" Gavrila sighed hopelessly in answer to the grim advice, and bitterly he added: "I'm a lost man!"

"Don't whine!" Chelkash whispered impressively.

This whisper deprived Gavrila of all power of grasping anything and transformed him into a senseless automaton, wholly absorbed in a chill presentiment of calamity. Mechanically he lowered the oars into the water, threw himself back, drew them out and dropped them in again, all the while staring blankly at his bast shoes. The waves splashed against the vessels with a sort of menace, a sort of warning in their drowsy sound that terrified him. The dock was reached. From its granite wall came the sound of men's voices, the splash of water, singing, and shrill whistles.

"Stop!" whispered Chelkash. "Give over rowing! Push along with your hands on the wall! Quietly, you devil!"

Gavrila, clutching at the slippery stone, pushed the boat alongside the wall. The boat moved without a sound, sliding alongside the green, shiny stone.

"Stop! Give me the oars! Give them here. Where's your passport? In the bag? Give me the bag! Come, give it here quickly! That, my dear fellow, is so you shouldn't run off. You won't run away now. Without oars you might have got off somehow, but without a passport you'll be afraid to. Wait here! But mind—if you peep—I'll find you at the bottom of the sea!"

And, all at once, clinging to something with his hands, Chelkash rose in the air and vanished over the wall.

Gavrila shuddered. It had all happened so quickly. He felt as though the cursed weight and horror that had crushed him in the presence of this lean thief with his mustaches was loosened and rolling off him. Now to run! And breathing freely, he looked round him. On his left rose a black hulk, without masts, a sort of huge coffin, a mole, untenanted, and desolate. Every splash of the water

CHELKASH

on its sides awakened a hollow, resonant echo within it, like a heavy sigh.

On the right the damp stone wall of the mole trailed its length, winding like a heavy, chill serpent. Behind him, too, could be seen black shapes of some sort, while in front, in the opening between the wall and the side of that coffin, he could see the sea, a silent waste, with the storm-clouds crawling above it. They were moving slowly, huge, ponderous, emanating terror, and ready to crush you with their weight. Everything was cold, black, sinister. Gavrila felt panic-stricken. This terror was worse than the terror inspired in him by Chelkash; it penetrated into Gavrila's bosom with icy keenness, huddled him into a cowering mass, and kept him nailed to his seat in the boat.

All around was silent. Not a sound but the sighs of the sea. The clouds were crawling over the sky as dismally as before; more of them still rose up out of the sea, and, gazing at the sky, one might believe that it, too, was a sea, but a sea in agitation and lay over that other sea beneath that was so drowsy, serene, and smooth. The clouds were like waves, flinging themselves with curly gray crests down upon the earth and into the abysses of space, from which they were torn again by the wind, and tossed back upon the rising billows of cloud, that were not yet hidden under the greenish foam of their furious agitation.

Gavrila felt crushed by this gloomy stillness and beauty, and felt that he longed to see his master come back quickly. And what if he failed to return? The time passed slowly, more slowly than those clouds crawled over the sky. And the stillness grew more sinister as time went on. From the wall of the mole came the sound of splashing, rustling, and something like whispering. It seemed to Gavrila that he would die that moment.

"Hi! Asleep? Hold it! Carefully!" sounded the hollow voice of Chelkash.

From the wall something cubical and heavy was let down. Gavrila took it into the boat. Something else like it followed. Then across the wall stretched Chelkash's long figure, the oars appeared from somewhere, Gavrila's bag dropped at his feet, and Chelkash, breathing heavily, settled himself in the stern.

Gavrila gazed at him with a glad and timid smile.

"Tired?"

"Bound to be that, calf! Come now, row your best! Put your back into it! You've earned good wages, mate. Half the job's done. Now we've only to slip under the devils' noses, and then you can take your money and go off to your Mashka. You've got a Mashka, I suppose, eh, kiddy?"

"No-o!" Gavrila strained himself to the utmost, working his chest like a pair of bellows, and his arms like steel springs. The water gurgled under the boat, and the blue streak behind the stern was broader now. Gavrila was soaked through with sweat at once, but he still rowed on with all his might. After living through such terror twice that night, he dreaded now having to go through it a third time, and longed for one thing only—to make an end quickly of this accursed task, to get on to land, and to run away from this man, before he really did kill him, or get him into prison. He resolved not to speak to him about anything, not to contradict him, to do all he told him, and, if he should succeed in getting successfully quit of him, to pay for a thanksgiving service to be said tomorrow to Nikolai the Wonder-worker. A passionate prayer was ready to burst out from his bosom. But he restrained himself, puffed like a steam-engine and was silent, glancing from under his brows at Chelkash.

The latter, with his lean, long figure bent forward like a bird about to take flight, stared into the darkness ahead of the boat with his hawk eyes, and turning his rapacious, hooked nose from side to side, gripped with one hand the rudder handle, while with the other he twirled his mustache, that was continually quivering with smiles which crooked his thin lips. Chelkash was pleased with his success, with himself, and with this youth, who had been so frightened of him and had been turned into his slave. He watched how he was toiling, and felt sorry for him, wanted to encourage him.

"Eh!" he said softly, with a grin. "Were you awfully scared, eh?"

"Oh, no!" sighed Gavrila, and he cleared his throat.

"But now you needn't work so at the oars. Ease off! There's only one place now to pass. Rest a bit."

Gavrila obediently paused, rubbed the sweat off his face with the sleeve of his shirt, and dropped the oars again into the water.

"Now, row more slowly, so that the water shouldn't bubble. We've only the gates to pass. Softly, softly. For they're serious people here, mate. They might take a pop at one in a minute. They'd give you such a bump on your forehead, you wouldn't have time to call out."

The boat now crept along over the water almost without a sound. Only from the oars dripped blue drops of water, and when they trickled into the sea, a blue patch of light was kindled for a minute where they fell. The night had become still darker and more silent. The sky was no longer like a sea in turmoil, the clouds were spread out and covered it with a smooth, heavy canopy that hung low over the water and did not stir. And the sea was still more calm and black, and stronger than ever was the warm salt smell from it.

"Ah, if only it would rain!" whispered Chelkash. "We could get through then, behind a curtain as it were."

On the right and the left of the boat, like houses rising out of the black water, stood barges, black, motionless, and gloomy. On one of them moved a light; someone was walking up and down with a lantern. The sea stroked their sides with a hollow sound of supplication, and they responded with an echo, cold and resonant, as though unwilling to yield anything.

"The coastguards!" Chelkash whispered hardly above a breath.

From the moment when he had bidden him row more slowly, Gavrila had again been overcome by that intense agony of expectation. He craned forward into the darkness, and he felt as though he were growing bigger; his bones and sinews stretched with a dull ache, his head, filled with a single idea, ached, the skin on his back twitched, and his legs seemed pricked with sharp, chill little pins and needles. His eyes ached from the strain of gazing into the darkness, whence he expected every instant something would spring up and shout to them: "Stop, thieves!"

Now when Chelkash whispered: "The coastguards!" Gavrila shuddered, and one intense, burning idea passed through him, and thrilled his taut nerves; he longed to cry out, to call men to his aid. He almost opened his mouth, and half rose from his seat, squared his chest, drew in a full draught of breath—and opened his mouth—but suddenly, struck down by a terror that smote him like a whip, he shut his eyes and rolled off his seat.

Far away on the horizon, ahead of the boat, there rose up out of the black water of the sea a huge fiery blue sword; it rose up, cleaving the darkness of night, its blade glided through the clouds in the sky, and lay, a broad blue streak on the bosom of the sea. It lay there, and within the path of its light there sprang up out of the darkness ships unseen till then, black and mute, shrouded in the thick night mist. It seemed as though they had lain long at the bottom of the sea, dragged down by the might of the tempest; and now behold they had been drawn up at the will of this blue fiery sword, born of the sea—had been drawn up to gaze upon the sky and all that was above the water. Their rigging wrapped about the masts and looked like clinging seaweeds, that had risen from the depths with these black giants caught in their snares. And it rose upward again from the sea, this terrible blue sword, —rose, cleft the night again, and again fell in another direction. And again, where it lay, there rose up out of the dark the outlines of vessels, unseen before.

Chelkash's boat stopped and rocked on the water, as though perplexed. Gavrila lay at the bottom, his face hidden in his hands, until Chelkash poked him with his boot and whispered furiously, but softly:

"Fool, it's the customs cruiser. That's the electric light! Get up, blockhead! Why, they'll turn the light on us in a minute! You'll be the ruin of yourself, you devil, and of me! Come!"

And at last, when a blow from the heel of the boot struck Gavrila's back more violently, he jumped up, still afraid to open his eyes, sat down on the seat, and, fumbling for the oars, rowed the boat on.

"Quietly! I'll kill you! Didn't I tell you? There, quietly! Ah, you fool, damn you! What are you frightened of? Eh, pig face? A lantern, that's all it is. Softly with the oars! You sour devil! They're on the look-out for smugglers. They won't get us, they've sailed too far off. Don't be frightened, lad, they won't catch us. Now we—" Chelkash looked triumphantly round. "It's over, we've rowed out of reach! Phe-ew! Come, you're in luck, you blockhead!"

Gavrila sat mute; he rowed, and breathing hard, looked askance where that fiery sword still rose and sank. He was utterly unable to believe Chelkash that it was only a reflector. The cold, blue brilliance, that cut through the darkness and made the sea gleam with silver light, had something about it inexplicable, portentous, and Gavrila now fell into a trance of miserable terror. He rowed automatically, huddled up as though expecting a blow from above, and there was no thought, no desire in him now, he was empty and soulless. The emotions of that night had gnawed away at last all that was human in him.

But Chelkash was triumphant again. His nerves, accustomed to strain, had already relaxed. His mustaches twitched voluptuously, and there was an eager light in his eyes. He felt splendid, whistled through his teeth, drew in deep breaths of the damp sea air, looked about him in the darkness, and smiled good-naturedly when his eyes rested on Gavrila.

The wind blew up and waked the sea into a sudden play of fine ripples. The clouds had become, as it were, finer and more transparent, but the sky was still covered with them. The wind, though still light, blew freely over the sea, yet the clouds were motionless and seemed plunged in some gray, dreary reverie.

"Come, mate, pull yourself together! It's high time! Why, what a fellow you are; as though all the breath had been knocked out of your skin, and only a bag of bones was left! It's all over now! Hey!"

It was pleasant to Gavrila to hear a human voice, even though Chelkash it was that spoke.

"I hear," he said softly.

"Come, then, milksop. Come, you sit at the rudder and I'll take the oars, you must be tired!"

Mechanically Gavrila changed places. When Chelkash, as he changed places with him, glanced into his face, and noticed that he was staggering on his shaking legs, he felt still sorrier for the lad. He clapped him on the shoulder.

"Come, come, don't be scared! You've earned a good sum for it. I'll pay you richly, mate. Would you like twenty-five rubles, eh?"

"I—don't want anything. Only to be on shore."

CHELKASH

Chelkash waved his hand, spat, and fell to rowing, flinging the oars far back with his long arms.

The sea had waked up. It frolicked in little waves, bringing them forth, decking them with a fringe of foam, flinging them on one another, and breaking them up into fine spray. The foam, melting, hissed and sighed, and everything was filled with the musical plash and noise. The darkness seemed more alive.

"Come, tell me," began Chelkash, "you'll go home to the village, and you'll marry and begin digging the earth and sowing corn, your wife will bear you children, food won't be too plentiful, and so you'll grind away all your life. Well? Is there such sweetness in that?"

"Sweetness, indeed!" Gavrila answered, timid and trembling. "Not much!"

Here and there the wind tore a rent in the clouds and through the gaps peeped blue bits of sky, with one or two stars. Reflected in the frolicking sea, these stars danced on the waves, vanishing and shining out again.

"More to the right!" said Chelkash. "Soon we shall be there. Well, well! It's over. A haul that's worth it! See here. One night, and I've made five hundred rubles! Eh? What do you say to that?"

"Five hundred?" Gavrila drawled, incredulously, but he was scared at once, and quickly asked, prodding the bales in the boat with his foot, "Why, what sort of thing may this be?"

"That's a costly thing. All that, if one sold it for its value, would fetch a thousand. But I sell cheap. Is that smart business?"

"Ye-es," Gavrila drawled dubiously. "If I had all that!" he sighed, recalling all at once the village, his poor little bit of land, his poverty, his mother, and all that was so far away and so near his heart; for the sake of which he had gone to seek work, for the sake of which he had suffered such agonies that night. There came back to him a flood of memories of his village, running down the steep slope to the river and losing itself in a whole forest of birch trees, willows, and mountain-ashes. "Ah, it would be grand!" he sighed mournfully.

"To be sure! I expect you'd bolt home by the railway! And wouldn't the girls make love to you at home, aye, aye! You could choose which you liked! You'd build yourself a house. No, the money, maybe, would hardly be enough for a house."

"That's true—it wouldn't do for a house. Wood's dear down our way."

"Well, never mind. You'd mend the old one. How about a horse? Have you got one?"

"A horse? Yes, I have, but a wretched old thing it is."

"Well, then, you'd have a horse. A first-rate horse! A cow—sheep—fowls of all sorts. Eh?"

"Don't talk of it! If I only could! Oh, Lord! What a life I should have!"

"Aye, mate, your life would be first-rate. I know something about such things. I had a home of my own once. My father was one of the richest in the village."

Chelkash rowed slowly. The boat danced on the waves that sportively splashed over its edge; it scarcely moved forward on the dark sea, which frolicked more and more gaily. The two men were dreaming, rocked on the water, and pensively looking around them. Chelkash had turned Gavrila's thoughts to his village with the aim of encouraging and reassuring him. At first he had talked grinning skeptically to himself under his mustaches, but afterward, as he replied to his companion and reminded him of the joys of a peasant's life, which he had so long ago wearied of, had forgotten, and only now recalled, he was gradually carried away, and, instead of questioning the peasant youth about his village and its doings, unconsciously he dropped into describing it himself:

"The great thing in the peasant's life, mate, is its freedom! You're your own master. You've your own home—worth a farthing, maybe—but it's yours! You've your own land—only a handful the whole of it—but it's yours! You're king on your own land! You're a person in your own right. You can demand respect from everyone. Isn't that so?"

Gavrila looked at him with curiosity, and he, too, warmed to the subject. During this conversation he had succeeded in forgetting with whom he had to deal, and he saw in his companion a peasant like himself—cemented to the soil for ever by the sweat of generations, and bound to it by the recollections of childhood—who had willfully broken loose from it and from its cares, and was bearing the inevitable punishment for this separation.

"That's true, brother! Ah, how true it is! Look at you, now, what you've become away from the land! Aha! The land, brother, is like a mother, you can't forget it for long."

Chelkash awaked from his reverie. He felt that scalding irritation in his chest, which always came as soon as his pride, the pride of the dare-devil, was touched by anyone, and especially by one who was of no value in his eyes.

"His tongue's set wagging!" he said savagely. "You thought, maybe, I said all that in earnest. Never fear!"

"But, you strange fellow!" Gavrila began, overawed again, "was I speaking of you? Why, there's lots like you! Ah, what a lot of unlucky people there are in the world! Tramps—"

"Take the oars, you sea-calf!" Chelkash commanded briefly, for some reason holding back a whole torrent of furious abuse which surged up into his throat.

They changed places again, and Chelkash, as he crept across the bales to the stern, felt an intense desire to give Gavrila a kick that would send him flying into the water.

The brief conversation dropped, but now Gavrila's silence even was eloquent of the country to Chelkash. He recalled the past, and forgot to steer the boat, which was turned by the current and floated away out to sea. The waves seemed to understand that this boat had missed its way, and played lightly with it, tossing it higher and higher, and kindling their gay blue light under its oars. While before Chelkash's eyes floated pictures of the past, the far past, separated from the present by the whole barrier of eleven years of vagrant life. He saw himself a child, his village, his mother, a red-cheeked plump woman, with kindly gray eyes, his father, a red-bearded giant with a stern face. He saw himself betrothed, and saw his wife, black-eyed Anfisa, with her long braid, plump, soft, and good-humored; again himself a handsome soldier in the Guards; again his father, gray now and bent with toil, and his mother wrinkled and bowed to the ground; he saw, too, the picture of his welcome in the village when he returned from the service; saw how proud his father was before all the village of his Grigory, the bewhiskered, stalwart soldier, so smart and handsome. Memory, the scourge of the unhappy, gives life to the very stones of the past, and even into poison drunk long ago pours drops of honey. . . .

Chelkash felt a rush of the softening, caressing air of home, bringing back to him the tender words of his mother and the weighty utterances of the venerable peasant, his father; many a forgotten sound and many a lush smell of mother-earth, freshly thawing, freshly plowed, and freshly covered with the emerald silk of the corn. And he felt crushed, lost, pitiful, and solitary, torn up and cast out for ever from that life which had distilled the very blood that flowed in his veins.

"Hey! But where are we going?" Gavrila asked suddenly.

CHELKASH

Chelkash started and looked round with the wary look of a bird of prey.

"Ah, the devil's taken the boat! No matter. Row a bit harder. We'll be there directly."

"You were dreaming?" Gavrila inquired, smiling.

"I'm tired," said Chelkash.

"But now, I suppose, we shan't get caught with this?" Gavrila kicked the bale with his foot.

"No. You can be easy. I shall hand it over directly and get the money. Oh, yes!"

"Five hundred?"

"Not less, I dare say."

"I say—that's a sum! If I, poor wretch, had that! Ah, I'd have a fine time with it."

"On your land?"

"To be sure! Why, I'd be off—"

And Gavrila floated off into daydreams. Chelkash was silent. His mustaches drooped, his right side was soaked by the splashing of the waves, his eyes looked sunken and had lost their brightness. All that bird-of-prey look in his figure seemed somehow eclipsed under a humiliated moodiness, that showed itself in the very folds of his dirty shirt.

He turned the boat sharply about, and steered it toward something black that stood up out of the water.

The sky was again all covered with clouds, and fine, warm rain had come on, pattering gaily on the crests of the waves.

"Stop! Easy!" commanded Chelkash.

The boat's nose knocked against the hull of the vessel.

"Are they asleep, the devils?" grumbled Chelkash, catching with his boat-hook on to some ropes that hung over the ship's side. "Hey! Let down the ladder! And this rain, too. As if it couldn't have come before! Hi, you sponges! Hi! Hi!"

"Is that Selkash?" they heard a soft purring voice say overhead.

"Come, let down the ladder."

"*Kalimera*, Selkash."

"Let down the ladder, you smoked devil!" roared Chelkash.

"Ah, how angry he is today. Ahoy!"

"Get up, Gavrila!" Chelkash said to his companion.

In a moment they were on the deck, where three dark-bearded figures, eagerly chattering together in a strange sibilant tongue, looked over the side into Chelkash's boat. The fourth, clad in a long gown, went up to him and pressed his hand without speaking, then looked suspiciously round at Gavrila.

"Get the money ready for me by the morning," Chelkash said to him shortly. "And now I'll go to sleep. Gavrila, come along! Are you hungry?"

"I'm sleepy," answered Gavrila, and five minutes later he was snoring in the dirty hold of the vessel, while Chelkash, sitting beside him, tried on somebody's boots. Dreamily spitting to one side, he whistled mournfully between his teeth. Then he stretched himself out beside Gavrila, his hands under his head, and twitching his mustaches.

The vessel rocked softly on the frolicking water, there was a fretful creaking of wood somewhere, the rain pattered softly on the deck, and the waves splashed on the ship's side. Everything was melancholy and sounded like the lullaby of a mother, who has no hope of her child's happiness. . . .

Chelkash, showing his teeth, lifted his head, looked around, and whispering something to himself, lay down again. . . . His legs wide apart, he looked like a pair of large scissors.

CHELKASH 33

III

He was the first to wake, he looked round him uneasily, but at once regained his self-possession and stared at Gavrila who was still asleep. He was sweetly snoring, and in his sleep smiled all over his childish, sunburned, healthy face. Chelkash sighed and climbed up the narrow rope-ladder. Through the port-hole he saw a leaden strip of sky. It was daylight, but a dreary autumn grayness.

Chelkash came back two hours later. His face was red, his mustaches curled up jauntily. He was wearing a pair of stout high boots, a short jacket, and leather breeches, and he looked like a sportsman. His whole costume was worn, but strong, and very becoming to him, making him look broader, covering up his angularity, and giving him a military air.

"Hi, little calf, get up!" He gave Gavrila a kick.

Gavrila started up, and, not recognizing him, stared at him in alarm with dull eyes. Chelkash guffawed.

"Well, you do look—" Gavrila brought out with a broad grin at last. "You're quite a gentleman!"

"We soon change. But, I say, you're easily scared! Aye! How many times were you ready to die last night, eh? Tell me!"

"Well, but just think, it's the first time I've ever been on such a job! I could have ruined my soul for life!"

"Well, would you go again? Eh?"

"Again? Well—that—how can I say? For what inducement? That's the point!"

"Well, if it were for two rainbows?"

"Two hundred rubles, you mean? Well—I might."

"But I say! What about your soul?"

"Oh, well—maybe one wouldn't lose it!" Gavrila smiled.

"One mightn't—and it would make a man of one for life."

Chelkash laughed good-humoredly.

"All right! That's enough joking. Let's row to land."

And soon they were in the boat again, Chelkash at the rudder, Gavrila at the oars. Above them the sky was gray, with clouds stretched evenly across it. The muddy green sea played with their boat, tossing it noisily on the waves that sportively flung bright salt drops into it. Far ahead from the boat's prow could be seen the yellow streak of the sandy shore, while from the stern there stretched away into the distance the free, gamboling sea, all furrowed over with racing flocks of billows, decked here and there with a narrow fringe of foam. Far away they could see numbers of vessels, rocking on the bosom of the sea, away on the left a whole forest of masts and the white masses of the houses of the town. From that direction there floated across the sea a dull resounding roar, that mingled with the splash of the waves into a full rich music. And over all was flung a delicate veil of ash-colored mist, that made things seem far from one another.

"Ah, there'll be a pretty dance by evening!" said Chelkash, nodding his head at the sea.

"A storm?" queried Gavrila, vigorously plowing the waves with his oars. He was already wet through from head to foot with the splashing the wind blew on him from the sea.

"Aye, aye!" Chelkash assented.

Gavrila looked inquisitively at him. . . .

"Well, how much did they give you?" he asked, at last, seeing that Chelkash was not going to begin the conversation.

"Look!" said Chelkash, holding out to Gavrila something he had pulled out of his pocket.

Gavrila saw the vari-colored notes and everything danced in brilliant rainbow tints before his eyes.

"I say! Why, I thought you were bragging! That's—how much?"

"Five hundred and forty!"

"Smart!" muttered Gavrila, with greedy eyes, watching the five hundred and forty rubles as they were put back again in Chelkash's pocket. "Well, I never! What a lot of money!" and he sighed dejectedly.

"We'll have a jolly good spree, my lad!" Chelkash cried ecstatically. "Eh, we've enough to. Never fear, mate, I'll give you your share. I'll give you forty, eh? Satisfied? If you like, I'll give it you now!"

"If—you don't mind. Well? I wouldn't say no!"

Gavrila was trembling all over with suspense and some other acute feeling that dragged at his heart.

"Ha—ha—ha! Oh, you devil's doll! 'I'd not say no!' Take it, mate, please! I beg you, indeed, take it! I don't know what to do with such a lot of money! You must help me out, take some, there!"

Chelkash held out some notes to Gavrila. He took them with a shaking hand, let go the oars, and began stuffing them away in his bosom, greedily screwing up his eyes and drawing in his breath noisily, as though he had drunk something hot. Chelkash watched him with an ironical smile. Gavrila took up the oars again and rowed nervously, hurriedly, keeping his eyes down as though he were afraid of something. His shoulders and his ears were twitching.

"You're greedy. That's bad. But, of course, you're a peasant," Chelkash said musingly.

"But see what one can do with money!" cried Gavrila, suddenly breaking into passionate excitement, and jerkily, hurriedly, as though chasing his thoughts and catching his words as they flew, he began to speak of life in the village with money and without money. Respect, plenty, joy!

Chelkash listened to him attentively, with a serious face and eyes filled with some dreamy thought. At times he smiled a smile of content. "Here we are!" Chelkash cried at last, interrupting Gavrila.

A wave caught up the boat and neatly drove it onto the sand.

"Come, mate, now it's over. We must drag the boat up farther, so that it shouldn't get washed away. They'll come and fetch it. Well, we must say good-by! It's eight versts from here to the town. What are you going to do? Coming back to the town, eh?"

Chelkash's face was radiant with a good-humoredly sly smile, and altogether he had the air of a man who had thought of something very pleasant for himself and a surprise to Gavrila. Thrusting his hand into his pocket, he rustled the notes there.

"No—I—am not coming. I—" Gavrila gasped, and seemed choking with something.

Chelkash looked at him in perplexity.

"What's the matter with you?" he asked.

"Why—" But Gavrila's face flushed, then turned gray, and he moved irresolutely, as though he were half longing to throw himself on Chelkash, or half torn by some desire, the attainment of which was hard for him.

Chelkash felt ill at ease at the sight of such excitement in this lad. He wondered what form it would take.

Gavrila began laughing strangely, a laugh that was like a sob. His head was downcast, the expression of his face Chelkash could not see; Gavrila's ears only were dimly visible, and they turned red and then pale.

"Well, damn you!" Chelkash waved his hand. "Have you fallen in love with me, or what? One might think you were a girl! Or is parting from me so upsetting? Hey, suckling! Tell me, what's wrong? Or else I'm off!"

"You're going!" Gavrila cried aloud.

The sandy waste of the shore seemed to start at his cry, and the yellow ridges of sand washed by the sea-

CHELKASH 37

waves seemed quivering. Chelkash started too. All at once Gavrila tore himself from where he stood, flung himself at Chelkash's feet, threw his arms round them, and drew them toward him. Chelkash staggered; he sat heavily down on the sand, and grinding his teeth, brandished his long arm and clenched fist in the air. But before he had time to strike he was pulled up by Gavrila's shame-faced and supplicating whisper:

"Friend! Give me—that money! Give it me, for Christ's sake! What is it to you? Why, you'll spend it one night —in only one night—while it would last me years— Give it me—I will pray for you! Continually—in three churches —for the salvation of your soul! Why, you'd cast it to the winds—while I'd put it into the land. Oh, give it me! Why, what does it mean to you? Did it cost you much? One night—and you're rich! Do a deed of mercy! You're a lost man, you see—you couldn't make your way—while I—oh, give it to me!"

Chelkash, dismayed, amazed, and wrathful, sat on the sand, thrown backward with his hands supporting him; he sat there in silence, rolling his eyes frightfully at the young peasant, who, with his head against Chelkash's knees, whispered his prayer to him in gasps. He shoved him away at last, jumped to his feet, and thrusting his hands into his pockets, flung the rainbow notes at Gavrila.

"There, cur! Swallow them!" he roared, shaking with excitement, with intense pity and hatred of this greedy slave. And as he flung him the money, he felt himself a hero.

"I'd meant to give you more, of myself. I felt sorry for you yesterday. I thought of the village. I thought: come, I'll help the lad. I was waiting to see what you'd do, whether you'd beg or not. While you!—Ah, you rag! you beggar! To be able—to torment oneself so—for money!

You fool. Greedy devils! They're beside themselves—sell themselves for five kopecks! Eh?"

"Dear friend! Christ have mercy on you! Why, what have I now! I'm a rich man!" Gavrila shrilled in ecstasy, trembling, as he stowed away the notes in his bosom. "Ah, you good man! Never will I forget you! Never! And my wife and my children—I'll bid them pray for you!"

Chelkash listened to his shrieks and wails of ecstasy, looked at his radiant face that was contorted by greedy joy, and felt that he, thief and rake as he was, cast out from everything in life, would never be so covetous, so base, would never so forget himself. Never would he be like that! And this thought and feeling, filling him with a sense of his own independence, kept him beside Gavrila on the desolate seashore.

"You've made me happy!" shrieked Gavrila, and snatching Chelkash's hand, he pressed it to his face.

Chelkash did not speak; he grinned like a wolf. Gavrila still went on pouring out his heart:

"Do you know what I was thinking about? As we rowed here—I saw—the money—thinks I—I'll give it him—you—with the oar—one blow! The money's mine, and into the sea with him—you, that is—eh! Who'll miss him? said I. And if they do find him, they won't be inquisitive how—and who it was killed him. He's not a man, thinks I, that there'd be much fuss about! He's of no use in the world! Who'd stand up for him? No, indeed—eh?"

"Give the money here!" growled Chelkash, clutching Gavrila by the throat.

Gavrila struggled away once, twice. Chelkash's other arm twisted like a snake about him—there was the sound of a shirt tearing—and Gavrila lay on the sand, with his eyes staring wildly, his fingers clutching at the air and his legs waving. Chelkash, erect, frigid, rapacious-looking, grinned maliciously, laughed a broken, biting laugh, and his mustaches twitched nervously in his sharp, angular face.

Never in all his life had he been so cruelly wounded, and never had he felt so vindictive.

"Well, are you happy now?" he asked Gavrila through his laughter, and turning his back on him he walked away in the direction of the town. But he had hardly taken two steps when Gavrila, crouched like a cat on one knee, and with a wide sweep of his arm, flung a round stone at him, viciously, shouting:

"O-one!"

Chelkash uttered a cry, clapped his hands to the nape of his neck, staggered forward, turned round to Gavrila, and fell on his face on the sand. Gavrila's heart failed him as he watched him. He saw him stir one leg, try to lift his head, and then stretch out, quivering like a bowstring. Then Gavrila rushed away into the distance, where a shaggy black cloud hung over the foggy steppe, and it was dark. The waves rustled, racing up the sand, melting into it and racing back. The foam hissed and the spray flew through the air.

It began to rain, at first slightly, but soon a steady, heavy downpour was falling in streams from the sky, weaving a regular network of fine threads of water that at once hid the steppe and the sea. Gavrila vanished behind it. For a long while nothing was to be seen but the rain and the long figure of the man stretched on the sand by the sea. But suddenly Gavrila ran back out of the rain. Like a bird he flew up to Chelkash, dropped down beside him, and began to turn him over on the ground. His hand dipped into a warm, red stickiness. He shuddered and staggered back with a face pale and distraught.

"Brother, get up!" he whispered through the patter of the rain into Chelkash's ear.

Revived by the water on his face, Chelkash came to himself, and pushed Gavrila away, saying hoarsely:
"Get—away!"
"Brother! Forgive me—it was the devil tempted me," Gavrila whispered, faltering, as he kissed Chelkash's hand.
"Go along. Get away!" he croaked.
"Take the sin from off my soul! Brother! Forgive me!"
"For—go away, do! Go to the devil!" Chelkash screamed suddenly, and he sat up on the sand. His face was pale and angry, his eyes were glazed, and kept closing, as though he were very sleepy. "What more—do you want? You've done—your job—and go away! Be off!" And he tried to kick Gavrila away, as he knelt, overwhelmed, beside him, but he could not, and would have rolled over again if Gavrila had not held him up, putting his arms round his shoulders. Chelkash's face was now on a level with Gavrila's. Both were pale and terrible-looking.
"Faugh!" Chelkash spat into the wide, open eyes of his companion.
Meekly Gavrila wiped his face with his sleeve. and murmured:
"Do as you will. I won't say a word. For Christ's sake, forgive me!"
"Sniveling idiot! Even wickedness is beyond you!" Chelkash cried scornfully, tearing a piece off his shirt from under his jacket, and without a word, clenching his teeth now and then, he began binding up his head. "Did you take the notes?" he filtered through his teeth.
"I didn't touch them, brother! I didn't want them! They bring ill luck!"
Chelkash thrust his hand into his jacket pocket, drew out a bundle of notes, put one rainbow-colored note back in his pocket, and handed all the rest to Gavrila.
"Take them and go!"
"I won't take them, brother. I can't! Forgive me!"

"T-take them, I say!" bellowed Chelkash, glaring horribly.

"Forgive me! Then I'll take them," said Gavrila, timidly, and he fell at Chelkash's feet on the damp sand, that was being liberally drenched by the rain.

"You lie, you'll take them anyhow, sniveler!" Chelkash said with conviction, and with an effort, pulling Gavrila's head up by the hair, he thrust the notes in his face.

"Take them! Take them! You didn't work for nothing, I suppose. Take it, don't be frightened! Don't be ashamed of having nearly killed a man! On account of people like me, no one will punish you. They'll say thank you, indeed, when they know of it. There, take it!"

Gavrila saw that Chelkash was laughing, and he felt relieved. He crushed the notes up tight in his hand.

"Brother! You forgive me? Won't you? Eh?" he asked tearfully.

"Brother of mine!" Chelkash mimicked him as he got, reeling, on to his legs. "What for? There's nothing to forgive. Today you do for me, tomorrow I'll do for you."

"Oh, brother, brother!" Gavrila sighed mournfully, shaking his head.

Chelkash stood facing him, he smiled strangely, and the rag on his head, growing gradually redder, began to look like a Turkish fez.

The rain streamed in bucketsful. The sea moaned with a hollow sound, and the waves beat on the shore, lashing furiously and wrathfully against it.

The two men were silent.

"Come, good-by!" Chelkash said, sarcastically.

He reeled, his legs shook, and he held his head queerly, as though he were afraid of losing it.

"Forgive me, brother!" Gavrila besought him once more.

"All right!" Chelkash answered, coldly, setting off on his way.

He walked away, staggering, and still holding his head in his left hand, while he slowly tugged at his brown mustache with the right.

Gavrila looked after him a long while, till he had disappeared in the rain, which still poured down in fine, countless streams, and wrapped everything in an impenetrable steel-gray mist.

Then Gavrila took off his soaked cap, made the sign of the cross, looked at the notes crushed up in his hand, heaved a deep sigh of relief, thrust them into his bosom, and with long, firm strides went along the shore, in the opposite direction from that Chelkash had taken.

The sea howled, flinging heavy, breaking billows on the sand of the shore, and dashing them into spray; the rain lashed the water and the earth; the wind blustered. All the air was full of roaring, howling, moaning. Neither the sea nor sky could be seen through the rain.

Soon the rain and the spray had washed away the red patch on the spot where Chelkash had lain, washed away the traces of Chelkash and the peasant lad on the sandy beach. And no trace was left on the seashore of the little drama that had been played out between two men.

1894.

ONE AUTUMN EVENING

ONE autumn evening I happened to be in a very inconvenient and unpleasant situation. I found myself penniless and without a roof over my head in the town where I had recently arrived and where I had not a single acquaintance.

Having sold, during the first few days, every scrap of clothing that I could do without, I left the town for the suburb called Ustye, where the wharves were. During the season of navigation the place seethed with activity, but now it was quiet and deserted—these were the last days of October.

Shuffling along the wet sand and examining it closely in the hope of finding some remains of food, I was roaming among the empty buildings and stalls, thinking how good it is to have a full stomach.

In our present state of culture the hunger of the soul can be satisfied more readily than that of the body. You wander through streets, you are surrounded by structures with pleasing exteriors and, you may be sure, agreeable interiors. This may start a trend of comforting ideas regarding architecture, hygiene, and other wise and sublime topics. You meet people suitably and warmly dressed—they are civil, they get out of your way, tactfully preferring not to notice the melancholy fact of your existence. Honestly, the soul of a hungry man is always better nourished than the soul of a well-fed man, a fact from which a very entertaining conclusion may be drawn in favor of the well-fed! . . .

. . . Evening was drawing in, it was raining, and a gust of wind was blowing from the north. It whistled through the empty stalls and shops, thumped against the boarded-up windows of inns, and under its blows the river foamed, its waves splashing noisily against the sandy shore, tossing their white crests, rushing into the dim distance, one leaping over the other. The river seemed to be feeling the approach of winter and fleeing in fear from the icy fetters with which the north wind could chain it that very night. The sky was heavy and lowering, and steadily exuded a fine drizzle. Two battered, deformed willow trees, and a boat turned upside down at their roots, stressed the elegiac sadness of Nature around me.

A boat with a broken bottom, pitiful, aged trees rifled by the cold wind . . . everything was ruined, barren, dead, and the sky was shedding incessant tears. Around me was but a gloomy waste. It seemed to me that soon I would be the only living thing amidst this death, and that cold death awaited me too.

And I was then only seventeen years old—a glorious age!

I kept on walking along the cold, wet sand, beating a tattoo with my teeth in honor of cold and hunger. Suddenly, as in my vain search for food, I rounded a stall, I noticed a crouching figure in woman's clothes that were wet with rain and that clung to its bent shoulders. Standing over her, I tried to see what she was doing. She was digging in the sand with her hands, trying to get under one of the stalls.

"Why are you doing that?" I asked, crouching beside her.

She cried out softly and jumped to her feet. Now that she stood and looked at me out of her wide-open gray eyes that were full of fear, I saw that she was a girl of my own age, with a very attractive face which was unfortunately embellished with three large bruises. This spoiled it, although they were placed with remarkable symmetry: two of equal size under the eyes, and one somewhat larger on the forehead above the bridge of the nose. This symmetry evi-

ONE AUTUMN EVENING 45

denced the work of an artist who had grown adept in the business of marring human faces.

The girl looked at me, and gradually the fear faded out of her eyes. . . . She shook the sand from her hands, adjusted the cotton kerchief on her head, hunched her shoulders, and said:

"I suppose you want to eat, too? . . . Go on digging. My hands are tired. Over there—" she nodded in the direction of a stall—"there must be bread. . . . They're still doing business at that stall."

I began digging. After waiting awhile and watching me, she sat down beside me and began to help me.

We worked in silence. I cannot say now whether at that time I had in mind the criminal code, morality, the rights of property, and the other things that, in the opinion of the well-informed, one must remember every moment of one's life. To be as truthful as possible, I must confess that I was so busy digging under the stall that I completely forgot about everything except what could be found in the stall.

With the advance of evening, the cold, damp, unwholesome darkness was thickening around us. The noise of the waves seemed to be somewhat muffled, but the rain thrummed against the boards of the stall more loudly and heavily. . . . The rattle of the night-watchman could already be heard. . . .

"Does it have a floor or not?" asked my helper in a low voice. I did not understand what she was talking about, and I said nothing.

"I say, does the stall have a floor? If it does, we're working for nothing. Suppose we do dig a pit and then we find heavy boards. . . . How are we going to pry them loose? It's better to break the lock . . . it isn't much of a lock."

Good ideas rarely enter women's heads, but, as you see, they do enter sometimes. I have always prized good ideas and as far as possible have tried to take advantage of them.

Having located the padlock, I pulled at it and wrenched it off together with the rings. My accomplice immediately stooped and wriggled like a snake into the square opening of the stall. From within came her approving voice:

"Good work!"

The smallest praise from a woman is dearer to me than a paean from a man, even if he have the eloquence of all the ancient orators taken together. But in those days I was less appreciative than I am now, and without paying any attention to the girl's compliment I asked her curtly and anxiously:

"Anything there?"

She began to enumerate her discoveries monotonously:

"A basket with bottles, empty sacks, an umbrella, an iron pail."

All this was not edible. I felt that my hopes were sinking. . . . Suddenly she cried excitedly:

"Aha! There it is!"

"What?"

"Bread . . . a loaf . . . only it's wet . . . take it!"

A loaf rolled to my feet and after it herself, my valiant accomplice. I had already broken off a piece, stuffed it into my mouth, and was chewing it . . .

"Give me some! . . . And we must get out of here. Where shall we go?" She peered into the wet, noisy darkness in every direction.

"There's a boat turned over, there. Shall we go to it?"

"Let's!" And we set off, tearing our booty to pieces as we went, and stuffing them into our mouths. . . . The rain was falling more heavily, the river roared; a long-drawn-out, mocking whistle sounded from far away, as though some fearless giant were hissing all earthly institutions and this wretched autumn evening, and us, its two heroes. The

ONE AUTUMN EVENING

whistling made my heart ache; nevertheless I ate greedily, and so did the girl, who walked to the left of me.

"What's your name?" I asked her, not knowing why.

"Natasha," she answered, chewing noisily.

I looked at her, and pain wrenched my heart. I looked into the dark in front of me, and it seemed to me as though the ironic phiz of my destiny were smiling at me enigmatically and coldly. . . .

. . . .

. . . The rain drummed tirelessly on the boat, and its soft patter brought on sad thoughts. The wind whistled as it drove through a hole in the broken bottom, where a loose splinter was vibrating with a disquieting, mournful sound. The waves splashed against the shore, and their roar was monotonous and hopeless, as though they were relating something intolerably tedious and depressing, something of which they had grown utterly weary and which they were trying to escape, but about which they must nevertheless keep on talking. The noise of the rain blended with the splashing of the waves, and above the turned-over boat there floated the long-drawn-out, heavy sigh of the earth, wearied and outraged by the eternal succession of warm bright summer and cold, damp, misty autumn. The wind moved over the deserted shore and the foaming river, moved and sang mournful songs. . . .

Our shelter under the boat was without any creature comforts: it was cramped, damp, and through the hole in the bottom came fine, cold drops of rain and gusts of wind. We sat silently and shivered with cold. I remember I wanted to sleep. Natasha leaned her back against the side of the boat, curled up into a little ball. Hugging her knees, and resting her chin on them, she stared at the river with wide-open eyes. On the pale patch of her face they seemed enormous, because of the bruises below them. She did not stir, and her immobility and silence gradually roused in me a kind of fear. I wanted to talk to her, but I did not know how to start.

She was the first to speak.

"What a cursed life!" she declared, speaking distinctly, deliberately, and with profound conviction.

It was not a complaint. There was too much indifference in her tone. It was simply that she had thought it over and had arrived at a certain conclusion, which she expressed aloud. As I could not deny it without contradicting myself, I held my peace, and she continued to sit there, motionless, as though not noticing me.

"If I could croak . . ." Natasha began again, this time in a quiet, reflective tone, and again there was no trace of complaint in her voice. It was clear that, having thought about life, and having considered her own case, she had calmly arrived at the conclusion that to protect herself from life's mockery, she could do nothing better than to "croak," as she put it.

The clarity of her thinking sickened me inexpressibly, and I felt that if I continued to be silent I was sure to cry. . . . And it would have been all the more shameful to do it before this woman, especially since she wasn't crying. I decided to engage her in conversation.

"Who beat you up?" I asked her, not having thought of anything better to say.

"It's all Pashka." she answered in an even, resonant voice.

"Who is he?"

"My lover. . . . A baker. . . ."

"Does he beat you often?"

"Every time he gets drunk he beats me up. . . ."

And suddenly, moving closer to me, she began telling me about herself, Pashka, and the relations that existed between them. She was a girl of the streets, and he, the baker, had a red mustache and played the harmonica very well. He had visited the house, and she had liked him very much because he was jovial and dressed neatly. He wore a fifteen-ruble coat and accordion-pleated boots. For these reasons she had fallen in love with him, and he had become her "man." And having established himself in this position, he proceeded to take away from her the money that other guests gave her for candy, and getting drunk on it, would beat her up. What was worse was that he began to take up with other girls before her very eyes. . . .

"Doesn't that hurt me? I'm no worse than the others. He is simply making a fool of me, the scoundrel. The day before yesterday I got leave of the madam to go for a walk, I came to his place, and there was Dunka sitting with him, drunk. And he, too, was soused. I says to him: 'You scoundrel, you crook, you!' He beat me up plenty. He kicked me and pulled me by the hair, and more. I wouldn't have minded that so much, but he tore my clothes. What can I do now? How can I show myself to the madam? He ripped everything . . . my dress, my jacket, and it was quite new . . . and he pulled the kerchief off my head. . . . Lord! What will become of me now," she suddenly wailed in an anguished, broken voice.

The wind was howling, growing colder and sharper. . . . Again my teeth began to jig, and she too shrugged together with cold. She pressed so close to me that I could see the gleam of her eyes through the darkness.

"What blackguards all you men are! I'd like to trample on you, I'd like to maim you! If one of you was croaking, I'd spit in his mug without any pity. Mean, nasty things! You wheedle and wheedle, you wag your tails like nasty curs, but once we're fools enough to give ourselves to you, it's all over with us! You step on us right away. . . . You mangy loafers!"

She cursed richly, but her curses were without strength; she had neither malice nor hatred toward these "mangy loafers," as far as I could hear. The tone of her speech was out of keeping with its substance, for she spoke calmly and there was no variation in her voice. But it affected me more forcibly than the most eloquent and convincing books and speeches of a pessimistic cast, of which I have read and heard enough in my day. And that, you see, is because an actual death-agony is always more natural and more affecting than the most exact and artistic descriptions of death.

I felt wretched, undoubtedly more because of the cold than because of my neighbor's words. I groaned softly and ground my teeth.

Almost instantly I felt two small cold hands upon me. One of them touched my neck and the other was laid upon my face, and at the same time I heard a gentle, anxious, affectionate voice:

"What's the matter?"

I was ready to believe that someone else was asking this question, not Natasha, who had just declared that all men were scoundrels, and who wanted to see them all destroyed. But already she spoke hurriedly.

"What's the matter, eh? Are you cold? Are you freezing? Oh, what a queer one you are, you sit there as silent as an owl! Why didn't you tell me that you were cold? Come . . . lie down . . . stretch out, and I'll lie down too . . . so! Now put your arms round me . . . tighter! Well, now you ought to be warm. . . . And then we'll lie back to back. . . . Somehow we'll get through the night. See here . . . have you been drinking? . . . Did they sack you? . . . That's nothing. . . ."

She was comforting me. . . . She was encouraging me.

May I be thrice damned! What irony there was in this for me! Think of it! I was seriously occupied at that time with the destiny of mankind; I dreamed of the reorganization of the social order, of political upheavals; I read all manner of devilishly clever books, whose profound depths were not to be fathomed even by their authors—in those days I was trying my best to make of myself "an active, significant force." And here a prostitute was warming me with her body, a miserable, bruised, hunted creature, worthless, without any place in life, whom I had never thought of helping until she helped me, and whom I would hardly have been able to help even if the thought had occurred to me. Oh! I was ready to believe that all this was happening to me in a dream, in an absurd, oppressive dream.

But, alas! I couldn't make myself believe that, for cold drops of rain were falling on me, a woman's breast was pressed to mine, I felt her warm breath on my face, a breath smelling slightly of vodka, and yet so vivifying. . . . The wind howled and groaned, the rain beat against the boat, the waves splashed, and both of us, pressed tightly together, nevertheless shivered with cold. All this was utterly real, yet I am sure that no one ever dreamed such an oppressive and ugly dream as that reality.

Natasha kept on talking, with a tenderness and sympathy of which only women are capable. Under the influence of her simple and friendly words a little fire was gently kindled within me, and it melted something in my heart.

Then tears poured from my eyes, washing my heart of much that was evil, much that was foolish, much uneasiness and filth that had accumulated long before that night. Natasha kept soothing me:

"There, there, darling, that's enough! Don't howl! That's enough! With God's help you'll be all right . . . you'll find another place. . . ."

And she kept on kissing me. She gave me countless, hot kisses. . . .

Those were the first kisses from a woman that life had offered me, and they were the best kisses, for all those that came after were terribly costly and gave me almost nothing.

"Come, stop howling, you queer fellow! Tomorrow I'll help you, if you have nowhere to go," I heard her gentle, persuasive whisper as though in a dream.

. . . Until dawn we lay in each other's arms.

And when day broke, we crawled out from under the boat and went to town. . . . There we said good-by to each other in a friendly fashion and never met again, although for half a year I searched all the low dives for that sweet Natasha with whom I had spent the autumn night I have just described.

If she is already dead—and well for her if it is so— may she rest in peace! And if she is living—peace be to her soul! And may she never awaken to the consciousness of her fall . . . for that would be unnecessary suffering, a pain that would not further life. . . .

1894.

THE AFFAIR OF THE CLASPS

WE were three friends, Syomka, Karguza, I, and Mishka, a bearded giant with large blue eyes which were always swollen with drink and beamed kindly on everyone. We lived on the outskirts of the city in an old, tumbledown building which for some reason was called "the glass factory," perhaps because there wasn't one whole pane in all of its windows.

We undertook all kinds of work: we cleaned courtyards, dug ditches, cellars, cess-pools, demolished old buildings and fences, and once we even attempted to build a hen-house. But in this we were unsuccessful. Syomka, who was always overly conscientious regarding the tasks we took upon ourselves to perform, grew doubtful about our knowledge of the architecture of hen-houses, and one day, during the noon rest-hour, he took the nails, the ax, and two new planks, all issued to us by our employer, and carried them off to the pot-house. We were sacked for it, but as we owned nothing, no compensation was demanded of us.

We were living from hand to mouth, and all three of us felt a dissatisfaction with our lot which was natural and legitimate under the circumstances. Sometimes it became so sharp as to rouse in us a hostility toward everything about us and inspire us to the somewhat riotous exploits covered by the "Code of Penalties Imposed by Justices of the Peace." Generally, however, worried about where the next meal was coming from, we were glumly stolid, and responded weakly to everything that did not promise material advantage.

All three of us had met in a doss-house some two

weeks before the occurrence I wish to relate because I think it interesting. Two or three days later we had already become friends. We went everywhere together, confided in each other our hopes and plans, shared whatever any one of us came by, and, in fact, concluded among us a tacit defensive and offensive alliance against life, which was treating us so harshly.

During the day we looked diligently for something to take apart, saw up, dig, carry from one place to another, and if such an opportunity turned up, at first we tackled the job with a will. But perhaps because at heart each of us considered himself destined for higher things, than, for example, the digging, or what is worse, the cleaning, of cess-pools, after a couple of hours the work was no longer attractive. Then Syomka would begin to express doubts as to its necessity.

"You dig a pit. What for? For slops. And why not just pour them out in the court-yard? It won't do, they say. It will smell. Pshaw! Slops smell! What rot people talk, from having nothing to do. You throw out a pickled cucumber, for instance. How can it smell, if it's a little one? It will lie there a day or two—rot away, and disappear. Of course, if you throw a dead man out into the sun, he will smell, to be sure, because man is a large beast."

Syomka's philosophizing considerably chilled our zeal for work. . . . And this was rather profitable for us if we were hired by the day. But when it was piece-work, we would take our pay in advance and spend it on food before the job was finished. Then we would go to our employer and ask for extra payment. In most cases he would tell us to get out and would threaten to force us, with the aid of the police, to complete the job already paid for. We would argue that we couldn't work if we were hungry, and with some heat insist on more money, which we generally succeeded in getting.

THE AFFAIR OF THE CLASPS

Of course, this was not right, but really it was very advantageous, and it isn't our fault if life is so awkwardly arranged that doing the right thing is almost always disadvantageous.

Syomka was the one who always took it upon himself to dispute with the employer, and he conducted the argument with an artist's skill, setting forth the proofs that he was right in the tone of a man worn out by work and crushed under its weight. As for Mishka, he looked on, held his peace, and blinked his blue eyes, now and then producing a kind, conciliatory smile as though he were trying to say something, but couldn't bring himself to do it. He usually spoke very little, and only when drunk was he capable of making something like a speech.

"Mates!" he would exclaim them, smiling, and his lips would twitch strangely, his throat would trouble him, and for some time after starting his speech, he would cough, pressing his hand to his throat.

"We-ell?" Syomka would encourage him impatiently.

"Mates, we live like dogs. . . . And really much worse. And why? Nobody knows. But, it must be, by the will of the Lord God. Everything happens in accordance with His will, eh, mates? Well, then . . . It proves that we deserve a dog's life because we are bad eggs. We are bad eggs, eh? Well, then . . . So now I say, it serves us right, dogs that we are. Am I right? So it turns out, we've got our deserts. And so now we must bear our lot, eh? Am I right?"

"Fool!" Syomka replied with indifference to his friend's anxious and searching questions.

Mishka would shrink guiltily, smile timidly, and say no more, blinking his eyes that were sticky with drunkenness.

One day a piece of luck came our way.

We were shoving our way through the market place in search of work, when we came upon a wizened little old woman with a stern, wrinkled face. Her head shook, and large silver-rimmed spectacles hopped on her nose, which was like an owl's beak; she kept adjusting them constantly, flashing sharp glances from her coldly glittering eyes.

"You're free? Looking for work?" she asked us, as all three of us fixed her with a look of longing.

"Very well," she said, having received from Syomka a respectful answer in the affirmative. "I have to have an old bath-house torn down and a well cleaned. How much do you want for the work?"

"We must first see how big your bath-house is, ma'am," Syomka said politely and reasonably. "Then again, the well. There are all kinds of wells. Some of them are very deep."

We were invited to examine the premises, and an hour later, armed with axes and wooden levers, we were lustily heaving at the rafters of the bath-house, having undertaken to tear it down and clean the well for the sum of five rubles. The bath-house was situated in the corner of an old neglected garden. Not far from it, among cherry-trees, stood a summer-house, and from the roof of the bath-house we could see the old woman sitting there on a bench, absorbed in a large book which lay open on her knees. Now and then she cast a sharp, attentive glance in our direction, the book shifted on her lap, and its massive clasps, evidently of silver, glittered in the sun.

No work goes as smoothly as that of destruction....

We were busily moving about in clouds of dry, biting dust, sneezing, coughing, blowing our noses, and rubbing our eyes; the bath-house, as aged as its owner, was crashing and falling to pieces.

"Come on, mates, all together!" Syomka ordered us, and the beams crashed to the ground, row after row.

"What's that book she's got, such a thick one?" asked Mishka, reflectively, leaning on his lever and wiping the sweat from his face with the palm of his hand. Suddenly

THE AFFAIR OF THE CLASPS

taking on the look of a mulatto, he spat on his hands, swung the lever, in order to drive it into a crack between two beams, drove it in, and added in the same reflective tone:

"If it's the Gospels, it seems too thick. . . ."

"What's that to you?" inquired Syomka.

"To me? Nothing. I like to hear them read a book, if it's a holy one. . . . In our village there was a discharged soldier, Afrikan was his name, and when he would begin reading the Psalms, it was like the roll of a drum. It was grand!"

"Well, what of it?" Syomka asked again, rolling a cigarette.

"Nothing. But it was fine! You couldn't quite make it out, but still . . . It was . . . You don't hear anything like that on the street. . . . You don't understand it, but you feel that these are words for the soul."

"You don't understand it, you say, but it's plain that you're as stupid as an ox," Syomka mimicked his companion.

"Of course you always swear at me," he sighed.

"How else can you talk to fools? Can they understand anything? Now take a whack at this rotten one. Ho!"

The pile of debris was growing around the bath-house as it was falling to pieces, and the structure was enveloped in clouds of dust which was turning the leaves of the nearby trees gray. The July sun was unmercifully baking our backs and shoulders.

"The book's got silver on it," Mishka returned to the subject.

Syomka raised his head and shot a keen glance in the direction of the summer-house.

"Looks that way," he declared briefly.

"Then it's the Gospels."

"Maybe the Gospels. . . . What of it?"

"Nothing."

"That's what my pockets are filled with. And if you're so keen on Scripture, why don't you go to her and say: 'Read me a little of it, Granny. There's no other way of our getting it. We don't go to church, we're not proper, we're dirty. . . . And we've got souls too, just as they ought to be . . . in the right place. . . .' Now you go and tell her that."

"Should I really?"

"Go ahead."

Mishka threw down the lever, pulled his shirt straight, smeared the dust over his face with his sleeve, and jumped down from the roof of the bath-house.

"She'll send you packing, you devil you," grumbled Syomka, grinning skeptically, but with extreme curiosity following with his eyes the figure of his comrade, who was making his way through the burdocks to the summer-house. Tall, stooped, his dirty arms bare, he was advancing clumsily, swaying as he walked, and brushing against the bushes, all the while smiling self-consciously and meekly. As the man approached, the old woman raised her head and calmly looked him up and down. The rays of the sun were playing on the lenses of her spectacles and on their silver rims.

Contrary to Syomka's prediction, she did not send him packing. Because of the rustling of the leaves we could not hear what Mishka was saying to the mistress, but presently we saw him lower himself heavily to the ground at the old woman's feet so that his nose almost touched the open book. His face was calm and composed; we saw him blow on his beard, trying to remove the dust from it, shift about and finally settle in an awkward position, craning his neck, and staring expectantly at the old woman's small dry hands as they methodically turned the leaves of the book.

THE AFFAIR OF THE CLASPS

"Look at the shaggy dog! He has it easy. Why don't we go down there too? Why not? He'll be having a soft thing of it, while we slave for him. Shall we go?"

Two or three minutes later Syomka and I too were sitting on the ground, flanking our comrade. The old woman didn't say a word to us, she only gave us a scrutinizing glance and continued turning the leaves of the book, looking for something in it. We sat amidst luxuriant, green, fragrant foliage and overhead there was a gentle, soft, cloudless sky. Now and then a breeze stirred and the leaves made that mysterious rustling sound which always soothes the soul, rouses in it a gentle, peaceful mood, moves one to thoughts of something vague yet deeply human, purging the spirit of all that is unclean or at least erasing the memory of it temporarily, and allowing one to breathe with a sense of ease and renewal.

" 'Paul, a servant of Jesus Christ,' " the old woman's voice was heard. It was halting and cracked with age yet full of piety and stern dignity. At the first sound of it Mishka crossed himself earnestly, while Syomka shifted about on the ground trying to find a more comfortable position. The old woman glanced at him without ceasing to read. " 'For I long to see you, that I may impart unto you some spiritual gift, to the end ye may be established; that is, that I may be comforted together with you by the mutual faith both of you and me.' "

Syomka, like the true heathen he was, yawned noisily, and his comrade shot a reproachful glance at him out of his blue eyes, and hung his shaggy, dusty head. The old woman, without ceasing to read, also looked severely at Syomka, and this embarrassed him. He twitched his nose, glanced aside, and apparently trying to efface the impression made by his yawn, drew a deep and pious sigh.

Several minutes passed quietly. The clear, monotonous reading acted soothingly.

" 'For the wrath of God is revealed from heaven against all ungodliness and . . .'

"What do you want?" the reader cried abruptly to Syomka.

"But . . . nothing! Have the goodness to go on reading. I am listening," he explained meekly.

"Why do you touch the clasps with your dirty paw?" the old woman asked angrily.

"I'm curious . . . because it's such fine work. I understand this sort of thing. I know locksmiths' work. . . . So I touched them."

"See here," the old woman commanded dryly. "Tell me, what was I reading about?"

"Why, of course, I know."

"Well, then, tell me."

"It's a sermon. . . . It teaches about faith, and also about ungodliness. . . . It's very simple, and it's all true! It goes straight to the soul."

The old woman shook her head sadly and looked at us reproachfully:

"You're lost souls—blockheads. Go back to your work."

"She seems to be . . . angry," declared Mishka, smiling guiltily.

Syomka scratched himself, yawned, and said thoughtfully, as he watched the old woman walk down the narrow garden path, without turning around:

"The clasps on the book are silver, sure enough. . . ." And he grinned from ear to ear, as if anticipating something pleasant.

Having spent the night in the garden near the ruins of the bath-house, which we had completely demolished in the course of the day, by noon of the following day we cleaned the well. Wet and muddy, we were sitting in the court-yard near the steps leading to the house, waiting to be paid off. We were talking to each other and pictur-

THE AFFAIR OF THE CLASPS   61

ing to ourselves the good dinner and supper in the offing. None of us had any desire to look further into the future. . . .

"Why the devil doesn't the old witch come?" Syomka was impatient and indignant, but he spoke under his breath. "Has she croaked?"

"There he is, swearing again," Mishka shook his head reproachfully. "And why should he swear? The old woman is the real thing, the god-fearing kind. But he has to swear at her. What a disposition the man has!"

"Smart, aren't you?" his companion said, with a smirk. "You scarecrow!"

This pleasant conversation between friends was interrupted by the appearance of our employer. She came up to us, and holding out her hand with the money in it, said contemptuously:

"Take it, and clear out. I was going to have you saw up the planks for firewood, but you don't deserve it."

Deprived of the honor of sawing up the planks, a job we didn't need now, we took the money without a word, and went off.

"Oh, you old hag!" began Syomka, as soon as we were beyond the gate. "That's a good one! We don't deserve it! The putrid toad! Go ahead and squeak over your book now!"

Putting his hand into his pocket, he pulled out two shining metal objects and showed them to us triumphantly.

Mishka halted, craning his neck inquisitively in the direction of Syomka's upraised hand.

"You broke off the clasps?" he asked in astonishment.

"There they are. Silver ones! Even if he didn't want them, a man would give a ruble for them."

"What a fellow! When did you get the chance? You'd better hide them, out of harm's way!"

"You bet I will."

We walked on down the street in silence.

"Smart work," Mishka muttered to himself, reflectively. "He went and broke them off! M-yes. But it's a good book. . . . I'm thinking the old woman will be sore at us."

"Why, no, the idea! She'll call us back and tip us," Syomka jested.

"What do you want for them?"

"Nine ten-kopeck pieces . . . that's the rock-bottom price. I won't take a kopeck less. They cost me more. Look —I broke my nail."

"Sell them to me," said Mishka timidly.

"To you? Want to make studs of them? Buy them! They'll make a dandy pair, just to suit your mug!"

"No; honest, sell them to me!" And Mishka spoke in a lower, more pleading tone.

"All right, buy them. What will you give?"

"Take. . . . What's my share?"

"A ruble, twenty."

"And what do you want for them?"

"One ruble."

"Make it less, for a friend."

"You thumping blockhead, you! What the devil do you want with them?"

"Never mind; you sell them to me."

Finally, the deal was closed, and the clasps went to Mishka for ninety kopecks.

He stopped, and began turning them over in his hands, bending his tousled head, knitting his brows, and scrutinizing the two silver pieces.

"Hang 'em on your nose," Syomka advised him.

"What for?" Mishka replied seriously. "No. I'll take them back to the old woman. 'Here, Granny,' I'll say to her. 'We carried these things off with us by mistake, so you put them back again where they belong,' I'll say, 'on that book there.' Only you've torn out a piece of stuff with them; what about that?"

"Are you really going to take them back, you devil?" Syomka gaped in amazement.

"Why not? You see, such a book—it ought to be whole. It isn't right to tear pieces off of it. And the old woman, too, she'll be hurt. . . . And she'll be dead soon. . . . So I'll just . . . You wait for me a minute, mates. I'll run back."

And before we could stop him, he strode off, disappearing round the corner.

"What a wood-louse! The dirty rotter!" Syomka stormed, after the occurrence and its possible consequences had come home to him. And cursing furiously at every third word, he began persuading me:

"Let's go, hurry up. He'll get us in bad. . . . He's probably sitting there now, with his hands tied behind him, and the old witch must have sent for the police already! . . . That's what it is to have dealings with such a nasty fellow. Why, he'll get you in jail for a trifle! But just think, what a scoundrel! What dirty beast would act this way to a comrade? Good Lord! What people are like nowadays! Come on, you devil, what are you sticking around for? Waiting for him? All right, wait, and the devil take you all—crooks! Faugh! Damn you! Not coming? All right, then . . ."

Calling hideous curses down on me, Syomka poked me furiously in the ribs, and strode off rapidly.

. . . .

I wanted to know what was happening between Mishka and our former employer, and walked quietly towards her house. I did not think that I would run into any danger or unpleasantness.

And I was not mistaken.

As I approached the house, I looked through a crack in the fence, and saw and heard what follows:

The old woman sat on the steps, holding the clasps of her Bible in her hand, and looking keenly and sternly at Mishka's face through her spectacles. He was standing with his back to me.

In spite of the severe, cold gleam in her sharp eyes, there were soft folds at the corners of her mouth; it was plain that the old woman wanted to hide a kindly smile, a smile of forgiveness.

From behind her back showed three heads. Two belonged to women; one had a red face and wore a motley kerchief; the other woman was bare-headed and wall-eyed; above her shoulders appeared a man's face, wedge-shaped, with gray side-whiskers and a forelock across his forehead. He was continually blinking both eyes in a curious fashion, as though saying to Mishka: "Run, brother! Quick!"

Mishka was hemming and hawing, trying to explain.

"Such a rare book! It says we're all beasts and curs, dogs. So I thought to myself: it's true, Lord. Truth to tell, we are riff-raff . . . damned souls . . . wretches! And then, too, I thought to myself, the mistress, she's an old lady; perhaps this book is her one comfort, and she's got nothing else. . . . Now, these clasps—how much could we get for them? But if they are on the book, then they amount to something. So I thought it over, and I said to myself, 'I'll go and give some pleasure to the godly old lady—take these back to her. . . .' Besides, glory be to God, we've earned a bit to buy bread with. Well, good-day; I'll be going."

"Wait," the old woman stopped him. "Did you understand what I read yesterday?"

"Me? How could I understand it? I heard it, that's true, but even then, how did I hear it? Have we ears for God's Word? We can't understand it. Good-by to you."

THE AFFAIR OF THE CLASPS

"So-o!" drawled the old woman. "No, just wait a minute."

Mishka sighed unhappily, so that he could be heard all over the yard, and shifted his weight from one foot to the other like a bear. This explanation was evidently getting to be too much for him.

"And would you like me to read some more to you?"

"M'm! My comrades are waiting for me."

"Drop them. You are a good fellow. Have no more to do with them."

"All right," Mishka agreed in a low voice.

"You will leave them? Yes?"

"I'll leave them."

"That's a sensible fellow. What a child you are! And look at your beard, it's almost down to your waist! Are you married?"

"I'm a widower. My wife's dead."

"And why do you drink? You're a drunkard, aren't you?"

"I am. I drink."

"Why?"

"Why I drink? Because of foolishness. I'm foolish, and so I drink. Of course, if a man had sense, would he himself work his own ruin?" Mishka said despondently.

"You have spoken the truth. Well, then, acquire sense, acquire it, and straighten yourself out. . . . Go to church. Listen to God's Word. Therein is all wisdom."

"Yes, of course," Mishka almost groaned.

"And I will read to you some more. Would you like that?"

"Please, ma'am."

The old woman produced her Bible from somewhere in back of her, paged it, and the courtyard resounded with her tremulous voice:

" 'Therefore thou art inexcusable, O man, whosoever thou art that judgest; for wherein thou judgest another, thou condemnest thyself; for thou that judgest doest the same things.' "

Mishka shook his head and scratched his left shoulder.

" 'And thinkest thou this, O man, that judgest them which do such things, and doest the same, that thou shalt escape the judgment of God?' "

"Ma'am," Mishka began with tears in his voice, "let me go, for God's sake. . . . I'll come some other time to listen. But now I'm awfully hungry. My stomach is rumbling something terrible. We've had nothing to eat since last night."

The old woman shut the book with a bang.

"Get along with you! Go!" sounded sharply and curtly through the yard.

"Thank you kindly." And he almost ran to the gate.

"Unrepentant souls, hearts of beasts," she hissed after him.

. . . . . .

Half an hour later all three of us were sitting in a tavern, having tea and white bread.

"It was as though she were screwing a gimlet into me," said Mishka, smiling kindly at me with his gentle eyes. "I stood and thought to myself, 'My God! Why in heaven's name did I go there?' It was torture. Instead of taking the clasps and letting me go, she began talking. How queer people are! You want to be decent with them, but they follow their own tack. . . . In the simplicity of my heart I said to her: 'Here, mistress, are your clasps. Don't hold it against me.' But she said, 'No, wait. You tell me why you brought them back to me,' and then she went on pitching into me. I broke into a sweat listening to her, honest I did."

And he kept on smiling in that infinitely gentle way of his.

Syomka, disheveled, sulky, and sullen, said to him earnestly:

"You'd better die straight off, my dear blockhead! Or else, with these doings of yours, the flies or cockroaches will eat you up."

"Well! The things you say! Come, let's drink a glass to the end of the affair!"

And we drank heartily to the end of this curious affair.

1895.

CREATURES THAT ONCE WERE MEN

THE street leading into the town is flanked by two rows of miserable-looking one-story huts, with warped windows and crooked walls pressing against each other. The roofs of these time-worn habitations are full of holes, have been patched up here and there with laths, and are overgrown with moss. Here and there above them project boxes for starlings on tall poles, shaded by dusty-leaved elder-trees and gnarled white willows—the pitiable flora of suburbs inhabited by the poor.

The dull-green, time-stained panes of the windows look upon each other with the glances of cowardly cheats. Along the street a sinuous path runs hillward, winding its way through deep gullies formed by the rains. Here and there lie piles of crushed stone and all kinds of rubbish—the remains or the beginnings of structures raised by the inhabitants in a vain struggle against the streams of rainwater rushing impetuously from the town. On the top of the hill, among green gardens with dense foliage, beautiful stone houses lie hidden, belfries of churches rise proudly towards the blue sky, and their gilded crosses shine dazzlingly in the rays of the sun.

During the rainy weather, the town pours all its mud into this street; when the weather is dry it covers it with dust, and all these dingy houses, too, seem, as it were, thrown down from the hill, swept together like refuse by someone's powerful hand. Crushed to the ground, they dot the sides of the hill; half rotten, sickly-looking, they have acquired, in the sun, the dust, and the rain, the dirty gray color of old wood.

At the end of the street, as though pushed out of the

town, stood a rambling two-story house belonging to Petunikoff the merchant. It was the last one in the line, right at the foot of the hill; behind it lay an open field, which about half a mile away ended in a steep slope descending to the river. The large old house seemed the most dismal of all its neighbors. It was bent to one side and not one in its two rows of windows had kept its shape; the remaining fragments of glass in the broken frames of the windows had the dull green shine of water from the marshes. The spaces of plastered wall between the windows were covered with rents and dark stains as if time had written the history of the old house in hieroglyphics. The tottering roof added still more to its pitiable aspect. It seemed as if the whole building bowed towards the ground, meekly awaiting the last stroke of that fate which would transform it into a shapeless mass of rotting remains.

The gates were open. One side, torn off its hinges, was lying on the ground at the entrance, and between its bars grew the grass, which covered up all the large and empty courtyard. In the depths of this yard stood a low, iron-roofed, smoke-begrimed building. The house itself was unoccupied, but this structure, formerly a smithy, was now turned into a doss-house, kept by a retired captain named Aristid Fomich Kuvalda.

The interior of the doss-house was a long sinister den measuring twenty-eight by forty-two feet. It was lighted on one side only by four small square windows and a wide door. The unplastered brick walls were black with smoke and so was the ceiling, built out of the remains of a barge. In the middle stood a large stove, the foundation of which was a furnace, and around the stove and along the walls were wide shelves with piles of rags, which served as beds for the lodgers. The walls smelt of smoke, the earthen floor of dampness, and the shelves of rotting rags. The proprietor's nook was on the top of the stove; the boards surrounding it were places of distinction and occupied only by those who were on good terms with him.

The Captain spent most of his day sitting on a brick bench which he had built for himself at the entrance to the doss-house, or else, across the road, in the eating-house belonging to Egor Vaviloff, where he took all his meals and drank vodka.

Before renting this house, Aristid Kuvalda had kept a registry office for servants in the town. If we look further back into his life, we shall find that he once owned printing works, and, previous to this, in his own words, he "just lived, and lived well too—by Jove, and like one who knew how!"

He was a tall broad-shouldered man about fifty, with a pock-marked face, bloated with drunkenness, framed by a large beard of a dirty-yellow hue. His eyes were huge, gray, insolently cheerful. He spoke in a deep bass voice, with a grumbling sound in his throat, and almost without fail a German china pipe with a crooked bowl protruded from his teeth. When he was angry, the nostrils of his big red hooked nose swelled out and his lips quivered, exposing to view two rows of large and wolf-like yellow teeth. He had long arms, bandy legs, always wore an old officer's cloak, a dirty greasy cap with a red band, but without a brim, and felt boots, with holes in them, which reached almost to his knees. He usually had a heavy drunken headache in the morning, and was slightly tipsy by night. But regardless of the amount of wine he absorbed he never got really drunk, and never lost his merry disposition.

In the evening, sitting on his brick bench with a pipe in his mouth, he received lodgers. "Now, what sort of a man is that?" he would ask the ragged and depressed object approaching him, evicted from the town for drunkenness or cast down for some still more legitimate reason. And after the man had answered him, he would say: "Let me see the legal papers that confirm your lies." If there were such papers, they were produced. The Captain would put them close to his breast, seldom taking any interest in their contents and would say: "All right. Two kopecks for the night, ten kopecks for the week, and thirty kopecks for the month. Go and find a place, and see that it is not somebody else's, or you'll get a hiding. My lodgers are people with strict views."

"Don't you sell tea, bread, other eatables?"

"I trade only in walls and roofs, for which I pay the swindling proprietor of this hole—Judas Petunikoff, merchant of the second guild—five rubles a month," explained Kuvalda in a business-like tone. "Only those come to me who are not used to luxuries . . . but if you are in the habit of guzzling every day, there is the eating-house opposite. You'd do better, however, you fragment of mankind, to abandon this fad. You see, you are not a gentleman. So what is it you eat? It is yourself you eat!"

Such speeches, delivered in an artificially business-like manner, but always with smiling eyes, and also the solicitude shown to his lodgers, made the Captain very popular among the paupers of the town. It often happened that a former client of his would appear, ragged and depressed, but more respectable-looking and with a happier face.

"Good day, your honor, and how are you keeping?"

"Alive, in good health! What next?"

"Don't you know me?"

"I do not."

"Don't you remember that I lived here for nearly a month last winter . . . when the police came and three men were taken away?"

"Oh, well, the police come often enough under my hospitable roof."

"But don't you remember you cocked a snook at the district Police Inspector?"

"Now, stop these reminiscences. Say straight away what you want, my lad."

"Won't you accept a small entertainment from me? When I lived with you, you were . . ."

"Gratitude must be encouraged, my friend, because it is so seldom to be found in the world. You must be a good fellow, and though I don't remember you, I will go with you to the pub and drink to your success in life with the greatest delight."

"You are just the same, always joking."

"What else can one do, living among you sad 'uns?"

They went to the pub. Sometimes the Captain's former customer, distracted and unsettled by the entertainment, returned to the doss-house and the next day they would again begin treating each other to drinks, till the Captain's companion would wake up one bright morning to realize that all his money had been spent on drink.

"Your honor, see, I 'ave joined your company once more! What shall we do?"

"The position, no doubt, is not one that should be encouraged, still one should not grouse if one gets into it," reasoned the Captain. "One should be indifferent to all things, my friend, not spoil one's life with philosophy, and not ask oneself any questions. To philosophize is always foolish; to philosophize with a drunken headache indescribably so. Drunken headaches require more vodka, not more remorse, or gnashing of teeth . . . save your teeth, they may come in useful when you are beaten up. Here are twenty kopecks, go and buy a bottle of vodka, some hot tripe or lungs for five kopecks, one pound of bread and two cucumbers. When we have lived off our drunken headaches we will discuss the situation."

As a rule the discussion of the situation lasted for two

CREATURES THAT ONCE WERE MEN 73

or three days, and only stopped when the Captain had not a kopeck left of the three or five rubles which were in his pocket at the arrival of his grateful customer.

"Well, we're in the soup now all right," he then would say. "Now that we have drunk with you to the last penny, you fool, let us try once more to regain the path of virtue and sobriety. It has been justly said that if you do not sin, you will not repent, and if you do not repent, you shall not be saved. We have done the first, and to repent is useless. Let us make straight for salvation. Go to work on the river, and if you think you cannot rely on your wisdom, tell the contractor to keep your money, or else give it to me. When we shall have gathered sufficient capital, I shall get you a pair of trousers and other things necessary to make you look like a respectable and hard-working man, persecuted by fate. With decent-looking trousers you can go far once more. Now then, be off!"

Then the client would go to the river to work as a boatman, pondering humorously over the Captain's speeches. He did not fully understand them, but saw in front of him two merry eyes, felt an encouraging influence, and knew that in the loquacious Captain he had an arm that would assist him in time of need.

And it actually happened that, after a month or so of hard work, owing to the strict surveillance of the Captain, the client managed to raise himself slightly from the condition to which, thanks to the same Captain's kind co-operation, he had sunk.

"Now then, my friend!" said the Captain, glancing critically at the restored client, "we have a coat and a jacket. They are factors of immense importance—trust my word for it. When I had respectable trousers I lived in a town like a respectable man. But as soon as the trousers fell to pieces, I, too, fell in the opinion of my fellow men, and had to come down here from the town. Men, you precious idiot, judge everything by outward appearances, the real essence of things escapes them, for they are born stupid. Bear this in mind, and pay me at least half of your debt. Then go in peace, seek, and you may find."

"How much do I owe you, Aristid Fomich?" asked the client, in confusion.

"One ruble and seventy kopecks . . . now, give me one ruble only, or, if you like, seventy kopecks, and for the rest, I shall wait until you have earned more than you have now, whether by stealing or by hard work."

"I thank you humbly for your kindness!" said the client, touched to the heart. "Truly you are a kind man . . . ; Life has persecuted you unjustly. . . . What an eagle you would have been in your right place!"

The Captain could not live without eloquent speeches.

"What does 'in my right place' mean? No one really knows his right place in life, and every one of us crawls into another one's harness. The place of the merchant Judas Petunikov ought to be in penal servitude, but he still walks through the streets in broad daylight, and even intends to build a factory. The place of our teacher ought to be beside a good wife and half-a-dozen children, but he lies groveling in the public-house of Vaviloff. And then, there is yourself. You are going to seek a situation as boots or waiter, but I know that what you really ought to be is a soldier, for you are no fool, patient and understanding discipline, see the irony of it? Life shuffles us like cards, and it is only accidentally, and that only for a time, that we fall into our proper places!"

These farewell conversations often served as a preface to the continuation of their friendship, which again began with a good booze and got to the stage where the client much to his amazement would again find that he had spent his last farthing, the Captain would stand him a treat in return and they would drink away all they had.

CREATURES THAT ONCE WERE MEN 75

Such repetitions did not affect in the least the good relations of the parties.

The teacher mentioned by the Captain was another of those customers who were reformed only in order that they should sin again. He had more in common with the Captain than any of the others, as far as his education was concerned, and this was probably why, having fallen as low as doss-house life, he was unable to rise again. It was only with him that Aristid Kuvalda could philosophize with the certainty of being understood. He valued this, and when the reformed teacher, having earned some money, prepared to leave the doss-house in order to get a corner in town for himself, Aristid Kuvalda took the news so sorrowfully and sadly, with such innumerable protestations of friendship, that the whole thing ended, as a rule, in their both getting drunk and spending all their savings. Probably Kuvalda arranged matters on purpose so that, much as the teacher desired it, he could not leave the doss-house. Was it possible for Aristid Kuvalda, a man of education (the remains of which still sparkled in his speeches) in whom the vagaries of fate had developed the habit of thinking, was it possible for him not to desire to keep the company of a man more like himself? We all know how to be sorry for ourselves.

This teacher had once taught at a normal school in a city on the Volga, but had been dismissed from his job. After this he had been a clerk in a tannery, a librarian, tried a few other professions, and finally, after passing examinations for the bar, and becoming a lawyer, he took to drink, and this brought him to the Captain's doss-house. He was tall, round-shouldered, with a long pointed nose and a bald head. In his bony yellow face, on which grew a wedge-shaped beard, shone a pair of restless eyes, deeply sunk in their sockets, and the corners of his mouth drooped down sorrowfully. He earned his bread, or rather his drink, by reporting for the local papers. Sometimes he earned as much as fifteen rubles a week. These he gave to the Captain and said:

"Enough of all this. I am going back to the bosom of culture."

"Very fine. As I heartily sympathize with your decision, Philip, I shall not give you another glass," the Captain warned him sternly.

"I shall only be grateful to you . . ."

The Captain heard a timid demand of concession in his voice, and became still sterner.

"You may clamor for it, but I won't."

"As you like, then," sighed the teacher, and went back to his reporting. But after a day or two he would stare with dreary and thirsty eyes from some corner at the Captain, anxiously waiting for his friend's heart to soften.

The Captain, with crushing irony, spoke then of the shameful weakness of some characters, on the animal delight of intoxication, and on other subjects that suited the occasion. One must do him justice: he was genuinely captivated by his rôle of mentor and moralist, but the skeptical lodgers, watching him and listening to his exhortations to virtue, would whisper aside to each other:

"The fox! What a tongue he has! 'I told you so,' says he, 'but you would not listen to me. Now you have only yourself to thank!'"

"His honor is indeed a good soldier, always first in line, but keeping an eye on the road back."

The teacher would then get hold of his friend in a dark corner, clutching at his dirty cloak, trembling and passing his tongue over his dry lips, and look into his face with a deep, inexpressibly tragic glance.

"Can't you bear it any longer?" the Captain would ask sullenly.

The teacher would answer by shaking his head.

"Wait another day . . . perhaps you'll get over it," Kuvalda would propose. The teacher would sigh, and shake his head hopelessly once more.

The Captain, seeing that his friend's thin body trembled with the thirst for the poison, would take some money from his pocket.

"In the majority of cases it is impossible to fight against fate," he would say, as if trying to justify himself before someone. The teacher, however, did not spend all his money on drink. At least half of it went to the children of the street. The poor are always rich in children, and in the dirt and ditches of this street there were crowds of them noisily seething from morning to night, hungry, naked and dirty. Children are the living flowers of the earth, but these had the appearance of flowers prematurely faded. Often the teacher would gather them round him, would buy them bread, eggs, apples and nuts, and take them into the fields by the riverside. There they would sit and first greedily eat everything he offered them, and then begin to play, filling the fields for a mile around with noise and laughter. The tall, gaunt figure of the drunkard seemed to shrink among these small people, who treated him as if he were of their own age. They called him "Philip" and did not trouble to prefix "Uncle" to his name. Playing around him, like little sprites, they pushed him about, jumped upon his back, beat him upon his bald head, caught hold of his nose. All this must have pleased him, as he did not protest against such liberties. He spoke very little to them, and when he did so it was cautiously and timidly as if afraid that his words would hurt or contaminate them. He passed many hours thus as their companion and plaything, watching their lively faces with his gloomy eyes. Then he would thoughtfully direct his steps to Vaviloff's pub where he would drink himself silently into unconsciousness.

· · · · · · ·

Almost every day after his reporting he would bring a newspaper, and then gather round him all these creatures that once were men. They would come towards him drunk, or suffering from drunken headaches, in different stages of disorder, but equally pitiable and filthy. There would come Aleksei Maksimovitch Simtsoff, stout as a barrel, at one time had been a forester, but now traded in matches, ink, and blacking. He was an old man of sixty, in a canvas overcoat and a wide-brimmed hat, the creased borders of which concealed his fat, red face with its thick white beard, from which a small red nose peered gaily heavenwards and a pair of watery eyes gleamed cynically. They called him "Spinning Top," a name which well described his round figure and wheezing speech. After him "Bad End" appeared from some corner—a dark, sinister, silent drunkard; then the former prison warden, Luka Antonovitch Martyanoff, a man who existed by gambling at "strap," "three-leaves," "bank-note," and by other arts equally cunning and equally disapproved of by the police. He would throw his hard and oft-scourged body on the grass beside the teacher, and, flashing around with his black eyes, point to the bottle, and ask in a hoarse, bass voice: "May I?"

Then appeared the mechanical engineer Pavel Solntseff, a man of some thirty years of age, suffering from consumption. His left ribs had been crushed in a quarrel, and his sharp, yellow, foxy face wore a malicious smile. The thin lips exposed two rows of black teeth, decayed by illness, and the rags on his narrow and bony shoulders swayed backwards and forwards as on a clothes pole. They called him "Bag of Bones." He hawked brushes and bath brooms of his own manufacture, made from a peculiar kind of grass, very useful for brushing clothes.

Then followed a tall and bony man with a frightened expression in his large solitary right eye. He was silent and timid, and had been imprisoned three times for theft by order of a Justice of the Peace and a District Court. His family name was Kiselnikoff, but he was nicknamed "Taras-and-a-Half," for being almost twice as tall as his bosom friend, Deacon Taras, who had been degraded from his office for drunkenness and immorality. The Deacon was a short, thick-set person, with the chest of an athlete and a round curly head. He danced with skill, and was still more skillful at swearing.

He and Taras-and-a-Half sawed wood on the banks of the river, and in free hours he told his friend or anyone who cared to listen, "Tales of my own composition," as he used to call them. Listening to these stories, the heroes of which were always saints, kings, priests, or generals, even the inmates of the doss-house spat with disgust and opened their eyes in amazement at the imagination of the Deacon, who unrolled tales of lewd, shameless adventures, his eyes half closed. The phantasy of this man was powerful and inexhaustible; he could go on relating and improvising all day, from morning to night, without once repeating himself. A great poet might have been buried in his person, certainly a remarkable story-teller, capable of putting life and soul even into stones with his obscene, but strong and effective words.

There was also a crazy young man whom Kuvalda called Meteor. One night he came to sleep in the doss-house and had remained ever since among these men, much to their astonishment. At first they did not take much notice of him. In the daytime, like all the others, he went to search for earnings, but at night he always loitered around this friendly company till at last the Captain took notice of him.

"Boy! What business have you here on this earth?"

The boy answered boldly and stoutly: "I am a barefooted tramp. . . ."

The Captain looked critically at him. This youngster had long hair, a naïve face, with prominent cheek-bones and a turned-up nose. He was dressed in a blue blouse without a belt, and on his head he wore the remains of a straw hat. His feet were bare.

"You are a fool!" decided Aristid Kuvalda. "What are you knocking about here for? . . . Do you drink vodka? . . . No! . . . Well, then, can you steal? Again, No. Go away, learn to be a man and then come back to us. . . ."

The youngster smiled.

"No. I shall go on living with you."

"Why?"

"Just because . . ."

"Oh, you . . . Meteor!" said the Captain.

"I will break his teeth for him," said Martyanoff.

"What for?" asked the youngster.

"Just because . . ."

"And I will take a stone and hit you on the head," the young man answered respectfully.

Martyanoff would have broken his bones, had not Kuvalda interrupted with:

"Leave him alone. . . . We are all birds of one feather. You have no good reason to break his teeth for him. He has no better reason to want to live with us. Well, then, the devil take him! . . . We all live in the world without any good reason for it."

"But it would be far better for you, young man, to go away from here," the teacher advised him, watching with his sad eyes. The latter gave no answer, but remained. They soon became accustomed to his presence, and ceased

CREATURES THAT ONCE WERE MEN 81

to take any notice of him. But he went on living among them, noticing everything.

All the above-mentioned men were the chief members of the Captain's general staff, and he called them with kind-hearted sarcasm "Creatures that once were men." Beside them there always were about five or six rank and file tramps in the doss-house. They could not boast of the same past as the "creatures," but were more complete human beings, less dislocated ones, although they, too, had experienced many hard kicks from fate. They were almost all of them former peasants. A respectable man of a cultured class may be superior to his equivalent among peasants, but an urban man of dissolute, low life is always worse than his rural counterpart.

The most vivid representative of the latter class was an old mujik called Tyapa. Tall and hideously angular, he held his head so that his chin touched his breast, and this gave his silhouette the shape of a poker. His face could be distinguished only in profile; one then saw his crooked nose, hanging lower lip and gray shaggy eyebrows.

He was the Captain's first lodger, and it was rumored that he had a great deal of money hidden in a secret place. About two years ago someone tried to cut his throat on account of this money: his head had been bent since that day. He denied that he had the money, and said that they only tried to cut his throat out of malice, and that it had only made his job of collecting rags—which meant bending to the ground—an easy one for him. When he went about with his unsteady gait and without a stick in his hand, or a bag behind his back—he seemed just a man buried in meditation, and, at such times, Kuvalda would say, pointing at him with his finger:

"Look, there goes the runaway conscience of Merchant Judas Petunikoff. See how disorderly, dirty, and low it is."

Tyapa spoke in a hoarse voice, his speech was indistinct,

and probably for that reason he spoke very seldom, and loved to be alone. But whenever a fresh example of mankind, compelled through need to leave the village, appeared in the doss-house, Tyapa grew restless and angry and followed the unfortunate man about with biting jeers emerging from his throat with an angry chuckle. He either set some other fresh beggar against him, or himself threatened to rob and beat him up till finally the frightened man would disappear from the doss-house. Then Tyapa would be quiet again, and would sit in a corner mending his rags, or reading his Bible, which was as dirty, worn, and old as himself. Only when the teacher brought a newspaper and began reading did he come from his corner once more. He listened to what was read silently and sighed deeply, without asking any questions. But when the teacher, having read the paper, wanted to put it away, Tyapa would stretch out his bony hand, and say, "Give it to me. . . ."

"What do you want it for?"

"Give it to me. . . . Perhaps there is something in it about us. . . ."

"About whom?"

"About the village."

They laughed at him and threw him the paper. He would take it and read in it how the hail had destroyed the cornfields in one village, how in another one fire had brought down thirty houses, and in a third a woman had poisoned her husband—in fact, everything that it is customary to say about the countryside which depicts it as wicked, miserable and ignorant. Tyapa read all this silently and grunted, perhaps expressing sympathy with that sound, perhaps delight.

He spent Sunday reading his Bible, and never went out collecting rags on that day. He propped the book against his breast, and was angry when anyone interrupted him or touched his Bible.

"Well, blasted book-worm," Kuvalda would say to him, "what do you understand of it all?"

"And what about you?"

"I don't understand anything, but then I do not read books. . . ."

"Well, I read them."

"Therefore you are a fool . . ." said the Captain decidedly. "When insects get in your head, it is bad enough, but what if thoughts would crawl into it too, what would you do, you old toad?"

"I have not long to live," said Tyapa, quietly.

Once the teacher asked how he had learned to read.

"In prison," answered Tyapa, shortly.

"Oh, you've been there, have you?"

"Yes, I have."

"What for?"

"Just a mistake of mine . . . but I got the Bible there. A lady gave it to me. . . . It is good to be in prison, brother."

"Is that so? And why?"

"It teaches one. . . . I learned to read there. . . . I also got this book. . . . And all this for nothing."

When the teacher appeared in the doss-house, Tyapa had already lived there for some time. He started watching him intently. In order to look into a man's face, Tyapa had to bend all his body sideways. He listened greedily to his conversation, and once, sitting down beside him, he said:

"I see you are very learned. . . . Have you read the Bible?"

"I have. . . ."

"I see; I see. . . . Can you remember it?"

"Yes. . . . I do. . . ."

Then the old man leaned to one side and gazed at the other with a stern, suspicious glance in his gray eyes.

"There were the Amalekites, do you remember?"

"Well?"

"Where are they now?"

"Disappeared . . . Tyapa . . . died out . . ."

The old man was silent, then asked again: "And where are the Philistines?"

"They, too . . ."

"Have they all died out?"

"All . . ."

"So—so, so we, too, shall die out?"

"There will come a time when we also shall die out," said the teacher placidly.

"And to what tribe of Israel do we belong?"

The teacher looked up at him, thought for a moment, and began telling him about Scythians and Slavs and Cimmerians.

The old man bent lower and lower down and glanced into his face, with frightened eyes.

"Lies, all of it!" he said scornfully, when the teacher had finished.

"What do you mean?" the latter said in amazement.

"You speak of tribes that are not mentioned in the Bible."

He got up and walked away, muttering to himself angrily.

"You're going crazy, Tyapa," called the teacher after him with conviction.

Then the old man came back again and threatened him with his crooked and dirty finger.

"Adam came from God—from Adam descended the Jews, that means that all people come from the Jews . . . and we do too."

"Well?"

"Tartars come from Ishmael, but he also came from a Jew."

"What are you telling me all this for?"

"Nothing! Only why tell lies?"

And he walked away, leaving his companion in perplexity. But two days later he came again and sat by him.

"You are learned. . . . Tell me, then, who are we?"

"We are Slavs, Tyapa," said the teacher.

"Quote the Bible to me. There are no such men there. Are we Babylonians?"

Then the teacher started pulling the Bible to pieces. The old man listened for a long while and interrupted him.

"Stop. . . . Wait! That means that among the people known to God there are no Russians? We are not known to God? Is it so? God knew all those who are mentioned in the Bible. . . . He destroyed them by sword and fire. He destroyed their cities; but He also sent prophets to teach them. That means that He also pitied them. He scattered the Jews and the Tartars, but protected them as well. . . . But what about us? Why have we no prophets?"

"Well, I don't know!" replied the teacher, trying to understand what the old man was saying. But the latter put his hand on the teacher's shoulder, slowly pushed him backwards and forwards, and there was a hoarse rattle in his throat as if he were swallowing something. . . .

"That is so. You do not know. You talk so much, as if you knew everything. It makes me sick to listen to you. You just darken my soul, that is all. Better if you were silent. Who are we, eh? Why is it we have no prophets? Ha! Ha! Where were we when Christ walked the earth, eh? And you are lying, too. A whole people cannot die out, they can't. The Russian people can't die out. . . . It is a lie. . . . They have been written down in the Bible, only it is not known under what name they go. . . . Can't you see what a huge people they are? How many villages we have . . . and people live in them, real people, strong and powerful, and you say they will die out. . . . A man can die—a people can't. . . . God needs them. It is they who build up the earth. . . . The Amalekites did not die out. They are now called German or French, that is all . . . and you . . . Now, tell me why is it we are abandoned by God? Why have we no punishments or prophets from him? Who is there to teach us?"

Tyapa's speech sounded very powerful—there was deep faith, reproach and scorn in his words. He spoke for a long time to the teacher, who, being drunk as usual and in a gloomy state of mind, could stand it no longer. He felt as though the words entered his body like a wooden saw. He listened to the old man, looked at his disfigured body, felt the curious penetrating power of his words and suddenly a great self-pity overcame him. He wanted to say something convincingly strong in return, something at the same time which would influence Tyapa in his favor and make him speak to him, not in this reproachful and stern voice, but gently, as a father. Tears rose to his throat, smothering him.

"What sort of a man are you? Your soul is all torn asunder. Still you go on talking as though you knew something. You would do better to keep silent."

"Ah, Tyapa, what you say is true," replied the teacher, sadly. "The people . . . you are right . . . they are numberless . . . but I am a stranger to them . . . and they are strangers to me. . . . Do you see where the tragedy lies? But never mind! I shall go on suffering . . . and there are no prophets, as you say. . . . No. You are right, I talk a great deal. . . . But it does no good to anyone. I shall be silent. . . . Only don't speak to me like this. . . . Ah, old friend, you do not know. . . . You do not know. . . . You cannot understand."

And in the end the teacher cried. He cried easily and

freely, with torrents of flowing tears and soon found relief in them.

"You ought to go to the village . . . try and become a clerk or a teacher. . . . You would be well fed there and see something different. Why waste your time here?" asked Tyapa sternly.

But the teacher was crying away, finding delight in his tears.

From this day they became friends, and the "creatures that once were men," seeing them together, said, "The teacher is getting on well with Tyapa. . . . He is after his money. Kuvalda must have pushed him to it—to nose about and find out where the old man's fortune is. . . ."

They probably said this without believing it. There was one strange thing about these men, they painted themselves in front of others worse than they actually were. A man who has nothing good in himself to advertise does not mind sometimes showing off the bad sides of his nature.

. . . .

When all these people were gathered round the teacher, the reading of the newspaper would begin.

"Well, what does the newspaper discuss today? Is there any fiction-page?"

"No," the teacher informed them.

"Your publisher seems stingy. . . . Is there any editorial maybe?"

"There is one today. . . . By Gulyaeff."

"Aha! Come, out with it. He writes cleverly, the rascal, curse him!"

"'The taxation of immovable property,'" reads the teacher, "'was introduced some fifteen years ago, and up to the present it continues to serve as the basis for collecting these taxes in aid of the city revenue. . . .'"

"That is all very naïve," comments Captain Kuvalda.

"Continues to serve, indeed. . . . That is ridiculous. It is profitable to the merchant who is in the city that it should continue to serve, therefore, it does."

"The article, in fact, is written on this subject," says the teacher.

"Is it? That is strange, it is more a subject for a story . . . it must be treated with plenty of pepper."

Then a short discussion begins. The people listen attentively, as only one bottle of vodka has been drunk until now.

After the editorial, they read the local events, then the court proceedings, and, if it is reported in the police court that the defendant or plaintiff is a merchant, then Aristid Kuvalda sincerely rejoices. If someone has robbed a merchant, "That is good," says he. "It is only a pity that they robbed him of so little." If his horses bolt—pleasant to hear, but "it is sad that he is still alive." If the merchant lost his suit in court, "It is a pity that the costs were not double the amount."

"That would have been illegal," remarks the teacher.

"Illegal! But is the merchant himself legal?" inquires Kuvalda, bitterly. "What is the merchant? Let us investigate this coarse and absurd phenomenon. First of all, every merchant is a mujik. He comes from a village, and in course of time becomes a merchant. In order to be a merchant, one must have money. Where can the mujik get the money from? It is well known that he does not get it by honest hard work, and that means that the mujik, somehow or other, has been dishonest. That is to say, a merchant is simply a dishonest mujik."

"Splendid!" cries the audience, approving the orator's deduction, and Tyapa bellows all the time, scratching his breast. He bellows like this every time on drinking his first glass of vodka after having been drunk. The Captain beams with joy. They next read the correspondence. This is, for the Captain, the opening of the floodgates, as he says. He sees everywhere how abominably the merchants build up this life, and how cleverly they spoil everything that has been done before. His speeches thunder at the merchants and annihilate them. His audience listens to him with great pleasure, because he swears atrociously. "If I wrote for the papers," he shouts, "I would show up the merchant in his true colors. . . . I would show that he is a beast, temporarily performing the functions of man. He is a rough boor, has no real taste for life, does not know the meaning of patriotism, and five kopecks is all he cares about."

Bag of Bones, knowing the Captain's weak point, and fond of making other people angry, maliciously adds:

"Yes, since the nobility began to die of hunger, men have disappeared from the world. . . ."

"You are right, you son of a spider and a toad. Yes, from the time that the noblemen collapsed, there have been no men. Only merchants have remained and I *hate* them."

"That is easy to understand, brother, because you, too, have been brought down by them. . . ."

"I? It was love of life that ruined me, you fool. I loved life, but the merchant robs it of everything, and I cannot bear him, simply for this reason, and not because I am a nobleman. But if you want to know the truth, it's not a nobleman that I am, but a *ci-devant*. I care now for nothing and nobody . . . and treat life as a mistress that has jilted me, for which I despise her."

"You lie!" says Bag of Bones.

"I lie?" roars Aristid Kuvalda, crimson with anger.

"Why shout?" comes in the cold sad voice of Martyanoff. "Why judge others? Merchants, noblemen . . . what have we to do with them?"

"Seeing that we are neither meat nor fish . . ." puts in Deacon Taras.

"Be quiet, Bag of Bones," says the teacher, good-naturedly. "Why turn the sword in the wound?"

He does not love discussion or noise, and when quarrel arises around him his lips fold into a painful grimace, he endeavors quietly and reasonably to reconcile each with the other, and if he does not succeed, leaves the company. Knowing this, the Captain, if he is not very drunk, controls himself, not wishing to lose, in the person of the teacher, one of his best listeners.

"I repeat," he continues, in a quieter tone, "that I see life in the hands of enemies, not only enemies of the noble class, but of everything fine, acquisitive enemies, incapable of adorning existence in any way."

"But all the same," says the teacher, "merchants too created Genoa, Venice, Holland, the merchants of England conquered India, the Stroganoff merchants . . ."

"What do I care about these? I am thinking of Judas Petunikoff, and Co. . . ."

"And what do you care about him?" asks the teacher quietly.

"But am I not alive? Aha! I am, so I cannot help being indignant that life is desecrated by these barbarians who have got hold of it."

"And dare to laugh at the noble anger of the Captain, a man out of office?" says Bag of Bones, teasingly.

"Very well! I agree that this is foolish. Being a creature who was once a man, I ought to blot out from my heart all those feelings and thoughts that once were mine. You may be right, but then how could I or any of you defend ourselves if we did away with all these feelings?"

"Now then, you are talking sense," says the teacher, encouragingly.

"We want other feelings and other views on life. . . .

We want something new because we ourselves are a novelty in this life. . . ."

"No doubt that is what we need," remarks the teacher.

"Why?" asks Bad End. "Is it not all the same whatever we say or think? We have not got long to live. . . . I am forty, you are fifty . . . there is no one among us younger than thirty, and not even at twenty can one go on for long living such a life."

"And what kind of novelty are we?" asks Bag of Bones, mockingly. "There have always been beggars!"

"Yes, and they were responsible for Rome," says the teacher.

"Yes, of course," says the Captain, beaming with joy. "Romulus and Remus, eh? We also shall do something when our time comes. . . ."

"Disturb public order and peace," interupts Bag of Bones. He laughs insolently. His laughter is evil, destructive, it is echoed by Simtsoff, the Deacon, and Taras-and-a-Half. The naïve eyes of young Meteor light up, and his cheeks flush crimson.

Bad End speaks, and it seems as if he were driving nails into their heads.

"All these are foolish illusions . . . fiddlesticks!"

It was strange to hear them reasoning in this manner, these outcasts from life, tattered, sodden with vodka and wrath, irony and filth. Such conversations were a feast for the Captain's heart. They gave him an opportunity of speaking more than the rest and therefore he thought himself better than the rest. And, however low he may fall, a man can never deny himself the delight of feeling cleverer, more powerful, or even better-nourished than his companions. Aristid Kuvalda abused this pleasure, and never could have enough of it, much to the disgust of Bag of Bones, Kubar, and others of these creatures that once were men, who were less interested in such matters.

Politics, however, were more to the general taste. The discussions as to the necessity of conquering India or of subduing England could last any amount of time. Nor did they speak with less enthusiasm of the radical measures for clearing Jews off the face of the earth. On this subject Bag of Bones always scored in proposing merciless plans, so that the Captain, desirous to be first in every argument, avoided this one. They also spoke readily, abundantly and impudently about women, but the teacher always defended the sex, and was very angry when they went beyond the limits of decency. They all, as a rule, gave in to him, because they looked upon him as an exceptional person, and also because they wished to borrow from him on Saturdays the money which he had earned during the week. He had many privileges. They never beat him, for instance, on these frequent occasions when the conversation ended in a free fight. He had the right to bring women into the doss-house; a privilege accorded to no one else, as the Captain had previously warned them.

"No bringing women to my house," he had said. "Women, merchants and philosophers, these are the three causes of my ruin. I will horsewhip anyone bringing in women. I'll horsewhip the woman too. . . . And if I find anyone philosophizing, I'll knock his head off for him." And notwithstanding his age he could have knocked anyone's head off, for he possessed wonderful strength. Besides, whenever he fought or quarreled, he was assisted by Martyanoff, who during a general fight would stand silently and solemnly as a tombstone back to back with Kuvalda, and then they became an all-destroying and impregnable engine of war. Once when Simtsoff was drunk, he rushed at the teacher for no reason whatever, and tore out a handful of hair. Kuvalda, with one stroke of his fist in the other's chest, made him unconscious for almost half an hour, and when he came to himself, Kuvalda forced him to eat the teacher's hair. He ate it, preferring this to being beaten to death.

Besides reading newspapers, fighting and indulging in general conversation, they entertained themselves by playing cards. They played without Martyanoff because he could not play honestly. After having been caught cheating several times, he openly confessed:

"I cannot play without cheating . . . it is a habit of mine."

"Habits do get the better of you," assented Deacon Taras. "I used to beat my wife every Sunday after Mass, and when she died I cannot describe how empty the day seemed on Sunday. I lived through one, it was bad enough . . . the second I still controlled myself, the third Sunday I struck my cook. . . . She protested and threatened to have me summoned. Just imagine if she had! On the fourth Sunday, I beat her just as if she were my own wife! Then I gave her ten rubles, and beat her after that regularly, till I married again."

"You are lying, Deacon! How could you marry a second time?" interrupted Bag of Bones.

"Aye, just so. . . . She looked after my house. . . ."

"Did you have any children?" asked the teacher.

"Five of them. . . . One was drowned . . . the eldest . . . he was an amusing boy! Two died of diphtheria. . . . One of the daughters married a student and went with him to Siberia. The other decided to study and died in St. Petersburg of consumption, they say. Ye-es, there were five of them. . . . Ecclesiastics are prolific, you know." He began explaining why this was so, and produced hysteric laughter. When the laughter stopped, Aleksei Maksimovitch Simtsoff remembered that he too had once had a daughter.

"Her name was Lidka . . . she was a stout girl." More than this he did not seem to remember, for he looked at them all, smiled in a guilty way, and remained silent.

Those men spoke very little to each other about their past, recalled it very seldom, and then only in its general outlines, and in a more or less cynical tone. Probably this was just as well, since, in many people, remembrance of the past kills all present energy and deadens all hope for the future.

. . . .

And on the rainy, cold, gray autumn days these "creatures that once were men" gathered in the eating-house of Vaviloff. They were well known there, a little feared as thieves and rogues, a little despised as hard drinkers, but believed to be clever and, therefore, respected and listened to.

The eating-house of Egor Vaviloff was the club of the street and the "creatures that once were men" were its intelligentsia. On Saturday evenings or Sunday mornings, when the eating-house was packed, the "creatures that once were men" were welcome guests. They brought with them, into the poverty- and sorrow-stricken crowd, consisting of the inhabitants of the street, their own atmosphere, in which there was something that brightened up the lives of men exhausted and perplexed by the struggle for existence, just as heavy drunkards as the inhabitants of Kuvalda's den, and, like them, outcasts from the town. Their ability to talk on all subjects and jeer, the fearlessness of their opinions, their sharp repartee, courage in the presence of things of which the whole street was in terror, the whole daring demeanor of these men could not but fascinate their companions. Then, too, they were well versed in law, and could advise, write petitions, and help to swindle without being caught. For all this they were paid with vodka and with a flattering admiration of their talents.

The inhabitants of the street were divided into two par-

CREATURES THAT ONCE WERE MEN

ties, according to their affections. One was in favor of Kuvalda, who was thought "a real warrior and much braver than the teacher," the other was convinced that the teacher, a man of great courage too, was in all ways "superior" to Kuvalda. The latter's admirers were to be found in the crowd of well-known inveterate drunkards, thieves and rascals, for whom the road from beggary to prison was inevitable. Those who respected the teacher were steadier men, who still had expectations, still hoped for better things, eternally plotted something and were nearly always hungry.

The nature of the teacher's and Kuvalda's relations with the street may be gathered from the following:

They were discussing one day in the pub the resolution passed by the municipal authorities regarding the street. The inhabitants were to fill up all the pits and ditches, but neither manure nor carrion were to be used for the purpose, only rubbish and crushed stone from building premises.

"Where on earth am I going to get this crushed stone when the only thing I ever wanted to build was a starling-house and that I haven't done yet?" Mokei Anisimoff complained. He traded in loaves of white bread baked by his wife.

The Captain decided to make a statement on the subject and banged his fist on the table to attract attention.

"Where can you get crushed stone and rubbish? Go and pull the Town Hall to pieces, my boys. It is so old that it is of no use to anyone, and you will thus be doing two good deeds for the adornment of the city. Firstly, by repairing our street; and secondly, by forcing them to erect a new Town Hall. If you want horses, get them from the Lord Mayor, and take his three daughters as well. They seem quite suitable for harness. Or else destroy the house of Judas Petunikoff and pave the street with its timber.

By the way, Mokei, I know where your wife got the fire to bake today's loaves; she used the shutters of the third window and the two steps of the porch of Judas' house."

When all present had laughed over this sufficiently, the grave market gardener, Pavlyugin, asked:

"No, truly, what are we to do, your honor? . . . Eh? What do you think?"

"Move neither hand nor foot. Let the street be ruined. . . ."

"Some of the houses are almost coming down. . . ."

"Let them fall; don't interfere; and when they fall ask assistance from the city. If you don't get it, bring a suit in court. Where does the water come from? From the city? Let the city then be responsible for the destruction of the houses."

"They will say the water comes from the rain. . . ."

"Does rain destroy the houses in the city? Eh? They take taxes from you but they do not let you speak of your rights. They destroy your life and property and at the same time force you to repair it! Fiddlesticks!"

And half the street, convinced by Kuvalda, the radical, decided to wait till the rain water swept away their houses. The others, more sensible, found in the teacher a man who composed for them a convincing report for the town authorities. In this report the refusal of the street's inhabitants to comply with the resolution was so well founded that the authorities actually responded to it. The street was allowed to use the rubbish left after the repairs to the barracks, and for the transport of this five horses were given by the fire brigade. Still more, they even saw the necessity of laying a drain-pipe through the street at the earliest opportunity. This and many other things vastly increased the popularity of the teacher. He wrote petitions for them and published notices in the newspapers.

For instance, on one occasion Vaviloff's customers noticed that the herrings and other provisions of the pub were not up to the mark, and after a day or two they saw Vaviloff standing at the bar with the newspaper in his hand making a public apology.

"It is true, I must acknowledge, that I bought moldy, not very fresh herrings, and the cabbage . . . well, that too was a bit withered. It is only too well known that everyone wants to put as many a five-kopeck piece in his pocket as he can. And what is the result? It has not been a success; I was greedy, I own, but the cleverer man has exposed my greed, so we are quits. . . ."

This confession made a very good impression on the people, and it also gave Vaviloff the opportunity of getting rid of his herrings and cabbages, for so much were they impressed that they failed to notice what they were eating.

This incident was very significant, because it not only increased the teacher's popularity, but also acquainted the man in the street with the effect of press opinion.

It often happened, too, that the teacher delivered lectures on practical morality in the public house.

"I saw you," he said to the house painter Yashka Tyurin, "I saw you, Yakov, beating your wife. . . ."

Yashka was not a little tight after two glasses of vodka, and was in a dare-devil mood.

The people around looked at him, expecting him to "kick up" a row, and all were silent.

"Did you see me? And how did you like it?" asked Yashka.

This was met with subdued laughter.

"I did *not* like it," replied the teacher. His tone was so earnest that the people around kept silent.

"Sorry, I was doing my best," said Yashka, with bravado, scenting that the teacher would get the better of him. "The wife is satisfied. . . . She has not been up today yet. . . ."

The teacher, who was drawing pictures absently with his fingers on the table, and examining them, said, "Don't you see, Yakov, why I don't like it? . . . Let us go into the matter thoroughly, and find out what you are really doing, and what the result for you may be. Your wife is pregnant. You struck her last night on her sides and chest. That means that you beat not only her but the child too. You may have killed it, and your wife might have died or else have become seriously ill. To have the trouble of looking after a sick woman is not pleasant. It is wearying, and expensive because illness requires medicine, and medicine money. If you have not killed the child, you may have crippled it, and it will be born deformed, lop-sided, or hunch-backed. That means that it will not be able to work, and it is only too important to you that he should be a good workman. Even if he is born ill, it will be bad enough, because he will keep his mother from work, and will require medicine. Do you see what you are doing to yourself? Men who live by hard work must be strong and healthy, and they should have strong and healthy children. Is all this right?"

"Yes," assented the listeners.

"But all this can't happen," said Yashka, rather frightened at the prospect held out to him by the teacher. "She is big and healthy, I could not possibly have got at the child. She is a devil—a hag, I tell you!" he shouted angrily. "She just eats me away as rust eats iron, whenever she gets a chance!"

"I understand, Yakov, that you cannot help beating your wife," the teacher's sad and thoughtful voice again broke in. "You have many reasons for doing so. . . . It is not your wife's nature that causes you to beat her so carelessly . . . but your own dark and sad life. . . ."

"You are right!" shouted Yakov. "We do live in darkness, like under a chimney sweep's shirt."

"You are angry with your life, but you vent your anger on your wife, on your closest of kin, and you make her suffer all this simply because you are stronger than she is. She is always handy and cannot get away. Don't you see how unreasonable you are?"

"That is so. . . . Devil take it! But what shall I do? Am I not a man after all?"

"Just so! You are a man. . . . Well, I only wish to tell you that if you cannot help beating her, then beat her carefully and always remember that you may injure her health or that of the child. It is not good to beat pregnant women . . . on their belly or on their sides and chest. . . . Beat her, say, on the neck . . . or else take a rope and beat her on some soft place. . . ."

The orator finished his speech and looked upon his hearers with his dark, deep-sunken eyes, seeming to apologize to them for some unknown crime.

They reacted to the speech with animation. They understood the ethics of this creature who was once a man, the ethics of the public house and much misfortune.

"Well, brother Yashka, did you understand? See how true all this is!"

Yakov understood. One should be careful how one beats one's wife or one might do oneself a wrong. He is silent, replying to his companions' jokes with confused smiles.

"Then again, what is a wife?" philosophizes the baker, Mokei Anisimoff. "A wife . . . is a friend . . . if we look at the matter in that way. She is like a chain, chained to you for life . . . and you are both just like two galley slaves. Try to walk in step with her, or else you will feel the chain. . . ."

"Wait a moment," says Yakov, "but you, you too beat your wife."

"Did I say that I did not? I beat her. . . . There is nothing else handy. . . . Do you expect me to thump against the wall with my fist when I just can't stand it all any longer?"

"That's how I feel, too . . ." says Yakov.

"What a foul and narrow life we lead, brothers! There is no real fling for us anywhere!"

"Even when beating one's wife, one has to be on the watch," someone remarks humorously. And thus they speak till far on in the night, or till they have quarreled, the usual result of drink or of passions engendered by such discussions.

The rain beats on the windows, and outside the cold wind is blowing hard. The pub is reeking with tobacco smoke, but it is warm, while the street is cold, wet and dark. Now and then the wind beats threateningly on the windows, as if impudently bidding these men to come out and be scattered like dust over the face of the earth. Sometimes a stifled and hopeless groan is heard in its howling, then again it is drowned by cold, cruel laughter. This music fills one with gloomy thoughts of the approaching winter, of tedious short days without sun, of interminable nights, of the need for warm garments and plenty to eat. It is hard to sleep through the long winter nights on an empty stomach. Winter is approaching. Yes, it is approaching. . . . How to live through it?

These gloomy forebodings created a strong thirst among the inhabitants of the street, and the heavy sighs of "the creatures that once were men" increased together with the wrinkles on their brows, their voices became thick and their behavior to each other coarser. And suddenly a fierce anger would break out amongst them, awakening the cruelty of persecuted people wearied by their hard fate. They began beating each other roughly and brutally and, then making it up, drank again till there was nothing more to pawn with undiscriminating Vaviloff. Thus in dumb anger and misery, which was squeezing their hearts, they spent the days of autumn, not knowing how to find a way out of this vile life, and in dread of the still crueler days of winter.

Kuvalda in such cases came to their assistance with his philosophy.

"Don't lose heart, brothers, everything has its end, this is the chief quality of life. The winter will pass, summer will follow . . . a glorious time, when, as they say, the sparrows themselves get their fill of beer." But his speeches did not have any effect—a mouthful of the freshest water will not satisfy a hungry man.

Deacon Taras also tried to entertain his friends by singing his songs and relating his tales. He was more successful, and sometimes his endeavors ended in a wild and desperate orgy at the pub. They sang, laughed and danced, and for hours behaved like sheer madmen. After this they again fell into gloom and despair, sitting at the tables of the pub, in the black smoke of the lamp and the tobacco, sullen and tattered, lazily speaking to each other, listening to the wild howling of the wind, and thinking only of getting enough drink to deaden their senses.

And each was filled with disgust for the other and fondled a helpless hatred against the whole world.

II

All things are relative in this world, and a man cannot sink into a condition so bad that it could not be any worse.

One bright day, towards the end of September, Captain Aristid Kuvalda was sitting, as was his custom, on the bench near the door of the doss-house, looking at the stone building in process of being erected by the merchant Petunikoff close to Vaviloff's pub, and thinking deeply.

This building, which was still unfinished, was intended for a soap factory and had for a long time been an eyesore for the Captain, with the dark, bare gaps made by the long rows of windows and the cobweb of scaffolding surrounding it from roof to foundation.

Painted red, as if with blood, it looked like a cruel machine which, though not working yet, had already opened a row of deep, hungry, gaping jaws, as if ready to devour and swallow anything. The gray wooden eating-house of Vaviloff, with its bent roof overgrown with moss, leaned against one of the brick walls of the factory, and looked like a large parasite clinging to it. The Captain was thinking that they would soon be putting up new houses to replace the old buildings as well. "They will also destroy the doss-house," he reflected. "One will have to look for another, but such a cheap and convenient one is not to be found. It seems a great pity to have to leave a place to which one has grown so used, only because some merchant has got it into his head to manufacture candles and soap." And the Captain felt that if he could only make the life of such a foe miserable, even for a while, oh! with what pleasure he would do it!

Yesterday, Ivan Andreyevitch Petunikoff was in the doss-house yard with his son and an architect. They measured up the yard and put some small wooden sticks here and there which, after the exit of Petunikoff and at the order of the Captain, Meteor pulled out and threw away.

The Captain could still see the merchant in front of him, small, dry, in a long garment like a frock coat, a velvet cap, and high, dazzlingly shining boots. He had a bony face with prominent cheekbones, a wedge-shaped grayish beard, and a high forehead seamed with wrinkles, from beneath which shone two narrow, half-closed, alert and observant gray eyes . . . a sharp, gristly nose, a small mouth with thin lips . . . altogether an appearance which was rapaciously pious and respectably wicked.

"Cursed cross-breed of fox and pig!" swore the Captain under his breath, recalling his first meeting with Petunikoff. The merchant had come with one of the town councilors to buy the house, and, seeing the Captain, asked of his companion:

"Is this piece of junk that lodger of yours?"

And from that day, a year and a half ago, there had been a keen competition among the two as to which could insult the hardest. Last night there had been a "slight skirmish with hot words," as the Captain called his conversations with Petunikoff. Having dismissed the architect, the merchant approached the Captain.

"Still squatting there?" he asked, putting his hand to his cap, so that one would have hesitated to say whether it was to adjust it or in way of a greeting.

"Still knocking about?" asked the Captain in the same tone, with a jerk of his chin which brought his beard into movement, and a careless person might have taken it for a nod, or for an attempt on his part to move his pipe from one corner of his mouth to the other.

"Well, having plenty of money, I can knock about the world. Money asks to be spent, so I am just giving it a free hand," the merchant teased the Captain, throwing a cunning glance at him.

"So it's you who serve the money, not the money you," Kuvalda retorted, fighting the desire to punch the merchant's belly.

"Isn't it all the same? Money puts everything right, but when you have none," . . . and the merchant looked at the Captain with feigned and impudent compassion. The latter's upper lip curled up and exposed large, wolfish teeth.

"With brains and a conscience, it is possible to live without it. Money usually comes to people just when their consciences begin to wither . . . the less conscience the more money!"

"Just so; but then there also are men who have neither money nor conscience."

"That's what you were like when you were young?" asked Kuvalda innocently. The other man's nostrils twitched. Ivan Andreyevitch sighed, half closed his eyes and said:

"Oh! When I was young I had to undergo many a hardship . . ."

"I suppose so . . ."

"How I worked . . ."

"And made others overwork?"

"People like you? Nobles? I should think so! Many of them begged for mercy."

"You went in only for robbing, not murder, I suppose?" hissed the Captain. Petunikoff turned green and hastily changed the subject.

"You are a bad host. Here you sit while your guest stands."

"There's nothing to prevent him from sitting," said Kuvalda.

"But what am I to sit on?"

"On the ground . . . it will stand any rubbish. . . ."

"You are a proof of that yourself," said Petunikoff, quietly. "I should say it's time I left you and your language," and his eyes shot forth cold, poisonous glances.

And he went away, leaving Kuvalda under the pleasant impression that the merchant was afraid of him. If he were not afraid he would long ago have evicted him from the doss-house. The five rubles a month could not possibly be a reason for keeping him. Following him with his eyes, he noticed how the merchant circled round the factory, and walked up and down the scaffolding, and he wished very much that he would fall and break all his bones. He sat imagining many horrible forms of disaster while watching Petunikoff climbing about like a spider in its web. Last night it had almost seemed to him that a plank gave way under the merchant, and he had jumped up in his excitement—but it came to nothing, alas.

And today, as always, the red building stood out before the eyes of Aristid Kuvalda, so plain, so massive, and clinging so strongly to the earth, as though it were already sucking away all its juice. It appeared, with its gaping walls, to be laughing coldly and in sinister fashion at the Captain. The sun poured its rays on them as generously as it does on the miserable hovels of the street.

"Devil take the thing!" exclaimed the Captain, thoughtfully measuring the walls of the factory with his eyes. "If only . . ." Trembling with excitement at the thought that had just flashed across his mind, Aristid Kuvalda jumped up and ran to Vaviloff's pub, smiling and muttering to himself all the time.

Vaviloff met him at the bar and gave him a friendly welcome.

"I wish your honor good health!" He was of middle height, and had a bald head with a crown of gray hair, and only a small bristling mustache like a tooth-brush. Upright and neat in his leather jacket, he showed in every movement that he was an old sergeant.

"Egorka, you have the deed to your property and the map, haven't you?" demanded Kuvalda, impatiently.

"I have." Vaviloff looked up suspiciously with his thievish little eyes and closely scanned the Captain's face, which seemed to have an unfamiliar expression.

"Show them to me!" shouted the Captain, striking the bar with his fist and sitting down on a stool close by.

"But what for?" asked Vaviloff, feeling that it was better to keep his wits about him with Kuvalda so excited.

"You fool! Bring them at once."

Vaviloff wrinkled up his forehead and turned his eyes questioningly to the ceiling.

"Where are those papers of mine?"

There was no answer to this on the ceiling, so the old sergeant looked down at his belly, and began drumming with his fingers on the bar in a worried and thoughtful manner.

"It's no good your playing the fool like this," shouted the Captain, who had no great affection for him, thinking that it befitted more a former soldier to become a thief than a pub-keeper.

"Oh! Yes! I remember now, Aristid Fomich. They were left at the District Court at the time when I came into possession."

"No nonsense, Egorka! It is in your own interest to show me the plan, the title-deeds, and everything you have immediately. You will probably clear a few hundred rubles over this, do you understand?"

Vaviloff did not understand at all; but the Captain spoke in such serious and convincing tones that the sergeant's eyes lit up with curiosity, and, telling him that he would see if the papers were in his desk, he went out through the door behind the bar. Two minutes later he returned with the papers in his hand and an expression of extreme astonishment on his face.

"Here they are, the blasted deeds, at home after all!"

"Ah! You . . . clown! And a former soldier too."

Kuvalda could not help rebuking him, as he snatched the blue file from his hands. Then, spreading out the papers in front of him and thus exciting all the more Vaviloff's curiosity, the Captain began reading, examining and ominously grunting at the same time. At last, he got up resolutely, and went to the door, leaving all the papers on the bar and saying to Vaviloff:

CREATURES THAT ONCE WERE MEN 107

"Wait! Don't put them away!"

Vaviloff gathered them up, put them into the cash box, locked it, then felt the lock to see if it were secure. After that he scratched his bald head thoughtfully and went out on the porch of the eating-house. From there he saw the Captain measuring the front of the house, and watched him anxiously, as he snapped his fingers, and began measuring the same line over again—thoughtful, but satisfied with the result. Vaviloff's face became strained, then puzzled, until finally a radiant smile appeared on it.

"Aristid Fomich, is it possible?" he shouted, when the Captain came up to him.

"Of course it is possible. There is more than an arshin cut off in the front alone, and as to the depth I shall see immediately."

"The depth . . . is thirty-two arshins."

"So, you have guessed, you barefaced mug?"

"Of course, Aristid Fomich! But what eyes you have, my word! You can see under the ground, you can!" shouted Vaviloff joyfully.

A few minutes later, they sat opposite each other in Vaviloff's parlor, and the Captain, consuming large quantities of beer, was telling the bar-keeper:

"Thus, one wall of the factory stands on your ground; now, mind you show no mercy! The teacher will be here presently, and we will get him to draw up a petition to the court. As to the amount of the damages, you will name a very moderate sum in order not to waste money in stamp duties, but we will ask to have the factory torn down. This, you see, you ass, is what it means to encroach on other people's property. It is a splendid piece of luck for you. Smash, indeed! It will cost him a penny to smash or move a thing like that. He'll want to settle. That will be the moment to bring pressure to bear on Judas. We will calculate in detail how much it will cost to bring the factory down, crushed brick, foundation, all! Even the time will be taken account of. Then, Judas, if you please, hand over two thousand rubles!"

"He will never give it!" cried Vaviloff, his eyes anxiously blinking and shining with a greedy light.

"Fiddlesticks! He will give it. . . . Use your brains. . . . What else can he do? Tear it down? But look here, Egorka, mind you don't let yourself be done in. They are sure to try to buy you off. Don't sell yourself cheap. They will probably use threats, but rely upon us . . ."

The Captain's eyes were alight with a fierce happiness, and his face, red with excitement, twitched nervously. He worked upon Vaviloff's greed, and urging upon him the importance of immediate action in the matter, went away in a very triumphant and unrelenting frame of mind.

. . . .

In the evening everyone was told of the Captain's discovery, and they all began to discuss Petunikoff's future predicament, painting in vivid colors his anger and astonishment on the day the court messenger would hand him the copy of the summons. The Captain felt himself a hero. He was happy and all his friends intensely pleased. The large heap of dark and tattered figures lay in the court-yard and made noisy demonstrations of pleasure. They all knew the merchant, Petunikoff, who passed them every day, contemptuously half-closing his eyes and giving them no more attention than he bestowed on the other rubbish in the street. He reeked with satiety, which exasperated them still more. He shone with superiority even down to his boots; and now one of them had struck a hard blow at his purse and pride! Was that not enough reason for rejoicing? Malice had a particular attraction for these men. It was the only weapon in their hands which they could handle. They all had fostered a subconscious, vague but sharp hostility towards well-fed and well-dressed people.

For a fortnight the inhabitants of the doss-house lived in expectation of further developments, but Petunikoff never once visited his building during that time. It became known that he was not in town and that the copy of the petition had not yet reached him. Kuvalda raged at the delays of the civil court. Surely nobody had ever awaited the merchant with such concentrated impatience as did this bare-footed brigade.

"He doesn't dream of coming, oh my darling! He does not love me, he does not!" sang Deacon Taras, resting his chin on his hand and casting a humorously sorrowful glance towards the hill.

At last one evening Petunikoff appeared. He came in a very presentable cart with his son playing the rôle of a groom. The latter was a red-cheeked youngster, in a long checkered overcoat. He wore dark eyeglasses. They tied the horse to a post of the scaffolding, the son took a measuring instrument out of his pocket and gave it to his father, and they began to measure the ground. Both were silent and looked preoccupied.

"Aha!" shouted the Captain, gleefully.

All those present in the doss-house at the moment came to the gate to watch and expressed themselves loudly in reference to the matter.

"What a strange thing the habit of thieving is. A man may steal without any intention to do so and lose thereby more than he gets," said the Captain, causing much laughter among his staff and eliciting various murmurs of assent.

"Take care, you devil!" shouted Petunikoff, exasperated at last by the jeers, "lest I have you in the police court for your words!"

"You can do nothing without witnesses. . . . Your son cannot give evidence on your side . . ." the Captain warned him.

"Look out all the same, you old wretch, one day justice will be meted out to you." Petunikoff shook his fist at him. His son, calmly engrossed in his calculations, took no notice of the dark group of men taking such a wicked delight in adding to his father's discomfiture. He did not even once look in their direction.

"The young spider has himself well in hand," remarked Bag of Bones, watching young Petunikoff's every movement and action.

Having taken all the measurements he desired, Ivan Andreyevitch knit his brows silently, got into the cart, and drove away. His son went with a firm step into Vaviloff's pub, and disappeared behind the door.

"Ho, ho! That's a determined young thief! . . . What will happen next, I wonder . . . ?" asked Kuvalda.

"Next? Young Petunikoff will buy off Egor Vaviloff," said Bag of Bones, with an air of conviction on his sharp face, and smacked his lips as if the idea gave him great pleasure.

"And you are glad of that, are you?" Kuvalda asked him, gravely.

"I am always pleased to see human calculations miscarry," explained Bag of Bones, closing his eyes and rubbing his hands with delight.

The Captain spat angrily on the ground and was silent. They all stood in front of the tumbledown building and silently watched the doors of the pub. More than an hour passed thus. Then the doors opened and Petunikoff came out as calmly as he had entered. He stopped for a moment, coughed, turned up the collar of his coat, glanced at the men, who were following all his movements with their eyes, and then went up the street towards the town.

The Captain watched him for a moment, and, turning to Bag of Bones, said with a scowl:

"You were probably right after all, you son of a scorpion

CREATURES THAT ONCE WERE MEN 111

and an earwig! You have a nose for every evil thing. Yes, the face of that young swindler shows that he has got what he wanted. . . . I wonder how much Egorka has got out of them. He has evidently taken something. . . . He is the same sort of rogue. . . . I'm damned if I did not arrange the whole thing for him! It is hard to realize one's own folly. . . . Yes, life is against us all, my miserable brothers . . . and even when you spit at your fellow-creature the spittle rebounds and hits your own face."

Having comforted himself with this reflection, the worthy Captain looked round at his staff. They were all disappointed, because they all knew that some arrangement had taken place between Petunikoff and Vaviloff. To know that you have failed in harming someone is more humiliating than to know that you have failed to do any good, because to do harm is so much easier and simpler.

"Well, why are we loitering here? We have nothing more to wait for . . . except the reward that I shall get out of Egorka . . ." said the Captain, looking gloomily at the pub. "So our peaceful life under the roof of Judas has come to an end. Judas will now turn us out. . . . This I announce to the Department of Sans-culottes which is entrusted to me."

Bad End smiled sadly.

"What are you laughing at, jailer?" Kuvalda asked.

"Where shall *I* go then?"

"That, my angel, is a question that fate will settle for you, so do not worry," said the Captain, thoughtfully, entering the doss-house. The "creatures that once were men" lazily followed him.

"We can do nothing but await the critical moment," said the Captain, pacing along among them. "When they turn us out we shall seek a new shelter for ourselves, but at present there is no use spoiling our life by thinking of it. . . . In times of crisis one becomes energetic . . . and if life were nothing but a crisis and every moment of it so arranged that we were compelled to tremble for our lives all the time . . . by God! it would be livelier and men more interesting than they are!"

"That means that they would cut each other's throats more viciously," explained Bag of Bones, smilingly.

"Well, what about it?" asked the Captain, hotly. He did not like to hear his thoughts explained.

"Oh! Nothing! You are right, when one wants to get anywhere quickly one whips up the horses, and pokes up the fire in the engines. . . ."

"Well, let everything go to the Devil as quickly as possible. I'm sure I should be pleased if the earth suddenly blew up or was consumed or blown to pieces, if I were to be the last left and could watch the others perish. . . ."

"Ferocious creature!" smiled Bag of Bones.

"Well, what of that? I . . . I was once a man . . . now I am an outcast . . . that means I have no ties or obligations. It means that I am free to spit on everything. The nature of my present life means the rejection of my past . . . giving up all means of intercourse with men who are well fed and well dressed, and who look upon me with contempt because I am inferior to them in the matter of feeding or dressing. I must develop something new within myself, do you understand? Something that will make the managers of life, such as Judas Petunikoff, and his kind, tremble in their guts before my imposing figure."

"Ah! you have a bold tongue!" jeered Bag of Bones.

"You worm!" And Kuvalda looked at him contemptuously. "What do you understand? What do you know? Are you able to think? I have thought and read . . . books of which you would not understand one word."

"Of course! I haven't learned how to eat soup with my shoe. . . . But though you have read and thought, and

I have done neither, we both seem to have got into pretty much the same condition, haven't we?"

"Go to the devil!" shouted Kuvalda. His conversations with Bag of Bones always ended like that. When the teacher was absent his speeches, that he knew, merely fell into thin air and infected it, receiving no approval or attention, but still he could not help speaking. Now, having quarreled with his companion, he felt rather deserted among these men, but still longing for conversation, he turned to Simtsoff with the following question: "And you, Aleksei Maksimovitch, where will you lay your gray head?"

The old man smiled good-humoredly, rubbed his nose, and replied, "I do not know . . . I will see. I do not require much, just a little drink now and then."

"Plain, but honorable fate!" the Captain said encouragingly. Simtsoff, after a silence, added that he would find a means of living sooner than any of them, because women loved him so. This was true. The old man had, as a rule, two or three prostitutes at his disposal, who kept him days on end on their very scant earnings. They very often beat him, but he took this stoically. For some reason they never beat him too hard, probably because they pitied him. He was a great lover of women, and said they were the cause of all his misfortunes. The intimacy of his relations with them and of their attitude to him was revealed by the appearance of his clothes, which were more neatly mended and cleaner than those of his companions, also by his frequent illnesses. And now, sitting at the door of the dosshouse, he boasted to his friends that for a long time Radish had been asking him to go and live with her, but he had not done so, because he did not want to part with their company. They heard this with jealous interest. They all knew Radish. She lived close by at the foot of the mountain and had recently had some months of prison for repeated theft. She was a *ci-devant* wet-nurse, a tall, stout peasant woman, with a face marked by smallpox, but with lovely, though always drunken eyes.

"Just look at the old devil!" swore Bag of Bones, looking at Simtsoff, who was smiling in a self-satisfied way.

"And do you know why they love me? Because I know how to cheer up their souls."

"Do you?" inquired Kuvalda.

"And I can make them pity me. . . . And a woman, when she pities, she is capable of killing you out of pity. . . . Go and weep to her, and ask her to kill you . . . she will pity you—and kill you too."

"It is I who feel like murder," declared Martyanoff, with his gloomy laugh.

"Whom would you murder?" asked Bag of Bones, edging away from him.

"It's all the same to me . . . Petunikoff . . . Egorka . . . or even you!"

"But why?" inquired Kuvalda.

"I want to get to Siberia. . . . I have had enough of this vile life. . . . There, at least, you have to live as you are told."

"Yes, they do, indeed, tell you that very thoroughly," agreed the Captain dejectedly.

They spoke no more of Petunikoff, or of the future ejection from the doss-house. They all knew that they would have to leave soon, therefore they did not think the matter worth discussion. Sitting in a circle on the grass, they conversed lazily about various things, passing from one subject to another, giving only so much attention to views expressed as was necessary to go on with the discussion. It was too dreary to keep silent and too dreary to sit listening. This group of "creatures that once were men" had one fine characteristic—no one made any effort to prove that he was better than the others, nor urged the other to such an effort.

The August sun jealously warmed their tatters as they sat with their backs and unkempt heads exposed to it . . . a chaotic mixture of the vegetable, mineral and animal kingdoms. In the corners of the yard tall burdock and other useless weeds gladdened the sight of this group of useless people.

. . . .

The following was the scene that took place in Vaviloff's eating-house:

Young Petunikoff entered without haste, slowly took off his gray hat, looked around him with a sneering glance, and said to the pub-keeper, who was greeting him obsequiously and smilingly:

"Egor Terentievitch Vaviloff? Is that you?"

"It is," answered the sergeant, leaning on the bar with both arms as if preparing to jump over it.

"I have some business with you," said Petunikoff.

"Delighted. Please come this way into my private room."

They went in and sat down, the guest on the oilcloth sofa in front of a round table, and his host on the chair opposite him. In one corner a lamp was burning before a gigantic icon—more icons hung on the wall around it. The silver frames were well polished and shone as new. The room, crowded with trunks and old miscellaneous furniture, smelt of tobacco, sour cabbage, and olive oil. Petunikoff looked around him with a grimace. Vaviloff glanced up at the icon, with a sigh, and then they scrutinized each other, and both seemed to be favorably impressed. Petunikoff liked Vaviloff's frankly thievish eyes, and Vaviloff the open, cold, determined face of Petunikoff, with its broad cheekbones and white teeth.

"I presume you guess what I am about to say to you," began Petunikoff.

"The lawsuit? . . . I presume?" remarked the ex-sergeant respectfully.

"Exactly! I am glad to see you are not beating about the bush, but going straight to the point like a straightforward man," said Petunikoff, encouragingly.

"I am a soldier," answered Vaviloff, with a modest air.

"That is easy to see, and I am sure we shall be able to settle this job quickly and without much trouble."

"Just so."

"Good! You have the law on your side, and will, of course, win your case. I want to tell you this from the first."

"Many thanks," said the sergeant, blinking in order to hide the smile in his eyes.

"But tell me, why did you have to make the acquaintance of your future neighbors in this brusque manner, through the law courts?"

Vaviloff shrugged his shoulders and did not answer.

"It would have been better to come straight to us and settle the matter peacefully, eh? What do you think?"

"That would have been better, of course, but you see there is a hitch . . . I was not acting on my own, but on the advice of others. . . . I found out later that it would have been better if . . . But it was too late."

"Oh! I suppose some lawyer advised you on this?"

"Someone of that sort."

"Aha! Do you really wish to settle the affair peacefully?"

"With all my heart!" cried the soldier.

Petunikoff was silent for a moment, then looked at him, and suddenly asked, coldly and dryly, "And why do you wish to do so?"

Vaviloff did not expect such a question, and therefore had no reply ready. In his opinion the question was quite a futile one, under the circumstances, so he grinned at young Petunikoff, feeling very superior.

"That is easy to understand. Men should try to live peacefully with one another."

CREATURES THAT ONCE WERE MEN 117

"Oh, no!" interrupted Petunikoff, "that is not exactly the reason why. As far as I can see, you do not distinctly understand why you wish to be on good terms with us. . . . I will tell you."

The soldier was a little surprised. This youngster, dressed in a checked suit, in which he looked slightly ridiculous, spoke as if he were Colonel Rakshin, of happy memory, who used to knock three of the soldiers' teeth out every time he was angry.

"You want to be friends with us because we should be such useful neighbors to you . . . because there will be less than a hundred and fifty workmen in our factory, and in course of time even more. If a hundred men come and drink one glass at your place, after receiving their weekly wages, that means you will sell every month four hundred glasses more than you sell at present. This is of course the lowest estimate. And then you have the eating-house besides. You are not an inexperienced fool, and you can understand for yourself what profitable neighbors we shall be."

"That is true," Vaviloff nodded, "I knew that."

"Well, what then?" asked the merchant, loudly.

"Nothing . . . Let us be friends!"

"It is nice to see you have decided so quickly. See here, I have already prepared a notification to the court on the withdrawal of the summons against my father. Here it is; read it, and sign it."

Vaviloff looked at his interlocutor with his round eyes and started, as if scenting something unpleasant.

"Pardon me . . . sign it? How is that?"

"Quite simple . . . just write your Christian name and surname, nothing more," explained Petunikoff, pointing obligingly with his finger to the place allotted for the signature.

"Oh! It is not that . . . I was alluding to the compensation I was to get for my ground."

"But this ground is of no use to you," said Petunikoff, calmly.

"But it is mine all the same!" exclaimed the soldier.

"Of course, and how much do you want for it?"

"Well, say the amount stated in the document," said Vaviloff, falteringly.

"Six hundred!" and Petunikoff smiled softly. "You are a funny bloke!"

"The law is on my side. . . . I can even demand two thousand. I can insist on your pulling down the building . . . and enforce it too. That is why my claim is so small. I demand that you should pull it down!"

"Very well, go on. Probably we shall do so . . . after three years, and after having dragged you into enormous law expenses. And then having paid up, we shall open our own public-house, far better than yours, and you will be ruined . . . done for like the Swedes at Poltava. We shall see that you are done for . . . we shall take good care of that, you may be sure."

Egor Terentievitch looked at his guest, clenching his teeth, and felt that his fate was in his hands. Vaviloff was overwhelmed with self-pity at having to deal with this calm, relentless figure in the checked suit.

"Being such a near neighbor you might have gained a good deal in remaining friendly with us, and we should have done our best to make it worth your while. For instance, I would advise you even now to open a small shop for tobacco, you know, bread, matches, cucumbers, and so on. . . . All these are sure to be in great demand."

Vaviloff listened, and, being a clever fellow, knew that to throw himself on the enemy's generosity was the better plan. He ought to have done this from the start. Now, unable to relieve his mind otherwise, the soldier began to swear at Kuvalda.

"Curses be upon your head, you drunken rascal! May the Devil take you!"

"Do you mean the lawyer who composed your petition?" asked Petunikoff, calmly, and added, with a sigh, "I have no doubt he would have landed you in a rather awkward fix . . . had we not taken pity on you."

"Ah!" And the distressed soldier raised his hand. "There are two of them. . . . One of them discovered it, the other wrote the petition, the accursed reporter!"

"Why the reporter?"

"He writes for the papers. . . . He is one of your lodgers . . . what vermin they are. . . . Clear them away for Christ's sake! The robbers! They rouse and egg on everyone in the street. One cannot live for them. . . . Desperate fellows, all of them. . . . One has to look out or they'll rob or set fire to you."

"And this reporter, who is he?" asked Petunikoff, with interest.

"He? A drunkard. He was a teacher, but got kicked out, drank himself to destruction . . . now he writes for the papers and composes petitions. A trickster."

"H'm! And did he write your petition too? So-so, I suppose it was he who wrote of the flaws in the building. The scaffolding was not safe, or what was it?"

"He did! I know it for a fact! The dog! He read it aloud in here and boasted: 'Now I have caused Petunikoff some trouble.' "

"Ye-es . . . Well, then, do you want to make peace?"

"To make peace?" The soldier lowered his head and pondered. "Ah! This is a dark life!" he said in an injured voice, scratching his head.

"One should get enlightened," Petunikoff advised him, lighting a cigarette.

"Enlightened? It is not that, my dear sir; but don't you see there is no freedom? Don't you see what a life I lead? I live in fear and trembling . . . deprived of the so desirable freedom in my movements. And why is that? Because this miserable little teacher writes about me in the papers. . . . Sanitary inspectors are summoned . . . fines have to be paid. . . . Then your lodgers might at any moment set fire to the place or rob and kill me. . . . I am powerless against them. They are not afraid of the police, they rather like going to prison, they get their food for nothing there."

"Well—we will have them turned out if we come to terms with you," promised Petunikoff.

"What terms do you suggest then?" asked Vaviloff, sadly and sullenly.

"Tell me yours."

"Well, give me the six hundred mentioned in the claim."

"Won't you take a hundred rubles?" asked the merchant, calmly, looking fixedly at his companion, and smiling softly. "I will not give one ruble more . . ." he added.

After this, he took out his eyeglasses, and began slowly cleaning them with his handkerchief. Vaviloff looked at him with despair and respect at the same time. The calm face of Petunikoff, his big gray eyes, the large cheekbones, every line of his thickset body betokened self-confidence and a well-balanced mind. Vaviloff liked Petunikoff's straightforward and friendly manner of addressing him, without pretensions, as if he were an equal, though Vaviloff understood well enough that Petunikoff was his superior, he being only a soldier. Looking at him, almost with admiration, he felt a rush of curiosity overcome him, and, forgetting for a moment the matter in hand, he respectfully asked Petunikoff:

"Where did you study?"

"In the technological institute. Why?" answered the other, smiling.

"Nothing. Only . . . excuse me!" The soldier lowered his head, and then suddenly exclaimed, with envy and exhilaration, "What a splendid thing education is! Science is light. Whereas, we poor folk are as stupid as owls in the sunlight. . . . Your honor, let us settle up this job."

With an air of decision he stretched out his hand to Petunikoff and said:

"Well, five hundred?"

"Not more than one hundred rubles, Egor Terenticvitch."

Petunikoff shrugged his shoulders as if regretting his inability to give more, and clasped the soldier's hairy hand with his large white palm. They soon ended the matter, for the soldier suddenly gave in and promptly met all Petunikoff's wishes. As to the latter, he was inexorable, and Vaviloff, after receiving the hundred rubles and signing the paper, threw the pen down on the table and said bitterly:

"Now I will have a nice time with those hooligans! They will laugh at me and cry shame, the devils!"

"You can tell them that I paid up all your claim," suggested Petunikoff, calmly puffing out ringlets of smoke and watching them float upwards.

"But do you think they will believe it? They are as clever swindlers, if not worse . . ."

Vaviloff stopped in time before making the intended comparison, and looked anxiously at the merchant's son. The other smoked on, and seemed to be absorbed in that occupation. He went away soon, promising to destroy the nest of restless vagabonds. Vaviloff followed him with a glance and sighed, feeling acutely as if he would like to shout some gross insult at the young man who was going with such firm steps towards the steep road, encumbered with its ditches and heaps of rubbish.

In the evening, the Captain appeared in the pub. His eyebrows were sternly knit and his right fist firmly clenched. Vaviloff smiled at him in a guilty manner.

"Well, worthy descendant of Judas and Cain, tell us . . ."

"It's all been decided . . ." said Vaviloff, sighing and lowering his eyes.

"I don't doubt it; how many pieces of silver did you receive?"

"Four hundred rubles . . ."

"Lying, of course . . . But all the better for me. Without any further words, Egorka, ten per cent of it for my discovery, twenty-five rubles to the teacher for writing the petition, one bucket of vodka to all of us, and decent refreshments all round. Give me the money now, the vodka and refreshments will do at eight o'clock."

Vaviloff turned green and stared at Kuvalda with wide-open eyes.

"This is humbug! This is robbery! I will do nothing of the sort. What do you mean, Aristid Fomich? Keep your appetite for the next feast! I like that! I need not be afraid of you now! I . . ."

Kuvalda looked at the clock.

"I give you ten minutes, Egorka, for your idiotic talk. Finish delivering your nonsense by that time and give me what I demand. If you don't, I'll make an end of you! Has Bad End sold anything to you? Did you read in the paper about the theft at Basoff's? Do you understand? You won't have time to hide anything, we will see to that . . . and this very night . . . you understand?"

"Aristid Fomich, have pity!" sobbed the cowering sergeant.

"No more words! Did you understand or not?"

Tall, gray, and imposingly stern Kuvalda spoke in a whisper, and his hoarse bass voice rang through the empty house in sinister notes. Vaviloff had always feared him, not only as a retired soldier, but also as a man who had nothing to lose. But now Kuvalda appeared before him in a new rôle. He did not speak as much and as jocosely as usual, but in the tone of a commander, convinced of the other's obedience, and that was no poor threat. And Vaviloff felt that the Captain could and would ruin him with the greatest delight. He must incline himself before this power. Nevertheless, boiling with rage, the soldier decided to make a last desperate attempt. He sighed deeply, and began with apparent meekness.

"It is justly said that a man's sin will find him out. . . . I lied to you, Aristid Fomich . . . I tried to be cleverer than I am . . . I only received one hundred rubles."

"Go on!" said Kuvalda.

"And not four hundred as I told you. . . . That means . . ."

"It does not mean anything. I don't know whether you are lying now or lied before. You owe me sixty-five rubles. That is not much, eh?"

"Oh! Good God! Aristid Fomich! I have always been attentive to your honor's wishes and done my best to please you."

"Drop all that, Egorka, grandchild of Judas!"

"All right! I will give it to you . . . only God will punish you for this. . . ."

"Silence! You pimple on the face of the earth!" shouted the Captain, rolling his eyes fiercely. "He has punished me enough already in forcing me to talk with you . . . to see you . . . I will kill you on the spot like a fly!"

He shook his fist in Vaviloff's face and gnashed his teeth.

After he had gone Vaviloff began grimacing and blinking

nervously. Then two large tears rolled down his cheeks. They were of a grayish hue, and when they had hid themselves in his mustache, two others followed them. Then Vaviloff went into his own room and stood before the icon, without praying, immovable, letting the salt tears run down his wrinkled brown cheeks. . . .

. . . .

Deacon Taras, whose favorite occupation was to loiter among woods and prairies, proposed to the "creatures that once were men" to go into the fields to a ravine there and drink Vaviloff's vodka in the bosom of Nature. But the Captain and all the rest unanimously swore both at the Deacon and at Nature, and decided to drink it in the court-yard.

"One, two, three," counted Aristid Fomich. "We are thirteen, the teacher is not here . . . but probably many other brigands will join us. Let us count, say, twenty persons, and to every person two-and-a-half cucumbers, a pound of bread, and a pound of meat. . . . That's not so bad! One bottle of vodka each, and there is plenty of sour cabbage, apples, and three watermelons. I ask you, what the devil could you want more, my scoundrels of friends? Now then, let us prepare to devour Egorka Vaviloff, because all this is his flesh and blood!"

They spread some old clothes on the ground, setting the delicacies and the drink on them, and sat around the feast, solemnly and quietly, almost unable to control the craving for drink that shone in their eyes.

The evening began to fall, and cast its shadows on the refuse littering the court-yard of the doss-house; the last rays of sun lit up the roof of the tumble-down building. The air was cool and soft.

"Let us begin, brothers!" commanded the Captain. "How many cups have we? Six . . . and there are thirteen of us! Aleksei Maksimovitch, pour it out. Ready? Now then, the first toast. . . . Come on!"

They drank, grunted, and began to eat.

"The teacher is not here. . . . I have not seen him for three days. Has anyone seen him?" asked Kuvalda.

"No one."

"It is unlike him. Well, never mind, let us drink, let us drink to the health of Aristid Kuvalda . . . the only friend who has never deserted me for one moment of my life! Devil take him all the same! I might have been the winner, had he left my society at least for a little while."

"You are witty . . ." said Bag of Bones, and coughed.

The Captain, with a keen sense of his superiority, glanced at the others, but said nothing, for he was eating.

Having drunk twice, the company began to grow merry; the food was copious.

Taras-and-a-Half expressed a timid desire to hear a tale, but the Deacon was arguing with Spinning Top about the superiority of thin women over stout ones, and paid no attention to his friend's request. He was asserting his views on the subject to Spinning Top with all the impetuousness and passion of a man deeply convinced of being right.

The naïve face of Meteor, who was lying on the ground near by, showed in its rapture that he was enjoying the Deacon's strong language.

Martyanoff sat clasping his knees with his huge hands covered with black hairs. He looked silently and sadly at the bottle of vodka, and tried to catch his mustache with his tongue and pinch it between his teeth while Bag of Bones was teasing Tyapa.

"I have spied the place where your money is hidden, you sorcerer."

"Your luck," growled Tyapa.

"I'll jolly well lay my hand on it, my lad."

"All right, you're welcome to it. . . ."

Kuvalda was bored with these men. Among them there was not one worthy of hearing his oratory or of understanding him.

"I wonder where the teacher is?" he asked, thinking aloud.

Martyanoff looked at him and said: "He'll soon come."

"I am positive that he will come on foot and not drive up in a carriage. Let us drink to your future health, you future jail-bird. If you kill any rich man go halves with me . . . then I shall go to America, brother. To those —what do you call them? Limpas? Pampas?—I will go there, and work my way up until I become the President of the United States, and then I will challenge the whole of Europe to war and will blow it up! I will buy an army . . . in Europe that is . . . I will invite the French, the Germans, the Turks, and so on, and will have them kill their own relatives . . . just as Ilya Morometz used Tartar against Tartar. With money it would be possible to be an Ilya, destroy the whole of Europe and take Judas Petunikoff for one's valet. He'd do it. . . . Give him a hundred rubles a month and he'd do it! But he would be a bad valet, because he would soon begin to steal. . . ."

"Another reason why the thin woman is better than the stout one is that she costs less," the Deacon was saying convincingly. "My first Deaconess used to buy twelve arshins for her clothes, the second only ten . . . And so on even in the matter of food."

Taras grinned guiltily. Turning his head towards the Deacon and looking straight at him with his one eye, he said in confusion:

"I had a wife once, too."

"Oh! that might happen to anyone," remarked Kuvalda; "but go on with your lies."

"She was thin, but she ate a lot, and even died from overeating."

"You poisoned her, you cripple!" said Bag of Bones, confidently.

"No, by God! It was from eating sturgeon," said Taras.

"But I tell you, you poisoned her!" declared Bag of Bones, decisively.

It often happened, that having said something quite absurd, he kept on repeating it, without any attempt to support his argument, beginning in a childish capricious tone, and gradually raising his voice to a frenzied shriek.

The Deacon stood up for his friend. "No, he did not poison her. He had no reason to do so."

"But I say he poisoned her!" swore Bag of Bones.

"Silence!" shouted the Captain, threateningly, his boredom intensifying his ill-temper. He looked at his friends with a fierce stare, and not discovering anything to further provoke his rage in their half-tipsy faces, he lowered his head, sat still for a little while, and then turned over on his back on the ground. Meteor was nibbling cucumbers. He took a cucumber in his hand without looking at it, pushed nearly half of it into his mouth, and bit it with his yellow teeth, so that the juice spurted out in all directions and ran over his cheeks. He did not seem to want to eat, but this game amused him. Martyanoff sat motionless in the position he had taken when he first sat down on the ground, like a statue, and looked in a fixed sullen manner at the huge bottle, already half empty. Tyapa stared at the ground, trying to chew a piece of meat too hard for his old teeth. Bag of Bones lay on his belly and coughed, shaking his meager little body. The rest of the dark, silent figures sat and lay around in various positions; their tatters made them look like monstrous animals, created by some strange, uncouth and fanciful force to make a mockery of man.

A lady there was in Suzdal
Whose family was not quite seemly;
She was stricken with cramps, sad to tell,
And found it unpleasant, extremely.

sang the Deacon in low tones, embracing Aleksei Maksimovitch, who was smiling blissfully into his face.

Taras-and-a-Half giggled voluptuously.

The night was approaching. High up in the sky stars flared up, and so did the lanterns on the mountain and in the town. The mournful whistles of steamers were heard from the river, and the doors of Vaviloff's pub opened with a screech and a rattle of glass. Two dark figures entered the court-yard, came up to the carousing crowd, and one of them asked in a hoarse whisper:

"Drinking?"

And the other said in a jealous aside:

"See, what devils!"

Then a hand stretched over the Deacon's head and took away the bottle, and the characteristic ripple of vodka being poured into a glass was heard. Then came a grunt.

"Oh, this is too glum!" shouted the Deacon. "Taras, let us remember ancient times and sing 'By the Rivers of Babylon.'"

"But can he sing?" asked Simtsoff.

"He? He was a soloist in the Bishop's choir. Now then, Taras! . . . 'By the r-i-v-e-r-s' . . ." The Deacon's voice was loud and hoarse and cracked, and his friend sang in a shrill falsetto.

The grimy building loomed large in the darkness and seemed to be pressing with all its rotten timber nearer to the singers, who were arousing its dull echoes with their wild shrieks. Heavy, sumptuous clouds were slowly floating in the sky over their heads. One of the "creatures that once were men" was snoring; the rest, not yet drunk enough, ate and drank silently or spoke to each other at long intervals in a whisper.

It was unusual for them to be in such low spirits during such a feast, with so much vodka. Somehow the drink tonight did not seem to have its usual exhilarating effect.

"Stop howling! you dogs!" said the Captain to the singers, raising his head from the ground to listen. "Someone is passing . . . in a droshky . . ."

A droshky in the street at such a late hour could not but attract general attention. Who would risk crossing the gullies and pits on the way from the town, and what for? They all raised their heads and listened. In the silence of the night the sound of the wheels touching the hard ground was heard distinctly. It gradually came nearer. A voice was heard asking brusquely:

"Well, where is it?"

Someone answered, "It must be that house over there."

"I shall not go any further."

"They are coming here!" shouted the Captain.

"The police!" someone whispered in great alarm.

"In a droshky! You fool!" said Martyanoff, softly.

Kuvalda got up and went to the entrance.

"Is this a doss-house?" asked someone, in a shaky voice.

"Yes," grunted the Captain, ungraciously.

"Oh! Did a reporter, one Titoff, live here?"

"Aha! Have you brought him?"

"Yes . . ."

"Drunk?"

"Ill."

"That means he is very drunk. Aye, teacher! Now, then, get up."

"Wait, I will help you. . . . He is very ill. . . . He has been with me for the last two days. . . . Take him under the arms. . . . The doctor has seen him. He is very bad."

Tyapa got up and slowly walked to the gates while Bag of Bones laughed, and took another drink.

"Strike a light over there!" shouted the Captain.

Meteor went into the house and lighted the lamp. Then a large stripe of light illuminated the court-yard, and the Captain, together with a small stranger, managed to get the teacher into the doss-house. His head was hanging limply on his breast, his feet trailed on the ground, and his arms hung in the air as if broken. With Tyapa's help they placed him on a shelf. He was shivering all over and moaned as he stretched himself out on it.

"We worked on the same paper . . . he is very miserable. . . . I said, 'Stay in my house, you are not in my way,' . . . but he begged me to send him 'home.' He was so troubled about it that I brought him here, thinking it might do him good. . . . Home! This is it, isn't it?"

"Do you suppose he has a home anywhere else?" asked Kuvalda, roughly, staring fixedly at his friend. "Tyapa, fetch me some cold water."

"I fancy I am of no more use," remarked the man in some confusion. The Captain looked at him critically. His clothes were rather shiny, and tightly buttoned up to his chin. His trousers were frayed, his hat almost yellow with age and crumpled like his lean and hungry face.

"No, you are not needed! We have plenty like you here," said the Captain, turning away.

"Then, good-by!" The man went to the door, and said softly from there, "If anything happens . . . let me know in the office. . . . My name is Ryzhoff. I might write a short obituary. He was after all a member of the Press."

"H'm, an obituary, you say? Twenty lines forty kopecks? I will do more than that. When he dies I will cut off one of his legs and send it to you. That will be of more profit to you than an obituary. It will last you for three days. His legs are fat. You devoured him, all of you, when he

CREATURES THAT ONCE WERE MEN 131

was alive. You may as well continue to do so after he is dead. . . ."

The man sniffed in an odd way and disappeared. The Captain sat down on the wooden shelf beside the teacher, felt his forehead, his breast, and called "Philip!"

The sound re-echoed from the dirty walls of the doss-house and died away.

"This is absurd, brother," said the Captain, gently stroking the teacher's untidy hair with his hand. Then he listened to his breathing, very rapid and uneven, and peered into his sunken gray face. Then he sighed and glanced around him, knitting his eyebrows. The lamp gave a poor, tremulous light and threw dark flickering shadows on the doss-house walls. The Captain stared at their silent dance, stroking his beard. Tyapa returned, bringing a pail of water, and, placing it on the shelf by the teacher's head, raised his arm as if weighing it in his hand.

"No need for the water," and the Captain shook his head.

"A priest, that's what's needed," said the old rag-collector.

"No! nothing," said the Captain decidedly.

They sat silently looking at the teacher.

"Let us go and drink, old devil!"

"And what about him?"

"Can you do him any good?"

Tyapa turned his back on the teacher, and both went out into the court-yard to join their companions.

"What is it?" asked Bag of Bones, turning his sharp nose to the Captain.

"Nothing in particular. . . . The man is dying . . ." remarked the Captain, shortly.

"Has he been beaten up?" asked Bag of Bones, with interest. The Captain gave no answer. He was drinking. "He must have known we had something to commemorate him with after his death!" continued Bag of Bones, lighting a cigarette. A laugh was heard, then a deep sigh. The Deacon suddenly drew himself up straight, moved his lips, rubbed his forehead, and howled wildly:

" 'Where the righteous r-e-s-t!' "

"You!" hissed Bag of Bones. "What are you howling for?"

"Give him a knock on the jaw," advised the Captain.

"You fool!" said Tyapa's hoarse voice. "When a man is dying one should be quiet. . . ."

It was quiet enough around. Both in the cloudy sky that threatened with rain and on the earth enveloped in the sinister darkness of an autumn night. One could hear the snoring of the sleepers and the tinkling sound of pouring vodka, chewing . . . The Deacon was muttering something. The clouds floated so low down that it seemed as if they would touch the roof of the old house and knock it over the group of men.

"Ah! It's sad when a friend is dying," stammered the Captain, sinking his head. No one answered him.

"He was the best man among you all . . . the cleverest, the most decent . . . I'll miss him."

" 'With the Saints give rest.' . . . Sing, you crippled scoundrel!" roared the Deacon, digging his drowsy friend in the ribs.

"Be quiet!" shouted Bag of Bones, jumping wrathfully to his feet.

"I will give him one on the head," proposed Martyanoff, raising his head from the ground.

"You are not asleep?" Aristid Fomich asked him with unexpected gentleness. "Have you heard about our teacher?"

Martyanoff lazily and heavily got up from the ground, looked at the streams of light coming out of the doss-

CREATURES THAT ONCE WERE MEN 133

house, shook his head and silently sat down beside the Captain.

"Let's have a drink!" proposed Kuvalda, groping for the glasses.

"I will go and see if he wants anything," said Tyapa.

"He wants a coffin!" came wryly from the Captain.

"Don't speak like that," begged Bag of Bones in a low voice.

Meteor rose and followed Tyapa. The Deacon tried to get up, but fell and swore loudly.

When Tyapa had gone the Captain touched Martyanoff's shoulder and said in low tones:

"Well, Martyanoff . . . you must feel it more than the others. You were . . . But to the Devil with that. . . . Won't you miss Philip?"

"No," said the ex-jailer, after a moment's silence, "I do not feel things of that sort, brother. . . . I have lost the habit . . . this life is disgusting, it is really, I mean it when I say I want to kill someone."

"Do you?" said the Captain vaguely. "Well . . . let's have another drink. . . ."

"Ours is a small job, a little drink and then one more . . ."

Simtsoff had waked up and drawled this in a rapt voice: "Is there someone there to pour out a glass for an old man!"

They poured out a glass and gave it to him. Having drunk it, he tumbled down again, knocking against another body as he fell. Two or three minutes' silence ensued, dark and eerie as the autumn night.

"What do you say?" a voice was heard asking.

"I say that he was a good man . . . with brains and so gentle," whispered another.

"Yes, and he had money too . . . and never refused it to a friend. . . ." Again came silence.

"He is sinking fast," said Tyapa, hoarsely, from behind the Captain's head. Aristid Fomich got up, and went with exaggeratedly firm steps into the doss-house.

"Don't go!" Tyapa stopped him. "Don't go! You are drunk! It is not right." The Captain stopped and thought for a moment.

"And what is right on this earth? Go to the Devil!" And he pushed Tyapa aside.

On the walls of the doss-house the shadows were creeping as though chasing one another. The teacher lay stretched out on the shelf at full length and rattled. His eyes were wide open, his naked breast rose and fell heavily, foam stood out at the corners of his mouth, and on his face was a tense expression as if he wished to say something grave, very important, but could not utter it and was tormented by it. The Captain stood with his hands folded behind his back and looked at him in silence for a moment. Then he spoke, wrinkling his forehead in distress.

"Philip! Say something to me . . . a word of comfort to a friend . . . come . . . I love you, brother! . . . All men are beasts. . . . You were the only man for me . . . though you were a drunkard. Ah! how you drank, Philip! That was the ruin of you! You ought to have listened to me and controlled yourself. . . . Did I not say to you . . . ?"

The mysterious, all-destroying reaper, called Death, as if insulted by the presence of this drunken man at the dark and solemn act of its struggle with life, made up its mind to finish the unrelenting work quickly. The teacher sighed deeply, moaned, quivered all over, stretched himself out, and then all was silent. The Captain stood staggering on his feet and continued to talk to him.

"Do you want me to bring you some vodka? It would be better of course if you did not drink, Philip . . . pull yourself together. Or perhaps better drink! On the whole, why control yourself? For what reason, Philip? For whose sake, eh?"

He took him by the feet and pulled him nearer to himself.

"Are you dozing, Philip? Well, then sleep . . . Good night. . . . Tomorrow I shall explain everything to you, and you will see that there is no real need to deny oneself anything. . . . But go on sleeping now . . . if you are not dead."

He went out to his friends, followed by the deep silence, and informed them:

"He is asleep or dead, I do not know. . . . I am a little drunk."

Tyapa bent further forward than usual and crossed himself. Martyanoff shivered, dropped to the ground and lay there in silence. Bag of Bones began to fidget about and said in a low and fierce tone:

"May you all go to the Devil! Dead? What of that? Why should I care? Why should I hear about it? My time will come too. . . . I am no worse than the rest."

"That is true," said the Captain loudly, sinking down to the ground. "The time will come when we shall all die like the others. Ha! Ha! How we live? That is nothing . . . But we shall die like everyone else, and this is the whole aim of life, take my word for it. A man lives only to die, and he dies . . . and if this be so, what does it matter how he lived? Am I right, Martyanoff? Let us therefore drink . . . whilst we are still alive!"

The rain began to fall. Thick, close darkness covered the figures that lay scattered over the ground, paralyzed by drink and sleep. The light in the windows of the doss-house flickered, paled, and suddenly vanished. Maybe the wind blew it out or the oil was exhausted. The drops of rain rapped timidly and falteringly on the iron roof of the doss-house. From the mountain over the town a slow, mournful ringing of bells was heard, the night guard was keeping watch. The metallic sound coming from the belfry softly swam through the darkness and slowly died away, but before its last tremulously sighing note was drowned in the shadows, another stroke was born and the silence of the night was again broken by the melancholy sigh of metal.

The next morning Tyapa was the first to wake up. Lying on his back, he looked up into the sky. Only in such a position did his deformed neck allow him to see the clouds above his head.

This morning the sky was of a uniform gray. The damp cold mist of dawn had gathered up there, extinguishing the sun, concealing the blue infinity behind and pouring despondency over the earth. Tyapa crossed himself, and, leaning on his elbow, looked round to see whether there was any vodka left. The bottle was empty. Crawling over his companions, he looked into their glasses, found one of them almost full, emptied it, wiped his lips with his sleeve, and began to shake the Captain.

The Captain raised his head and looked at him with lusterless eyes.

"We must inform the police. . . . Get up!"

"About what?" asked the Captain, sleepily and angrily.

"Why, that he is dead. . . ."

"Who?"

"The learned one . . ."

"Philip? Ah, yes!"

"Did you forget so soon? . . . Good Lord! . . ." croaked Tyapa, in a tone of reproach. The Captain rose to his feet, yawned loudly and stretched himself till all his bones cracked.

"Well, then! Go and make the declaration. . . ."

CREATURES THAT ONCE WERE MEN 137

"I will not go. . . . I do not like them," said Tyapa, morosely.

"Well, then, wake up the Deacon. . . . I'll go and have a look at him."

The Captain entered the doss-house, and stood at the teacher's feet. The dead man lay at full length, his left hand on his breast, the right hand thrown back as if ready to strike someone.

The Captain thought that if the teacher got up now, he would be as tall as Taras. Then he sat by the side of the dead man and sighed, as he remembered that they had spent the last three years together. Tyapa entered, holding his head like a goat ready to butt.

He sat down on the opposite side of the teacher's body, looked into the dark face, quiet and serious with its compressed lips, and began to groan:

"So . . . he is dead. . . . I too shall die soon. . . ."

"High time too!" said the Captain gloomily.

"It is," Tyapa agreed. "You too ought to die. . . . Anything better than this . . ."

"But perhaps death might be worse? How do you know?"

"It could not be worse. When you die you have God to deal with . . . but here you deal with men . . . and men—what are they worth?"

"Enough! . . . Be quiet!" interrupted Kuvalda, angrily.

And in the darkness which filled the doss-house reigned a solemn stillness. They sat for a long time at the feet of their dead companion, glancing at him, now and then, both plunged in thought. Then Tyapa asked:

"Will you bury him?"

"I? No, let the police bury him!"

"Better if you do it. . . . You took the money from Vaviloff for his petition after all . . . and I will give you some if you have not enough. . . ."

"Though I have his money . . . still I shall not bury him."

"That is not right. You are robbing the dead. I will tell them all that you want to pinch his money," Tyapa threatened him.

"You are a fool, you old devil!" said Kuvalda, contemptuously.

"I am not a fool . . . but it is not right or friendly."

"Enough! Be off!"

"How much money is it?"

"Twenty-five rubles . . ." said Kuvalda, absently.

"So! . . . You might give me a five-ruble note."

"You are an old scoundrel! . . ." And staring vacantly into Tyapa's face the Captain swore.

"Well, what? Won't you give it?"

"Go to the Devil! . . . I am going to spend this money in putting up a monument to him."

"What does he want that for?"

"I will buy a stone and an anchor. I shall place the stone on the grave, and attach the anchor to it with a chain. It will be heavy."

"Why? What's the joke?"

"Well . . . It is no business of yours."

"Look out! I shall tell . . ." again threatened Tyapa.

Aristid Fomich looked at him sullenly and said nothing.

"Listen. . . . They are coming!" Tyapa got up and went out of the doss-house.

Then the Doctor, the Police Inspector, and the Coroner appeared at the door. All three came up in turn, looked at the dead teacher, and then went out, throwing suspicious glances at Kuvalda. He sat there, without taking any notice of them, until the Police Inspector asked him:

"What did he die from?"

"Ask him. . . . I think from lack of habit."

"What?" asked the Coroner.

"I say that he died because he wasn't used to the disease which struck him."

"H'm, yes. Had he been ill long?"

"Bring him out here, I cannot see him properly in there," said the Doctor in a bored voice. "There may be signs . . ."

"Now then, tell someone to carry him out!" the Police Inspector ordered Kuvalda.

"Go and tell them yourself! He is not in my way here . . ." the Captain replied indifferently.

"Well, I never!" shouted the Inspector, pulling a ferocious face.

"Phew!" snarled Kuvalda, without moving from his place, in a state of quiet anger.

"The Devil take it!" shouted the Inspector, so maddened that the blood rushed to his face. "I'll make you pay for this! I'll . . ."

"Good morning, gentlemen!" said the merchant Petunikoff, with a sweet smile, making his appearance in the doorway.

He looked round, with a sharp glance, shivered, took off his cap and crossed himself piously. Then a triumphant, wicked smile crossed his face, and looking straight at the Captain, he inquired:

"What has happened? Has there been a murder here?"

"Yes, something of that sort," replied the Coroner.

Petunikoff sighed deeply, crossed himself again, and spoke in a distressed tone.

"God almighty! It is just as I feared. Every time I looked in I left with cold fear in my heart. . . . Aye, aye, aye! God protect us all, I would say, as I got home. Times without number I wanted to refuse to rent the house to that gentleman over there, the commander-in-chief of that crew of toughs, but I was afraid. You know . . . they are such unruly people . . . better give in to them, I thought, or else . . ."

He made a vague gesture with his hand, passed it over his face, tugged at his beard, and sighed again.

"Dangerous men they are and this fellow here is a sort of leader . . . the robbers' chief, in fact."

"We will sound him all right!" promised the Inspector, looking at the Captain with a revengeful eye. "He is well known to me too."

"Yes, old man, we are old friends . . ." said Kuvalda in a tone of familiarity. "How many times have I overpaid you and your kind to keep quiet?"

"Gentlemen!" shouted the Inspector, "did you hear this? I'll make him pay for this. Ah, my friend, you'll remember it! Aha, I shall make short work of you, my friend, remember!"

"Don't count your chickens before they are hatched," said Aristid Fomich, calmly.

The Doctor, a young man with eyeglasses, looked at him curiously, the Coroner with an attention that bodied him no good, Petunikoff with triumph, while the Inspector shouted and almost went for him with his fists.

The dark figure of Martyanoff appeared at the door of the doss-house. He entered quietly, and stood behind Petunikoff, so that his chin was on a level with the merchant's head. Behind him stood the Deacon, opening wide his small, swollen, red eyes.

"Let us be doing something, gentlemen," suggested the Doctor. Martyanoff made an awful grimace, and suddenly sneezed on Petunikoff's head. The latter gave a yell, crouched, and then jumped hurriedly aside, almost knocking down the Inspector, into whose open arms he fell.

"You see," said the frightened merchant, pointing to Martyanoff, "you see what kind of men they are?"

Kuvalda burst out laughing. The Doctor and the Coroner smiled too, and at the door of the doss-house the group of figures was increasing . . . sleepy figures, with swollen faces, red inflamed eyes, and disheveled hair, staring rudely at the Doctor, the Coroner, and the Inspector.

"Keep out!" warned the policeman on guard at the door, pulling at their tatters and trying to push them aside. But he was one against many, and, without taking any notice, they all entered and stood there, reeking of vodka, silent and sinister.

Kuvalda glanced at them, then at the authorities, who were taken aback by the interruption of these ragamuffins, and said, smiling wryly, "Gentlemen, perhaps you would like to make the acquaintance of my lodgers and friends? Would you? Anyhow, whether you wish it or not, you will have to learn to know them sooner or later in the course of your duties."

The Doctor smiled with embarrassment. The Coroner pressed his lips together, and the Inspector saw that it was time to go, and shouted:

"Sidoroff! Whistle! Tell them to bring a cart here."

"I will go now," said Petunikoff, coming forward from a corner. "You had better leave these lodgings today, my good gentlemen, I want to pull down this shack. See that it is done or else I'll apply to the police!"

The policeman's whistle echoed shrilly across the courtyard. At the door of the doss-house its inhabitants stood in a group, yawning and scratching.

"So you do not wish to be introduced? That is rather rude of you!" laughed Aristid Fomich.

Petunikoff took his purse from his pocket, fumbled in it, took out two five-kopeck pieces, put them at the feet of the dead man, and crossed himself.

"God have mercy . . . for the burial of the sinful dust. . . ."

"What!" yelled the Captain, "you give this for the

burial? Take this money away, I say, you scoundrel! How dare you give your stolen kopecks for the burial of an honest man? I will tear you limb from limb!"

"Your Honor!" cried the terrified merchant to the Inspector, seizing him by the elbow. The Doctor and the Coroner rushed outside. The Inspector shouted:

"Sidoroff, come here!"

The "creatures that once were men" stood at the door in a close wall, looking and listening with an interest which lit up their sad countenances.

Kuvalda, shaking his fist at Petunikoff's head, roared and rolled his bloodshot eyes like a wild beast.

"Scoundrel and thief! Take back your money! Dirty worm! Take it back, I say . . . or else I shall cram it down your throat. . . . Take your five-kopeck pieces!"

Petunikoff stretched out a trembling hand for his mite and, with the other protecting himself from Kuvalda's fist, said:

"You are my witnesses, Sir Inspector, and all you good people!"

"We are not good people, merchant!" said the trembling voice of Bag of Bones.

The Inspector whistled impatiently, blowing out his cheeks like a balloon; his other hand was stretched protectingly over Petunikoff, who was crouching in front of him as if trying to hide inside his belly.

"You dirty toad! Shall I force you to kiss the dead man's feet? How would you like that?" And catching Petunikoff by the neck, Kuvalda hurled him against the door as if he had been a mere kitten.

The "creatures that once were men" sprang aside quickly to give the merchant enough space to fall. And down he fell at their feet, crying in wild terror:

"Murder! Help! Murder!"

Martyanoff slowly raised his foot, aiming it at the merchant's head. Bag of Bones spat in his face with a voluptuous grin. The merchant rolled himself into a ball and helped himself with hands and feet into the court-yard, rousing general laughter. But by this time two policemen had arrived, and pointing to Kuvalda, the Inspector cried:

"Arrest him and bind him, hand and foot!"

"Tie him up," implored Petunikoff.

"You dare not! . . . I will not run away . . . I will go on my own," said Kuvalda, freeing himself from the policemen who had rushed up to him.

The "creatures that once were men" disappeared one after the other. A cart entered the yard. Some ragged wretches carried out the dead man's body.

"I'll teach you! You just wait!" thundered the Inspector at Kuvalda.

"What now, robbers' chief?" asked Petunikoff, maliciously, exhilarated and happy at the sight of his enemy in bonds. "Caught, are you? Eh? You just wait. . . ."

But Kuvalda was quiet now. He stood imposingly straight and silent between the two policemen, watching the teacher's body being placed in the cart. The man who was holding the corpse under the arms was very short, and could not manage to place the head on the cart at the same time as the legs were being lifted onto it. For a moment the body hung as if it wanted to fall headlong and hide itself beneath the earth, away from these foolish and wicked men, disturbers of its peace.

"Take him away!" ordered the Inspector, pointing to the Captain.

Kuvalda, with a frowning face, silently moved forward without protestation, passing the cart on which the teacher's body lay. He bowed his head before it without looking up. Martyanoff, with his stone-like face, followed him. The court-yard of the merchant Petunikoff emptied quickly.

"Now then, go on!" called the driver, pulling the horses'

reins. The cart clattered along the rough surface of the court-yard. The teacher's stretched-out body was covered with a heap of rags, and his belly was shaking beneath them. It seemed as if he were laughing softly and contentedly at the prospect of leaving the doss-house at last, never to return to it, never.

Petunikoff, who was following him with his eyes, crossed himself, and then carefully began to shake off with his cap the dust and rubbish which had clung to his clothes. As the dust disappeared from his cloak a quiet smile of self-satisfaction appeared on his face. He could still see the tall gray figure of the Captain, in a cap with a red band, which looked like a stripe of blood, his arms tied behind his back, being led away along the street up the mountain.

Petunikoff smiled the smile of the conqueror, and walked back to the doss-house, but suddenly he stopped and staggered. At the door facing him stood an old man with a stick in his hand and a large bag on his back, a terrible old man in rags and tatters, which covered his bony figure. He stooped under the weight of his burden, and bent his head towards his breast, as if preparing to attack the merchant.

"What are you? Who are you?" cried Petunikoff.

"A man . . ." came in a hoarse voice. This hoarseness reassured Petunikoff, he even smiled.

"A man! Are there such men as you?" Stepping aside, he let the old man pass. He pursued his way, muttering slowly:

"There are men of different kinds . . . as God wills them to be. . . . There are some even worse than me . . . even worse. . . . Yes. . . ."

An overcast sky hung silently over the dirty yard and over the neatly dressed little man with the pointed gray beard, who was walking about the earth measuring everything with his steps and with his sharp little eyes. On the roof of the old house a crow perched and solemnly croaked, thrusting its head forward and rocking to and fro. In the gray, stern clouds, which entirely concealed the sky, there was something tense and merciless, as if they had gathered together in order to pour out streams of rain, firmly set on washing all the filth from this unfortunate, suffering and sorrowful earth.

1897.

NOTCH

THE round window of my cell looked out upon the prison-yard. It was a very high window, but by placing the table against the wall and climbing on it, I could see everything that was going on in the yard. Above the window, under the eaves, pigeons had built themselves a nest, and when I looked out of my window into the court below, they cooed above my head.

I had sufficient time to acquaint myself from my vantage-point with the inmates of the prison, and I knew that the merriest member of that sullen and humdrum crew went by the nickname of Notch.

He was a square-set, stout fellow, with a ruddy face and high forehead from under which his large eyes always shone brightly. He wore his cap on the back of his head, and his ears struck out on both sides of his funny head in a funny fashion. He never fastened the strings of his shirt-collar, he never buttoned his jacket, and every movement of his muscles made it plain that he housed a soul incapable of dejection and bitterness.

Always on the go, always full of laughter and noise, he was the idol of the prison; he was always surrounded by a crowd of gray-clad comrades, and he amused and entertained them by various curious pranks, brightening up their dull, bleak days with his hearty gaiety.

On one occasion he emerged from his cell for his walk with three rats ingeniously harnessed with strings as if they were horses. He ran after them through the yard, shouting that he was driving a troika. The rats, maddened by his shouts, rushed about, while the prisoners laughed like children, looking at this stout man and his troika.

NOTCH

Apparently he believed that he existed solely to divert people. To achieve this he stopped at nothing. Sometimes his inventiveness assumed cruel forms. Thus, for instance, he once managed to glue to the wall the hair of a prisoner, a mere boy who was sitting on the ground asleep against the wall, and when the glue had dried, he suddenly awoke him. The lad quickly leaped to his feet, and clutching his head with his slim, lean hands, fell weeping to the ground. The prisoners guffawed, and Notch was content. Afterwards—I saw it through the window—he comforted the boy, who had left quite a tuft of his hair on the wall. . . .

Besides Notch, there was yet another favorite in the prison—a plump auburn kitten, a playful little animal pampered by all. When they came out for their regular walk, the prisoners invariably hunted it up and played with it for a long time. They would pass it on from hand to hand, run after it in the yard, let it scratch their hands and faces which were animated by this sport with the pet.

When the kitten appeared on the scene, it diverted the general attention from Notch, and the latter was by no means pleased with this preference. At heart Notch was an artist, and as such he had an inordinate amount of amour-propre. When his public devoted itself to the kitten, he, left alone, would sit down in a corner of the court-yard and from there watch his comrades, who in those moments forgot him. And from my window I watched him and felt everything that filled his soul during such moments. It seemed to me that Notch was bound to kill the kitten at the first opportunity, and I was sorry for the jolly prisoner. The desire to be the center of attention is pernicious to man, for nothing deadens the soul so quickly as the desire to please.

When you are in prison even the growth of mold on its walls seems interesting. It is therefore easy to understand the interest with which I followed from my window the little drama below, a man's jealousy of a kitten, and it is easy to understand, too, the impatience with which I awaited the denouement. It came in this way.

One bright, sunny day, when the prisoners had poured out of their cells into the yard, Notch noticed in a corner a pail of green paint, left by the men who were painting the prison roof. He went up to it, pondered over it, and dipping his finger into the paint, smeared his mustaches with it. The green mustaches on his red phiz caused an outburst of laughter. A lad in the group, in imitation of Notch, proceeded to paint his upper lip; but Notch dipped his whole hand into the pail and dexterously smeared the boy's entire face with the paint. The lad sputtered and shook his head, Notch danced around him, and the public roared, encouraging its entertainer with shouts of approval.

Just at that moment the auburn kitten appeared in the court-yard. It walked across the yard without haste, gracefully lifting its paws; it waved its arched tail, and was evidently unafraid of getting under the feet of the crowd which was milling around Notch and the bespattered boy, who was energetically rubbing his face with his palm and smearing the sticky mixture of oil and verdigris all over it.

"Fellows!" someone exclaimed. "Mishka is here."

"Ah, the little rascal!"

"Hi, there, Ginger! Pussy!"

They seized the kitten and passed it from hand to hand; everybody fondled it.

"They don't starve him! See how fat he is!"

"How fast he's growing!"

"He scratches, the little devil!"

"Leave him alone. Let him jump!"

"I'll hump my back for him. Jump, Mishka!"

Nobody paid any attention to Notch. He stood alone,

rubbing the paint off his mustaches with his fingers, and glancing at the kitten which was jumping on the shoulders and backs of the prisoners. This amused everybody very much, and there was continual laughter.

"Mates! Let's paint the cat!" Notch's voice was heard. There was an imploring note in his suggestion.

The crowd's response was noisy.

"But he'll croak!" declared one.

"From paint? What an idea!"

"Go on, Notch, paint him!" a broad-shouldered chap with a flaming red beard cried enthusiastically. "Such a thing to think of! What a devil of a fellow!"

Notch already had the kitten in his hands and was walking over to the pail of paint.

> Look, mates, look at that, [sang Notch]
> Watch me paint the ginger cat.
> We'll paint it green, it will be great,
> And do a dance to celebrate.

There was a burst of laughter, and the prisoners, holding their sides, made way for Notch. I saw plainly how, grasping the kitten by its tail, he dipped it into the pail, and dancing, sang:

> Stop your mewing, kitty, cease!
> Give your godfather some peace!

The laughter was louder than ever.

"Oh, cock-eyed Judas!" piped a thin voice.

"Oh, gracious!" another groaned.

They were choking with laughter, suffocating with it; it twisted the bodies of these men, bent them double, shook them, and it rumbled through the air, powerful, carefree, growing louder and louder until it reached the pitch of hysteria. From the windows of the women's wing of the prison peered smiling faces, framed in white kerchiefs. The guard, backed against the wall, thrust out his bulging middle, and clasping it with both hands, let out volleys of thick, low-pitched laughter that fairly choked him.

The laughter scattered the men in all directions. Cutting astounding capers, Notch did a squatting jig, singing by way of accompaniment:

> Oh, Life is a funny thing!
> Once there was a cat all gray,
> But her son, the auburn puss,
> Leads a life that's green today!

"Enough, devil take you!" groaned the man with the flaming beard.

But Notch was in high feather. Around him rioted the wild laughter of these men in gray, and Notch knew that it was he, and he alone, who was making them laugh.

His awareness of this was evident in every gesture of his, in every grimace of his mobile, clownish face, and his whole body twitched with the joy of his triumph. Now he held the kitten by the head, and shaking the excess paint from its coat, he went on dancing and improvising with the ecstasy of an artist conscious of his victory over the crowd:

> Come, dear brothers, let us look
> At the saints' names in the book;
> Pussy needs a name, I vow.
> Pray, what shall we call her now?

Everything laughed around the crowd of prisoners, possessed by insane gaiety; the sun laughed on the window-panes through the grating; the blue sky smiled above the prison-yard, and even its old, dirty walls seemed to be smiling with the smile of one who must suppress his gaiety, no matter how it may riot within him. From behind the gratings of the windows in the women's wing, women's faces peered down into the yard; they too laughed and their teeth sparkled in the sun. Everything was reborn, as it were, having shaken off the dull grayness that weighed one down with ennui and dejection; everything came alive, suffused with this purifying laughter which, like the sun, makes even dirt seem more decent.

Having set the green kitten on the grass, little islands of which, springing up between the stones, gave a motley look to the prison-yard, Notch, excited, out of breath, and sweating, continued to perform his wild jig.

But the laughter was already dying down. There had been too much of it, and it was beginning to tire people. Some were still shrieking hysterically; some continued laughing, but not so steadily. Finally a moment came when all were silent, except Notch, who was still singing a dance-tune, and the kitten, which, crawling on the grass, was mewing softly and plaintively. It was almost indistinguishable from the grass in color, and the paint must have blinded it and interfered with its movements; the sticky, big-headed creature tottered stupidly on its trembling paws, stopping now and then as if glued to the grass, and mewing continually. Notch commented thus on the kitten's movements:

> Christian people, look at that!
> The green puss don't know where he's at.
> Mishka, once the ginger cat,
> Cannot find a place to squat!

"Very clever, you beast," said a red-headed fellow.

The audience was looking at its artist with sated eyes.

"He's mewing," declared the youth, nodding in the direction of the kitten, and looked at his comrades. They watched the kitten in silence.

"Is he going to stay green the rest of his life?" asked the lad.

"How long do you think he'll live?" spoke up a tall, gray-haired prisoner, squatting near Mishka. "He'll get dry in the sun, his fur will be glued together, and he'll croak."

The kitten kept on mewing piercingly, causing a change in the mood of the prisoners.

"He'll croak?" asked the lad. "And what about giving him a wash?"

No one answered him. The little green ball was writhing at the feet of these coarse men, and was piteous in its helplessness.

"Phew! I'm all in a sweat!" cried Notch, throwing himself on the ground. No one paid any attention to him.

The lad edged over to the kitten and took him up in his hands, but immediately set him down on the grass again, declaring:

"He's awfully hot."

Then he looked at his comrades and said sadly:

"Poor Mishka! No more Mishka for us. Why did you have to kill the beast?"

"Maybe he'll get over it," said the red-headed man.

The hideous green creature kept crawling on the grass, while twenty pairs of eyes watched it, and by now there was not the trace of a smile on a single face. All were sullen and silent, all looked as wretched as the kitten, as though it had communicated its suffering to them and they felt its pangs.

"Get over it!" grinned the lad, raising his voice. "That's likely! There was Mishka, we all liked him. . . . Why are you torturing him? Maybe we'd better put him out of his misery."

"And who did it all?" cried the red-headed prisoner angrily. "It's him, this devil of a clown!"

"Well," said Notch soothingly, "didn't we all do it together?"

And he hugged himself as if he were cold.

"All together!" said the lad, mockingly. "That's good! You're the only one to blame! You are!"

"Don't you bellow, you calf!" Notch advised him meekly.

The old man took up the kitten, and having examined it carefully, suggested:

"If you bathe him in kerosene, the paint will come off."

"I say, take him by the tail and throw him over the wall," said Notch, and added, with a smirk, "Simple matter."

"What!" roared the red-headed man. "Suppose I threw you over the wall, would you like it?"

"The devil!" cried the lad, and, snatching the kitten from the old man's hands, set off at a run. The old man and several others followed him.

Notch remained alone among the men, who looked at him with angry, sullen eyes. They seemed to be waiting for him to make a move.

"It wasn't just me, mateys," Notch whined.

"Shut up!" cried the red-headed man, glancing round the court-yard. "Not just you! And who else was there?"

"But you were all in it," said the clown distinctly.

"You dog!"

The red-headed man punched Notch on the mouth. The artist backed away, only to receive a blow in the neck.

"Mates! . . ." he begged pitifully. But his mates saw that the two guards were a good distance away, and huddling in a thick crowd around their idol, knocked him down with a few blows. From afar the crowd could have been taken for a group engaged in lively conversation. Surrounded and hidden by them, Notch lay at their feet. From time to time a muffled sound was heard: they were kicking Notch in the ribs, kicking without haste, without anger, waiting until the man, writhing like a snake in the grass, should expose a particularly choice spot for a kick.

This lasted some three minutes. Suddenly the guard shouted:

"Hey, you devils! Don't go too far!"

The prisoners did not stop the torture all at once. One by one they left Notch, and every one of them took leave of him with a kick.

When they had gone, he remained lying on the ground. He lay prone, his shoulders shook—he must have been crying—and he kept coughing and expectorating. Then, cautiously, as though afraid of falling apart, he began to raise himself from the ground. He leaned on his left hand, then bent one leg, and howling like a sick dog, he sat up.

"Don't you pretend!" shouted the red-headed man threateningly.

Notch swayed and rose quickly to his feet.

Then, staggering, he walked to one of the walls of the prison. One hand was pressed against his chest, the other was stretched out in front of him. He reached the wall, and standing erect, he bowed his head. He was coughing.

I saw dark drops falling on the ground; I could see them distinctly against the gray background of the prison wall.

In order not to soil the public building with his blood, Notch made an obvious effort to shed it on the ground so that not a drop of it should get on the wall.

They laughed at the clown. . . .

The kitten was not seen any more. And Notch had no rival for the attention of the inmates of the prison.

1897.

CHUMS

ONE of them was called Jig-Leg, the other Hopeful, and both were thieves by trade.

They lived on the outskirts of the city, in a suburb that straggled queerly along a ravine, in one of the dilapidated shanties built of clay and half-rotten wood, which looked like heaps of rubbish that had been thrown down into the ravine. The pals did their thieving in the nearby villages, for in the city it was difficult to steal, and in the suburb the neighbors had nothing worth taking.

Both of them were cautious and modest: having nabbed a piece of linen, a coat, or an ax, a piece of harness, a shirt, or a hen, for a long time they would keep away from the village where they had made their haul. But in spite of this prudent way of working, the suburban peasants knew them well, and threatened on occasion to beat the lives out of them. The occasion, however, did not present itself to the peasants, and the bones of the two friends remained whole, although they had been hearing these threats for full six years.

Jig-Leg was a man of forty, tall, somewhat bent, lean and muscular. He walked with his head bowed, his long arms crossed behind his back, with a long leisurely stride, and as he moved along, he kept glancing restlessly and anxiously from side to side with his sharp, puckered-up eyes. He wore his hair clipped short and shaved his beard; his thick, grayish, military mustaches covered his mouth, lending his face a bristling, dour look. His left leg must have been dislocated or broken, and it mended in such a way that it was longer than the right one. When he lifted it in walking, it jumped up in the air and jerked sideways. This peculiarity of his gait earned him his nickname.

Hopeful was about five years older than his comrade; he was shorter, and broader in the shoulders. But he had a persistent, hollow cough, and his knobby face was covered with a large black beard, streaked with gray, which did not hide his sickly, yellow complexion. He had large, black eyes, which looked at everything with a guilty and amiable expression. As he walked, he would press his thick lips together in the shape of a heart, and he whistled softly a sad, monotonous melody, always the same. His shoulders were covered by a short garment made of motley rags, something resembling a wadded pea-jacket; Jig-Leg wore a long, gray kaftan, with a belt.

Hopeful was by birth a peasant, his comrade was the son of a sexton, and had at one time been a footman and a marker. They were always together, and the peasants, seeing them, would say: "There are the chums again! . . . Watch out."

The chums would tramp along some country road, keeping a sharp look-out, and avoiding people. Hopeful coughed and whistled his tune; his comrade's leg jigged in the air, as though trying to wrench itself loose and dash away from its master's dangerous path. Or else they lay on the edge of a forest, in the rye, or in a gully, and quietly discussed how to steal something in order to eat.

· · · · · · ·

In winter even the wolves, who are better adapted to the struggle for life than the two friends, have a hard time of it. Lean, hungry, and vicious, they stalk the roads, and though people kill them, these same people are afraid of them: they have claws and fangs for self-defense, and, above all, their hearts are softened by nothing. This last point is very important, for, in order to be victorious in the struggle for existence, man must have either keen intelligence or the heart of a beast.

In winter the chums were hard put to it. Often both of them went into the streets in the evening and begged, trying not to be noticed by the police. They rarely succeeded in stealing anything; it was inconvenient to go into the country because it was cold, and because one left traces in the snow; besides, it was useless to visit the villages when everything there was locked up and snowbound. In winter the comrades lost much strength fighting hunger, and perhaps no one awaited spring as eagerly as they did.

And then, at last, spring would come! The pals, exhausted and ailing, crawled out of their ravine, and gazed joyfully at the fields, where, every day, the snow thawed more rapidly, brown patches began to appear, the puddles shone like mirrors, and streams babbled gaily. The sun lavished upon the earth its disinterested caresses, and both friends warmed themselves in its rays, figuring out how soon the earth would get dry and at last it would be possible to "do business" in the villages. Often Hopeful, who suffered from insomnia, would wake his friend in the early morning, and would announce joyfully:

"Hey! Get up! The rooks have come!"

"They have?"

"Honest. You hear them cawing?"

Leaving their shanty, they would watch eagerly for a long time how the black messengers of spring were weaving new nests and repairing old ones, filling the air with their loud, anxious chatter.

"Now it's the larks' turn," Hopeful would say, and set about mending his old, half-rotten bird-net.

The larks would come. The comrades would go into the fields, set up the net on a brown patch, and racing through the wet, muddy field, would drive into the net the hungry birds, exhausted by their long flight and looking for food on the moist earth that had just been released from the snow. Having caught the birds, they would sell them for five and ten kopecks apiece. Then nettles appeared. They picked them and took them to the marketplace to sell them to the women who traded in greens. Almost every spring day brought them something new, some additional, if small, earnings. They knew how to take advantage of everything: pussy-willows, sorrel, mushrooms, strawberries —nothing escaped them. The soldiers would come out for rifle practice. When the shooting was over the friends would dig in the earthworks looking for bullets, which they would afterwards sell at twelve kopecks a pound. All these odd jobs, although they prevented the friends from dying of hunger, very rarely gave them a chance to relish the sense of having eaten their fill, the pleasant feeling of a full stomach busily digesting the food it held.

· · · · · ·

One day in April, when the trees were only beginning to bud, when the woods were enveloped in a bluish haze, and on the brown, rich, sun-flooded fields the grass was just starting to show, the friends were walking on the highroad, smoking cheap cigarettes that they themselves had rolled, and engaged in talk.

"Your cough is getting harder," Jig-Leg calmly warned his comrade.

"I don't give a damn! The sun will warm me, and I'll be myself again."

"H'm! Maybe you ought to go to the hospital."

"Nonsense! What do I need a hospital for? If I have to die, I'll die anyway!"

"True enough."

They were walking along through a birch grove, and the trees cast upon them the patterned shadows of their delicate branches. Sparrows hopped on the road, chirping gaily.

"You don't walk as well as you used to," observed Jig-Leg, after a pause.

"It's because I have a choky feeling," explained Hopeful. "These days the air is thick and rich, and it's hard for me to swallow it."

And, stopping short, he had a coughing-fit.

Jig-Leg stood by, smoked away, and looked at him uncertainly. Hopeful shook with coughing and rubbed his chest with his hands. His face turned blue.

"It clears my lungs, anyway!" he said, when he had stopped coughing.

And they went further, scaring away the sparrows.

"Now we are on the way to Mukhina," said Jig-Leg, tossing away the cigarette-butt and spitting. "We'll go round it the back way: maybe we'll be able to pick up something. Then across the Sivtsova woods we'll make for Kuznechikha. . . . From there we'll turn off to Markovka, and then we'll strike out for home."

"That will make a good thirty versts," said Hopeful.

"If only we get something out of it!"

To the left of the road there was a forest that looked dark and forbidding; among the naked branches there was not a single green patch to cheer the eye. A small horse with a shaggy, matted coat and woefully fallen-in flanks was straying along the edge of the wood. Its ribs were as prominent as the hoops of a barrel. The friends halted again and for a long time watched it slowly putting one foot after the other, lowering its muzzle toward the ground, getting hold of the faded grass-blades with its lips and carefully munching them with its worn-down yellow teeth.

"She's gotten thin, too," observed Hopeful.

"Whoa-whoa!" cried Jig-Leg coaxingly.

The horse looked at him, and shaking its head, bent it earthwards again.

"She doesn't like you," Hopeful interpreted the horse's tired movement.

"Come on. If we turn her over to the Tartars . . . they might give us some seven rubles for her," said Jig-Leg pensively.

"No, they won't! What good would she be to them?"

"What about the hide?"

"The hide? Will they give all that for the hide? They won't give more than three for it."

"Still . . ."

"But look at that hide. It's not a hide, it's an old rag."

Jig-Leg looked at his comrade, and, after a pause, said: "Well?"

"There might be trouble . . ." Hopeful said, doubtfully.

"Why?"

"We'd leave tracks. . . . The earth is damp. . . . They could see where we'd gone."

"We could put bast shoes on her feet."

"If you like."

"Come along! Let's drive into the wood and wait in the ravine until dark. At night we'll take her out and drive her to the Tartars. It's not far—only three versts."

"Well," Hopeful nodded, "let's go. A bird in the hand, you know . . . But what if . . . ?"

"Nothing will happen," said Jig-Leg confidently.

They left the road, and glancing about them, walked toward the wood. The horse looked at them, snorted, waved its tail, and again began to crop the faded grass.

· · · · · · ·

At the bottom of the deep ravine in the wood it was dark, damp, and quiet. The murmur of a stream was wafted through the stillness, sad and monotonous, like a lament. Naked branches of hazel, snowball trees, and honeysuckle were hanging down the steep sides of the ravine; here and there roots, washed out by spring freshets, were helplessly sticking out of the ground. The forest was still dead; the evening twilight added to the lifeless monotony of its hues and the mournful stillness that lurked in it filled it with the gloomy, solemn peace of a cemetery.

For a long time the chums had been sitting in the damp and silent dusk, under a clump of aspens which had slid down to the bottom of the ravine together with a huge mass of earth. A small fire burned brightly before them, and, warming their hands over it, they fed it twigs, from time to time, taking care that the flame should burn evenly and not smoke. The horse stood not far off. They had wrapped its muzzle with a sleeve torn from Hopeful's rags, and had tied it by the bridle to the trunk of a tree.

Hopeful, crouching by the fire, looked pensively into it and whistled his tune; his comrade, having cut a bunch of osier-twigs, was weaving a basket out of them, and, busy with his task, he was silent.

The melancholy sound of the stream and the low whistle of the luckless man blended together and floated piteously on the stillness of the evening and the forest; sometimes the twigs crackled in the fire, crackled and hissed, as if they were sighing out of pity for the two men whose life was more painful than their own death in the flames.

"Are we starting out soon?" asked Hopeful.

"It's too early. Wait till it gets quite dark, and then we'll start," said Jig-Leg, without lifting his head from his work.

Hopeful sighed and began to cough.

"Chilly, eh?" asked his comrade, after a long pause.

"No. . . . I'm not quite right."

"So?" and Jig-Leg shook his head.

"My heart bothers me."

"Sick, eh?"

"I suppose so . . . and maybe it's something else."
Jig-Leg said:
"See here! . . . Don't think!"
"What about?"
"Oh, about everything."
"You see—" Hopeful suddenly grew animated— "I can't help thinking. I look at her—" he pointed to the horse—"I look at her and it comes home to me. I too used to have one like that. . . . She's not much to look at, but on a farm, she's worth everything. At one time I had a pair of them. . . . I worked hard in those days."

"What did you get out of it?" asked Jig-Leg. "I don't like this streak in you. Once you tune up, you don't stop playing. And what's the good of it?"

Hopeful silently threw a handful of twigs, broken up small, into the fire, and watched the sparks fly upward and go out in the damp air. He kept on blinking, and shadows ran across his face. Then he turned his head in the direction of the horse and looked at it for a long time.

The horse was standing motionless, as though rooted in the earth; her head, disfigured by the cloth, was drooping dejectedly.

"We must look at things more simply," Jig-Leg said, sternly and impressively. "Our life is like this—a day and a night, and twenty-four hours are gone! If there is food—good; if not—squeal a bit, and then stop, it doesn't get you anywhere. . . . But you, once you start, you never stop. It's disgusting to listen to. It's because you're sick, that's why."

"It must be sickness," Hopeful agreed meekly, but after a pause he added, "And maybe because my heart is soft."

"And your heart is soft because of sickness," declared Jig-Leg categorically.

He bit off a twig, waved it, cut the air with a swish, and said sternly:

"I'm all right, and I don't act up that way."

The horse shifted from one leg to another; a twig creaked; some earth plumped into the stream with a splash that brought a new note into its soft melody; then from somewhere two little birds started up and flew along the ravine, screeching uneasily. Hopeful followed them with his eyes and spoke quietly:

"What birds are those? If they are starlings they have no business in the woods. They must be waxwings. . . ."

"And maybe they're cross-bills," said Jig-Leg.

"It's too early for cross-bills, and besides, cross-bills like evergreens. They have no business here. They're sure to be waxwings."

"Who cares?"

"You're right!" agreed Hopeful, and for some reason drew a deep sigh.

Jig-Leg was working rapidly; he had already woven the bottom of the basket, and he was deftly making the sides. He cut the twigs with a knife, bit them through with his teeth, bent and wattled them with quick movements of his fingers, and wheezed from time to time, bristling his mustaches.

Hopeful looked at him and at the horse, petrified in its dejected pose, at the sky, already almost dark, yet starless.

"The peasant will look for the horse," he suddenly spoke up in a strange voice, "and it won't be there—he'll look here, and there—no horse!"

Hopeful spread his arms wide. There was a foolish look on his face, and his eyes blinked rapidly as though he were looking at a bright light that had suddenly flared up before him.

"What are you driving at?" asked Jig-Leg sternly.

"I was reminded of something . . ." said Hopeful guiltily.

"What is it?"

"Well, it's this way. . . . They stole a horse . . . from a neighbor of mine . . . Mikhaila was his name . . . he was a tall fellow . . . pock-marked. . . ."

"Well?"

"Well, it was stolen. It was grazing in the pasture, and then it was gone. So when he, Mikhaila that is, understood that he had lost his horse, he threw himself on the ground, and he howled! Brother, how he howled! . . . And he plumped down as though he had broken his legs. . . ."

"Well?"

"Well . . . he carried on like that for a long time."

"What's that to you?"

At this sharp question, Hopeful moved away from his comrade and answered timidly:

"Nothing. . . . I just happened to think of it. Because without a horse, a peasant is done for."

"Let me tell you something," began Jig-Leg sternly, looking pointblank at Hopeful, "give it up! This kind of talk gets you nowhere, understand? Your neighbor, Mikhaila! It's not your affair."

"But it's a pity," Hopeful objected, shrugging his shoulders.

"A pity! Does anybody pity us?"

"That's true."

"Well, then, shut up! We'll soon have to go."

"Soon?"

"Yes."

Hopeful edged toward the fire, poked it with a stick, and looking out of the corner of his eye at Jig-Leg, who was again absorbed in his work, he said in a soft, beseeching tone:

"Hadn't we better let that horse go?"

"You have a mean nature!" exclaimed Jig-Leg, aggrieved.

"But honest," said Hopeful softly and persuasively. "Think of it, it's dangerous! We'll have to drag her along for a distance of four or five versts. . . . And what if the Tartars don't take her? Then what!"

"That's my business."

"As you please. But it would be better to let her go. She can go and roam about. Look what an old nag she is!"

Jig-Leg held his peace, but his fingers moved faster than ever.

"What are we going to get for her?" Hopeful drawled, softly but stubbornly. "And this the best time. It will be dark soon. If we go along the ravine we'll come out at Dubenka, and there we may pick up something worth while."

Hopeful's monotonous murmur, blending with the babble of the stream, floated down the ravine, and irritated the industrious Jig-Leg.

He was silent, his teeth clenched, and because of his excitement the osier-twigs snapped under his fingers.

"The women are bleaching their linen at this time."

The horse sighed audibly and grew restive. Wrapped in the darkness, it looked uglier and more pitiable than ever. Jig-Leg looked at it and spat into the fire.

"And the poultry is at large now . . . there are geese in the puddles. . . ."

"How long will it take you to dry up, you devil!" Jig-Leg asked savagely.

"It's God's truth. . . . Don't be angry at me, Stepan. To the devil with her. Really!"

"Did you have any grub today?" cried Jig-Leg.

"No," answered Hopeful, abashed and frightened by his comrade's shout.

"Then, deuce take you, you may starve here, for all I care."

Hopeful looked at him silently, while he, collecting the

osier-twigs into a heap, tied them up into a sheaf, and snorted angrily. The fire threw a reflection on his whiskered face, and it looked red and angry.

Hopeful turned away and heaved a deep sigh.

"Look here, I don't care, do as you please," said Jig-Leg angrily, in a hoarse voice. "But let me tell you this," he went on, "if you go on that way, I'm no company for you! All right, it's enough. I know you, that's what . . ."

"You're a queer fellow. . . ."

"Not another word."

Hopeful shrank together and coughed; then when his fit of coughing was over, he said, breathing heavily:

"Why do I insist? Because it's dangerous."

"All right!" Jig-Leg shouted angrily.

He picked up the twigs, threw them on his shoulder, took the unfinished basket under his arm, and rose to his feet.

Hopeful also rose, looked at his comrade, and quietly went over to the horse.

"Whoa! Christ be with you! Don't be afraid!" his hollow voice resounded through the ravine.

"Whoa! Whoa! Stop! Well—go now—go along. There you are, you fool!"

Jig-Leg watched his comrade fussing over the horse, unwinding the rag from its muzzle, and the thief's mustache twitched.

"Let's go," he said, moving forwards.

"Let's," Hopeful agreed.

And, forcing their way through the bushes, they went silently along the ravine in the darkness which filled it to the brim.

The horse followed them.

Presently behind them they heard a splash which broke the murmur of the stream.

"The fool! She slipped into the stream," said Hopeful. Jig-Leg snorted angrily, but said nothing.

In the darkness and the morose silence of the ravine, resounded the gentle cracking of twigs; the sound floated from the spot where the red heap of embers shone on the ground like a monstrous eye, malicious and mocking.

The moon rose.

Its transparent radiance filled the ravine with a smoky gloom; there were shadows everywhere, making the forest all the denser, and the silence fuller and more severe. The white stems of birches, silvered by the moon, stood out like wax candles against the dark background of oaks, elms, and brushwood.

The chums walked along the bottom of the ravine in silence. It was hard going; sometimes their feet slipped, or sank deep in the mud. Hopeful frequently breathed fast, and a whistling, wheezing, rattling sound came from his chest, as though a large clock that had not been cleaned for a long time were hidden there. Jig-Leg walked ahead; the shadow of his tall, straight figure fell upon Hopeful.

"Going, are we?" he broke out, in a hurt, petulant tone. "Where to? What are we looking for? Eh?"

Hopeful sighed, and said nothing.

"And these nights are shorter than a sparrow's beak. It will be dawn before we get to the village. . . . And how are we walking? Like ladies . . . taking a stroll."

"I don't feel well, brother," said Hopeful quietly.

"Don't feel well!" exclaimed Jig-Leg ironically. "And why?"

"I have trouble breathing," replied the sick thief.

"Breathing? Why do you have trouble breathing?"

"It's the sickness, I suppose."

"You're wrong! It's your foolishness."

Jig-Leg halted, turned his face to his comrade, and wagging his finger under his nose, added:

"It's because of your foolishness that you have trouble breathing. Yes. . . . Yes! Understand?"

Hopeful bowed his head low and said guiltily:

"You're right!"

He wanted to add something, but a fit of coughing seized him. He clasped a tree-trunk with his trembling hands, and coughed for a long time, stamping about on one spot, tossing his head, opening his mouth wide.

Jig-Leg looked attentively at his face, which stood out haggard, earthy, and greenish in the moonlight.

"You'll wake up all the wood-sprites," he said at last in a surly tone.

And when Hopeful had done coughing, and, throwing back his head, breathed freely, he spoke peremptorily:

"Take a rest. Let's sit down."

They sat down on the damp earth in the shadow of the bushes. Jig-Leg rolled a cigarette, lit it, looked at the glow of it, and began slowly:

"If we had something to eat at home . . . we could go back. . . ."

"That's true," Hopeful nodded.

Jig-Leg looked at him out of the corner of his eye and continued:

"But since there's nothing at home, we must go on."

"So we must," sighed Hopeful.

"Although we've nowhere to go, because no good will come of it. And the main reason is, we're foolish. What fools we are!"

Jig-Leg's dry voice cut through the air, and must have greatly disturbed Hopeful: he kept writhing on the ground, sighing, and making strange rumbling sounds.

"And I'm so damn hungry," Jig-Leg concluded his reproachful speech.

Hopeful resolutely rose to his feet.

"What's the matter?" asked Jig-Leg.

"Let's go!"

"Why so lively all of a sudden?"

"Let's go!"

"All right—" Jig-Leg rose too—"only it's no use. . . ."

"What will happen will happen!" and Hopeful waved his hand.

"So you've plucked up courage again?"

"What? Here you've been nagging and nagging me, and scolding and scolding me. . . . Oh, Lord!"

"Then why do you act foolishly?"

"Why?"

"Yes."

"Well, don't you see, I felt so sorry."

"For whom? For what?"

"For whom? For that peasant, I suppose."

"Peasant?" drawled Jig-Leg. "That's an idea to chew on! You've a heart of gold, but no brains. What's the peasant to you? Understand? Why, he'd nab you and crack you under his nail like a flea! That's the time for you to be sorry for him! Go and show him what a fool you are, and in return for your pity he'll torture you seven ways at once. He'll wind your guts round his wrist, and pull your veins out, an inch an hour. . . . And you talk of . . . pity! You'd better pray God that they do you in without any 'pity,' at one blow, and make an end of it! Oh, you! To the devil with you! Pity . . . faugh!"

He was indignant, this Jig-Leg.

His cutting voice, full of irony and contempt for his comrade, resounded through the wood, and the branches of the bushes waved with a gentle rustle, as if confirming his stern, just words.

Hopeful, crushed by these reproaches, was walking slowly, his legs trembling, his hands in the sleeves of his jacket, and his head bent low over his chest.

"Wait!" he said at last. "Never mind. I'll be all right.

We'll get to the village. . . . I'll go, I'll go all alone. . . . You needn't come at all. . . . I'll nab the first thing that comes to hand. . . . Then we'll make for home! We'll get there and I'll lie down! I'm feeling bad."

He spoke almost inaudibly, gasping for breath, with a rattling and gurgling in his chest. Jig-Leg looked at him suspiciously, stopped, and was about to say something, but waved his arm, and without a word walked on again.

For a long time they walked in silence.

Nearby cocks were crowing; a dog howled; then the melancholy sound of the watchman's bell floated towards them from a distant village church, and was swallowed by the silence of the forest. A large bird, like a big black spot, rushed into the murky moonlight, and in the ravine the sweep of wings made an eerie sound.

"It must be a crow, or a rook," observed Jig-Leg.

"Listen," said Hopeful, lowering himself heavily to the ground, "you go, I'll stay here. . . . I can't go on. . . . I'm choking. . . . I'm dizzy."

"Well, that's a fine thing!" said Jig-Leg crossly. "You really can't go on?"

"I can't."

"Congratulations. Faugh!"

"I'm so weak."

"Of course; we've been walking since morning on an empty stomach."

"No, it's not that. . . . I'm done for . . . look how the blood gushes!"

And Hopeful raised his hand to Jig-Leg's face, all smeared with something dark. The other looked askance at the hand and, lowering his voice, asked:

"What are we going to do?"

"You go ahead. . . . I'll stay here. . . . Maybe if I rest, I'll feel better."

"Where can I go? Suppose I go to the village and say there's a man in the woods who's taken sick?"

"Look out. . . . They'll beat you up."

"True enough. Just give them the chance."

Hopeful lay on his back, coughing a hollow cough, and spitting out whole gobs of blood.

"Is it still coming?" asked Jig-Leg, standing over him, but looking aside.

"It's flowing fast," said Hopeful, almost inaudibly, and was seized with another fit of coughing.

Jig-Leg swore loudly and cynically.

"If only we could call someone!"

"Whom?" asked Hopeful, his voice like a dismal echo.

"Maybe you could get up . . . and walk . . . slowly? . . ."

"No chance. . . ."

Jig-Leg sat beside his comrade's head, and clasping his own knees with his hands began to look into his face. Hopeful's chest rose convulsively with a hollow rattle, his eyes sank into his head, his lips gaped strangely and seemed to cling to his teeth. From the left corner of his mouth a dark living stream was trickling down his cheek.

"Still flowing?" asked Jig-Leg quietly, and in the tone of his question there was something akin to respect.

Hopeful's face quivered.

"Flowing," came a weak rattle.

Jig-Leg leaned his head on his knees and was silent.

Above them was the wall of the ravine, deeply furrowed by the spring freshets. From the top of it a shaggy row of moonlit trees looked down into the ravine. The other side of the ravine, which sloped more gently, was overgrown with shrubs; here and there above their dark mass rose the gray stems of aspens, and on their naked branches rooks' nests were clearly visible. . . . The ravine, flooded by moonlight, was like a tedious dream, lacking the colors of life; and the gentle murmur of the stream emphasized its lifelessness and brought out the melancholy silence.

"I am dying," said Hopeful, in a hardly audible whisper, and then immediately afterwards repeated in a loud, clear voice: "I am dying, Stepan!"

Jig-Leg shuddered, squirmed, snorted, and raising his head from his knees spoke in an awkward, gentle voice, as if he were afraid of creating a disturbance:

"Oh, it's not that bad . . . don't be afraid. . . . It's nothing. . . . Maybe it's just . . . It's nothing, brother!"

"Lord Jesus Christ!" Hopeful sighed heavily.

"It's nothing," whispered Jig-Leg, bending over his face. "Just stick it for a little while . . . maybe it will pass over!"

Hopeful began to cough again; there was a new sound in his chest: it was as though a wet rag were slapping against his ribs. Jig-Leg was looking at him and was silently bristling his mustaches. When the coughing-fit was over, Hopeful began to pant loudly and jerkily, as though he were running with all his might. He went on breathing that way for a long time. Then he said:

"Forgive me, Stepan . . . if anything I . . . about that horse, you know. . . . Forgive me, brother!"

"You forgive me!" interrupted Jig-Leg, and after a pause, added:

"And I . . . where shall I go now? What will I do?"

"It's all right. . . . May the Lor . . ." He broke off in the middle of the word, and was silent.

Then he began to make a rattling sound . . . he stretched out his legs . . . one of them jerked sideways.

Jig-Leg looked at him without blinking. Minutes passed that were as long as hours.

Then Hopeful lifted his head, but at once it fell helplessly back onto the ground.

"What is it, brother?" Jig-Leg bent over him. But he did not answer, he lay quiet and motionless.

For a while Jig-Leg sat at his comrade's side. Then he rose, took off his cap, crossed himself, and slowly went on his way along the ravine. His face was drawn, his eyebrows and mustaches bristled, and he strode firmly as though he were striking the earth with his feet, as though he were trying to hurt it.

It was already daybreak. The sky was gray and harsh; a sullen silence reigned in the ravine; only the stream was talking monotonously and tediously.

But suddenly there was a noise—a clump of earth must have rolled down to the bottom of the ravine. A rook awoke, and with a cry of alarm, flew off. Then a titmouse piped. In the damp chill air of the ravine sounds did not last long; they arose and immediately died away. . . .

1898.

TWENTY-SIX MEN AND A GIRL

A Poem

THERE were six-and-twenty of us—six-and-twenty living machines locked up in a damp basement, where from morning till night we kneaded dough and rolled it into pretzels and cracknels. Opposite the windows of our basement was a bricked area, green and moldy with moisture. The windows were protected from outside with a close iron grating, and the light of the sun could not pierce through the windowpanes, covered as they were with flour dust.

Our employer had bars placed in front of the windows, so that we should not be able to give a bit of his bread to passing beggars, or to any of our fellows who were out of work and hungry. Our employer called us crooks, and gave us half-rotten tripe to eat for our midday meal, instead of meat. It was swelteringly close for us cooped up in that stone underground chamber, under the low, heavy, soot-blackened, cobwebby ceiling. Dreary and sickening was our life within its thick, dirty, moldy walls.

Unrefreshed, and with a feeling of not having had our sleep out, we used to get up at five o'clock in the morning; and at six, we were already seated, worn out and apathetic, at the table, rolling out the dough which our mates had already prepared while we slept. The whole day, from early morning until ten at night, some of us sat round that table, working up in our hands the unyielding dough, swaying to and fro so as not to grow numb; while the others mixed flour and water. And the whole day the simmering water in the kettle, where the pretzels were being cooked, sang low and sadly; and the baker's shovel scraped harshly over the oven floor, as he threw the slippery bits of dough out of the kettle on the heated bricks.

From morning till evening wood was burning in the oven, and the red glow of the fire gleamed and flickered over the walls of the bake-shop, as if silently mocking us. The giant oven was like the misshapen head of a monster in a fairy tale; it thrust itself up out of the floor, opened wide jaws, full of glowing fire, and blew hot breath upon us; it seemed to be ever watching out of its black air-holes our interminable work. Those two deep holes were like eyes—the cold, pitiless eyes of a monster. They watched us always with the same darkened glance, as if they were weary of seeing before them such slaves, from whom they could expect nothing human, and therefore scorned them with the cold scorn of wisdom.

In meal dust, in the mud which we brought in from the yard on our boots, in the hot, sticky atmosphere, day in, day out, we rolled the dough into pretzels, which we moistened with our own sweat. And we hated our work with a bitter hatred; we never ate what had passed through our hands, and preferred black bread to pretzels. Sitting opposite each other, at a long table—nine facing nine—we moved our hands and fingers mechanically during endlessly long hours, till we were so accustomed to our monotonous work that we ceased to pay any attention to our own motions.

We had all stared at each other so long, that each of us knew every wrinkle of his mates' faces. It was not long also before we had exhausted almost every topic of conversation; that is why we were most of the time silent, unless we were chaffing each other; but one cannot always find something about which to chaff another man, especially when that man is one's mate. Neither were we much given to finding fault with one another; how, indeed, could one of us poor devils be in a position to find fault with another, when we were all of us half dead and, as it were, turned to stone? For the heavy drudgery seemed to crush all feeling out of us. But silence is only terrible and fearful for those who have said everything and have nothing more to say to each other; for men, on the contrary, who have never begun to communicate with one another, it is easy and simple.

Sometimes, too, we sang; and this is how it happened that we began to sing: one of us would sigh deeply in the midst of our toil, like an overdriven horse, and then we would begin one of those songs whose gentle drawn-out melody seems always to ease the burden on the singer's heart.

At first one sang by himself, and we others sat in silence listening to his solitary song, which, under the heavy vaulted roof of the basement, died gradually away and became extinguished, like a little fire in the steppes, on a wet autumn night, when the gray heaven hangs like a leaden roof over the earth. Then another would join in with the singer, and now two soft, sad voices would break into song in our narrow, dull hole of a basement. Suddenly others would join in, and the song would surge up like a wave, would grow louder and swell upward, till it would seem as if the damp, foul walls of our stone prison were widening out and opening. Then, all six-and-twenty of us would be singing; our loud, harmonious song would fill the whole shop; the song felt cramped, it was striking, as it were, against the walls in moaning sobs and sighs, moving our hearts with a soft, tantalizing ache, tearing open old wounds, and awakening longings.

The singers would sigh deeply and heavily; suddenly one would become silent and listen to the others singing, then let his voice flow once more in the common tide. Another would exclaim in a stifled voice, "Ah!" and would shut his eyes, while the deep, full sound waves would show him, as it were, a road, in front of him—a sunlit, broad road in the distance, which he himself, in thought, wandered along.

But the flame flickers once more in the huge oven, the baker scrapes incessantly with his shovel, the water simmers in the kettle, and the flicker of the fire on the wall dances as before in silent mockery. While in other men's words we sing out our dumb grief, the weary burden of live men robbed of the sunlight, the heartache of slaves.

So we lived, we six-and-twenty, in the vault-like basement of a great stone house, and we suffered each one of us, as if we had to bear on our shoulders the whole three storys of that house.

But we had something else good, besides the singing—something we loved, that perhaps took the place of the sunshine.

In the second story of our house there was established a gold-embroiderer's shop, and there, living among the other embroidery girls, was Tanya, a little maid-servant of sixteen. Every morning there peeped in through the glass door a rosy little face, with merry blue eyes; while a ringing, tender voice called out to us:

"Little prisoners! Have you any pretzels, please, for me?"

At that clear sound we knew so well, we all used to turn round, gazing with good-natured joy at the pure girlish face which smiled at us so sweetly. The sight of the little nose pressed against the windowpane, and of the small white teeth gleaming between the half-open lips, had become for us a daily pleasure. Tumbling over each other we used to jump up to open the door, and she would step in, bright and cheerful, holding out her apron, with her head bent to one side, and a smile on her lips. Her thick, long chestnut braid fell over her shoulder and across her breast. We, ugly, dirty and misshapen as we were, looked up at her—the door was four steps above the floor—looked up at her with heads thrown back, wishing her good morning, and speaking strange, unaccustomed words, which we kept for her only. Our voices became softer when we spoke to her, our jests were lighter. For her—everything was different with us. The baker took from his oven a shovelful of the best and the brownest pretzels, and threw them deftly into Tanya's apron.

"Be off with you now, or the boss will catch you!" we warned her each time. She laughed roguishly, called out cheerfully: "Good-by, poor prisoners!" and slipped away as quick as a mouse.

That was all. But long after she had gone we talked about her to one another with pleasure. It was always the same thing as we had said yesterday and the day before, because everything about us, including ourselves and her, remained the same—as yesterday—and as always.

Painful and terrible it is when a man goes on living, while nothing changes around him; and when such an existence does not finally kill his soul, then the monotony becomes with time, even more and more painful. Generally we spoke about women in such a way that sometimes it was loathsome to us ourselves to hear our rude, shameless talk. The women whom we knew deserved perhaps nothing better. But about Tanya we never let fall an evil word; none of us ever ventured so much as to lay a hand on her, even too free a jest she never heard from us. Maybe this was so because she never remained with us for long; she flashed on our eyes like a star falling from the sky, and vanished; and maybe because she was little and very beautiful, and everything beautiful calls forth respect, even in coarse people. And besides—though our life of drudgery had made us dull beasts, oxen, we were still men, and, like all men, could not live without worshiping something or other. Better than her we had none, and none but her took any notice of us, living in the basement—no one, though there were dozens of people in the house. And then, too—most likely, this was the chief thing —we all regarded her as something of our own, something existing as it were only by virtue of our pretzels. We took on ourselves in turns the duty of providing her with hot pretzels, and this became for us like a daily sacrifice to our idol, it became almost a sacred rite, and every day it bound us more closely to her. Besides pretzels, we gave Tanya a great deal of advice—to wear warmer clothes, not to run upstairs too quickly, not to carry heavy bundles of wood. She listened to all our counsels with a smile, answered them by a laugh, and never took our advice, but we were not offended at that; all we wanted was to show how concerned we were for her welfare.

Often she would apply to us with different requests, she asked us, for instance, to open the heavy door into the cellar, to chop wood: with delight and a sort of pride, we did this for her, and everything else she wanted.

But when one of us asked her to mend his solitary shirt for him, she said, with a laugh of contempt:

"What next! A likely idea!"

We made great fun of the queer fellow who could entertain such an idea, and—never asked her to do anything else. We loved her—all is said in that. Man always wants to give his love to someone, though sometimes he crushes, sometimes he sullies, with it. We were bound to love Tanya, for we had no one else to love.

At times one of us would suddenly begin to reason like this:

"And why do we make so much of the wench? What is there in her, eh? What a to-do we make about her!"

The man who dared to utter such words we promptly and coarsely cut short—we wanted something to love: we had found it and loved it, and what we twenty-six loved must be for each of us unshakable, as a holy thing, and anyone who acted against us in this was our enemy. We loved, maybe, not what was really good, but you see there were twenty-six of us, and so we always wanted to see what was precious to us held sacred by the rest.

Our love is not less burdensome than hate, and maybe that is just why some proud souls maintain that our hate is more flattering than our love. But why do they not run away from us, if it is so?

. . . .

Besides our department, our employer had also a bakery where they made rolls; it was in the same house, separated from our hole only by a wall; but the bakers—there were four of them—held aloof from us, considering their work superior to ours, and therefore themselves better than us; they never used to come into our workroom, and laughed contemptuously at us when they met us in the yard. We, too, did not go to see them; this was forbidden by our employer, for fear that we should steal the fancy rolls. We did not like the bakers, because we envied them; their work was lighter than ours, they were paid more, and were better fed; they had a light, spacious workroom, and they were all so clean and healthy—and that made them hateful to us. We all looked gray and yellow; three of us had syphilis, several suffered from skin diseases, one was completely crippled by rheumatism. On holidays and in their leisure time the bakers wore pea-jackets and creaking boots, two of them had accordions, and they all used to go for strolls in the public park—we wore filthy rags and torn leather shoes or bast slippers on our feet, the police would not let us into the public park—could we possibly like the bakers?

And one day we learned that one of their men had gone on a spree, the master had sacked him and had already taken on another, and that this other was an ex-soldier, wore a satin waistcoat and a watch and gold chain. We were anxious to get a sight of such a dandy, and in the hope of catching a glimpse of him we kept running one after another out into the yard.

But he came of his cwn accord into our workroom. Kicking at the door, he pushed it open, and leaving it ajar, stood in the doorway smiling, and said to us:

"God help the work! Good morning, mates!"

The frosty air, which streamed in through the open door, curled in streaks of vapor round his feet. He stood on the threshold, looked down upon us, and under his fair, twisted mustache gleamed big yellow teeth. His waistcoat was really something quite out of the common, blue-flowered, brilliant with shining little red stone buttons. He also wore a watch chain.

He was a fine fellow, this soldier; tall, healthy, rosy-cheeked, and his big, clear eyes had a friendly, cheerful glance. He wore on his head a white starched cap, and from under his spotlessly clean apron peeped the pointed toes of fashionable, well-blacked boots.

Our baker asked him politely to shut the door. The soldier did so without hurrying himself, and began to question us about the master. We explained to him, all speaking together, that our employer was a thoroughgoing brute, a crook, a knave, and a slave-driver; in a word, we repeated to him all that can and must be said about an employer, but cannot be repeated here. The soldier listened to us, twitched his mustache, and watched us with a friendly, open-hearted look.

"But haven't you got a lot of girls here?" he asked suddenly.

Some of us began to laugh deferentially, others leered, and one of us explained to the soldier that there were nine girls here.

"You make the most of them?" asked the soldier, with a wink.

We laughed, but not so loudly, and with some embarrassment. Many of us would have liked to have shown the soldier that we also were tremendous fellows with the girls, but not one of us could do so; and one of our number confessed as much, when he said in a low voice:

"That sort of thing is not in our line."

"Well, no; it wouldn't quite do for you," said the soldier with conviction, after having looked us over. "There is something wanting about you all. You don't look the right sort. You've no sort of appearance; and the women, you see, they like a bold appearance, they will have a well-set-up body. Everything has to be tip-top for them. That's why they respect strength. They want an arm like that!"

The soldier drew his right hand, with its turned-up shirt sleeve, out of his pocket, and showed us his bare arm. It was white and strong, and covered with shining golden wool.

"Leg and chest, all must be strong. And then a man must be dressed in the latest fashion, so as to show off his looks to advantage. Yes, all the women take to me. I don't call to them, I don't beckon them, yet with one accord, five at a time, they throw themselves at my head."

He sat down on a flour sack, and told at length all about the way women loved him, and how bold he was with them. Then he left, and after the door had creaked to behind him, we sat for a long time silent, and thought about him and his talk. Then we all suddenly broke silence together, and it became apparent that we were all equally pleased with him. He was such a nice, open-hearted fellow; he came to see us without any stand-offishness, sat down and chatted. No one else had ever come to us like that, and no one else had talked to us in that friendly sort of way. And we continued to talk of him and his coming triumph among the embroidery girls, who passed us by with contemptuous sniffs when they saw us in the yard, or who looked straight through us as if we had been air. But we admired them always when we met them outside, or when they walked past our windows; in winter, in fur jackets and toques to match; in summer, in hats trimmed with flowers, and carrying colored parasols. Among ourselves, however, we talked about these girls in a way that would have made them mad with shame and rage, if they could have heard us.

"If only he does not get hold of little Tanya!" said the baker, suddenly, in an anxious tone of voice.

We were silent, for these words troubled us. Tanya had quite gone out of our minds, supplanted, put on one side by the strong, fine figure of the soldier.

Then began a lively discussion; some of us maintained that Tanya would never lower herself so; others thought she would not be able to resist him, and the third group proposed to break his ribs for him if he should try to annoy Tanya. And, finally, we all decided to watch the soldier and Tanya, and to warn the girl against him. This brought the discussion to an end.

Four weeks had passed by since then; during this time the soldier baked white rolls, walked out with the gold-embroidery girls, visited us often, but did not talk any more about his conquests; only twisted his mustache and licked his lips lasciviously.

Tanya called in as usual every morning for "little pretzels," and was as gay and as nice and friendly with us as ever. We certainly tried once or twice to talk to her about the soldier, but she called him a "goggle-eyed calf," and made fun of him all round, and that set our minds at rest. We saw how the gold-embroidery girls carried on with the soldier, and we were proud of our girl; Tanya's behavior reflected honor on us all; we imitated her, and began in our talks to treat the soldier with small consideration. She became dearer to us, and we greeted her with more friendliness and kindliness every morning.

One day the soldier came to see us, a bit drunk, and sat down and began to laugh. When we asked him what he was laughing about, he explained to us:

"Why, two of them—that Lydka girl and Grushka—have been clawing each other on my account. You should have seen the way they went for each other! Ha! ha! One got hold of the other one by the hair, threw her down on the floor of the passage, and sat on her! Ha! ha! ha! They scratched and tore each others' faces. It was enough to make one die with laughter! Why is it women can't fight fair? Why do they always scratch one another, eh?"

He sat on the bench, in fine fettle, fresh and jolly; he sat there and went on laughing. We were silent. This time he made an unpleasant impression on us.

"Well, it's a funny thing what luck I have with the women-folk! Eh? One wink, and it's all over with them! It's the d-devil!"

He raised his white arms covered with golden wool, and dropped them down on his knees. And his eyes seemed to reflect such frank astonishment, as if he were himself quite surprised at his good luck with women. His fat, red face glistened with delight and self-satisfaction, and he licked his lips more than ever.

Our baker scraped the shovel violently and angrily along the oven floor, and all at once he said sarcastically:

"There's no great strength needed to pull up fir saplings, but try a real pine-tree."

"Why—what do you mean by saying that to me?" asked the soldier.

"Oh, well . . ."

"What is it?"

"Nothing—it slipped out!"

"No, wait a minute! What's the point? What pine-tree?"

Our baker did not answer, working rapidly away with the shovel at the oven; flinging into it the half-cooked pretzels, taking out those that were done, and noisily throwing them on the floor to the boys who were stringing them on bast. He seemed to have forgotten the soldier and his conversation with him. But the soldier had all at once grown uneasy. He got up onto his feet, and went to the oven, at the risk of knocking against the handle of the shovel, which was waving spasmodically in the air.

"No, tell me, do—who is it? You've insulted me. I? There's not one could withstand me, n-no! And you say such insulting things to me?"

He really seemed genuinely hurt. He must have had nothing else to pride himself on except his gift for seducing women; maybe, except for that, there was nothing living in him, and it was only that by which he could feel himself a living man.

There are men to whom the most precious and best thing in their lives appears to be some disease of their soul or body. They fuss over it all their lives, and only living by it, suffering from it, they feed on it, they complain of it to others, and so draw the attention of their fellows to themselves. For that they extract sympathy from people, and apart from it they have nothing at all. Take from them that disease, cure them, and they will be miserable, because they have lost their one resource in life —they are left empty then. Sometimes a man's life is so poor, that he is driven instinctively to prize his vice and to live by it; one may say for a fact that often men are vicious out of boredom.

The soldier was offended, he went up to our baker and roared:

"No, tell me, do—who?"
"Tell you?" the baker turned suddenly to him.
"Well?"
"You know Tanya?"
"Well?"
"Well, there then! Only try."
"I?"
"You!"
"Her? Why, that's nothing to me—pooh!"
"We shall see!"
"You will see! Ha! ha!"
"She'll—"
"Give me a month!"
"What a braggart you are, soldier!"
"A fortnight! I'll prove it! Who is it? Tanya! Pooh!"
"Well, get out. You're in my way!"
"A fortnight—and it's done! Ah, you—"
"Get out, I say!"

Our baker, all at once, flew into a rage and brandished his shovel. The soldier staggered away from him in amazement, looked at us, paused, and softly, malignantly said, "Oh, all right, then!" and went away.

During the dispute we had all sat silent, absorbed in it. But when the soldier had gone, eager, loud talk and noise arose among us.

Someone shouted to the baker: "It's a bad job that you've started, Pavel!"

"Do your work!" answered the baker savagely.

We felt that the soldier had been touched to the quick, and that danger threatened Tanya. We felt this, and at the same time we were all possessed by a burning curiosity, most agreeable to us. What would happen? Would Tanya hold out against the soldier? And almost all cried confidently: "Tanya? She'll hold out! You won't catch her with your bare arms!"

We longed terribly to test the strength of our idol; we were forcibly trying to persuade each other that our divinity was a strong divinity and would come victorious out of this ordeal. We began at last to fancy that we had not worked enough on the soldier, that he would forget the dispute, and that we ought to pique his vanity further. From that day we began to live a different life, a life of nervous tension, such as we had never known before. We spent whole days in arguing together; we all grew, as it were, sharper; and got to talk more and better. It seemed to us that we were playing some sort of game with the devil, and the stake on our side was Tanya. And when we learned from the bakers that the soldier had begun "running after our Tanya," we felt a sort of delighted terror, and life was so interesting that we did not even notice that our employer had taken advantage of our preoccupation to increase our work by three hundred pounds of dough a day. We seemed, indeed, not even tired by our work. Tanya's name was on our lips all day long. And every day we looked for her with a certain peculiar impatience. Sometimes we pictured to ourselves that she would come to us, and it would not be the same Tanya as of old, but somehow different. We said nothing to her, however, of the dispute regarding her. We asked her no questions, and behaved as well and affectionately to her as ever. But even in this a new element crept in, alien to our old feeling for Tanya—and that new element was keen curiosity, keen and cold as a steel knife.

"Mates! Today the time's up!" our baker said to us one morning, as he set to work.

We were well aware of it without his reminder; but still we became alert.

"Have a good look at her. She'll be here directly," suggested the baker.

One of us cried out in a troubled voice, "Why! as though one could see anything! You need more than eyes."

And again an eager, noisy discussion sprang up among us. Today we were at last to discover how pure and spotless was the vessel into which we had poured all that was best in us. This morning, for the first time, it became clear to us that we really were playing for high stakes; that we might, indeed, through the exaction of this proof of purity, lose our divinity altogether.

All this time we had been hearing that Tanya was stubbornly and persistently pursued by the soldier, but not one of us had thought of asking her what she thought of him. And she came every morning to fetch her pretzels. and was the same toward us as ever.

This morning, too, we heard her voice outside: "You poor prisoners! Here I am!"

We opened the door hastily, and when she came in we all remained, contrary to our usual custom, silent. Our eyes fixed on her, we did not know what to say to her, what to ask her. And there we stood in front of her, a gloomy, silent crowd. She seemed to be surprised at this unusual reception; and suddenly we saw her turn white and become uneasy, then she asked, in a choking voice:

"Why are you—like this?"

"And you?" the baker flung at her grimly, never taking his eyes off her.

"What about me?"

"N-nothing."

"Well, then, give me the little pretzels quickly."

Never before had she bidden us hurry.

"There's plenty of time," said the baker, not stirring and not removing his eyes from her face.

Then, suddenly, she turned round and disappeared through the door.

TWENTY-SIX MEN AND A GIRL

The baker took his shovel and said, calmly turning away toward the oven:

"Well, that settles it! There's a soldier for you—the low cur!"

Like a flock of sheep we all pressed round the table, sat down silently, and began listlessly to work. Soon, however, one of us remarked:

"Perhaps, after all—"

"Shut up!" shouted the baker.

We were all convinced that he was a man of judgment, a man who knew more than we did about things. And at the sound of his voice we were convinced of the soldier's victory, and our spirits became sad and downcast.

At twelve o'clock—while we were eating our dinners —the soldier came in. He was as clean and as smart as ever, and looked at us—as usual—straight in the eyes. But we were all awkward in looking at him.

"Now then, honored sirs, would you like me to show you a soldier's prowess?" he said, chuckling proudly.

"Go out into the passage and look through the crack —do you understand?"

We went into the passage, and stood all pushing against one another, squeezed up to the cracks of the wooden partition of the passage that looked into the yard. We had not to wait long. Very soon Tanya, with hurried footsteps and an anxious face, walked across the yard, jumping over the puddles of melting snow and mud: she disappeared into the cellar. Then whistling, and not hurrying himself, the soldier followed in the same direction. His hands were thrust in his pockets; his mustaches were quivering.

Rain was falling, and we saw how its drops struck the puddles, and the puddles were wrinkled by them. The day was damp and gray—a very dreary day. Snow still lay on the roofs, but on the ground dark patches of mud had begun to appear. And the snow on the roofs too was covered by a layer of brownish dirt. The rain fell slowly with a depressing sound. It was cold and disagreeable for us waiting.

The first to come out of the cellar was the soldier; he walked slowly across the yard, his mustaches twitching, his hands in his pockets—the same as always.

Then—Tanya, too, came out. Her eyes—her eyes were radiant with joy and happiness, and her lips—were smiling. And she walked as though in a dream, staggering, with unsteady steps.

We could not bear this calmly. All of us at once rushed to the door, dashed out into the yard and—hissed at her, reviled her viciously, loudly, wildly.

She started at seeing us, and stood as though rooted in the mud under her feet. We formed a ring round her, and maliciously, without restraint, abused her with vile words, said shameful things to her.

We did this quietly, slowly, seeing that she could not get away, that she was hemmed in by us, and we could rail at her to our hearts' content. I don't know why, but we did not beat her. She stood in the midst of us, and turned her head this way and that, as she heard our insults. And we—more and more violently flung at her the filth and venom of our words.

The color had left her face. Her blue eyes, so happy a moment before, opened wide, her bosom heaved, and her lips quivered.

We in a ring round her avenged ourselves on her, for she had robbed us. She belonged to us, we had lavished on her our best, and though that best was beggar's crumbs, still there were twenty-six of us, she was one, and so there was no pain we could give her equal to her guilt! How we insulted her! She was still mute, still gazed at us with wild eyes, and a shiver ran through her.

We laughed, roared, yelled. Other people ran up from

somewhere and joined us. One of us pulled Tanya by the sleeve of her blouse.

Suddenly her eyes flashed; deliberately she raised her hands to her head and straightening her hair she said loudly but calmly, straight in our faces:

"Ah, you miserable prisoners!"

And she walked straight at us, walked as directly as though we had not been before her, as though we were not blocking her way.

And hence none of us did actually block her way.

Walking out of our circle without turning round, she added loudly, with pride and indescribable contempt:

"Ah, you scum—brutes."

And—was gone, erect, beautiful, proud.

We were left in the middle of the yard, in the rain, under the gray sunless sky.

Then we went mutely away to our damp stone basement. As before—the sun never peeped in at our windows, and Tanya came no more. Never!

1899.

CAIN AND ARTYOM

CAIN was a nimble little Jew, with a head running up to a point, and a lean, sallow face. Tufts of coarse red hair grew on his cheek-bones and chin, giving his face the appearance of being set in a frame of crumpled plush, the upper part of which was formed by the visor of his dirty cap.

Under the visor could be seen two bright, little gray eyes, ornamented with red eyebrows, which looked as if they had been plucked. These eyes very rarely rested for any length of time on the same object; they wandered with quick, furtive glances from one side to the other, casting timid, obsequious smiles in all directions.

It was impossible to see these and not at once become aware that the dominant feeling in the man who smiled that way was a fear of everything and everybody, a fear which in a moment could grow to abject terror.

Hence, all those who were not too lazy to do so, increased this tenseness of the Jew by cuffs and cruel jokes. Everything about him seemed to participate in this feeling, from his nerves to the folds of the canvas garment that hung loosely over his thin body, from shoulder to heel, and which seemed continually quivering.

The Jew's name was Khaim Aaron Purvitz, but he was known as Cain. It was a simpler and more familiar name than Khaim, and, added to this, it was very insulting. Little as it suited his frail and timid figure, everybody seemed to think that it exactly described the Jew, both in body and soul, and that at the same time it was humiliating.

He lived in the midst of those who had suffered at

the hands of fate, and such as these always find pleasure in offering offense to their neighbors, and, what is more, they always know how to do it—it is the only means they have of avenging themselves. And it was an easy thing with Cain; when they mocked him, he only gave a deprecating smile, and at times, he even took part himself in their ridicule of him, as if he wished to pay his tormentors in advance for the right to live among them. He lived, of course, by trade. He went about the streets with a wooden box before him, calling out in a thin, mawkish voice: "Shoe polish! Matches! Pins! Needles! Haberdashery! Notions!"

He had another characteristic feature; he had very large ears, which stood out from his head, and which were continually moving like those of a sensitive horse.

He carried on his trade at Shikhan, the suburb where the poorest and raggedest lived, all kinds of riffraff. Shikhan consisted of one narrow street, lined with old, high, and repulsive-looking houses. Among these were night-refuges, taverns, bakers' shops, groceries and places where they sold old iron and various utensils. The population consisted of thieves and receivers of stolen goods, small second-hand dealers, and female costermongers. There was always plenty of shadow, thanks to the height of the houses, and plenty of mud, and drunkards; in summer the street continually reeked with the heavy smell of decaying matter and brandy. The sun looked in only at early morning, and then cautiously and for a very short time, as if fearing the contact with the mud would soil its rays.

The street, which ran along the slope of the hill beside a large river, was always full of dockyard workers, sailors on shore leave, and stevedores. Here they got drunk and amused themselves in their own way, and here, too, pickpockets lurked in convenient corners waiting their opportunity when the drink should have done its work. Along the foot-paths stood the earthenware pots, filled with little meat patties, and here, too, were the trays belonging to the confectioners and the liver-sellers. The workmen from the docks crowded round and eagerly devoured the hot food; those among them who were tipsy sang in loud coarse voices and reviled one another; the vendors cried their wares in strident tones, puffing up their goods; carts rumbled along, with difficulty making their way through the press of people who were either bent on buying or selling, waiting for work, or watching an opportunity for this or that. The chaos of sounds whirled through the street, which was as narrow as a ditch, breaking against the filthy walls of the houses which looked as though they were covered with sores, their decaying plaster falling away everywhere in little bits.

In this ditch, reeking with its impurities, in the midst of the deafening noise and the filthy language, children were always darting about, children of every age, but all equally dirty, famished, and degraded. They ran about there from morning till evening; depending for their livelihood on the kindness of the vendors, and on the nimbleness of their own little hands: at night they slept where they could, in the shelter of doorways, under the counter used by a pastry-vendor, in the embrasure of a cellar-window. No sooner had the dawn appeared, than these emaciated victims of rickets and scrofula were again on their feet, beginning their work of stealing what they could get hold of in the way of choice bits, and of begging for those which were no longer salable. To whom did these children belong? To everyone. It was here, in this street, that Cain prowled about day after day, crying his goods, which he sold to the women. They were in the habit of borrowing twenty kopecks from him for a few hours, under obligation of paying back twenty-two, and they never failed in their payments. Cain as a rule did a big business in the street; he bought shirts, caps, boots, and accordions from men on a spree, and from the women their petticoats, bodices, and cheap ornaments; he then exchanged these goods, or sold them at a profit of ten kopecks. And all the while he was exposed to their ridicule and blows; at times they even stripped him of his goods, but he never uttered a complaint; all he did was to smile, with that smile so tragically gentle.

Again, it happened sometimes that two or three youths, driven to excess by hunger and drink, would fall upon the Jew in one of the dark recesses of the town, and either from fear or from their blows he would fall to the ground, and lie there trembling at the feet of his assailants, digging convulsively in his pockets, and crying in a supplicating voice: "Sirs, good sirs, do not take all my kopecks—how then can I carry on my trade?"

And his thin face would be quivering with his endless smiles.

"Well, leave off whining! Just give us thirty kopecks." These good gentlemen quite understood that the cow must be allowed to keep her udder if more milk is to be got from her. Sometimes Cain would rise and walk amicably beside them down the street, joking and smiling, the youths condescending so far as to exchange conversation with him and to make fun of him; and it was all done as naturally and frankly as possible.

Cain always looked a little thinner after an episode of this kind—that was all.

He did not appear to be on good terms with the Jewish community. He was but seldom seen walking with one of his coreligionists, and on these rare occasions it was noticed that the latter treated Cain with haughty contempt. There was even a rumor spread abroad that Cain was under the ban, and at one time the women peddlers called him cursed.

This, however, was not very likely, although Cain showed unmistakable signs of heresy; he did not observe Sabbath, and he ate meat that was not kosher. He was besieged with questions; first one and then another insisted or commanded that he should explain why he dared to eat things which were forbidden by his religion. He shrank into himself, smiled, and put off his questioners with some joking answer, or got away somehow without giving them any information concerning the beliefs and customs of the Jews.

Even the wretched children pursued him along the streets, throwing handfuls of mud, melon rinds, or other dirty objects at his back or into his box. He would try to stop them by speaking kindly to them, but more often he would plunge into the thick of the crowd, whither they dared not follow him, for fear of being trampled under foot.

And so Cain lived on from day to day; known to all and persecuted by all, he carried on his trade, he trembled with fear, he smiled—and then all at once fortune in her turn smiled on him.

There is no corner of the universe without its despot. At Shikhan this part was played by the handsome Artyom, a colossal fellow, with a round head covered by a forest of dark, curly hair, that fell in soft wayward ringlets over his forehead down to the beautiful velvety eyebrows, and the huge, dark, almond-shaped eyes which were always veiled by a soft dew. The nose was straight, of a classic correctness of form, the lips red and fresh, and surmounted by a large black mustache; the pure oval of his somewhat swarthy face was of a marvelous regularity and simple beauty of feature, and the eyes, with the misty shadow over them, suited it exactly, seeming as it were to explain, as well as to complete, its beauty. Broad-chested, tall and well-proportioned, always wearing a smile of unconscious contentment, he was a terror to the men of Shikhan, and an object of delight to the women. He passed the best part of his day lying about, he did not care where, provided that the spot was well in the sun, and there, massive and indolent, he drank in short draughts of the fresh air and the light, his powerful chest rising and falling with the regularity of his strong, steady breathing.

He was twenty-five years of age, and had come into the town three years previously with a crew of stevedores from Promzino;* and the shipping season once over, he stayed on through the winter, having ascertained that, thanks to his strength and beauty, he could lead an agreeable life without working. And so, from being a mere peasant and stevedore, he became the favorite of the female peddlers of patties, the shopkeepers and other women of Shikhan. This occupation provided him with ample supplies of food, vodka, and tobacco, whenever he wanted them, and he wanted nothing else, and so his days passed.

Women abused each other because of him, fought over him, and bore tales to husbands of his doings with their wives, which resulted in unmerciful beatings. Artyom remained perfectly indifferent to all this; he lay, at full length, like a cat warming himself in the sun, waiting until he was moved by one of the few desires which he was capable of feeling.

As a rule, he chose the hill on which the street abutted for his couch. Right in front of him lay the river, beyond which he could see the fields stretching away to the horizon, their smooth green surface broken here and there by gray patches, which were villages. Down there, in the midst of that verdant expanse, it was always cool and clear. By turning his head to the left he could see down the whole length of the street, overflowing with noisy life. If he looked

* Promzino, a village in the province of Simbirsk, which supplies the best, i.e., the strongest, stevedores employed on the Volga.

attentively at this dark, surging mass, he could distinguish the outlines of well-known figures, he could hear the street's hungry roar, and possibly a thought or two may have passed through his mind. Thick, high grasses grew up all around the spot where he reclined; a few decayed-looking birch trees stood in solitary wretchedness, with some uprooted elder-bushes. Here the rowdies came to sleep themselves sober and to play cards, to patch up their rags, and to rest themselves from work and tavern broils.

Artyom enjoyed no good reputation among them. In the assurance of his irresistible strength, he was often insolent towards them; and then he earned his bread with far too little trouble. These things combined awakened a spirit of envy; what was more, he very seldom shared his booty with anyone else. Comradeship was not a sentiment highly developed in him, and he was not fond of the society of his fellow-men. If anyone came up to him and began to talk, he was quite willing to answer, but he never was the one to begin a conversation; if money was begged of him for drink he gave it, but never took the initiative in standing treat, though among his friends it was the custom to eat and drink every kopeck's worth in company.

It was there, as he lounged among the bushes, that Artyom received the messengers of love, who appeared in the guise of a dirty raggedly-dressed girl from the neighborhood, or of a boy in all respects equally filthy. They were usually of tender age, from seven to eight, rarely as old as ten, but they were nevertheless always profoundly impressed with the importance of their mission; they spoke in whispers, and there was an air of mystery on their ugly little faces.

"Uncle Artyom, Aunt Marya has told me to let you know that her husband has gone away, and that you are to hire a boat to take her into the fields—today."

"Oh!" Artyom would drawl, lazily, and a smile would appear in his sleepy, beautiful eyes.

"You are to be sure and do this."

"Yes, I will come—but tell me now—what is she like—this Aunt Marya?"

"Why, she is one of the shopkeepers in the town, of course," answered the messenger in a tone of reproach.

"Ah, yes! her shop is next the one where they sell old iron."

"No, the one beside that belongs to Anissa Nicolaevna."

"Yes, yes, I know, little brother. I only asked you in fun—as if I could forget. I know Marya very well."

But the messenger does not feel thoroughly convinced of this, and, anxious to execute his orders conscientiously, he insists on explaining further to Artyom:

"Marya is the little red-cheeked woman next to the fish-shop."

"Quite so, the one next to the fish-shop. What a queer little monkey you are. Did you think I should make a mistake? Well, run and tell Marya that I am coming. Now, be off!"

Then the messenger puts on his most beguiling expression, and says:

"Uncle Artyom, give me a kopeck."

"A kopeck! And suppose I have not got one?" says Artyom, at the same time plunging his two hands into the pockets of his trousers. He never fails to find some coin. With a merry laugh, the messenger runs away at full speed to bring word to the amorous liver-seller that he has carried out her orders, and to receive his reward. He knows the value of money, and he has need of it, not only because he is hungry, but because he smokes cigarettes, drinks brandy, and has also his own little affairs of the heart. During a day following a scene of this kind, Artyom is even more inaccessible than usual to all impressions from the outside world, and even more splendid in the serene strength of his rare animal beauty.

And so he carried on his surfeited existence, from day to day, in a state, as it seemed, of almost dreamy unconsciousness, undisturbed by the jealousy and envious hatred of the men and women around him, whom he had made his enemies, but, above all, in perfect calmness, for he knew himself to be under the protection of his own formidable fist.

But in spite of this, at times the brown eyes of the handsome young man bore a dark, threatening expression, the velvet eyebrows became contracted, and a deep line furrowed the swarthy forehead.

He would rise and leave his lair to go towards the street. The nearer he approached its tumult, the rounder became the pupils of his eyes, and the more frequently delicate nostrils quivered. A yellow vest of coarse material hung over his left shoulder, the right one was covered by his shirt, under which could be distinguished his powerful shoulder. He did not like boots, and always wore bast shoes; the strips of white linen, neatly wound crossways round his legs in place of stockings, threw the muscles of his legs into relief. He walked forward slowly, like a huge threatening cloud.

His habits were well known in the suburb, and everyone could tell by the look on his face what to expect of him. A murmured warning would be heard: "Artyom is coming!"

Everyone hastened to clear the way before the handsome youth. The baskets and goods set out for sale, the portable stoves and the earthenware pots full of hot meats, are drawn back, while flattering smiles and greetings are showered upon him—the whole population, meanwhile, standing in awe of him. Sulky and silent he strides along amid these mingled signs of admiration for his person and fear of his strength, like a huge beast of the forest in his wild beauty.

His foot catches in a basket laden with tripe, liver, and lungs, and the contents are scattered over the muddy pavement. The owner cries out and curses.

"And why do you get in my way then?" asks Artyom calmly but ominously.

"And does the road belong to you, you ox?" howls the huckster.

"And suppose I want to walk here."

The muscles over Artyom's cheek-bones swell, and his eyes look like white-hot nails. The huckster takes note of these signs and murmurs:

"The street is not wide enough for you then!"

Artyom goes slowly forward. His victim turns into a public-house, asks for hot water, washes his goods, and five minutes later is heard crying at the top of his voice:

"Liver! Lungs! Hot heart! Come and buy, sailor! Cut you a slice of tongue for five kopecks! Have some of this neck, Aunt! Who wants hot heart? Liver? Lung?"

The indistinct sound of the mingled voices rises and falls in the thick air laden with the odor of rotten stuff, brandy, sweat, fish, tar, and onions. The people pass to and fro on the street, hindering the passage of the vehicles, crying their wares, buying, selling, and laughing. Above them winds a blue strip of sky, which shows dim behind the cloud of dust and soot that rises from the street, where even the shadows of the houses seem damp and saturated with mud.

"Haberdashery! Thread! Needles!" calls the shrill voice of the Jew as he walks behind Artyom, who is an object of even greater terror to him than to the others.

"Pear tarts sweet! Buy and eat!" sings out a little pastry-cook clearly.

"Onions, green onions!" squeaks another peddler.

"Kvass! Kvass!" croaks a hoarse voice belonging to a fat, little old man with a red face, seated in the shade of his barrel.

Another man, known by the curious nickname of the Ragged Bridegroom, is busy selling a shirt, dirty but whole, from his own back, to one of the dockyard workers, shrieking at him in a tone of assurance:

"You blockhead! where would you get such a showpiece as that for twenty kopecks? Why, with that on your back you could go and ask a rich merchant's widow in marriage! A woman with millions, you devil!"

Suddenly the universal howling is pierced by the sound of a child's clear, ringing voice:

"For Christ's sake, give a kopeck to a homeless child who has neither father nor mother."

The name of Christ sounds strange and alien to the ears of the crowd assembled in the street.

"Artyusha! Come here!" It is the affable voice of a soldier's grass widow, the buxom Darya Gromova, who sells meat patties. "Where have you been hiding? Have you forgotten us?"

"Has business been good?" Artyom asks her, quietly; and with a touch of his foot he upsets her wares. The yellow, shining patties roll steaming over the stones of the pavement, and Darya, ready to fight, shrieks furiously:

"Impudent wretch! Murderer! How can the earth bear you, you camel of Astrakhan!"

Those around her laugh. They know that Artyom will have no difficulty in obtaining pardon from her. And on he goes again, jostling everybody out of his way, upsetting some, and treading on the toes of others.

And ever as he goes, the warning murmur glides along ahead like a serpent: "Artyom is coming!"

Even he who hears these three words for the first time is aware of the menace in them and makes room for

Artyom, as he gazes with fear and surprise at the powerful figure of the handsome youth.

Artyom comes across a loafer of his acquaintance. They greet one another, and Artyom squeezes the hand of his friend in such fashion that the latter cries out in pain and swears at him. Then Artyom grips his shoulder with fingers of iron, or invents some other way of hurting him, and looks quietly at the man as, half suffocated, he shrieks and groans in the enemy's grasp, and with stifled voice cries:

"Let me go, you cursed hangman!"

But the hangman is as inexorable as a judge.

Cain had often fallen into the rough hands of the giant, who played with him as an inquisitive child might play with a beetle.

This particular and inexplicable mode of behavior on the part of the athlete was known in Shikhan as "Artyom's sortie." It earned him many enemies, but in spite of their efforts, they could not break his superhuman strength.

Thus, on one occasion seven husky fellows, with the approval of the whole neighborhood, agreed to give Artyom a lesson which would keep him quiet for a while.

Two of the number paid dearly for the affair; the others came off lightly. On another occasion some shopkeepers, injured husbands, hired a butcher from the town, known to have come off victorious several times in matches with circus athletes. The butcher, in return for a large reward, undertook to beat up Artyom within an inch of his life. The two men were confronted, and Artyom, who was always ready to fight "for the pleasure of it," dislocated the butcher's arm, and dealt him such a blow under the heart that the butcher fell unconscious to the ground. These deeds of prowess, while they increased Artyom's prestige, naturally added to the number of his enemies. He continued his "sorties" as before, crushing all and everything in his path. What feelings did he thus express? Did the native of the woods and fields, torn from his natural environment, seek thus perhaps to revenge himself on the town and its manner of life? Perhaps he had some dim consciousness that the town was gradually working his destruction, that body and soul were being inoculated with its poison, and with this feeling he fought, as his nature prompted him, against the deadly forces that were enslaving him. His "sorties" came to an end sometimes at the police station, where he was treated better than the other inhabitants of Shikhan; the police were astonished at his fabulous strength and drew amusement from it; they knew he was no thief—he was not clever enough for that. It happened more often, however, that his "sortie" being over, he turned into some low dive, and was there taken under the wing of one of his lady-loves. He fell into moody fits after these exploits. A certain look of wildness came into his eyes, and the immobility of his face gave him the appearance of an idiot. Then one of the shopkeepers, soaked with grease to her marrow, a robust female of the age celebrated by Balzac, would assume airs of proprietorship over this untamed beast, and take him under her care, not without a certain feeling of fear.

"Shall I ask for another two glasses of beer, Artyusha? or a liqueur? And won't you eat something? You are not up to the mark today."

"Leave me alone," Artyom would answer in a thick voice. For a few minutes she would stop fussing over him and then again start plying him with drinks, for she knew that when sober he was miserly with his caresses.

And now, it pleased fate, which is fond of playing tricks, to bring Cain and Artyom together.

. . . .

This is how it came to pass.

It was after one of his "sorties," which had been followed by a heavy feast, that Artyom and his female companion made their way home, with unsteady steps, to the latter's dwelling, which was situated in a narrow alley in a lonely suburb. But there an ambush awaited him. Several men threw themselves upon him and immediately knocked him down. Weakened by drink, he was unable to defend himself; and then, for nearly an hour, these men revenged themselves upon him for the innumerable outrages to which he had subjected them.

Artyom's companion had fled; the night was dark, and the place a deserted one. His assailants had all the leisure they could desire for squaring their accounts with Artyom, and they worked without sparing their strength. When at last, tired out, they ceased, two motionless bodies were lying on the ground; one was Artyom, the other a man familiarly known as Red Buck.

After consulting together as to what was the best way of disposing of the bodies, the men decided that they would hide Artyom in an old barge which had been damaged by the ice, and was lying keel upwards beside the river; as to Red Buck, who was still groaning, they determined to take him along with them.

The pain caused by being dragged towards the shore brought Artyom to life again, but thinking that the best thing for him was to pretend to be dead, he stifled the cry which had nearly escaped him. They jostled him, they hurled invectives at him, and each boasted to the others of the blows they had inflicted on the athlete. Artyom heard Mishka Vavilov relating to his comrades how he had kept trying to kick Artyom under the left shoulder-blade, in order to burst his heart. Sukhopluyev said that he had leveled his blows at the victim's belly, for if the intestines are once injured, food, however great a quantity a man may take, ceases to nourish him, and he loses his strength. Lomakin also had, as he declared, leapt twice onto Artyom's belly. Not one of them, in short, but what could boast of having distinguished himself in an equally brilliant manner; their exploits continued to be the subject of their conversation until they reached the barge, under which they then pushed Artyom's body. He had missed nothing of their talk, and he heard his assailants assuring themselves, as they walked away, that undoubtedly Artyom would never get up again.

And now he was alone in the dark, on a wet heap of refuse cast up under the barge when the river was in flood. It was a cool night in May, and at intervals Artyom recovered consciousness, revived by the freshness of the air. But when he tried to crawl down to the river overcome by the terrible pain that shot through every fiber of his body, he swooned afresh. He came to himself again, torn by pain, and with an agony of thirst upon him. Close at hand he could hear the river lapping against the shore as if in mockery of his powerlessness to move. He lay thus the whole night through, fearing to groan or make the least movement.

At last, coming to himself once more, he was conscious that something had been done to him that had brought him relief. He could with great difficulty open one eye, and just move his torn and swollen lips. It must be daytime, he thought, for the rays of the sun were shining through the cracks of the barge, and making a twilight round him where he lay. He managed to raise his hand to his face, and felt that it was covered with wet rags. There were wet cloths, too, on his chest and his abdomen. His clothes had all been taken off, and the cool air assuaged his sufferings.

"Drink," he said, with a vague sense that there must be someone near him. A trembling hand was passed over his head, and the neck of a bottle put to his lips. The hand that held it shook so that the bottle knocked against

Artyom's teeth. Having drunk, Artyom was curious to know who was there, but he turned so sick with the effort of moving his head that he was obliged to lie still. Then, in a hoarse voice, he began to stammer out a few words.

"Brandy—let me have a glass of it to drink—and rub my body with it—perhaps then I shall be able to get up."

"To get up? You can't get up. Your whole body is as blue and swollen as that of a drowned man. As to brandy, that is possible—there is some brandy—I have a whole bottle."

The words were spoken quickly, in a soft timid voice. Artyom recognized it, but could not remember to what woman it belonged.

"Give me some," he said.

Again someone, who apparently did not wish to be seen, handed him a bottle over his head. As, with some difficulty, he was swallowing the brandy, Artyom's eyes wandered round the dark moist bottom of the barge, which was overgrown with fungi.

When he had drunk about a quarter of the contents of the bottle, he gave a deep sigh of relief; then in a low, feeble voice, his chest rattling the while, he said:

"They did nicely for me that time—but wait—I shall get over it—and then—look out!"

There was no answer, but he detected a slight movement as if someone was edging away from him, then all was silence; there was only the lapping of the waves and somebody in the distance was singing "Dubinushka," to the accompaniment of groans: apparently a heavy load was being dragged along. Then came, cutting through the air, the shrill whistle of a steamer, and a few seconds later he heard the melancholy wail of the siren as if the boat were bidding farewell forever to the land.

Artyom lay a long time waiting for an answer to his remarks, but the silence under the barge remained unbroken; the rotten, massive hull, green with mildew, heaved up and down above his head, looking as if at any moment it might fall over and mercilessly crush him to death.

Artyom was seized with pity for himself. He was suddenly conscious of his almost childish helplessness, and at the same time he felt aggrieved. He, so strong, so handsome, and they had thus maimed and disfigured him! He raised his weak hands and began to feel the bruises and swellings on his chest and on his face, and then he began to curse bitterly and to cry.

He sobbed and sniffled, swore dully, and hardly able to move his eyelids, he pressed out with them the tears that filled his eyes: they rolled, large, hot tears, down his cheeks, and fell into his ears, and he felt as if, thanks to them, something within him was being cleansed.

"Good—wait," he murmured through his sobs.

Then suddenly he heard sobs and stifled murmurs close beside him; it was as if someone were mimicking him.

"Who is it?" he cried in a threatening tone of voice, although for some reason or other he felt afraid.

No answer came to his question.

Then gathering all his strength together, Artyom turned on his side, roared with pain like an animal, raised himself on his elbows, and was then able to distinguish in the dark a little figure curled up into a ball on the edge of the barge. It was a man, who pressed his head against his knees, which he grasped tightly between his long skinny hands, his shoulders the while trembling violently. To Artyom he appeared to be a boy in his teens.

"Come here," he said.

But the other did not move; he continued to tremble as if shaken by fever.

A look of pain and horror came into Artyom's eyes at the sight of this figure, and he howled:

"Come!"

But the only answer was a hasty outpouring of trembling words.

"What harm have I done you? Why do you shout at me? Haven't I washed you and given you drink? Didn't I give you brandy? Didn't I cry when you cried? Didn't it hurt me when you were groaning? Oh, my God, my Lord! Even the good I do brings me nothing but suffering in return. What evil have I done either to your body or soul? How can I—I, harm you in any way?"

He broke off sobbing, and said no more.

He was seated on the ground, he took his head in his hands and began to sway from side to side.

"It's you, then, Cain, is it?"

"Well, what of it? It is I."

"You? So you did all that? Well, well! Come here, then. Come, you queer creature, you!"

Artyom was quite overwhelmed with surprise, and conscious at the same time of a feeling very nearly akin to joy. He even began to laugh when he saw the Jew creeping timidly towards him on all fours, the little eyes moving restlessly in the funny face that Artyom knew so well.

"Don't be afraid! I swear I will not touch you." He saw that it was necessary to reassure the Jew.

Cain crawled up to him, stopped, and looked up with a pleading, timorous smile, as if he had quite expected to have his fear-shrunken little body trampled under foot.

"And so it is you, then! You have done all this for me! And who sent you? . . . Anfissa?" asked Artyom, who could hardly move his tongue.

"I came of my own accord."

"Of your own accord? You lie!"

"I am not lying! I speak the truth!" replied Cain in a rapid whisper. "It was of my own accord. Please believe me. I will tell you how it happened. I heard about the affair in Grabilovka. I was drinking my tea, and I heard them say: 'Last night they did in Artyom.' I did not believe it. Is it possible to do you in? I laughed to myself. 'What fools they are,' I thought, 'that man is a Samson, and which of you could overcome him?' But first one and then another came in repeating the same thing. 'He's done for now! He's done for now!' They cursed you and laughed—everyone was pleased—and at last I was obliged to believe it true. Then I learnt that you were here. Some of them had already been round to look at you, and reported that you were dead. I came myself, and saw you. . . . You were groaning as I stood near you. I said to myself as I looked at you: 'And they have overcome him—the strongest man in the world!—Such strength, such strength!' I felt pity for you—forgive me for saying it! I thought your wounds ought to be washed—and I did it—and the water revived you. I was so delighted to see this—oh! so delighted. You do not believe me, I know. Why? Because I am a Jew. Isn't it so? But no, do believe me. I will tell you why I was so pleased, and all I thought at the time—I will tell you the truth—you won't get angry with me?"

"See, I make the sign of the cross! May a thunderbolt kill me!" swore the vanquished Artyom with energy.

Cain drew a little nearer to him and lowered his voice even further:

"You know what a fine life I lead—you know it, don't you? Haven't I—forgive me—endured blows from you? Haven't you often laughed at the dirty Jew? What? Isn't it true? You will forgive me if I speak the truth, you have sworn to do so. Do not get angry—I only say that you, like others, have persecuted the Jew. And why? Is not the Jew the son of your God, and was not my soul given to me by the same God as gave you yours?" Cain spoke rapidly, putting question after question without pausing for an answer. Words rose rapidly to his lips, as, with the remembrance of all the insults and outrages that had been heaped upon him, his heart all at once overflowed in a burning torrent of speech.

Artyom began to feel ill at ease.

"Listen, Cain," he said, "let all that be! Curse me if I ever touch you with a finger—and if anyone else harms you, I will tear him to pieces! Do you understand?"

"Ah!" exclaimed Cain in triumph, and even clicked his tongue. "There! You are guilty before me—forgive me! Do not get angry, because of the fact that you know that you are guilty before me. But still I know, yes, I am certain of it, that you are less guilty than the others! I understand it! And the others, they do nothing but cover me with their dirty spit. You spit at me too, but then you also spit at them. You dealt more cruelly with others than with me, and then I have thought to myself: 'This strong man insults and beats me, not because I am a Jew, but because I am like the others, no better than they are, and because I live among them.' And . . . I have always loved you, but my love was mixed with fear. I used to look at you and think that you could have torn open the lion's mouth and slain the Philistines. I saw you beating the others, and I admired the way you set about it, and I wanted to be strong too, but I am only like a flea."

Artyom gave a hoarse laugh.

"True—you are like a flea!"

He did not follow all that Cain was saying, but it was pleasant to see the Jew's little figure beside him. And as Cain wandered on in his excited whisper, many thoughts passed slowly through Artyom's mind.

"I wonder what time it is—about midday, I should think. And not one of them has come to see her sweetheart. But the Jew—he came—and he gave me help and says he loves me—and yet I have beaten and insulted him, how many times! And he praises my strength! Will that strength return to me? My God, if only it does!"

Artyom heaved a deep sigh. He pictured his enemies after he had given them a beating, lying swollen as he was now. And they, too, would be lying helpless somewhere, but it would be their own, their comrades who would come and look after them, not the Jew.

Artyom looked at Cain, and it seemed to him that his thoughts had brought a kind of bitterness into his mouth and throat.

He spat, and sighed heavily.

And Cain, his face contorted with excitement, and his whole body quivering, went on talking:

"And when you cried . . . I cried too . . . out of pity for your lost strength."

"And I thought someone was mimicking me," said Artyom with a gloomy smile.

"I always loved your strength, and I prayed to God: 'Our God, eternal in the heavens and on earth, let it come about that this strong man shall need me! Let me be of service to him, and let his strength become a protection to me! Let his strength stand between me and the continual persecution I suffer, and let my enemies perish by that strength!' That was my prayer, and I went on praying for a long, long time, asking God to turn my greatest enemy into my protector, as He had given Mordecai a defender in the person of the king, the conqueror of the nations. And just then you began to cry, and I cried too, but suddenly you shouted at me, and all my prayers vanished."

"Well, how should I know, you queer fellow," said Artyom, with a guilty smile on his face.

But Cain hardly heard his words. He swayed backwards and forwards, waving his hands, and continued to whisper. It was a low, passionate whisper, which vibrated with joy and hope, with worship of the strength of the maimed man, with fear and anguish.

"My day has come at last—and I am here along with you. . . . All of them have forsaken you—but I—I came. . . . You will get well, Artyom, won't you? There is nothing seriously the matter with you, is there? And your strength will come back?"

"I shall be all right again, do not fear! . . . And in return for your goodness, I will take care of you as I should of a little child."

By degrees Artyom began to feel better; the pains in his head seemed less severe, and his mind grew clearer. "I must take Cain's part," he said to himself. "Why not? He is so kind and frank, so straightforward in his talk." As this thought passed through his mind he suddenly smiled; he had been conscious for a long time of some vague longing within him, and now he knew what it was he wanted.

"I am hungry! Can you find me something to eat, Cain?"

Cain leapt up so quickly that he nearly knocked himself against the beams of the barge. His face was positively transformed. There was upon it an expression of energy, and at the same time of something naïve and childlike. Artyom, this famous athlete, had asked him—Cain—for something to eat!

"I'll do everything for you, everything. It is all ready here in the corner. I've prepared it. I know . . . when people are ill they ought to eat—I know that—and so on my way here I spent a whole ruble on food."

"We will settle our accounts later on. I will pay you back ten rubles. I shall be able to do it—the money is not mine, but I have only to say 'Give!' and I get as much as I want."

He laughed good-naturedly, and, hearing him, Cain beamed with happiness and grew merry himself.

"I know all about it! Now tell me what you want. I will do anything in the world for you—anything!"

"Good! Well, then, begin by rubbing me down with vodka. Don't give me any food. First rub me down. Can you do it?"

"Why can't I? You will see, I shall do it as well as the best doctor."

"Go ahead! Rub me, and then I shall get up."

"Get up? No, I don't think you will be able to do that."

"You don't think so? Well, wait and see. Do you think I am going to spend the night here? What a queer little body you are! Give me my rubbing first, and then go into the suburb to Mokevna, the baker-woman, and tell her I am moving into her shed, and she should put some straw down in it. There I shall get well. You shall be well paid for your pains, have no fear."

"I believe you," replied Cain, pouring some vodka onto Artyom's chest. "I believe you more than I do myself. Oh, I know you!"

"Oh! Oh! Rub, rub! It doesn't matter that it hurts. Keep on rubbing. Oh! Oh! Here! Here! . . . There! . . . Oh! Oh!" roared Artyom.

"I would throw myself into the water to please you," said Cain, continuing his protestations.

"That's right! Now on the shoulder! Harder! Cursed devils! They gave it to me! And all because of a woman. If there had been no woman, I should have been sober, and when I am sober just try and touch me."

"Women!" responded Cain, who had now quite taken up his rôle as a servant, "they are the sin of the world. We Jews—we have even a daily prayer which runs, 'Blessed be Thou, God eternal, Ruler of the universe, that Thou didst not create me a woman.'"

"Is that true?" exclaimed Artyom, laughing. "You really have a prayer like that? What singular people you are!

Well, a woman, after all, what is she? Foolish, no mistake about it, and yet one cannot live without her—but to pray like that—that's going too far, it is an insult to her. Do you think that women have no feelings?"

Artyom, huge, helpless, looking more enormous than ever from the swellings on his body, lay stretched upon the ground, while Cain, frail and thin, breathless with exertion, rubbed his sides, his chest, and his stomach, coughing the while from the smell of the vodka. They could hear the footsteps of people continually passing along beside the river, and caught scraps of conversation. The barge lay at the bottom of a sandy ravine that was over seven feet deep. It could only be seen from above if one stood at the very edge of the ravine. A narrow strip of sand, covered with splinters of wood and rubbish, separated it from the river. The place, as a rule, was quite deserted, but today the barge appeared to be an object of exceptional interest to the passers-by. Cain and Artyom saw them one after the other walk up to it and seat themselves on the upturned hull, kicking the sides the while. Cain grew rather uneasy; he left off talking, and creeping quietly up to Artyom he said with a frightened, piteous little smile on his face:

"Do you hear that?"

"I hear," said the athlete, laughing contentedly. "I know what they are up to. They want to find out whether I shall be about again soon; and why they want to know this, is in order to get their ribs ready. Ha! Ha! The devils! I suppose they're sorry that I haven't croaked! Their little piece of work came to nothing after all."

"I tell you what—" Cain whispered in his ear, with a grimace of terror and warning on his face—"I tell you what, suppose I leave you, and you remain all alone . . . then they will come to you and . . . and . . ."

Artyom opened his mouth to give vent to a whole volley of hoarse laughs.

"Why, you little imp you! do you imagine for a moment they are afraid of you? Of you?"

"Ah! But I can serve as a witness."

"They will give you a rap on the head. Ha! Ha! Ha! Then you can go and bear witness—in the next world."

His laughter drove away Cain's fear. A feeling of delightful security took possession of his shrunken and depressed heart.

His life henceforth would assume quite another complexion, for there would be a strong hand to ward off the blows and injustice which had hitherto been inflicted upon him with impunity.

. . . .

Nearly a month passed.

One day towards noon, the hour when life in Shikhan grows more intense and agitated, and reaches the highest pitch of activity, the hour when the vendors of food are surrounded by a swarm of men just up from the docks and landing-stages, all with empty stomachs and craving food, the hour when the whole street is rank with the hot smell of cooked, spoiled meat, at that hour someone called out in a low voice, "Artyom is coming!"

Some beggars prowling idly about the street in their rags, on the lookout for any opportunity that might offer of doing a little profitable business of some kind, quickly disappeared, no one knew where. On all sides the inhabitants of Shikhan were seen to turn their eyes in the direction whence the warning had come, with mingled expressions of curiosity and uneasiness.

Artyom's advent had been looked forward to with keen expectation for some time past, and there had been hot discussions as to how he would first appear on the scene.

As formerly, Artyom took possession of the middle of

the road, walking with his customary slow gait, which was that of a well-fed man taking a stroll. There was nothing new in his appearance. As usual, his yellow vest was hanging over his shoulder, his cap stuck on the side of his head, and his black curls were falling over his forehead. His right-hand thumb was stuck in his belt, his left hand thrust far down into his trousers pocket, and his athletic chest thrown out.

Only one change was noticeable, that his handsome face, as is always the case after an illness, seemed to have gained an expression of increased intelligence. He strolled along, responding to the greetings and congratulations with a careless nod of the head.

He was followed by all the eyes in the street, and by low murmurs of astonishment and admiration at the indestructible strength which had stood the beating so well. Many of the inhabitants of the suburb spoke regretfully of Artyom's recovery, and hurled scorn and insult on those who had failed to injure his lungs and break his ribs. There was no man alive whom it was impossible to do in! Others, again, took delight in picturing the way in which Artyom would settle his score with Red Buck and his gang. But the greater the strength, the greater its power of fascination, and the majority of his fellow-townsmen were under the spell of Artyom's strength.

Meanwhile, Artyom had entered Grabilovka, a tavern which was the club of Shikhan.

There were only a few people in the long, low brick-vaulted room as his tall, powerful figure crossed the threshold. One or two uttered an exclamation of surprise at the sight of him. There was a hasty scuffling of feet, and someone threw himself precipitately into a distant corner of the cellar-like room, which reeked with the fumes of bad tobacco, dirt, and damp.

Artyom, without appearing to notice anybody, let his eyes

travel slowly round the room, and in answer to the obsequious greetings of the tavern-keeper, Savka Khlebnikov, he asked:

"Has Cain been here?"

"He soon will be. He generally comes about this time."

Artyom took his seat near one of the iron-barred windows, ordered tea, and with his immense hands resting on the table, began to examine the company with an air of indifference.

There were about ten men in the room, all roughs; they had congregated together round two tables, and there sat watching Artyom. As their eyes met his, they all smiled in a constrained sort of way, as if anxious to secure his favor. They were evidently wishing to enter into conversation with him, but Artyom gave them only dark and surly looks in return. So they all held their tongues, unable to make up their minds who should first address him. Khlebnikov, busy at the bar, hummed behind his mustache; while his foxy eyes glanced furtively around.

The stupefying noise from the street penetrated through the window; abusive language, oaths, and vendors' cries could be heard, together with nearer sounds of bottles falling and breaking to pieces on the stones. Artyom began to be bored in this malodorous and airless den.

"You men there," he cried out suddenly in a loud, deliberate voice, "you wolves, why have you suddenly become so meek? . . . Have you nothing better to do than stare and keep mum?"

"We would gladly talk, most high and terrible one!" answered the Ragged Bridegroom, rising and going towards Artyom.

He was a thin, bald-headed man, with a pointed beard and small, red eyes that had a malicious way of blinking. He wore a canvas blouse and a pair of soldier's trousers.

"You have been ill, I hear," he said, seating himself opposite to Artyom.

"And what of that?"

"Nothing. . . . But we have not seen you for a long time. . . . And whenever we asked after you, we were told: 'Artyom has been pleased to fall ill.'"

"So! Well?"

"Well, let's proceed. What was the matter with you?"

"You don't know?"

"Was I treating you?"

"You are lying the whole time, you dog," said Artyom, laughing. "And why do you tell lies? You know well enough what happened."

"Yes, I know," answered the Bridegroom, laughing too.

"Well, then, why do you tell lies?"

"Because it is smarter."

"Smarter! You think so, you candle-end!"

"Yes. If I had spoken the truth, you would probably have been angry."

"I spit on you."

"Thank you! And you don't offer to treat us with a little vodka in honor of your recovery?"

"Order what you like."

The Ragged Bridegroom ordered half a bottle of vodka, and his spirits began to rise.

"You've got an easy time of it, Artyom. You are never in want of money."

"Well, what else?"

"Nothing. It is the women—devil take them—who get you out of trouble."

"And they won't even look at you, is that it?"

"What can we do? We haven't the feet to walk your beat," sighed the Bridegroom.

"No, it is because a woman likes a healthy man. And what are you? I am a clean man—there you have it."

This was the tone Artyom had adopted when he conversed with roughs. His slow, calm, and indifferent manner of speaking added a peculiar emphasis to his words, which never failed to be rude and wounding. Possibly he felt that the men of this class were worse than himself in many ways, but at all times, and as regarded all matters, more keen-witted.

Cain now appeared, carrying his peddler's box on his chest, and with a yellow cotton dress over his left arm. Unable to throw off his habitual feeling of fear, he stood a moment on the threshold, craning his neck, and looking into the room with an uneasy smile, but on catching sight of Artyom, his face beamed with joy. Artyom looked at him, and gave him a broad smile.

"Come here and sit with me," he called to Cain; and then, turning to the Bridegroom, said in a mocking tone of command:

"And you, clear out. Make room for a man."

The Bridegroom's ugly face, with its bristles of red hair, became for an instant petrified with astonishment and disgust. He rose slowly, looked towards his comrades, who were not less taken by surprise, then towards Cain, who was walking noiselessly and cautiously up to the table; then he suddenly spat upon the floor and exclaimed angrily, "Faugh!"

He went slowly and silently back to his own table, and immediately there arose a muffled murmur of voices, amid which could be clearly distinguished tones of fury and sarcasm.

Cain continued to smile, in joyful confusion, but at the same time he shot anxious glances across to where the Bridegroom and his companions were sitting.

Then Artyom addressed him good-humoredly.

"Well, let's have tea, you merchant. Let us get some patties; will you eat some? Why do you look that way?

Spit at them, don't be afraid. Wait a moment! I'll read them a lesson."

He rose, threw his waistcoat to the ground with a movement of his shoulder, and walked up to the table where the malcontents were. Tall and powerful, his chest thrown out, his shoulders squared for a fight, he stood before them in all the arrogance of his strength, a mocking smile on his lips; and they, on their guard, sat in watchful attitudes, not speaking a word, ready to flee before him.

"Well," said Artyom, "what are you grumbling about?"

He would have liked to say something very strong, but the words would not come, and he paused.

"Out with it," said the Ragged Bridegroom, with a grimace and a wave of his hand, "or else you had better leave us in peace and go—I don't care where, you club of God!"

"Be quiet," commanded Artyom, frowning. "You are angry and put out because I am the Jew's friend and chased you away; but I tell you all that the Jew there is a better man than any one of you. He has a feeling of kindness towards his fellow-men which you have not. He has been a martyr from the beginning, and now I take him under my protection; and if one of your lot, it does not matter which, dares to injure him, let him beware. I'm telling you straight, I will beat him, I will torture him. . . ." His eyes glittered savagely, the veins in his throat swelled, and his nostrils quivered.

"That some of them got the better of me while I was drunk—that I care nothing about. They have not lessened my strength, only made my heart a little harder than it was. But understand, I'll stand up for Cain, and if anyone insults him with a single word, he will not rise again after the thrashing I shall give him. Tell this to everybody."

He heaved a profound sigh as if ridding himself of a

heavy burden, and turning his back upon them, returned to his seat.

"Well spoken!" exclaimed the Ragged Bridegroom in a low voice; and as he saw Artyom take his place opposite Cain, he made a mournful grimace.

Cain, pale with emotion, still seated at the table, never took his eyes off Artyom, and as he gazed, they grew larger and were full of an indescribable expression.

"Did you hear that?" Artyom asked him in a stern voice. "You understand, then, that if anyone touches you, you only have to run and tell me. I will come and break his bones for him."

The Jew muttered something—he was either praying to God or thanking the man. The Ragged Bridegroom and his gang whispered together, and then one by one they went out. The Bridegroom hummed as he passed in front of Artyom's table:

> If I had as much money
> As I have wit,
> I could drink gaily
> And never once quit;

and then looking straight at Artyom, he suddenly wound up his song with words of his own, making a wry face the while, and beating time with his foot:

> I would buy up all the fools there be
> And drown them all in the Black Sea;

and turning quickly to the door, he disappeared.

Artyom swore and looked round the room—only three people were left in the dim, smoky, ill-smelling place—himself, Cain, and Savka at the bar.

Savka's foxy eyes met Artyom's gloomy look, and his long face assumed an expression of mawkish piety.

"You have done an excellent and magnificent thing,

CAIN AND ARTYOM

Artyom Mikhailovich!" he said, stroking his beard. "You have acted according to the gospel precepts, quite like the good Samaritan. Cain was covered with sores—and you turned not away from him."

Artyom took no notice of the words, but he heard their echo, and this echo, reflected by the vaulted ceiling, went floating through the foul air, and crawled into his ears. Artyom was silent and kept gently shaking his head, as if to drive the sound away from him. But the words still lingered on the air, penetrated his ears, irritating him. A heavy gloom fell upon him, and some strange weight seemed to crush his heart.

He stared at Cain, who found his tea too hot and was blowing on it in the saucer. The Jew, bending over the table, drank with avidity, holding the saucer with trembling hands. Now and again Artyom caught Cain looking furtively at him, and as the athlete felt the Jew's gaze upon him, he grew more depressed still. A dull feeling of discontent, for which he could assign no cause, more and more took possession of him; a deeper gloom settled in his eyes, and he looked wildly about him. Unspoken thoughts were turning round and round in his head like mill-stones. Formerly his thoughts had never troubled him, but they had come to him during his illness, and he could not shake them off.

The windows resembled those of a prison, being provided with iron bars, and through them came the deafening noise of the street. Overhead were the heavy damp stones of the arched vault; the brick floor was slippery with mud and covered with refuse; and there was the little scared figure all in rags. . . . He sat, trembled, and said nothing. . . . And out there in the country it would soon be time for mowing. Already, on the farther side of the river, in the fields facing the town, the grass came up to a man's waist, and when a breeze floated over from them, it carried such tempting odors. . . .

"Why do you never speak, Cain?" asked Artyom, with a look of annoyance on his face. "Are you still afraid of me? What a man you are!"

Cain lifted his head and started shaking it strangely, showing a face full of piteous discomfiture.

"And what am I to say? With what tongue can I speak to you? . . . With this?" And the Jew put out the tip of his tongue and pointed to it. . . . "With this, the same that I use in speaking to everyone else? Ought I not to be ashamed to speak to you with this tongue? Do you think I do not understand that you are ashamed to be seated here beside me? What am I, and what are you? Think of all that, you great-souled Artyom—you, the equal of Judas Maccabeus! What would you do if you knew the purpose for which God had created you? Ah, no one knows the great secrets of the Creator, and no one can guess why life has been given to him. You cannot imagine during how many days and nights of my existence I have asked myself: 'Of what good is life to me? Of what use my soul and mind? What am I to other men? I am but as a spittoon for their envenomed spit! And what are other men to me? . . . Vermin who wound me, body and soul, in every possible way. . . . Why am I on earth at all? And why should I have known nothing but unhappiness? And why is there not a single ray of light for me?'"

He spoke in a passionate half-whisper, and as usual when the spirit that had been overwrought with suffering was aroused, his whole face quivered.

Artyom did not understand what he was saying, but he heard and saw that Cain was complaining of something. As a result, Artyom's feeling of dullness and weariness grew more acute.

"Now, look here! You are at it again!" and he gave an

irritable shake to his head. "I have told you, have I not, that I will protect you?"

Cain laughed quietly and bitterly.

"How will you intercede for me before the face of my God? It is He who pursues me."

"Of course, I can't go against God," said Artyom, naïvely acquiescent; and then, in a compassionate tone, he advised the Jew: "Have patience, there is no way of going against God."

Cain looked at his protector and smiled—it was his turn now to feel pity. First the strong had pitied the intelligent, and now the intelligent pitied the strong, and a breath of something passed between the speakers which drew them a little closer to one another.

"Are you married?" asked Artyom.

"Yes, I have a large family, too large for my feeble strength." Cain sighed heavily.

"Really!" exclaimed the athlete. It was difficult for him to picture the woman who could love the Jew, and he looked with renewed curiosity at this sickly and diminutive, dirty and timid man.

"I have had five children, but only four are left—my little Khaia was always coughing—and then she died. My God! . . . My Lord! . . . And my wife is ill too—she keeps on coughing."

"You have a hard time," said Artyom, and he grew thoughtful.

Cain, his head sunk on his breast, also fell into a reverie. Old-clothesmen were now coming into the tavern. They went up to the bar, where they entered into a whispered conversation with Savka. The latter mysteriously communicated something to them, accompanying his words by significant glances in the direction of Cain and Artyom, which led his listeners to stare at them also with looks of mingled astonishment and ridicule. Cain had quickly taken note of these glances, and he grew alert. But Artyom was looking away again towards the fields beyond the river. He heard the whistling of the scythe and the soft rustle made by the grass as it fell.

"You had better go, Artyom; or if you want to stay, I will go. Some people have come in," whispered Cain, "and they are laughing at you on my account."

"Who is laughing?" roared Artyom, aroused from his dreams, as his eyes darted fiercely round the room.

But everyone present appeared perfectly serious and absorbed in his own affairs. Artyom did not catch a single glance turned in his direction. He frowned sternly, saying to the Jew:

"You are telling lies. . . . There is nothing to complain about. . . . But take care, that is not playing fair. Wait till you have been ill-treated before you complain to me. Or perhaps you were testing me? You said it on purpose?"

Cain gave a sickly smile, but said nothing. For some minutes neither spoke. Then Cain rose, and hanging his box round his neck, prepared to go. Artyom held out his hand to him.

"You are going? Well, be off, and get on with your trading. I shall stay on here."

With his two tiny hands Cain shook his protector's immense paw, and left hurriedly. Having reached the street, he chose a corner where he could stand and see what was going on around him. It commanded a view of the tavern door, and he had not to wait long, for Artyom soon appeared upon the threshold. His eyebrows were knotted, and he had the look of one who dreads to see something which he wishes to avoid.

He stood examining the groups of men and the passers-by for some time, then his face recovered its habitual expression of idle indifference, and he went on through the crowd towards the end of the street that abutted on the hill; he was evidently on the way to his favorite resting-place.

Cain followed him with mournful eyes, and then, covering his face with his hands, he leant his forehead against the iron door of the storehouse near which he had stationed himself.

. . . .

Artyom's weighty threat had produced its effect; the people were afraid, and stopped tormenting the Jew.

Cain became aware that there were now fewer thorns along the path of suffering he was treading to the grave. Indeed, it was as though people had ceased to notice his existence. As formerly, he went in and out among the crowd crying his goods, but nobody now tried to tread upon his toes, nor did anyone hit him over his thin flanks or spit into his box. But, on the other hand, formerly he had not been greeted by looks of such coldness and hostility as now met him on all sides.

Sensitive to everything that related to him, he became conscious of this altered attitude towards him, and asked himself what it could mean, and what it portended. He thought over the matter a great deal, but failed to understand why he was so treated. And then, again, he remembered that formerly, although on very rare occasions, someone would exchange a friendly word with him, and ask him how he was getting on, and sometimes even joke with him without any unkind intention. . . . Cain grew very thoughtful. For it is invariably the case that men love to recall the least particle of happiness they may have had in the past, although at the time it was hardly noticeable.

And so he became very pensive, listening with attentive ears and watching with vigilant eyes. One day he got wind of a new song composed by the Ragged Bridegroom, the troubadour of the street. This man earned his living by music and song; eight wooden soup-spoons served him for an instrument; he held them between his fingers, struck them together, or else executed roulades on his chest or on his inflated cheeks, thus obtaining all the accompaniment he needed for the jingles that he himself composed. If the music was scarcely pleasing, it nevertheless demanded a conjurer's deftness on the part of the performer, and skill of any kind was held in high estimation by the inhabitants of the suburb.

On one occasion Cain happened to come across a group of men assembled round the Bridegroom, who, armed with his spoons, was addressing them in a lively style:

"Honored sirs! Convicts to me! Here is a new song from me; you will get it steaming hot from the pot! I charge a kopeck a head; those who have mugs will pay two instead! I begin:

> When the sun comes in at the window
> Folks are glad.
> But if I who let myself in . . .

"We all know that old song!" called out one of the crowd.

"No doubt you have heard it before, but I don't give the patty gratis before the bread," was Bridegroom's answer, as he clacked his spoons one against the other and then went on singing:

> My life is bitter, I've had no luck,
> My dad and my brother had to choke,
> But when they tried to string me up,
> It wasn't my neck, but the cord that broke.

"That was a pity!" the public declared.

But people threw the Bridegroom their kopecks, for they knew him to be a conscientious man, and that if he had promised them a new song, he would not fail to produce it.

"Here is a new one," he said, and there was a brilliant outburst of spoon music.

> An ox made friends with a spider,
> A Jew made friends with a fool.
> The ox trots the spider on his tail,
> The Jew sells the fool to the girls.
> Oh, women!

"Stop! Mister Cain, our greetings! May you have many beatings. Have you deigned, Mister Merchant, to listen to my song? It is not for your ears. . . . Pass on, if you please!"

Cain smiled at the artist, and went on his way sighing, his heart oppressed with a presentiment of evil.

He prized these days, and he feared for them. Every morning he appeared on the street, sure that no one would dare to rob him of his kopecks. His eyes had grown a little brighter and less restless. He saw Artyom every day, but he did not go near the athlete unless the latter spoke to him.

Artyom did not often notice him; when he did, it was always to ask him how he was getting on.

"Oh! I am getting on, thanks to you," Cain would answer, his eyes sparkling with joy.

"They don't touch you?"

"As if they would dare, knowing that you are my protector!" the Jew would exclaim.

"That's all right! But mind, if anything happens, tell me."

"I will."

"Good!"

And then Artyom would look sullenly at the little figure of the Jew, and give him his dismissal.

"Now go—and look after your business."

And Cain would walk quickly away, catching sight, as

he passed along, of the mocking and malicious glances of the onlookers, which had not ceased to fill him with alarm.

Things went on like this for another month. And then one evening, as Cain was preparing to return home, he met Artyom. The handsome giant nodding to him, beckoned him with his finger. Cain ran up to him; he saw that Artyom was in a morose and gloomy frame of mind, looking like an autumnal cloud.

"You have finished your day's work?" he asked.

"Yes, I was just going home."

"Wait. Come with me a little way. I have something to say to you," said Artyom in a smothered voice.

Huge and heavy, he began walking on in front, while Cain followed at his heels.

They left the street, and took the path that led to the river, and Artyom soon found a suitable spot at the bottom of the ravine, close to the water's edge.

"Sit down," he said to Cain.

The Jew sat down, casting a sidelong, timid glance towards his protector. Artyom lowered himself to the ground, and then began slowly rolling a cigarette, while Cain looked first at the sky, and then at the forest of masts on the farther side of the river, and at the quiet waves, which seemed almost as if petrified amid the evening silence; and all the while he was wondering what Artyom could have to say to him.

"Well," said Artyom, "you're getting on?"

"Oh, yes, all goes well. I am not afraid of anything now."

"That's as it should be."

"I have you to thank for it."

"Wait!" said Artyom.

But a long time elapsed before he spoke; he sat puffing at his cigarette and breathing hard, while the Jew, full of cruel presentiments, sat waiting his words.

"And so they have left off hurting and insulting you?"

"Yes, they are afraid of you. They are like so many dogs, while you—you are like a lion. And I, now—"
"Wait!"
"What is it? What have you got to say to me?" asked Cain, fearfully.
"What have I got to say to you? It is not so simple."
"What is it, then?"
"Well, let us speak openly—say all that there is to be said—and get it over."
"Get what over?"
"I must tell you that I can no longer—"
"What is it that you can no longer? How?"
"I cannot go on with it. It disgusts me. It is not the right kind of thing for me," said Artyom, sighing.
"But I do not understand. What thing?"
"The whole business—you, and everything. I do not wish to know you any longer, simply because—it doesn't do for me."

Cain shrank back as if someone had struck him.

"And if anyone harms you, do not come and complain to me. I cannot help you any longer. You must not look upon me in future as your protector. Do you understand? I can't do it."

Cain sat silent as death.

Having thus spoken, Artyom gave a sigh of relief; then he continued to speak more clearly and connectedly:

"You took pity on me then; I can pay you for that. How much do you want? Tell me, and you will get it. But I can't be sorry for you. It isn't in me. I have tried all along to believe that I pitied you, but it was just pretense. I said to myself: 'I am sorry for him,' but it was a lie. There is no feeling of pity in me."

"Is it because I am a Jew?" Cain asked him gently. Artyom looked sideways at him, and answered simply, with one of those speeches which come direct from the heart:

"What's a Jew? Why, we are all Jews in the Lord's sight."

"Then why is it?" asked Cain quietly.

"Because I can't. Understand? I have no pity for you—or for anyone. Try to understand this. I wouldn't have said this to another. I would just have knocked him on the noodle. . . . But I am saying it to you. . . ."

" 'Who will rise up to defend me from the wicked ones? Who will deliver me from mine enemies?' " asked the Jew, in a sad, low voice, quoting the Psalmist's words.

"I . . . can't," Artyom replied, shaking his head. "It isn't because they laugh. I don't care a rap, let them laugh. . . . But I'm not sorry for you. . . . But in return for what you did for me, I should like to give you some money."

And Cain, bent double in anguish, cried out in imploring accents:

"Oh! Almighty God! Oh! Eternal One! God of vengeance! Arise, and let Thy light go forth, O Judge of the earth!"

The summer evening was warm and peaceful. The soft, sad rays of the setting sun were reflected in the river; the shadow from the gorge fell over Artyom and Cain.

"Think for a moment," began Artyom again, in a melancholy and persuasive voice, "what a task I have before me. You don't understand this! But I—I must revenge myself. They beat me up without mercy—you remember?"

He grew agitated and ground his teeth together; then he lay back on the sand, his feet stretched out towards the water, his hands clasped behind his head.

"I have found out the names of all of them."

"All of them?" asked Cain, in a dejected voice.

"All. Now I am going to begin to settle accounts with them. And you are in my way."

"How can I be in your way?" exclaimed the Jew.

"It is not that you are in my way, but . . . it's like this: I am bitter against everybody. Am I worse than they are? That's what it is. . . . Well, then, I don't need you now. Do you understand?"

"No," answered Cain meekly, shaking his head.

"You don't understand? You really are too queer. One should be sorry for you, isn't that so? Well, I can't be sorry for anybody now. I haven't any pity for anyone," and poking the Jew in the ribs, he added: "I haven't any! Understand?"

There was a long silence. The murmur of the splashing waters floated towards the two men through the warm and scented air; it seemed like the distant sighing and moaning of the dark, sleeping river.

"What is to become of me now?" asked Cain at last; but he received no response, for Artyom had dozed off or, perhaps, had fallen into a reverie.

"How am I to live without you?" continued the Jew in a louder voice. Artyom, gazing up at the sky, made answer:

"It is for you to decide what you will do."

"My God, my God!"

"One cannot tell other people offhand how to live," Artyom said, lazily.

Having said everything he had to say, all at once he grew serene and quiet.

"I knew it would end like this. I knew it when I first went to help you, when you were lying nearly dead. I knew that you could not continue to be my protector for any length of time."

He threw a supplicating look towards Artyom, but the latter was lying with his eyes closed.

"Perhaps you are doing this because they laugh at you on my account?" Cain put his question cautiously, and almost in a whisper.

"They? What do I care about them?" Artyom smiled, opening his eyes. "If I had wished to do so, I would have carried you through the streets on my shoulders. Let them laugh. . . . But all this leads to nothing. One must act according to one's true feelings, according to the dictates of one's own soul. What's not there, just isn't. And I, brother, I confess—it disgusts me that you are as you are! And that is the whole truth!"

"Ah! That's true! What about me, now? Shall I go?"

"Yes, go while it is still daylight—no one will touch you for the moment. No one has overheard our conversation."

"No! And you will say nothing about it to anyone?" asked Cain.

"Of course not! But remember not to come near me too often."

"Very well!" The Jew agreed quietly and mournfully, and rose to his feet.

"If you take my advice, you will go away from here altogether, and carry on your trade elsewhere," said Artyom, in a nonchalant tone of voice. "Life is very hard here, and everyone is trying to injure his neighbor in some way or other."

"But where can I go?"

"That's for you to find out."

"Good-by, Artyom."

"Good-by, brother."

And without rising, Artyom stretched out his large hand, and squeezed the skinny fingers of the Jew.

"Good-by, don't feel hurt."

"I won't," sighed the Jew, dejectedly.

"Good, then! it will be much better so: when you have time to think it over, you will see that I am right. You are not my equal, and you can be no companion to me. Am I to live only for you? It won't do!"

"Good-by."

"Get along."

Cain went off, walking beside the river with stooping shoulders and bent head.

Artyom looked after him for a few seconds, and then, resuming his former attitude, he lay face upwards, while the sky above him grew dark with approaching night.

Curious sounds came and went in the still air. There was the regular splash of the river breaking against the shore.

Cain turned back, went up to the massive figure stretched upon the sand, and standing beside him, said in a low, deferential voice:

"Perhaps you have changed your mind?"

But Artyom remained silent.

"Artyom," Cain called again, and waited patiently for a reply.

"Artyom, perhaps you only said all that to me in jest?" said Cain, again, in a trembling voice. "Artyom, remember that night—when I came and looked after you. No one came but me."

The only answer was a faint snore.

Cain remained for a long time standing over the athlete, staring at his vapidly handsome face, softened by sleep. The powerful chest rose and fell at regular intervals, and the black mustache, as it was parted by his breath, displayed the man's strong shining teeth. He seemed to be smiling.

With a profound sigh, and bending his head yet lower, the Jew once more turned and began walking along the river. He advanced cautiously; life was now full of terror for him, and he trembled; where the path was lit by the moon he walked more slowly, gliding swiftly along when he came to the darker stretches.

He was like a mouse, like a small, cowardly animal, returning to its hole, amidst many dangers threatening him on all sides. Night had already fallen, and the shore lay deserted.

1898.

RED

NOT so long ago a man of about forty by the name of Vaska, nicknamed Red, was employed in a house of prostitution in a city on the Volga. He owed his nickname to the fact that he had bright red hair and a heavy face the color of raw meat.

Thick-lipped, with big ears that struck out from his skull like handles on a wash-basin, he struck people by the cruel expression of his small colorless eyes. Sunk in fat, they shone like icicles, and in spite of his well-filled, stocky frame, they always had a ravenously hungry look. Short and thick-set, he wore a blue Cossack coat, wide woolen trousers and brightly shined top-boots with fine creases. His red hair grew in curls, and when he put on his smart cap, they showed from under it and fringed the band, and then it seemed as though Red were wearing a ruddy wreath.

He was called Red by his comrades; the girls called him the Hangman, because he liked to torture them.

There were several institutions of higher learning in the city, and many young people. For that reason, the houses of prostitution formed a whole district—a long street and several alleys. Vaska was known in all the houses. His name struck terror into the hearts of all the girls and when they quarreled among themselves, or with the madam, she would threaten them:

"Look out! Don't try my patience or I'll call Red!"

Sometimes this threat alone was sufficient to quiet the girls and make them give up their demands, often quite just and reasonable ones, as, for example, the demand for better food or for the right to leave the house to take a walk. But if the threat was not enough to subdue the girls, the proprietress called Vaska.

He would come walking with the slow gait of a man who is in no hurry, lock himself up with the proprietress in her room, and there she would name the girls who were to be punished.

He would listen to her complaint without a word, and simply say:

"All right. . . ."

Then he would go to the girls. They blanched and quailed at the sight of him. He saw this, and relished their fear. If the scene took place in the kitchen, where the girls dined and took their tea, he would stand for a long time at the door, looking at them, as silent and motionless as a statue, and these moments were no less painful than the tortures to which he subjected them.

After watching them for a while, he would say in an indifferent, husky voice:

"Mashka, come here. . . ."

"Vasily Mironych!" the girl would sometimes say imploringly and firmly. "Don't touch me! Don't touch me. . . . If you do, I'll strangle myself. . . ."

"Come here, you fool, I'll give you the rope. . . ." Vaska would say indifferently, without even a sneer.

He always insisted that the culprits should come to him of their own accord.

"I'll call for help! . . . I'll break the windows! . . ." The girl, choking with fear, would enumerate all the things she might do.

"Break the windows! . . . I'll make you eat the glass," Vaska would say.

And in most cases the stubborn girl would give in and go over to the Hangman. If she refused, Vaska would walk up to her, take her by the hair and throw her to the floor. Her own friends—often those who felt as she did—would tie her hands and feet, gag her, and right there, on the kitchen floor and before their eyes, the culprit would be flogged. If she was a spirited girl, capable of lodging a complaint, she was flogged with a heavy leather strap, so as not to cut the skin, and through a wet sheet, so as not to raise welts. Long thin bags filled with sand and gravel were also used. A blow on the buttocks with such a bag caused the victim a dull pain that lasted a long time. . . .

The cruelty of the punishment depended, however, not so much upon the culprit's character as upon the degree of her guilt and Red's sympathy. Sometimes he flogged even daring girls mercilessly, without taking any precautions. In the pocket of his trousers he always carried a three-tailed whip with a short crop of oak polished by frequent use. Into the leather of the tails were woven thin metal wires that formed a tassel at the end. The first blow with such a whip cut through the skin to the bone, and often, to increase the pain, a mustard plaster or rags soaked in brine were applied to the sore back.

When he punished the girls Vaska never showed any emotion; he was always equally taciturn and stolid, and his eyes never lost their expression of ravenous hunger. Sometimes he screwed them up, which made them look even sharper.

The methods of punishment were not confined to these. Vaska was inexhaustibly fertile in inventing new ones, and indeed, he reached creative heights in the refinements of the tortures he thought up.

Take, for example, the case of Vera Kopteva, a girl in one of the establishments who fell under the suspicion of having stolen 5000 rubles from a guest. This guest, a Siberian merchant, informed the police that he had been in Vera's room with her and another girl, Sara Sherman. After about an hour, the latter went away, and he spent the rest of the night with Vera and was in a drunken state when he left her.

The affair took its due course. The investigation dragged on and on. Both defendants were detained in prison, tried, and, because of insufficient evidence, acquitted.

When they returned to their employer after the trial, the two girls were subjected to another investigation. The madam was certain that they were guilty of the theft and wanted her share.

Sara succeeded in proving that she had had nothing to do with the theft. Then the madam began to work on Vera Kopteva. She locked her in a bath-house and kept her on a diet of salty caviar, but in spite of this, the girl would not confess where she had hidden the money. It became necessary to resort to Vaska's help.

He was promised a hundred rubles if he discovered the whereabouts of the money.

And so, one night, the devil appeared to Vera, as she lay crouched in the bath-house, tormented by thirst, darkness, and dread. From his black shaggy hide came a smell of phosphorus and a glowing bluish smoke. Two fiery sparks took the place of eyes. He stood before the girl and asked in a terrifying voice:

"Where's the money?"

She lost her mind from terror.

This happened in winter. Next morning, barefoot, and dressed in nothing but her chemise, she was taken through the deep snow from the bath-house to the house. She was laughing gently and saying happily:

"Tomorrow I shall go to mass with Mamma again, I shall go to mass again."

When Sara Sherman saw her in this state, she said before everybody in quiet bewilderment:

"But I was the one who stole the money."

· · · · · · ·

It is hard to say whether the girls hated or feared Vaska more.

They all made up to him, trying to curry favor with him. Everyone eagerly sought the honor of being his mistress. At the same time they egged on their pimps, the guests, and the bouncers whom they knew to beat Red up. But he was enormously strong, and never got drunk, so that it was hard to get the better of him. More than once arsenic was placed in his food, his tea, and his beer, and on one occasion to some effect, but he recovered. In some way he always got wind of every move against him. But apparently his realization of what he was risking by living among countless enemies neither increased nor diminished his cold cruelty toward the girls. With his usual stolidity he would say:

"I know that you'd tear me to pieces with your teeth if you got the chance. . . . But there's no use your getting worked up about it. Nothing will happen to me."

And shoving out his thick lips, he would snort into their faces. This was his way of laughing at them.

His companions were policemen, other bouncers, and detectives, of whom there are always many in houses of prostitution. But he had no friends among them, and there was not one of his acquaintances whom he wished to see more frequently than the rest. He treated all alike with complete indifference. He drank beer with them and talked of the scandals that occurred every night in the district. He never left the house of his employer unless he was called away on business, that is, to administer a beating, or, as they said, to put the fear of God into someone's girl.

The house in which he was employed was one of the establishments of the middling sort. The admission charge was three rubles, and the charge for the night, five. The proprietress, Fekla Yermolayevna, a stout woman of about fifty, was stupid and malicious, feared Vaska, prized him highly, and paid him fifteen rubles a month, in addition to his keep. He had a small, coffin-like room in the attic. Because of Vaska, perfect order prevailed among her girls. There were eleven of them and they were all as meek as sheep.

When she was in a good humor, and talking to a guest whom she knew, she often bragged of her girls as one brags about pigs and cows.

"My goods are first class," she would say, smiling with pride and satisfaction. "The girls are all fresh and sound. The oldest is twenty-six. Of course, she's not a girl you can have an interesting talk with, but what a body! Just take a look at her, sir—a marvel, not a girl! Ksyushka, come here. . . ."

Ksyushka would come up, waddling like a duck. The guest would examine her more or less carefully and always be satisfied with her body.

She was a girl of medium height, plump, and as firm as though she had been hammered out of one piece. She had an ample, high bosom, a round face, and a little mouth with thick bright red lips. Her eyes, which were expressionless and irresponsive, resembled the beady eyes of a doll, and her pug nose and the bangs over her eyebrows, by adding to her resemblance to a doll, quenched in the least exacting guest the desire for any conversation with her on any subject. Usually they simply said to her:

"Come."

And she would go, with her heavy swaying gait, smiling meaninglessly and rolling her eyes from right to left. She had been taught this by the madam. It was known as "luring the guest." Her eyes had gotten so accustomed to this movement that she began to "lure the guest" from the very moment when, gaudily dressed, she entered the still empty parlor in the evening, and her eyes continued to roll from side to side all the time she was there, whether alone, with other girls, or with a guest.

She had another strange habit: winding her long braid, the color of fresh bast, around her neck, she would let the end of it fall on her bosom, and hold on to it with her left hand all the while, as though carrying a noose around her neck. . . .

She could say of herself that her name was Aksinya Kalugina, that she hailed from the province of Ryazan, that she had once "sinned" with Fedka, had given birth to a child, and had come to the city with the family of an excise official, where she was employed as wet nurse, but that when her child died she had lost her position and then she had been "engaged" to work in the house. She had been there for four years. . . .

"Like it here?" she would be asked.

"It's all right. I have enough to eat, I get shoes and clothes. . . . Only you have no peace here. . . . And Vaska, too. . . . He beats you, the fiend. . . ."

"But then it's gay here?"

"Where?" she would answer, and turning her head, would examine the parlor, as though wishing to see where the gaiety was.

Around her there were drunkenness and noise, and everything—from the madam and the other girls to the cracks in the ceiling—was familiar to her.

She spoke in a thick bass voice and laughed only when she was tickled—she laughed loudly like a husky peasant and shook with laughter. The stupidest and healthiest of the girls, she was less unhappy than the others, for she was closer to the animal.

· · · · · · ·

Of course, it was especially the girls in the house where Vaska was employed as a bouncer who had accumulated fear of and hatred towards him. When they were drunk, the girls did not hide their feelings, and complained of Vaska openly to the guests, but since the guests came there not to protect them, their complaints had neither meaning nor results. When they took the form of hysterical screams and weeping, and Vaska heard it, his flaming head showed itself in the doorway of the parlor and he would say in his indifferent wooden voice:

"Hey, you, don't act like a fool."

"Hangman! Monster!" the girl would scream. "How do you dare disfigure me? Look, mister, see what he did to my back with a whip!" And the girl would try to tear off her bodice.

Vaska would go over to her, take her by the hand, and without changing his voice, which was particularly horrible, would expostulate with her:

"Don't make a noise! Hush! What are you gabbing about? You're drunk. Look out!"

This was almost always sufficient, and very rarely did Vaska have to take a girl out of the parlor.

Never did any of the girls hear from Vaska a single kind word, although many of them were his concubines. He took them without ado. If any of them caught his fancy, he would say to her:

"I'll stay with you tonight."

Then he would keep on going to her for some time, and break with her without a word.

"What a devil!" the girls said of him. "He's made of wood!"

In the establishment where he worked he lived with almost every girl in turn, including Aksinya. And it was while he was living with her that on one occasion he gave her a cruel flogging.

As she was healthy and lazy, she liked to sleep very much, and she often fell asleep in the parlor, in spite of the noise that filled it. Seated somewhere in a corner, she would suddenly cease to "lure the guest" with her stupid eyes. They would become fixed upon some object, then her eyelids would slowly droop and cover her eyes, and her lower lip would hang down, baring large white teeth. Comfortable snores would be heard, sending the other girls and the guests into peals of laughter, but the laughter would not wake Aksinya.

This happened frequently. Her mistress scolded her severely and slapped her face, but this did not frighten off sleep: she would cry a little afterwards, and fall asleep again.

Finally Red took matters in hand.

One night, when the girl fell asleep sitting on a divan next to a drunken guest, who was also dozing, Vaska went over to her, and taking her by the hand without a word, led her away with him.

"Are you really going to thrash me?" Aksinya asked him.

"I have to . . ." said Vaska.

When they came to the kitchen, he told her to undress.

"At least don't hurt me badly," the woman begged him.

"Go on, go on. . . ."

She stripped to her chemise.

"Take it off!" Vaska ordered.

"What a rowdy you are!" the girl sighed, and took off her chemise.

Vaska struck her over the shoulders with a strap.

"Into the court-yard with you!"

"What are you saying? It's winter. . . . I'll be cold. . . ."

He pushed her out of the kitchen door, led her through the entry, switching her with the strap, and in the court-yard he ordered her to lie down on a heap of snow.

"Vaska . . . how can you?"

"Go on, go on!"

And pushing her face into the snow, he forced her head down into it, so that her cries should not be heard, and for a long time he struck her with the strap, repeating these words:

"Don't sleep, don't sleep, don't sleep. . . ."

When he let her go, she sobbed to him through her tears:

"Wait, Vaska! Your time will come. . . . You will cry too! There is a God, Vaska!"

"Go on talking," he said calmly. "You fall asleep in the parlor once more! Then I'll take you out into the yard, give you a whipping and pour water over you. . . ."

. . . .

Life has its wisdom, its name is accident. Sometimes it rewards us, but more often it takes revenge on us, and just as the sun endows each object with a shadow, so the wisdom of life prepares retribution for man's every act. This is true, this is inevitable, and we must all know and remember it. . . .

The day of retribution arrived for Vaska too.

One evening when the half-dressed girls were having their supper before going into the parlor, one of them, Lida Chernogorova, a spirited and malicious girl with chestnut hair, looked out of the window and declared:

"Vaska's come."

Several girls swore unhappily.

"Look!" Lida shouted. "He's . . . drunk! He's with a policeman. . . . Look!"

All dashed to the window.

"He's being taken out of the droshky . . . he can't walk. . . . Girls!" Lida shouted with joy. "He must have had an accident!"

The kitchen resounded with oaths and malicious laughter—the joyous laughter of revenge. The girls, pushing each other, dashed into the entry to meet the fallen enemy.

There they saw Vaska supported by the policeman and the driver. His face was gray, and there were large beads of perspiration on his forehead, and he was dragging his left leg.

"Vasily Mironych! What's the matter with you?" cried the proprietress.

Vaska wagged his head helplessly and replied in a hoarse voice:

"I fell. . . ."

"He fell off a trolley . . ." explained the policeman. "He fell off, and his leg was caught under the wheel! Crack . . . and there you are!"

The girls held their peace, but their eyes burned like live coal.

They took Vaska upstairs to his room, put him to bed and sent for a doctor. The girls, standing beside the bed, exchanged glances, but did not say a word.

"Get out!" Vaska said to them.

No one budged.

"Ah! You're glad! . . ."

"We won't cry," replied Lida with a smirk.

"Mistress, chase them out of here. . . . What have they . . . come for?"

"Afraid?" asked Lida, bending over him.

"Go, girls, go downstairs . . ." the madam ordered.

They went. But as they were leaving, each one of them looked at him ominously, and Lida muttered under her breath:

"We'll come back!"

As for Aksinya, she threatened him with her fist, shouting at him:

"Oo, you **devil!** So you're crippled? Serves you right. . . ."

Such daring astounded the girls very much.

Downstairs they were seized with an ecstasy of malice, a vengeful ecstasy, the sharp sweetness of which they had never before experienced. Mad with joy, they jeered at

Vaska, scaring the proprietress by their violent mood and even infecting her with it to a degree.

She too was glad to see Red punished by fate. She too resented him, for he treated her not as an employer, but as though she were the subordinate and he the superior. But she knew that without him she could not keep the girls in hand, and she expressed her real feeling about Vaska cautiously.

The doctor came, bandaged up the patient, prescribed medicines, and went away, telling the proprietress that it would be better to send Vaska to a hospital.

"Well, girls, shall we pay a visit to our darling patient?" cried Lida in a dare-devil tone.

And they all dashed upstairs with laughter and shrieks.

Vaska lay with closed eyes. Without opening them, he said:

"You have come back. . . ."

"Aren't we sorry for you, Vasily Mironych! . . ."

"Don't we just love you! . . ."

"Remember how you . . . ?"

They spoke quietly but impressively, and standing around his bed they looked at his gray face with malicious and joyful eyes. He too looked at them, and never before had his eyes expressed so much unsatisfied, insatiable hunger, the incomprehensible hunger which always burned in them.

"Girls . . . look out! I'll get up. . . ."

"And, maybe, please God, you won't get up . . ." Lida interrupted him.

Vaska compressed his lips tightly and held his peace.

"Which little leg hurts you, darling?" asked one girl tenderly, bending over him. Her face was pale and her teeth showed. "Is it this one?"

And seizing Vaska by his injured leg, she pulled it hard towards her.

Vaska gritted his teeth and howled. His left arm, too,

was hurt, he swung his right, and wishing to strike the girl, slapped his own stomach.

A roar of laughter resounded about him.

"Huzzies!" he shouted, rolling his eyes frightfully. "Look out, I'll murder you!"

But they danced around his bed, they pinched him, pulled him by the hair, spat in his face, pulled his injured leg. Their eyes burned, they laughed, they swore, they howled like dogs. Their mockery was taking on an indescribably hideous and cynical character. They were drunk with revenge, they reached a state of frenzy.

All in white, half-dressed, heated by the jostling, they were monstrously terrible.

Vaska roared, waving his right arm; the proprietress, at the door, was screaming in a dreadful voice:

"Enough! Give it up. . . . I'll call the police! You'll kill him. . . . Oh, dear, oh, dear!"

But they did not listen to her. He had been tormenting them for years, they had minutes in which to retaliate, and they were in haste. . . .

Suddenly the noise and howling of the orgy was pierced by a thick imploring voice:

"Girls! Enough. . . . Girls, have pity. . . . He too is . . . he too . . . feels pain! My dears, for Christ's sake . . . my dears. . . ."

This voice acted like a cold shower on the girls; frightened, they left Vaska hastily.

It was Aksinya who had spoken; she stood at the window all atremble and she bowed low to them, now pressing her hands against her stomach, now stretching them out absurdly in front of her.

Vaska lay motionless. The shirt on his chest was torn, and this broad chest, with its thick red wool, was heaving rapidly as though something were beating in it, madly trying to escape from it. There was a rattle in his throat, and his eyes were closed.

Massed together, so that they seemed to form one large body, the girls stood at the door silent, listening to Aksinya's muffled mumbling and Vaska's rattling. Lida, standing in front of them all, was quickly wiping from her right hand the red hairs that stuck to her fingers.

"And . . . suppose he dies?" someone whispered. And there was silence again.

One after another, trying not to make any noise, the girls were cautiously leaving Vaska's room, and when they had all left, there were many rags and tatters on the floor. . . .

Only Aksinya remained there.

Sighing heavily, she went over to Vaska and in her usual deep voice asked him:

"What shall I do for you now?"

He opened his eyes, looked at her, but made no answer.

"You may talk now. . . . Should I clean up? . . . I'll clean up. . . . And maybe you want a drink of water? I'll give you a drink. . . ."

Vaska silently shook his head and moved his lips. But he did not say a word.

"So that's how it is—you can't even speak!" Aksinya said, winding her braid around her neck. "We were pretty nasty to you, all right. . . . Does it hurt, Vaska, eh? Be patient, you'll get over it . . . it's only at first that it hurts. . . . I know."

A muscle twitched in Vaska's face, he said hoarsely:

"Water. . . ."

And the expression of unappeased hunger disappeared from his eyes.

· · · · · · ·

Aksinya remained upstairs with Vaska, coming down only to eat, to have tea, or to fetch something for the patient. The other girls did not talk to her, asked her no questions, nor did the proprietress prevent her from nursing the sick man, and in the evening she did not call her out to the guests. Generally Aksinya sat at the window in Vaska's room and looked out at the snow-covered roofs, the trees white with hoarfrost, the smoke which rose in opal clouds to the sky. When she was tired of looking out, she fell asleep right there in the chair, with her elbows on the table. At night she slept on the floor, near Vaska's bed.

There was almost no talk between them. Vaska would ask for water or something else, she would bring it to him, look at him, sigh, and go over to the window.

Thus four days passed. The proprietress was trying her best to place Vaska in a hospital, but for the time being there was no bed for him there.

One evening when the shadows had already crowded into Vaska's room, he lifted his head and asked:

"Aksinya, are you there, eh?"

She was dozing off, but his question woke her.

"Where should I be?" she replied.

"Come here. . . ."

She went over to the bed and halted, as usual weaving her braid around her neck and holding on to the end of it.

"What do you want?"

"Take a chair, sit down here. . . ."

With a sigh she went over to the window to get the chair, brought it over to the bed, and sat down.

"Well?"

"Nothing, I. . . . Sit down here awhile. . . ."

On the wall hung Vaska's big silver watch, ticking away rapidly. A sleigh drove by in the street, and one could hear the crunching of the runners. Downstairs the girls were laughing, and one of them was singing in a high-pitched voice:

"A hungry student had my heart. . . ."

"Aksinya!" said Vaska.

"What?"

"See here . . . let's live together."

"Don't we now?" the girl answered lazily.

"No, wait, let's do it properly. . . ."

"All right," she agreed.

"That's good. . . ."

He grew silent again, and lay for a long time with closed eyes.

"Yes . . . we'll go away from here . . . and start over again."

"Where will we go?" asked Aksinya.

"Some place. . . . I'll sue the trolley company for my injury. . . . They've got to pay, it's the law. Besides, I have money of my own, about six hundred rubles."

"How much?" asked Aksinya.

"About six hundred rubles."

"You don't say!" said the girl, and yawned.

"Yes . . . with that money alone you can open a house of your own . . . and if I make the company cough up some money too . . . We'll go to Simbirsk, or Samara . . . and there we'll open a place. . . . It will be the best house in the city. . . . We'll get the best girls. . . . We'll charge five rubles admission."

"How you talk!" Aksinya smiled

"Why not? That's how it will be. . . ."

"Really! . . ."

"That's how it will be . . . if you like, we'll get married."

"Wha-at?!" Aksinya exclaimed, blinking stupidly.

"We'll get married," Vaska repeated, with some agitation.

"You and I?"

"Why, yes."

Aksinya laughed aloud. Swinging back and forth on her chair, she held her sides, now uttering a thick low laugh, now squeaking, which sounded quite unnatural from her.

"What's the matter with you?" asked Vaska, and again the hungry look came into his eyes. She kept on guffawing. "What's the matter?" he repeated.

Finally, somehow, through her squeaks and her laughter, she managed to say:

"It's about the wedding. Is that for the likes of us? I haven't been inside a church for three years, maybe more. What a funny fellow you are! Me, your wife. . . . Do you expect me to give you children too? Ha! ha! ha!"

The idea of children threw her into a fresh spasm of hearty laughter. Vaska looked at her in silence.

"And do you think I'll go anywhere with you? What an idea! You'll take me somewhere and do me in. Everybody knows how you torture people."

"Oh, keep still," said Vaska softly.

But she kept on talking to him about his cruelty, recalling various incidents.

"Keep still," he begged her. And when she did not obey him, he shouted hoarsely: "Keep still, I say!"

That evening they said nothing more to each other. At night Vaska was delirious; a rattling, a howling, came from his broad chest. He gritted his teeth and waved his right arm in the air, sometimes striking his chest with it.

Aksinya woke up, stood beside the bed and looked into his face fearfully for a long time. Then she waked him.

"What's the matter with you? Was the house-sprite choking you, or what?"

"Nothing, I was dreaming . . ." Vaska said weakly. "Give me some water."

When he had had a drink he wagged his head and declared:

"No, I'm not going to open a house. I'd rather have a shop. . . . That's better. I won't want a house."

"A shop . . ." said Aksinya pensively. "Yes, a shop . . . that's a good thing."

"Will you come with me? Will you?" Vaska asked with quiet urgency.

"Do you really mean it?" Aksinya exclaimed, moving away from the bed.

"Aksinya Semyonovna," said Vaska respectfully, in a ringing voice, lifting his head from the pillow, "I swear by . . ."

He waved his hand in the air and fell silent.

"I'll go nowhere with you," said Aksinya with a resolute shake of the head, after waiting a moment for him to finish, "nowhere!"

"If I want you to, you will," said Vaska quietly.

"I won't go anywhere!"

"But that's not what I mean. . . . But if I wanted you to, you'd go."

"Oh, no . . ."

"What the devil!" Vaska cried in irritation. "Here you're fussing over me, doing things for me, so why won't you . . ."

"That's different," Aksinya explained. "But as for living with you, no! I'm afraid of you. You're an evil man."

"Oh, you . . . What do you know about it?" Vaska exclaimed venomously. " 'Evil man!' You're a fool. 'Evil man,' you think, and that's all there is to it. Maybe you think it's easy to do evil."

He broke off, and was silent for a while, rubbing his chest with his sound hand. Then, quietly, with anguish in his voice and fear in his eyes, he spoke again.

"You're laying it on thick. 'Evil,' well, is that the whole

story? A-agh! What did they ask of me? Won't you come with me, Aksinya Semyonovna?"

"Don't say another word about it! I won't," Aksinya asserted stubbornly, and moved away from him with a look of suspicion.

Their talk ceased again. The moon was looking into the room and by its light Vaska's face looked gray. For a long time he lay silent, now opening his eyes, now closing them. Downstairs there was dancing, singing, laughter.

Soon Aksinya began to snore lustily. Vaska heaved a deep sigh.

Two more days passed, and the proprietress found a bed for Vaska in a hospital.

The ambulance, with a doctor's assistant and a hospital attendant, arrived to fetch him. They helped him carefully downstairs into the kitchen, and there he saw all the girls crowded in the doorway.

His face was convulsed, but he said nothing. They stared at him earnestly and grimly, but it was impossible to tell from their glances what they were thinking at the sight of Vaska. Aksinya and the madam were helping him into his coat, and everyone in the kitchen preserved a heavy, sullen silence.

"Good-by," Vaska said suddenly, lowering his head without looking at the girls. "Good- . . . by!"

Some of them nodded to him silently, but he did not see it. Lida said calmly:

"Good-by, Vasily Mironovych."

"Good-by. . . . Yes. . . ."

The doctor's assistant and the hospital attendant, placing their hands under his arm-pits, raised him from the bench and led him to the door. But he turned to the girls again:

"Good-by. It's true, I was . . ."

Two or three more voices replied:

"Good-by, Vasily."

"What's the use?" He shook his head, and on his face appeared an expression quite alien to him. "Forgive me. . . . For Christ's sake . . . those who . . . whom . . ."

"They're taking him! They'll take my darling away!" suddenly Aksinya shrieked savagely, falling onto the bench.

Vaska started and lifted his head. His eyes blazed frightfully. He stood listening eagerly to her howls, and with trembling lips he said softly:

"What a fool! What a crazy thing!"

"Come on, come on," the doctor's assistant hurried him, frowning.

"Good-by, Aksinya, see that you come to the hospital," Vaska said aloud.

But Aksinya kept on howling:

"Who-oo-o will co-omfort me-ee-ee?"

The girls surrounded her and looked stolidly at her face and the tears streaming from her eyes.

Lida, bending over her, soothed her sternly:

"What are you howling about, Ksyushka? He's not dead! You can go to see him. . . . You can go to him tomorrow. . . ."

1900.

EVIL-DOERS

ONCE at dinner Vanyushka Kuzin's mother said to him:

"Why don't you go to the city, Vanya?"

Vanya said nothing. He was peeling hot potatoes, blowing noisily on his fingers, his lips thrust out like a trumpet, and twitching his eyebrows angrily.

His mother looked at his round, boyish face, sighed, and repeated more quietly:

"Really, why don't you?"

"What for?" asked Vanya, tossing a potato from one hand to the other.

"Take the ax, and go."

"There are a lot like me there with axes already."

"Well, take a shovel. . . . They will soon be digging cellars. You will chop some wood here, you will do something else there, and so you'll earn your bread somehow. Why don't you go, Vanya?"

He wanted to go to the city, but he didn't say a word to the old woman. In the two weeks that had passed since his father's death, Vanya had come to consider himself completely independent. At the funeral feast he had drunk vodka for the first time with impunity, and now he walked through the village with his chest thrown out, his eyebrows knitted thoughtfully, and he talked to his mother curtly and abruptly, in imitation of his father. . . .

After dinner the old woman busied herself with the mending of her fur-coat, while Vanyushka climbed up onto the stove, and after lying there for a short half-hour, asked his mother:

"How much money have you?"

"A ruble and six ten-kopeck pieces."
"Give me the sixty kopecks."
"What for?"
"To take along."
"You're going then?"
"It looks as though I am."
"That's good. You go, sonny. . . . When will you start out?"
"Tomorrow."

At dawn his mother blessed him with a copper icon of St. Nicholas, Vanya drew his belt tight, stuck the ax into it, pulled his cap over his ears, and slapping his thighs with his mittened hands, said:

"I'm off. Good-by."

"God be with you, Vanya. Be on your guard against city folk. Take care how you behave with them—they're sly ones! And no drinking, do you hear?"

"All right," said Vanyushka, and tilting his cap at a dashing angle, he went out into the street.

It was still dark. He walked no more than ten steps away from the cottage, and when he turned, hearing the voice of his mother, who stood at the gate, he could no longer see her in the murk, and could only hear broken words which resounded anxiously in the stillness:

"City girls . . . bad sickness . . ."

"Good-by!" shouted Vanka.

And suddenly he felt sad about his mother, about the village, about his poor old cottage. He stopped, listened. . . . But already everything was quiet again, his mother had gone in. With a sigh he moved to meet the unstirring silent darkness, still untouched by dawn.

As he strode through the fields he was thinking of how he might earn good money in the city, and come home towards spring to marry Vasilisa Shamova. And he pictured Vasilisa, plump, sturdy, and cleanly. Or perhaps

EVIL-DOERS

he might find a position as a porter with some kind, rich merchant, and then he would marry not Vasilisa but a city girl. He was walking along, and behind him dawn was gently breaking, all around night's shadows were vanishing unseen, and the pale yellow rays of the winter sun were beginning to fall on the snow. Underfoot the snow creaked more loudly and cheerfully, and Vanyushka began singing. Three twenty-kopeck pieces were jingling in the pocket of his trousers, and thoughts and guesses about the future were slowly moving through his head, to the sound of the tune.

It was easy, pleasant walking; his feet did not stick in the packed snow of the road. The frosty air filled his lungs and gave him a sense of well-being. The blue haze of the distance was beautiful and inviting. Hoar-frost feathered Vanya's budding mustache, and he thrust out his upper lip, looking at it with pleasure—his mustache seemed to him long and handsome. . . . A large crow, black as a charred ember, was stepping heavily on the snow beside the road. Vanyushka whistled. But the gloomy bird only looked at him with one eye and waddled even nearer to the road. Then he slapped his mittens, making a sound like a rifle-shot, but even that did not frighten the bird.

"You devil!" Kuzin muttered, and walked faster.

By mid-day, when he had covered more than half the distance, a snow-storm set in. Light, transparent puffs of snow, torn from the hillocks by the wind, flung a cold, white dust into his face. At times a flock of snowflakes rose from under his feet, as if wanting to stop the boy, while the wind pushed him in the back as though hurrying him on. The far-off distance was blotted out by murky clouds. The wind shrieked, as it touched the ground, covering up all traces, and wailed in a sad, long-drawn-out manner. The people and horses that he encountered appeared before his eyes and vanished like stones thrown into water. Vanyushka closed his eyes and walked with a swaying gait amidst the noises and sad songs of the storm. His thighs ached, his feet were heavy, he thought angrily of his mother: "She is sitting there, and here am I walking!"

And then he grew so tired that he could think of nothing. The only thing he wanted was to get to the city, to rest in a warm room, to drink tea. His back bent, his head down, he walked without noticing anything around him until, through the thunder of the storm, he heard the sullen roar of a factory siren. He halted and, straightening up, sighed deeply. Then he pulled the three coins out of his pocket, and put them in his mouth, thrusting them into his cheek, so that he might not tempt city folk with their jingling.

Seen through the gray curtain of snow, the city looked like a heavy cloud that had settled on the ground. Vanyushka took off his cap, crossed himself, and said to himself: "Here I am!"

II

When he entered the tea-house, the thick, damp air touched his face and like a warm, wet rag wiped from his cheeks the stinging sensation of cold. A bluish, acrid smoke wavered under the low, vaulted ceiling and stung the eyes; the smell of vodka, tobacco, and burnt oil tickled the nose; the noise in the tea-house was dull and muffled, and made Vanya pleasantly dizzy. Making his way slowly among the tables, he was looking for a place, and could not find one. All the seats were occupied by red-faced cabbies, and hollow-cheeked, half-naked artisans. Ragged roughs with thievish eyes were sullenly scrutinizing Ivan. One of them, a tall, lean fellow with red mustaches, winked at him and said, thrusting out his hand:

"Hello, greenhorn! Come here!"

Vanya lunged away from him and brushed against a small, rotund girl. Her face was a bright red and her black eyebrows were as large as mustaches.

"Look out, you booby!" she shouted in a hoarse voice.

In the corner of the room under the burning icon-lamp a man sat alone at a table. Vanyushka went over to him.

"May I sit down here?"

"Suit yourself."

Kuzin sat down at the table, undid the collar of his caftan, and said:

"Lots of people here!"

"A place like this is never empty. You from the country?"

"Yes."

"Looking for work?"

"Why, yes."

"Nothing much doing here."

"That so?"

"It's the truth. This is my third week here. . . ."

"No work?"

"Fact is—you starve."

A waiter dashed past the table.

"I'd like tea!" Vanyushka shouted at him, and began to examine his companion.

He was a man of about twenty-five, wearing a woman's quilted jacket, greasy and ragged. Tall and thin, he was bent low over the table as though he were trying to hide from people his pock-marked, hairless face. At times, with a swift, strong movement of his neck, he lifted his close-cropped head and looked at Kuzin uneasily with his large, gray eyes, as though he were speculating about something. When he noticed that Vanyushka was scrutinizing him, he gave him a thin-lipped smile, and said in a whisper:

"I had an overcoat: I ate it up. I had a cap: I ate it up. What's left are my boots. . . ."

He thrust out from under the table a long leg in a sturdy leather boot, and added:

"Soon I'll have to sell these too. I'll trade them in."

Vanyushka pitied both the stranger and himself.

"But maybe you'll find something," he said.

"Small chance. There are as many of us around here as there are yellow leaves in autumn. Just look about you —so many people, and they all want to eat."

"Let's have tea together," Vanyushka offered.

"Thanks. I thank you very much. I've had tea. But if we could have a little glass of something . . ." He sighed heavily.

Vanyushka felt the money in his mouth with his tongue, deliberated a moment, beckoned to the waiter with his finger, and gave his order with an air of importance:

"See that we get a half-bottle—for two."

The pock-marked fellow smiled gaily, but said not a word.

"Where do you sleep?" asked Vanyushka.

"Not far from here, it costs three kopecks a night. And you?"

"But I've just arrived."

"Well, then, why don't we sleep in the same place?"

"Let's!"

"Good. What's your name?"

"Ivan . . . Kuzin."

"My name is Yeremey Salakin."

They grew silent and looked at each other, smiling. And when the waiter brought the vodka and Vanyushka poured out a glass for Salakin, the latter half rose, took the glass, and holding it towards Kuzin, said:

"Well, let's drink in token of the commencement of our friendship!"

Vanyushka liked these words very much. He dashingly

emptied his glass at a gulp, made a sound of satisfaction, and said gaily:

"Two are better off than one."

"Of course."

"I've come to the city to work for the first time. I used to come here on business, but not stay," Vanya was saying, refilling the glasses.

"I am here for the first time, too. I used to work on estates mostly. But I fell out with the steward at the last place, and he sacked me. The red-headed bastard!"

"My father died a little while ago. Now I am my own master."

At a table near them sat two truck drivers, both covered with a white dust. They were engaged in a loud argument, and one of them, a huge old man, kept striking the table with his fist and shouting:

"Serves him right then!"

"Why?" the other kept asking. He was a black-bearded man with a scar on his forehead.

"Because—he ought to understand! What kind of a worker was he? Workers—they're, you see, dough, God's bread! The others, good-for-nothings that is, they're offal, bran! Their end, you see, is to serve as food for the beasts!"

"All alike are to be pitied," said the black-bearded driver.

Salakin, who was lending an ear to the argument, said:

"It isn't true."

"What?"

"About pity. Take me, for instance: Matvey Ivanovich, the steward, is my enemy! Why did he sack me? I had worked two years, everything was as it should be! Suddenly he got furious with me, said that the cook Marya and me . . . And things like that. And then about the reins . . . that was my fault, too. The reins got lost. Look for them! Then he says to me: 'Go!' How's that? I'm no use to him, but I'm certainly of use to myself! I must live. And now—can I pity him, the steward?"

Salakin was silent for a while, and then declared with deep conviction:

"I can pity myself only, and no one else!"

"Of course," said Vanyushka.

After the third glass both of them leaned on the table, face to face, heated by the vodka and the noise. And Salakin began to tell Vanyushka his life-story in a long-winded, incoherent, and vehement manner.

"I am a foundling!" he said. "My life is a burden to me because of my mother's sin. . . ."

Vanyushka looked at his friend's excited, pock-marked face, and nodded in agreement so often that he was dizzy.

"Vanya! Order another half-bottle! It's all one!" shouted Salakin, waving his arm in despair.

"It c-can be done . . ." replied Vanyushka.

III

When Vanyushka woke up, he found himself lying on a plank bed in a dusky cellar with a vaulted ceiling as badly pitted as Salakin's face. He moved his tongue about in his mouth: there was no money, but only bitter, hot saliva. Vanyushka sighed deeply and looked around.

The entire cellar was occupied by low plank beds, and on them lay, like heaps of mud, ragged, dingy men. Some of them had awakened, and, moving heavily, were sliding onto the brick floor. Others were still asleep. The subdued hubbub of voices mingled with the snoring of the sleepers; the splashing of water could be heard. In the gray murk of early morning the men's disheveled figures resembled tatters of autumn clouds.

"You awake?"

Next to Vanyushka stood Salakin. His face was red,

apparently because he had just washed it with cold water. In his hands was a copper box with a number of wheels in it. With one eye he examined the wheels and with the other he looked at Vanyushka, smiling.

"We went the limit last night," said Kuzin, looking at his chum reproachfully.

"Yes, we wet our whistles plenty," the other replied with relish.

"I blew in all my dough!"

"That's nothing. We'll get along!"

"Yes, it's all right for you . . ."

"Don't worry. I have seventeen kopecks, and then I'll sell my boots. We'll get along."

"Well, if that's how it is . . ." said Vanyushka, looking distrustfully into his chum's face, and seeing that Salakin was silent, he added:

"You've got to help me now, I spent my money drinking with you, so you must . . ."

"That's all right. 'Goes without saying. Laugh together, cry together. We're no rich folk to quarrel over who should get what. There's not much to divide."

His eyes and voice reassured Vanyushka, and he said:

"What have you got in your hand?"

"Guess."

Kuzin glanced about and asked under his breath:

"Counterfeiting tools, eh?"

"You queer fish!" exclaimed Salakin, laughing. "The idea! What do you know about counterfeiting?"

"I know. Not far from our village there was a peasant in this business. . . . Well, he landed in Siberia."

Salakin grew thoughtful, was silent for a while, and turning the box about in his hands, said with a sigh:

"Yes, they deport you for it."

"So that's what it is?" asked Vanyushka quietly, nodding towards the box.

"Oh, no. That's the inside of a watch. . . . Get up, let's go and have tea."

Vanyushka climbed off the bed, smoothed his hair with his hand, and said:

"Let's."

But the copper box fascinated him and filled him with a kind of fear. Seeing that Salakin thrust it in his bosom, he asked him:

"Where did you get it?"

"I bought it at the marketplace, when I was selling my overcoat. I paid seventy kopecks . . ."

"What do you want it for?" Vanyushka pressed him.

"You see—" bending toward his ear, Salakin spoke mysteriously—"for a long time I've wanted to understand how the clock knows what time it is. Midday, and it strikes twelve! How's that? Plain copper and yet made so that it knows what time it is! A man can guess the time by the sun, and an animal is a living thing. But these are wheels, copper!"

Vanyushka's head was aching. He walked beside his chum, listened to his cryptic words, and tried to figure out with difficulty what Salakin would do after he had sold his boots. Would he pay back at least half the money that had been spent on drink, or wouldn't he? And looking up into Salakin's eyes, he asked him:

"When are you going to sell your boots?"

"As soon as we've drunk our tea, we'll go. I've been thinking about clocks for a long time, brother. I've asked many people, intelligent people, too. One says this, another says that—impossible to make it out."

"And why do you want to know?" asked Vanyushka, curiously.

"It's interesting. How can it be? Now take a human being, he moves, but then he's alive, that's simple."

EVIL-DOERS

Salakin spoke of the mystery of clocks so long and so vehemently that Vanyushka involuntarily was infected by his enthusiasm, and himself began to wonder how it was that a clock knew the time. And while the friends drank tea, they kept up persistently the discussion of clocks.

Then they went to sell the boots, and sold them for two rubles and forty kopecks. Salakin was chagrined by the low price the boots had fetched. Right there on the market square he invited Vanyushka into an eating-place and in despair spent a whole ruble at one stroke. And late at night, when both of them, unsteady on their feet and talking loudly, were on their way to the doss-house, only four five-kopeck pieces were jingling in Salakin's pocket. Vanyushka held him by the arm, pushed him with his shoulder, and spoke elatedly:

"Brother, I love you like one of my own people. . . . Honest! You're a brick! You can have the whole of me, there it is! Honest! Get on my back if you like, I'll carry you."

"L-little fool!" muttered Salakin. "Don't worry, we'll get along! Tomorrow we'll go and sell the clock's guts, the whole business. To the devil with it, eh!"

"Damn it all!" shouted Vanyushka, waving his arm, and in a thin voice he began singing:

> I'm ho-omely, I'm po-or.

Salakin halted, and joined in:

> My clothes are all o-old.

And tightly pressed against each other, they howled together savagely:

> That's why the poor gi-irl
> Is left out in the co-old.

"And Matveyka, the red-headed devil! I'll show him!" Salakin concluded suddenly, and raising his arm high, he shook his fist in the air ferociously.

IV

A week passed.

One night the friends, hungry and full of rancor, were lying side by side on their plank beds in the doss-house, and Vanyushka was quietly reproaching Salakin:

"It's all your fault! If it weren't for you, I would be working somewhere by this time. . . ."

"Go to the devil," Salakin curtly advised his friend.

"Shut up! I'm telling the truth: What's to be done now? Starve . . ."

"Go, marry a merchant's widow, and your belly will be full. . . . Milk-sop!"

"You pock-marked mug! You stitched nose! . . ."

It wasn't the first time that they used such language to each other.

During the day, half-naked, blue with cold, they roamed the streets, but very rarely succeeded in earning something. They hired themselves out to split wood, to chop away the dirty ice in court-yards, and receiving twenty kopecks a-piece, they immediately spent the money on food. Sometimes on the market-place a lady would hand Vanyushka her basket, heavily laden with meat and vegetables, and pay him five kopecks to trail after her through the market for an hour carrying it for her. On such occasions Vanyushka, so hungry he had cramps, always felt that he hated the lady, but fearing to show this feeling, he made a pretense of being deferential towards her and indifferent to the things in her basket that were rousing his hunger.

Sometimes Vanyushka begged alms, trying to keep out of sight of the police, while Salakin knew how to steal a piece of meat, a slab of butter, a head of cabbage, a weight from scales. On such occasions Vanyushka would tremble with fear and say to his comrade:

"You'll ruin me! They'll clap us into jail. . . ."

"In jail we'll be fed and clothed," Salakin would retort, reasonably enough. "Is it my fault that it is easier to steal than to find work?"

That day they were just able to scrape together six kopecks for the doss-house; Salakin had stolen a French bread and a small bunch of carrots, and they had nothing more to eat that day. Hunger was consuming their vitals, and, preventing sleep, exasperated them.

"How much did I spend on you?" Salakin asked Vanyushka reproachfully. "All you had to your name was an ax and a kaftan. . . .",

"And what about the six ten-kopeck pieces? You've forgotten!"

They growled at each other like two vicious dogs, and more than once Vanyushka gave Salakin a shove as though by accident. But he did not wish to quarrel with his comrade openly: during these days he had grown used to him, and he knew that without Salakin he would have an even harder time.

It was frightful to live alone in the city. And he was ashamed to return to the village ragged and half-naked, ashamed before his mother, and before the girls, before all. Besides, Salakin jeered at him every time Vanyushka spoke of returning to the village.

"Go, go!" he would say, baring his teeth. "Make your mother happy: 'I've earned a pile, I'm dressed like a gentleman!'"

Moreover, Vanyushka was kept in the city by a vague hope that his luck would turn. Sometimes he thought that a rich man would take pity on him and hire him as a handy man, or else he imagined that Salakin would find some way out of this painful, hungry life. Faith in his comrade's cleverness was supported by Salakin himself, who would often say:

"Don't worry. We'll get along. Just you wait, we'll make our way yet. . . ."

He spoke with great assurance, and he looked at Vanyushka with peculiar attentiveness. At such times it seemed to Vanyushka that his comrade knew a way out.

Nevertheless, that night, as he lay beside his comrade, it occurred to him that if a brick were to fall out of the ceiling and land on Salakin's head, it would be a good thing. And he recalled that a few days ago, in the dead of night there had been a wild scream that had frightened everybody, and he remembered a man's bloody face flattened by a brick that had fallen from the ceiling.

"That's a great fortune, your six ten-kopeck pieces!" Salakin muttered. "But, now, if you . . ."

"If I what?"

"If you had guts . . ."

"Well?"

"Well, never mind."

Vanyushka reflected, and said:

"You can't do anything. You just like to hear yourself talk."

"Me?"

"You."

"Oh, I could say something."

"What?"

"Suppose I were ready for anything, then what?"

"Then what?"

"Yes, I want to know."

"I *will* tell you."

"Go ahead, say it."

"I will, only . . ."

"You have nothing to say!" Vanyushka muttered with finality.

Salakin stirred on his bed, while Vanyushka, turning his back on him and sighing with desperate anguish, whispered:

"God, if there were at least a crust! . . ."

For a few moments both were silent. Then Salakin half-raised himself, bent his head over Vanyushka, and almost touching his ear with his own lips, said nearly inaudibly:

"Ivan, listen. Come with me."

"Where?" asked Vanyushka, also under his breath.

"To Borisovo."

"What for?"

"I'll tell you on the way."

"Tell me now."

"Well, let's go. I will tell you. . . . We'll get there, and . . . we'll rob Matvey Ivanovich. Honest!"

"Go to the devil!" said Vanyushka with fear and irritation.

But Salakin, pressed tight against him, began to whisper into his ear:

"Listen. It's simple enough. We'll do what has to be done and get back here. Who will suspect us? I know everything there, all the ins and outs. And where the money is kept. And there is silver. Spoons. Goblets in a cabinet behind glass. . . ."

Salakin's hot breath warmed Vanyushka's cheek and his terror began to melt away. Nevertheless, he repeated quietly:

"Get out, I say, you devil!"

"No, but wait! . . . What a life we could have! Just think! First of all, we eat, we have shoes, we have clothes!"

Vanyushka lay silent, and Salakin kept breathing into his ear and into his brain hot, confident words.

Finally, Vanyushka asked him:
"Is there much money in it?"

V

Two days later, early in the morning, they were walking along the highroad, shoulder to shoulder, and Salakin was talking excitedly to his companion, looking into his eyes.
"You understand? First thing we do, we set fire to the shed! And when it catches, everybody will run to the fire, and he too, Matvey, that is! He will run off, and we'll get into his house! And we'll clean him out. . . ."
"And if they catch us?" asked Vanyushka reflectively.
"They can't!" said Salakin. "Who would catch us?" And he added in a severe tone of voice: "You have to put out the fire, not catch thieves! Understand?"
Vanyushka nodded.
This was at the beginning of March. Soft, fluffy, heavy snowflakes were lazily dropping from the invisible sky and were fast obliterating the footsteps of the men, who were walking on the road between two rows of aged birches with broken boughs.
"If only we could do it!" said Vanyushka, sighing heavily.
"You'll see, we'll have it our way!" Salakin promised confidently.
"God grant it! I mean, if only we succeeded— Lord, I would never undertake anything like that again. . . ."
The comrades walked fast, because they were very poorly clothed. Salakin wore his woman's jacket embellished with innumerable holes from which dirty cotton peeped out; his feet swam in huge felt boots; and on his head was a cap gray with age. Vanyushka had acquired, instead of a kaftan, a brown woolen pea-jacket, but for some reason its right sleeve was black. Bast shoes, a cap with a broken visor, a cord for a belt, gave Vanyushka the appearance not of a

peasant, but of an artisan who had drunk all his earnings.

On the eve of the day when they decided to do the job, Salakin succeeded in hooking a copper pan and an iron, and sold them for eighty kopecks to a dealer in scrap-iron, and now he had a fifty-kopeck piece in his pocket.

"If only we could meet someone with a horse and get a lift," said Salakin. "Otherwise we won't get there before dark—it's a distance of over forty versts! We could even pay five kopecks apiece, for the lift. . . ."

The snow dropped on their heads, fell on their cheeks, pasted up their eyes, formed white epaulettes on their shoulders, stuck to their feet. Around them and above them a white porridge was seething, and they could see nothing in front of them. Vanyushka walked silently, like a sick old jade which is being led to the slaughter-house, while the lively, talkative Salakin kept glancing about him and chattered ceaselessly.

"I wonder how far we've gone! And there's no seeing what's in front of us! What a snow-fall. . . . Of course, the snow plays into our hands: there will be no traces. . . . If only it kept coming down! Only then it will be awkward to get the fire going! Well, you can't have everything. . . ."

The snowflakes were becoming smaller and drier. They did not fall slowly, straight to the ground, but circled uneasily and fussily in the air in larger quantities. Suddenly a rickety structure, looking as though it had been pressed into the ground by the heavy drifts on its roof, loomed before them like a dark, heavy cloud.

"That's Fokino," said Salakin. "Let's go into the pot-house and have a glass . . ."

"Let's," Vanyushka agreed, shuddering all over.

Two horses, each hitched to a sledge, stood motionless before the pot-house. Small, shaggy, they gazed sadly out of their meek eyes, shaking off the snow from their eyelashes. The unpainted shaft-bows were covered with black dust.

"Aha, a charcoal-burner!" said Salakin. "I hope he's going our way. . . ."

And indeed, in the pot-house, at a table near the window sat a young fellow drinking beer. Vanyushka was struck by his long funny nose on a thin face covered with black spots. The charcoal-burner was sprawling importantly on the chair with his legs wide apart, and sipping his beer slowly, but when he was through drinking, he started coughing, his whole body shook, and he at once lost his air of importance.

Vanyushka went over to the counter, swallowed a glass of fragrant, bitter vodka, and glanced from the charcoal-burner to Salakin with a wink.

"Going to town, my hearty?" asked Salakin, approaching the charcoal-burner.

The other looked at him and answered in a hollow voice:

"We don't go to town without a load."

"So you're coming from town?"

"What does it matter to you?"

"Me? Why, my chum and I, we're going to Borisovo, we've been hired by the oil-factory. Give us a lift, since we're going in the same direction!"

The man examined Salakin, then Vanyushka, poured himself some beer, and, fishing out pieces of cork with his finger, answered curtly:

"Doesn't suit me."

"Give us a lift, be a good fellow! We'll give you five kopecks apiece. . . ."

"I don't need it," said the young man, without looking at Salakin.

"Give us a lift, for Christ's sake!" begged Vanyushka gently and timidly.

The young man looked at them, frowned, and shook his head.

"What a fellow you are!" exclaimed Salakin. "Isn't it all one to you? We've a long way to go, we're tired, you can see what kind of clothes we have on. . . ."

"You should dress more warmly," the charcoal-burner said with a sneer.

"But if we haven't any money!" said Vanyushka persuasively. "You see, we're poor . . ."

"And why are you poor?" asked the charcoal-burner unconcernedly, and returned to his beer.

Vanyushka exchanged glances with his comrade, both grew silent, and stood cap in hand before the charcoal-burner.

Then the old woman who kept the pot-house spoke up:

"Don't put on airs, Nikolai, give them a lift. What's the matter? The horse is going to go anyway, and besides, they offer five kopecks apiece! You ask to be paid in advance, and let them ride."

The charcoal-burner again examined the two friends in turn. Then he sighed and said:

"Ten kopecks apiece."

"Very well!" shouted Salakin, waving his arm. "Here, take it, make the most of it!"

"Take a look at the money first," the old woman advised.

The charcoal-burner threw the coin on the table, listened to the ring of it, then bit it with his teeth, and going over to the counter, threw it to the old woman, saying:

"This is for the beer."

"What a dog!" Salakin whispered to Vanyushka.

"You sit in the empty one," said the charcoal-burner

to Vanyushka, having gotten the change from the old woman, "and you with me. . . ."

"Very well," agreed Salakin. "But why shouldn't we ride together?"

"And why together?" asked the charcoal-burner suspiciously.

"We'd be warmer. . . ."

"Well," the charcoal-burner sneered. "You do as I tell you. Because if your comrade gets it into his head to steal one of my horses, I'll knock you on the head with a weight, bind you, and . . ."

Without finishing his speech, he laughed, then began to cough long and painfully. . . .

VI

Having gone a distance of some five versts, the charcoal-burner at last spoke to his fare:

"Who are you?"

"A human being," said Salakin through his teeth.

It was cold, riding. Salakin was shivering all over. The snow had stopped falling, but a keen wind was blowing. Twice Salakin had jumped off the sledge and run alongside the road in the hope of getting warm. But it was difficult to run in the deep yielding snow, he tired quickly, piled into the sledge again, and after that felt even colder. And every time he jumped out of the sledge, the charcoal-burner, who was dressed in a sturdy sheepskin jacket and an overcoat, thrust out from the sleeve of the overcoat a short stout stick with a chain at one end, from which a pound weight was suspended. At the sight of this bludgeon a hatred as terrible as the cold crushed Salakin's heart.

"Everybody is a human being," said the charcoal-burner. "But I'm asking you, where do you belong?"

"I belong nowhere. I am without kith or kin," answered Salakin, and shouted:

"Vanya, are you alive?"

"Alive," answered Vanyushka rather softly.

"Are you cold?"

"Sort of . . ."

"I look at you—" the charcoal-burner spoke grumblingly— "I can see, you're unfortunates. Both in rags, queer fellows . . . loafers, I suppose. . . ."

Salakin sat hunched together and said nothing, trying to keep his teeth from chattering.

Looking back, he saw through the snowflakes, which were now few, a deserted, bluish waste. The sight pierced him with cold and anguish. There was nothing on it to arrest the eye.

"Take us, the Semakins, we are three brothers. We burn charcoal, understand, and take it to town, to the distillery. We live at peace. We have enough to eat, we have something to wear, shoes to our feet. . . . Everything is as it should be, thank God! A man who knows how to work, who isn't lazy, doesn't loaf, always lives well. . . . The older brothers are married, and I'm going to get married after the holidays. . . . That's how it is. A man who works can get along."

The horse moved with difficulty, straining against the collar; the sledge jerked; and Salakin was jolted like a nut held in the palm of the hand.

The charcoal-burner's dull, obtuse, heavy words dropped upon Salakin's soul like so many cold bricks, crushing it, and it was both painful and humiliating for him to listen to this man's hollow voice.

"Vanyushka!" he shouted.

"Eh?"

"Why don't you get down and run a bit?"

"What for?" asked Kuzin in a weak voice.

"So you don't freeze to death."

"Never mind."

The charcoal-burner sighed. Then he smiled sneeringly, wiped his nose with his sleeve, and spoke again:

"What people! What people! Why do you want to live? You're cold, hungry . . . It's crazy. Is that the way people should live? A man should live well."

"You share your money with me, and I'll live well," said Salakin viciously.

"What!"

"I say, share your money . . ."

"I'll share you! Did you see this?"

Before Salakin's eyes dangled the weight hanging at the end of the chain. He saw the charcoal-burner's face, black as the devil's, and twisted by his smirk. And suddenly it was as though Salakin had been set a-fire, as though the heart in his breast had burst and were shooting out flame, and this flame leapt to his head and colored everything before his eyes blood-red. He swung his right hand with all his might, and striking the charcoal-burner in the face with his elbow, threw him on his back. At the same time the weight struck Salakin between the shoulder-blades. A sharp pain entered his body and crushed the breath out of him.

"Help! Murder!" shouted the charcoal-burner.

But Salakin fell upon him with his whole weight, seized the charcoal-burner's throat with his fingers, and squeezing it, jammed his knees into the charcoal-burner's stomach.

"Now talk! Shout! Talk!"

The charcoal-burner's throat rattled; his teeth bit into Salakin's shoulder. He was writhing under him like a fish under a knife and was groping with his hands for Salakin's throat. The bludgeon fell out of his fingers and hung from a strap at his wrist. Now and then it touched Salakin's body, and every contact, though not painful, roused fear.

"Vanyushka, help!" shouted Salakin wildly.

Vanyushka, crushed by the cold, lay in the sledge, buried under empty coal-sacks, and when he heard the charcoal-burner's cry he was seized by terror. Instinctively he at once understood what was going on, and burrowed deeper into the sacks. . . .

"I'll say I was asleep, I didn't hear anything," he said to himself quickly.

But when he heard his comrade's shout for help he shuddered and flung out of the sledge like a clod of snow from under a horse's hoof. The thought shot through his brain that should the charcoal-burner get the better of Salakin, he would kill him too. And when he found himself near the two human bodies twisted in a huge knot, when he saw the charcoal-burner's face streaked with blood and yet still black, and the bludgeon that dangled from his right wrist while his hand convulsively tried to grasp it, Vanyushka seized his hand and began to turn and twist it. . . .

The small, shaggy horse with sad eyes trotted quietly along the road, shaking its head. It was carrying into the cold, dead distance three men who, grunting and grinding their teeth, were meaninglessly struggling in the sledge. The other horse, afraid that the men's feet would hit it on the muzzle, began to lag.

VII

When Vanyushka, tired and sweating, came to himself after the struggle, he whispered to Salakin, fear in his eyes:

"Look! Where's the horse? It's gone."

"It won't blab," mumbled Salakin, wiping the blood from his face.

His comrade's calm voice lessened Vanyushka's fear.

"We've done it now!" he said, looking at the charcoal-burner out of the corner of his eye.

"It was better to kill him than to have him kill us," observed Salakin with the same calmness, and forthwith added in a businesslike manner:

"Come, let's strip him! You get the sheepskin jacket, I the overcoat. We must hurry, or we may meet somebody, or be overtaken. . . ."

Vanyushka silently turned the charcoal-burner over and began taking off his clothes. He kept glancing at his chum. He was thinking: "Can it be that he isn't afraid?"

Salakin's calm and businesslike attitude toward the murdered man aroused Vanyushka's astonishment and made him timid in his comrade's presence. What amazed him even more was Salakin's pock-marked, scratched face: it twitched and grimaced as though with silent laughter, and his eyes shone in a peculiar way, as if he had had a drop too much or were overjoyed by something. In the struggle Vanyushka had lost his cap, and now Salakin took the charcoal-burner's cap, handed it to Vanyushka, and said:

"Put it on, you'll be cold! Besides, it isn't right—a man without a cap. How did that happen?"

He proceeded to turn the murdered man's trouser-pockets inside out, and he did it as quickly and deftly as though all his life his sole occupation had been killing and robbing.

"You've got to watch out for everything," he said, unfastening the charcoal-burner's tobacco pouch. "No one goes around without a cap. Look at that: a gold coin, five rubles, no, seven and a half . . ."

"Is . . ." Vanyushka spoke timidly, looking at the coin with eyes that had blazed up.

"What is it?" asked Salakin, glancing at him rapidly. And then he grumbled disdainfully:

"We'll have enough dough. Gee-up, little one! Shake

a leg." And Salakin struck the horse's rump with the flat of his hand.

"I didn't mean money," said Vanyushka. "I wanted to ask . . ."

"What?"

"Is this the first time?" Vanyushka winked at the stripped corpse of the charcoal-burner.

"You fool!" exclaimed Salakin, smiling. "What! am I a bandit?"

"I asked because you undressed him so quickly."

"It's hard to strip a living man, but a dead one, that's plain sailing."

And suddenly Salakin, who was on his knees, swayed and fell heavily across Vanyushka's feet. The latter shuddered as though he had suddenly been plunged into cold water, screamed, and started pushing his comrade away, while the horse, frightened by the outcry, bolted.

"It's nothing, nothing," Salakin mumbled, groping for Vanyushka. His face turned blue, his eyes grew dull.

"He hit me between the shoulder-blades. I have a pain in my heart. . . . It'll pass."

"Yeremey," said Vanyushka in a trembling voice, "let's go back, for Christ's sake!"

"Where?"

"To the city! I'm scared."

"To the city, no! We'll first sell the horse, and then we'll go on, to Matvey's."

"I'm scared," said Vanyushka mournfully.

"What of?"

"We're done for, brother. What's going to happen now? Was this what we were after?"

"Go to the devil!" shouted Salakin, and his eyes flashed angrily. "Done for! What do you mean, done for? Are we the only ones who ever killed man? Is this the first time this happened on earth?"

"Don't be angry," begged Vanyushka in a tearful voice, noticing that his comrade's face again wore a desperate, drunken look.

"How can I help getting angry!" exclaimed Salakin indignantly. "Here this thing has happened . . ."

"Wait! What are we doing?" Vanyushka spoke up forcibly, shuddering violently and looking around him in fear. "Where are we taking him? We'll soon get to Vishenki, and think of the load we are carrying!"

"Whoa, you devil!" Salakin shouted at the horse, and swiftly and lightly as a ball he jumped out of the sledge onto the road.

"You're right, brother," he muttered, seizing the charcoal-burner's right hand. "Take him, drag him, get hold of his legs! Pull him out!"

Vanyushka, trying not to look at the face of the corpse, lifted it by the legs and did catch a glimpse of something blue, round, and terrible where the charcoal-burner's face should have been.

"Dig a pit!" commanded Salakin, and jumped about in the yielding snow, shoving it to either side with quick vigorous movements of his feet. He did it in such a curious fashion that Vanyushka, dropping the body of the charcoal-burner on the snow, stood over it and watched his comrade without helping him.

"Bury him, bury him!" Salakin was saying, swiftly and diligently covering the murdered man's head and chest with snow. The comrades were working two paces away from the sledge, and the horse, turning its head, looked at them with one eye, and was as motionless as though it were petrified.

"We're done. Let's go."

"It's no good," objected Vanyushka.

"Why?"

"You notice it—the hillock."

"It doesn't matter."

They got into the sledge and drove on, tightly pressed against each other. Vanyushka looked back and it seemed to him that they were going at a terribly slow pace, because the hillock of snow over the body continued to remain in sight.

"Hurry the horse," he begged Salakin, closing his eyes tightly and keeping them shut for a long time. When he opened them he still saw, far off, to the left of the road, a little mound on the level snow.

"Oh, we're done for, Yeremey," said Vanyushka almost in a whisper.

"Don't worry," Salakin answered in a hollow voice. "We'll sell the horse, and then we'll go back to the city. . . . Go find us! And now, here's Vishenki."

The road led downhill into a shallow depression filled with snow. Bare black trees appeared on both sides of the road. A jackdaw screamed. The comrades shivered, and each looked silently at the other's face.

"Be careful," Vanyushka whispered to Salakin.

VIII

They entered the pot-house jauntily and noisily.

"Hey, old man, turn on the tap and give us a glass each."

"It can be done," said a tall, dark peasant with a bald spot, rising from behind the counter, and he looked at Vanyushka with such simple-hearted geniality that he stood still in the middle of the room and smiled guiltily.

"It's the custom here," said the tavern-keeper, setting the glasses down before Salakin, "that when a man comes into a place he says, 'Good day' or 'How are you?' Did you come a long way?"

"We? Oh, no, we . . . we don't hail from far away, about thirty versts," explained Salakin.

"In which direction?"

"This," and Salakin pointed to the door of the pot-house.

"So you're from near town?" asked the tavern-keeper.

"That's right. . . . Come, Vanya, drink."

"That your brother?"

"No," Vanyushka answered quickly. "We're no brothers."

In the corner, beside the door, sat a peasant, a short man with a sharp, beaklike nose and keen, gray eyes. He got up, slowly walked to the counter and unceremoniously stared at the comrades.

"What is it?" asked the tavern-keeper.

"Nothing," said the peasant in a creaking voice. "I thought maybe I knew them."

"Let's sit here awhile and get warm," said Salakin, leaving the corner and pulling Vanyushka by the sleeve.

They stepped aside and sat down at a table. The peasant with the beaklike nose remained at the counter and said something under his breath to the tavern-keeper.

"Let's go. Let's be off," whispered Vanyushka to Salakin.

"Wait," Salakin said loudly.

Vanyushka looked reproachfully at his comrade and shook his head. It seemed to him that under the circumstances it was dangerous, wrong, awkward to speak aloud in the presence of strangers.

"Another glass for each of us," Salakin ordered.

The door of the pot-house creaked, and two more peasants entered: an old man with a long, gray beard and a stocky, big-headed man in a short sheepskin coat, which reached to his knees.

"May you be in good health," said the old man.

"A welcome to you," responded the tavern-keeper, and glanced at Salakin.

"Whose horse is that?" asked the stocky peasant, nodding toward the door.

"It belongs to these two," the sharp-nosed peasant declared slowly, pointing his finger at Salakin.

"It's ours," Salakin said in confirmation.

Vanyushka heard the voices, and fear kept clutching at his heart. It seemed to him that all these people were talking in a peculiar way, too plainly, as though they knew everything, were surprised at nothing, and were waiting for something.

"Let's drive off," he whispered to his comrade.

"And who are you?" the stocky peasant asked Salakin.

"We? We're butchers," Salakin answered suddenly, and smiled.

"What are you saying?" exclaimed Vanyushka uneasily, vainly trying to lower his voice.

All the four peasants heard his exclamation, and slowly turning their heads, they stared at him with inquisitive eyes. Salakin looked at them calmly, only his tightly compressed lips quivering. But Vanyushka bowed his head over the table and waited, feeling as though he could not breathe. The silence, heavy as a cloud, did not last long. . . .

"So that's why," said the stocky peasant, "I noticed that the front of the sledge was stained with blood."

"What!" said Salakin boldly.

"As for me," said the old man, "I didn't notice any blood. Was there blood? I looked at the sledge and it was all black, so I thought to myself, these must be charcoal-burners. Pour me out a glass, Ivan Petrovich."

The tavern-keeper poured out a glass of vodka and slowly, like a well-fed tom-cat, walked out of the door. The peasant with the beaklike nose waited until he passed by him and then he also walked out of the door.

"Well," said Salakin, getting up from his chair, "well,

Vanya, we must be off. Where's the tavern-keeper? Doesn't he want his money?"

"He'll be right back," said the stocky peasant, turning away from Salakin, and began to roll a cigarette. Vanyushka too rose, but immediately sat down again. His knees turned to water and refused to support his body. He looked stupidly into his comrade's face and seeing that Salakin's lips were trembling, he wailed softly in fear and anguish.

The tavern-keeper returned alone. He went behind the counter again as slowly and quietly as he had left it, and leaning on it, he said to the old man:

"It's getting warmer again."

"It's the time of year."

"Well, we must be driving off," said Salakin aloud, approaching the counter. "Here's your money."

"Wait a while," the tavern-keeper said, smiling lazily.

"We're in a hurry," said Salakin, more quietly, dropping his eyes.

"Well, wait anyway," repeated the tavern-keeper.

"What for?"

"I sent for the bailiff."

Vanyushka jumped to his feet and sat down again.

"Your bailiff's nothing to me," declared Salakin, shrugging his shoulders and putting on his cap.

"But you're something to him," said the tavern-keeper lazily, moving away from Salakin.

The old man and the stocky peasant became interested in the conversation, which was unintelligible to them, and moved over toward the counter.

"He wants to ask you a question: how is it that you sell meat, but you carry coal-sacks?"

"Ah," drawled the old man, moving away from Salakin.

"So that's the way of it!" exclaimed the stocky peasant. "They have stolen the horse!"

"No!" exclaimed Vanyushka in a shrill voice.

Salakin waved his arm, and turning to him, said with a crooked smile:

"Here we are, we're through!"

Five more peasants entered the pot-house noisily, one of them a tall, red-headed man, with a long staff in his hands. Vanyushka looked at them with wide-opened eyes. It seemed to him that they were all swaying on their feet like drunken men and were making the room sway, too.

"Good day, my hearties!" said the peasant with the staff. "Well, tell us who you are. And where do you come from? Take me, for instance, I am the bailiff, and who are you?"

Salakin looked at the bailiff and gave a laugh that resembled the barking of a dog. His face blanched.

"So you are laughing?" said one of the peasants sternly, and proceeded to tuck up his sleeves.

"Wait, Korney," the bailiff halted him. "Everything in its turn. You needn't . . . Make a clean breast of it, men, where did you get the horse? Eh?"

Heavily and slowly, like snow that, having thawed underneath, slides off a roof, Vanyushka slipped from his chair to the floor, and on his knees began to mumble stammeringly:

"Orthodox folks—it isn't me! It's him! We didn't steal the horse—we killed the charcoal-burner. . . . He's there, not far away, buried in the snow. We didn't steal the horse—we were just driving along, honest! It's not me—all this! The horse itself dropped behind, it will come back! We didn't want to kill him—he was the one who started it —he used a bludgeon! We were on our way to Borisovo— we wanted to rob the steward—first set the house on fire— but we didn't touch the horses! He made me—he! . . ."

"Fire away!" shouted Salakin. He tore his cap off his

head and threw it down at the feet of the peasants who stood before him like a silent, thick, dark wall.

"Go to it, Vanka, bury me!"

Vanka stopped speaking, dropped his head on his chest, and let his arms hang down helplessly.

The peasants looked at them in sullen silence for a long time. At last one of them, the man with the beaklike nose and the creaking voice, sighed and said aloud with vexation:

"Such evil-doers—fools, ugh!"

1901.

BIRTH OF A MAN

THIS happened in 1892, a famine year, at a point between Sukhum and Ochemchiry, on the shore of the Kodor River, so near the sea that through the gay babble of the clear waters of the mountain stream the muffled thunder of the billows was distinctly heard.

It was an autumn day. Yellow cherry-laurel leaves were circling and glistening in the white foam of the Kodor like nimble salmon fry. I was sitting on some rocks near the bank and reflecting that the sea-gulls and cormorants, too, must be mistaking the leaves for fish, and that was why their cries were so fretful over there to the right, behind the trees where the sea was rumbling.

The chestnut trees overhead were decked out in gold; at my feet lay piles of leaves which looked like the palms of hands that had been cut off. On the opposite bank the hornbeam boughs were already bare, and hung in the air like a torn net; caught in it, as it were, a red and yellow mountain woodpecker hopped along, tapping the bark with his black beak, while adroit titmice and dove-colored nuthatches—visitors from the distant north—pecked the insects he drove out.

To the left, above the mountain peaks, hung smoky, heavy, rain-laden clouds; they cast shadows over the green slopes dotted with boxwood, "the dead tree." Here in the hollows of old beeches and lindens is found that "heady honey," the intoxicating sweetness of which nearly caused the downfall of the soldiers of Pompey the Great long ago, having overcome a whole legion of iron Romans. The bees make it from laurel and azalea blossoms, and tramps get it out of the hollows and eat it, spreading it on what the natives called *lavash*, a thin flat cake made of wheat flour. That is exactly what I was doing, as I sat under the chestnut trees. Stung all over by angry bees, I was dipping pieces of bread into a kettle full of honey and eating, while I admired the lazy play of the weary autumnal sun.

Autumn in the Caucasus is like a gorgeous cathedral built by great sages—these are always great sinners, too. To hide their past from the prying eyes of conscience, they have built an immense temple made of gold, turquoise, emeralds, hung the mountains with the finest carpets embroidered in silk by Turcomans at Samarkand, at Shemakha. They have plundered the whole world and brought everything here, to the sun, as if to say to it: "All these are Thine—from Thy people—for Thee!" I see bearded, white-haired giants with the huge eyes of merry children, descending from the mountains to embellish the earth. They generously scatter vari-colored gems, cover the mountain peaks with thick layers of silver, and their slopes with a living fabric of varied trees—and under their hands this piece of blessed earth becomes ravishingly beautiful.

It is a fine thing—to be a man of earth; you see so much that is marvelous; how painfully and sweetly the heart throbs in quiet ecstasy before beauty!

Of course, there are difficult moments: burning hatred fills the breast to overflowing, anguish greedily sucks the heart's blood, but these moments pass. Even the sun is often sad as it looks at human beings: it has worked so hard for them, yet they are failures. . . .

Of course, there are not a few good people, but even they need mending, or better still, should be made over completely.

Suddenly, above the bushes, to my left, there appeared dark heads swaying, while through the thunder of the sea and the noise of the river the faint sound of human voices

BIRTH OF A MAN

was heard. These were famine victims, tramping from Sukhum, where they had built a road, to Ochemchiry, where other work awaited them. I knew them: they were peasants from the province of Oryol. We had been working together and had been discharged together the previous day, but I had left before they did, at night, to meet sunrise on the beach.

Four men and a young peasant woman in the last stages of pregnancy were more familiar to me than the others. She had high cheekbones and gray-blue eyes bulging as though with fear. Above the bushes her head in a yellow kerchief was swaying like a blossoming sunflower in the wind. At Sukhum her husband had died, after eating too much fruit. I had lived in barracks with these people: according to the good Russian custom, they discussed their misfortunes so volubly and so loudly that their pitiful words must have been heard for five versts around.

These people were crushed by their sorrow. It had wrenched them from their native barren and exhausted lands and had carried them to this spot, the way a wind carries dry leaves in autumn. Here the exuberant and unfamiliar aspect of nature dazzled and bewildered them, while the oppressive conditions of work robbed them of the last ounce of courage. They looked at the land, blinking their dull, sad eyes forlornly, smiling piteously at each other and saying quietly:

"Ah . . . what rich soil. . . ."

"Things just push out of it."

"My—yes . . . still, rather stony. . . ."

"Not very easy to work, this soil, I must say. . . ."

And they recalled their native villages, where every handful of soil was the dust of their ancestors, and the land was memorable, familiar, dear—watered by their sweat.

There was with them a woman, tall, straight, flat as a board, with equine jaws and a dull look in her coal-black, squinting eyes. In the evening, together with the woman in the yellow kerchief, she would go off beyond the barracks, and sitting on a pile of crushed stone, her cheek in her palm, her head bent to one side, she would sing in a high, angry voice:

> By the graveyard,
> Where the shrubs grow green and thick,
> On the sand-bank
> I will spread a linen cloth.
> It may happen
> If I wait there I shall see him . . .
> If my love comes,
> Then I will bow down before him.

Her companion usually held her peace, staring down at her stomach, her head bent forward, but sometimes she would suddenly join in, with words like sobs, singing indolently and thickly in a mannish, somewhat hoarse voice:

> Darling, darling,
> Oh, my dear, my love, my own,
> I am fated
> Nevermore to look on thee.

In the stifling blackness of the Southern night these plaintive voices recalled the North, the snowy wastes, the wailing of snowstorms and the distant howling of wolves. . . .

Then the squint-eyed woman had been taken ill with a fever, and she had been carried to town on a tarpaulin stretcher. She shook and moaned, as though continuing her song about the churchyard and the sand-bank.

Ducking suddenly, the yellow head disappeared.

I finished my breakfast, covered the honey in the kettle with leaves, tied up my bundle, and without hurrying, set out after the others, who had left earlier, tapping my cornel stick against the hard path.

BIRTH OF A MAN

And now I too am on the narrow, gray strip of road. On my right, the dark blue sea is tossing; it is as though a thousand invisible carpenters were planing it—the white shavings roll up on the beach with a rustling sound, driven by a wind, moist, warm, and fragrant, like the breath of a healthy woman. A Turkish felucca, listing to port, is gliding toward Sukhum, her sails bellied, the way an important engineer at Sukhum used to puff out his fat cheeks as he shouted:

"Shut up! You may be smart, but I'll have you in jail in a jiffy!"

He was fond of having men arrested, and it is good to think that worms have surely long since gnawed him to the bone.

The going is easy—it is as though you walk on air. Pleasant thoughts, motley reminiscences, are circling gently. These thoughts in the mind are like white-caps on the sea. They are on the surface, while down in the depths it is quiet: there the bright, pliant hopes of youth are swimming gently, like silver fish in the deep.

The road is drawn toward the sea; coiling, it creeps closer to the strip of sand that the waves invade. The bushes, too, wish to peer into the face of the waves; they bend over the ribbon of road as though greeting the far-flung, watery waste.

The wind begins to blow from the mountains—it will rain.

. . . A low moan in the bushes—a sound of human distress, which always shakes the soul with sympathy.

Making my way through the bushes, I came upon the peasant woman with the yellow kerchief. She was sitting with her back against the trunk of a nut tree. Her head was resting on her shoulder, her mouth was gaping in an ugly way, her eyes were starting out of her head, and there was a crazy look in them. She was clutching her enormous abdomen with her hands and breathing so unnaturally that it moved up and down convulsively, and she was making a muffled, cow-like sound, baring yellow, wolf-like teeth.

"Someone gave you a beating?" I asked her, bending over her. Her bare legs, covered with ashen dust, were jerking like a fly's, and shaking her heavy head, she managed:

"Go away . . . you shameless fellow . . . go . . ."

I understood what it all meant, I had seen it happen before. Of course, I was frightened, jumped away, and the woman let out a long-drawn-out wail. From her eyes, which looked ready to burst, came troubled tears that ran down her purple, strained face.

This brought me back to her. I threw my bundle on the ground, together with the tea-pot and kettle, put her on her back, and tried to bend her knees. She pushed me away, hitting me on the face and chest, turned around, and roaring like a bear and cursing, crawled on all fours further into the bushes:

"You bandit . . . devil . . ." she brought out.

Her arms giving way under her, she fell, her face striking the earth, and again she howled convulsively, stretching out her legs.

In a fever of excitement, and quickly recalling everything I knew about this business, I turned her around and laid her on her back and bent her legs.

"Lie quiet," I said to her, "you will be delivered in no time. . . ."

I ran down to the sea, tucked up my sleeves, washed my hands, returned, and became an accoucheur.

The woman was writhing like birch-bark in the fire, she thrashed about with her hands, and, plucking the faded grass, tried to push it into her mouth. She strewed earth over her terrible, inhuman face with its wild, bloodshot eyes. Already the child's head was showing. I had to keep her legs from writhing, help the child, and see that she did not put grass into her wry, bellowing mouth.

We swore at each other a little, she through her teeth, I too under my breath, she from pain and, perhaps, also from shame, I because I was ill at ease and tormented by pity for her.

"L-lord!" she repeated, bringing out the word with a rattling sound. Her blue lips were bitten and frothy, and from her eyes, which looked as though they had suddenly been faded by the sun, tears kept pouring, the abundant tears of a mother's unbearable suffering, and her body was writhing, breaking, dividing in two. "G-go away, you devil . . ." she kept saying.

With weak, dislocated hands she kept pushing me away, while I repeated persuasively:

"Get through, you fool, get through quickly. . . ."

I was racked by pity for her, it was as though her tears were in my eyes, anguish squeezed my heart, I felt like shouting, and I shouted: "Come on, hurry up!"

At last, a human being was in my hands. Through my tears I saw that he was all red, and already he was discontented with the world. He struggled, carried on, and howled in a thick voice, although he was still tied to his mother. He had blue eyes, his nose was ludicrously crushed against his red, crumpled face, his lips moved, and he screamed: "I . . . I . . ."

He was so slippery that if I had not taken care, he would have slipped away from me. Kneeling, I looked at him and laughed—I was very glad to see him. And I had forgotten what must be done next.

"Cut it . . ." whispered the mother gently. Her eyes were closed, her face relaxed. It was earth-colored, as if she were dead, her blue lips barely moved:

"Cut it . . . with a knife. . . ."

My knife had been stolen in the barracks. I bit through

the cord. The baby howled in an Oryol bass, and the mother smiled; her bottomless eyes blossomed out marvelously and burned with a blue fire. Her dark hand fumbled in her skirt, feeling for the pocket, and her bleeding, bitten lips were barely able to produce:

"I haven't . . . strength . . . tape . . . in the pocket . . . to bind . . . the navel. . . ."

I got the tape and bound up the navel. Her smile was even brighter, it was indeed so warm and brilliant that it nearly dazzled me.

"Now set yourself to rights," I said, "and I'll go and give him a wash. . . ."

"But look out," she murmured, uneasily, "go gently. . . ."

This red fellow didn't have to be treated with care, not at all: he clenched his fists and bawled, bawled as if challenging someone to a fight: "I . . . I . . ."

"You . . . you! Assert yourself firmly, brother, or else your fellow men will break your neck for you straight off. . . ."

He gave a particularly loud and earnest yell when he was splashed for the first time by a frothy wave which gaily dashed against us both. Then, when I bathed his chest and back, he screwed up his eyes, struggled violently and screamed piercingly, while the waves kept splashing over him.

"Make a noise, old fellow! Shout at the top of your lungs. . . ."

When I took him back to his mother, she lay with her eyes closed again, biting her lips. She was undergoing the pangs of expelling the after-birth. Nevertheless, through her sighs and groans I heard her faint whisper:

"Give . . . give him to me. . . ."

"He'll wait."

"No . . . give him here."

And with unsteady, trembling hands she unbuttoned her

blouse. I helped her to free her breast, prepared by nature for a score of babies, and I placed the obstreperous fellow against her warm body. He grasped the situation at once and grew silent.

"Holy Mother of God, Most Pure Virgin," the woman repeated, shuddering, and rolled her disheveled head from side to side on my bundle.

And suddenly, with a gentle outcry, she grew silent. Then she opened her infinitely beautiful eyes, the hallowed eyes of a mother. Blue, they looked at the blue sky, and there burned and melted in them a grateful, joyous smile. With a heavy hand she was slowly making the sign of the cross over herself and the child. . . .

"Glory be to Thee, Most Pure Mother of God," she repeated; "oh . . . glory . . ."

Her eyes grew tired and sunken. For a long time she was silent, scarcely breathing. And suddenly she said in a matter-of-fact tone, her voice grown firm:

"Untie my sack, lad. . . ."

I did so. She looked at me attentively, smiled weakly, her drawn cheeks and damp forehead flushing slightly.

"Would you mind . . ."

"Don't you do too much. . . ."

"Just leave me. . . ."

I went off into the thicket. Birds were gently singing in my heart and, together with the noise of the sea, this was so wonderful that I thought I could listen to that music for a year on end. . . .

Not far off a stream was babbling: it was as though a girl were telling her friend of her beloved.

Presently above the bushes the woman's head appeared, with the yellow kerchief properly tied.

"Eh, is that you, sister?" I shouted. "It's too soon for you to be stirring about."

Holding on to a bough, she was sitting like a statue,

white-faced, with huge blue lakes instead of eyes, and she whispered with emotion:

"Look—how he sleeps. . . ."

He looked well asleep, but as far as I could judge, no better than other babies, and if there was any difference it was due to the surroundings. He lay under a bush, such as do not grow in the province of Oryol, on a heap of bright autumn leaves.

"You had better lie down now, mother . . ." I advised her.

"No," she said, shaking her head, which seemed to be loosely screwed to her neck; "I must tidy up and be off for what-d'ye-call-it. . . ."

"Ochemchiry?"

"That's it. My people must have gone quite a distance. . . ."

"But can you walk?"

"And what of the Virgin? She will help. . . ."

Well, if she has the Virgin with her, there is nothing more to be said!

She looked at the little pouting face under the bush, and warm rays of caressing light poured from her eyes. She licked her lips and passed her hands slowly over her chest.

I made a fire and set up stones to put the tea-kettle on.

"Now I am going to treat you to tea, mother."

"Do . . . my throat is dry. . . ."

"And what about your people? Have they left you in the lurch?"

"They haven't . . . no. I just stayed behind. They have had a drop too much, and . . . it's better, this way. . . . What would it have been like with them around?"

Glancing at me, she covered her face with her elbow; then spat blood, and smiled bashfully.

"Is this your first one?" I asked.

BIRTH OF A MAN

"The first.... And who are you?"
"A human being, sort of...."
"Of course, a human being! Married?"
"Haven't had the honor...."
"That's not true."
"What do you mean?"
She dropped her eyes, thought awhile, and said:
"And how is it you know about these things?"
This time I decided to lie, and I said:
"I studied these things. I am a student, understand?"
"Yes, yes. Our priest's eldest son is also a student. He studies to be a priest...."
"Yes, that's the kind I am. Well, I'll fetch some water...."

The woman bent her head in the direction of the child, listening to his breathing for a while, then looked off toward the sea.

"I would like to have a wash, too," she said, "but this queer water ... What kind is it? It's salt and bitter...."

"You wash yourself with it; it's good for you!"
"Is it?"
"Sure. It's warmer than the stream; the streams hereabouts are like ice...."
"You know best...."

Here an Abkhasian came riding slowly by, his head drooping sleepily. His small sinewy horse looked at us out of the corner of its round black eye, pricking up its ears. Suddenly it snorted and the rider warily jerked up his head in its shaggy fur cap, looked in our direction too, and dropped his head again.

"How queer people are here, and frightening," said the woman quietly.

I went off. A stream of clear water as alive as quicksilver flowed over the stones, and in it autumn leaves were gaily cavorting. It was wonderful. I washed my hands and face, filled my tea-kettle, and went back. Through the bushes I noticed that the woman was crawling on her knees, casting uneasy glances about her.

"What is it?" I shouted to her.

She turned gray with fright and proceeded to hide something under her skirts. I understood what it was.

"Give it to me," I said; "I'll bury it."

"Oh, dear! But how will you do it? It should be buried in the bath-house entry, under the floor. . . ."

"And how soon do you think they'll build a bath-house here?"

"This is a joke to you, but I am afraid! Maybe, a beast will devour it . . . it must be given back to the earth, you know. . . ."

She turned aside and, handing me a damp, heavy bundle, begged me shamefacedly, under her breath:

"You bury it well, as deep as possible, for Christ's sake. . . . Out of pity for my little son, do it well. . . ."

When I came back, she was returning from the beach. Her gait was unsteady and one of her arms was stretched out in front of her; her skirt was wet up to her waist; her face was somewhat flushed and lit by an inner light, as it were. I helped her to walk to the fire, thinking to myself: "What animal strength!" Then we drank tea with honey and she questioned me gently:

"You've given up school?"

"I have."

"After drinking away everything?"

"Yes, I drank away everything, mother, to the last shred!"

"That is the kind of fellow you are! I remember you; I noticed you at Sukhum when you were arguing with the chief over the food; I thought to myself then: he is afraid of nothing, must be a drunk!"

BIRTH OF A MAN

And appreciatively licking the honey off her swollen lips, she kept glancing at the bush under which the latest addition to the population of Oryol was quietly asleep.

"What will his life be like, I wonder?" she said with a sigh, looking at me. "Here you've helped me, and I thank you for it . . . but is it good for him? I don't know. . . ."

She finished her tea and her food, crossed herself, and while I was getting my things together, she was staring at the ground with her faded eyes, swaying sleepily, and thinking. Then she started getting up.

"Are you really going to walk?" I asked her.

"I am."

"Look out, mother!"

"And what of the Virgin? Let me have him!"

"No, I will carry him."

After some argument she gave in, and we set off, shoulder to shoulder.

"I hope I don't drop," she said, smiling guiltily, and laid her hand on my shoulder.

Meanwhile the new inhabitant of the Russian land, a person with an unknown future, was lying in my arms, breathing noisily like a solid citizen. The sea was splashing and swishing, laced with white shavings; the bushes were whispering to each other; the sun, which had already passed the zenith, was shining.

We were walking, slowly. Now and then the mother would stop to draw a deep breath. She would lift up her head and look about, at the sea, the forest, the mountains, and then she would peer into her son's face. Her eyes, thoroughly washed by tears of suffering, were again amazingly clear, again blossoming and burning with the blue fire of inexhaustible love.

Once, as she halted, she said:

"Lord, dear God! How good it all is, how good! I could

walk like this, I could walk to the end of the world, and he, my little son, would grow, would grow freely amidst plenty, near his mother's breast, my darling. . . ."

. . . The sea was booming. . . .

1912.

GOING HOME

A MIGHTY wind is blowing gustily out of Khiva; it strikes the black mountains of Daghestan, and, thrust back, hits the cold waters of the Caspian, raising a short, jagged wave near the shore.

The sea is heaving with thousands of white hillocks that circle, that dance as though molten glass were fiercely seething in a giant vat. Fishermen describe this game of sea and wind as "huddle."

White spray flies over the sea in muslin clouds, bespattering an aged, two-masted schooner. She is on her way from Persia to Astrakhan with a cargo of dried fruit. She is also carrying about a hundred fisherfolk, people who follow "God's trade."

They all hail from the forests of the upper Volga, a sturdy race, with thews of iron, scorched by hot winds,— seasoned by the bitter brine of the deep, bearded, kindly animals. They are glad to be going home with substantial earnings in their pockets, and they are romping on the deck like bears.

The green body of the sea is seen breathing through the white garments of the waves; the schooner's sharp prow cleaves it like a plow cutting the earth, and plunging into the snowy froth, soaks the slanting jibs in the cold, autumn seas. The sails belly out, their patches crackle, the yards creak, the taut rigging twangs like strings, everything is strained in the forward dash, the clouds too scurry across the sky, the silver sun bathing in them. The sea and the sky are curiously alike, the sky too is seething.

Whistling angrily, the wind wafts over the sea people's voices, thick laughter, the words of a song—they have been singing it for a long while but are still unable to do it properly, in tune. The wind dashes a fine salt spray into the singers' faces, and only now and then is heard the cracked voice of a woman, singing lingeringly and plaintively:

Like a fiery serpent . . .

There is a powerful, sweet odor of dried apricots, even the strong smell of the sea cannot overcome this fragrance.

The boat has already passed Uch Hook, soon Chechen Island will heave into view, a region known to Russians since time immemorial—thence men from Kiev went forth to raid Tabaristan. On the port side, through autumn's transparent blue, the dark mountains of the Caucasus keep looming up and vanishing.

Leaning his broad back against the mainmast, sits a stalwart youth, his cheeks still hairless, wearing a white linen shirt and blue Persian trousers; he has full red lips, the clear, pale-blue eyes of a child, that shine with the intoxication of young joy. His legs are flung wide across the deck, and on his knees lies a young peasant woman. She is one of those employed to gut the fish. She is as large and heavy as he, with a face reddened and roughened by sun and wind; she has large, thick, black eyebrows like the wings of a swallow; her drowsy eyes are half-shut, her head is hanging languidly over the lad's leg, and from the folds of her unbuttoned red bodice rise her breasts, as firm as if they were carved out of bone. . . .

The youth's long, knotty arm is bare to the elbow, and he has laid his broad paw upon her left breast and is heavily stroking the woman's robust body. In his other hand he holds a tin mug of thick wine, from which purple drops fall onto the white breast of his shirt.

Men circle enviously about them, their eyes greedily touching the sprawling woman, while they hold on to the

GOING HOME

caps that the wind is trying to tear from their heads, and wrap their coats about them. Shaggy green waves peer through the railing, now on the right, now on the left; clouds scurry across the motley sky; insatiable gulls are crying; the autumn sun is dancing on the frothy water, now covering it with blue shadows, now kindling all manner of gems in it.

The people on the schooner are shouting, singing, laughing. On a heap of sacks filled with dried fruit lies a large skin of Kakhetian wine, around which huge, bearded peasants are noisily jostling each other. Everything has an air of legendary antiquity about it. One thinks of the return of Stenka Razin from his Persian campaign.

Blue-clad Persian seamen, with the bony look of camels, are watching the merry-making of the Russian folk, and bare their pearly teeth in friendly grins—the sleepy eyes of the men of the East glow with strange smiles.

A sullen old man, rumpled by the wind, with a crooked nose protruding from the hairy face of a sorcerer, stumbles over the woman's foot as he passes by the couple. He stops, shakes his head with a vigor unusual for an old man, and shouts:

"Devil take you! What are you blocking the way for! The shameless creature, look at her, faugh!"

The woman does not even budge, does not so much as open her eyes, only her lips quiver slightly, and the lad, straightening up, sets the mug down on the deck, places the other hand too on the woman's breast, and says firmly:

"What, Yakim Petrov, you're envious? Be off with you! Don't burst with envy, don't pine in vain. This sugar isn't for your tooth."

He lifts his paws and placing them again on the woman's breast, he says triumphantly:

"We'll nurse the whole of Russia!"—

At this the woman gives a slow smile, and just then

everything, the schooner and all the people on it, heave up, like one swelling breast, a wave crashes against the side of the boat and splashes everybody, including the woman, with salty spray. Then she half-opens her dark eyes, casts a friendly glance at the old man, the lad, and everything about her, and unhurriedly starts to cover herself.

"Don't," says the lad, seizing her hands. "Let them look. Don't begrudge it to them."

Astern, men and women are playing a dance-tune. A clear, thrilling, young voice sings in rapid tempo:

> I do not want your silver and gold;
> My darling's more precious than wealth untold . . .

Boots are thumping on the deck, someone is hooting like a huge owl, a triangle chimes thinly, Kalmuck pipes are sounding, and a woman's voice, rising higher and higher, sings gaily:

> Wolves are howling in the wood,
> Howling because hunger hurts;
> Father-in-law should be their food,
> Then he'd get his just deserts!

People are shrieking with laughter, and someone shouts deafeningly:

"How do you like it, old men?"

The wind is sowing the waves with holiday laughter.

The stalwart youth has lazily covered the woman's breast with the skirt of his coat, and meditatively rolling his round, childlike eyes, he says, looking ahead of him:

"When we get home we'll make things hum! Oh, Marya, won't we make things hum!"

On fiery wings the sun is flying westward. The clouds chase it, and unable to overtake it, settle in snowy hills upon the black ribs of the mountains.

1912.

LULLABY

ONE sultry summer night, in an out-of-the-way alley on the outskirts of the town, I saw a strange sight. A woman, standing in the middle of an enormous puddle, was stamping her feet, splashing the mud as little boys do— she was stamping and singing a bawdy song in a nasal voice.

During the day a storm had swept mightily over the town. The heavy downpour had turned the clayey earth of the alley into mud. The puddle was deep. The woman was almost up to her knees in it. To judge by her voice, the singer was drunk. If, tired with dancing, she had dropped, she might easily have drowned in the liquid mud.

I pulled up my high boots, got into the puddle, grabbed her by the arms and dragged her to a dry spot. At first, apparently, she was scared. She followed me obediently, without a word. But then with a vigorous movement of her whole body she wrenched her right arm free, struck me on the chest, and screamed: "Help!"

Then she resolutely made for the puddle again, dragging me with her.

"You devil!" she mumbled, "I won't go! I'll get along without you. . . . You get on without me. . . . He-elp!"

The night watchman emerged from the darkness, stopped five steps away from us and asked in a surly tone:

"Who's making that racket there?"

I told him that I was afraid the woman would drown in the mud, and that I wanted to pull her out. The watchman looked closely at the drunken woman, spat noisily, and commanded:

"Mashka, come on out."

"I won't."

"And I'm telling you, come on out!"

"I won't do it."

"I'll give you a beating, you slut!" the watchman promised her without enmity, and turned to me affably. "She lives around here—she picks oakum for a living. Mashka's her name. Got a smoke?"

We lit cigarettes. The woman was bravely striding through the puddle, shouting now and then:

"Bosses! I'm my own boss! I'll take a bath here, if I want to."

"I'll give you a bath!" the watchman—a sturdy, bearded old man—warned her. "That's the way she carries on almost every night, and she has a crippled son at home."

"Does she live far from here?"

"She ought to be shot," said the watchman, without answering me.

"She ought to be taken home," I suggested.

The watchman sniggered in his beard, held his cigarette up to my face, and clumped away on the soggy path.

"Take her, but look at her mug first."

Meanwhile the woman sat down in the mud, paddling it with her hands, and squawked fiercely in a nasal voice:

> Over the dee-eep sea-ea-ea. . . .

Not far from where she sat, a huge star was reflected from the black emptiness above us in the greasy muddy water. When a ripple ran across the puddle, the reflection vanished. Again I stepped into the puddle, took the singer by the arm-pits, lifted her, and shoving her with my knees, led her over to the fence. She held back, waved her arms, and challenged me:

"Well, hit me, hit me! Never mind! Hit me! Ah, you beast! Ah, you butcher! Go ahead, hit me!"

Propping her against the fence, I asked her where she lived. She lifted her drunken head and looked at me out of the dark spots that were her eyes. I noticed that her nose had caved in and what was left of it stuck out like a button, that her upper lip, pulled askew by a scar, bared small teeth, and that her little bloated face wore a repellent smile.

"All right, let's go," she said.

We walked on, lurching against the fence. The wet hem of her skirt kept slapping across my legs.

"Come, dear," she mumbled, as though sobering up. "I'll let you in, I'll comfort you."

She brought me into the court-yard of a large, two-story house. Carefully, like one blind, she walked among the carts, barrels, boxes, and piles of firewood, stopped before a hole in the foundation, and invited me:

"Go in."

Holding on to the slimey wall, grasping the woman by her waist, hardly able to keep her sprawling body together, I lowered myself down the slippery steps, found the felt strip and the latch of the door, opened it, and stood on the threshold of a black pit without having the courage to go further.

"Mammy, is it you?" a soft voice asked in the dark.

"It's me."

A warm stench of decay and a smell of tar struck my nostrils. A match was lit and for a second the small flame illumined a pale childish face, and then went out.

"Who else would be coming to you? It's me," said the woman, swaying against me.

Another match was struck, there was a clink of glass and a thin funny hand lit a small tin lamp.

"Darling," said the woman, and swaying, tumbled into the corner. There, hardly raised above the brick floor, was a wide bed.

Watching the flame of the lamp closely, the child adjusted the wick as it began to smoke. He had a grave little face with a sharp nose and full lips like a girl's. It was a little face that looked as though it were painted with a fine brush, and it was startlingly out of place in this dark damp hole. Having taken care of the lamp, he looked at me with eyes so heavily fringed that they looked shaggy, and asked:

"She drunk?"

His mother, who lay across the bed, was hiccuping and snoring.

"She ought to be undressed," I said.

"Undress her," the boy replied, lowering his eyes. And when I began to pull the wet skirt off the woman, he asked quietly and in a businesslike fashion:

"The lamp—shall I put it out?"

"What for?"

He did not answer. While I was handling his mother like a sack of flour, I was watching him. He sat on the floor in a box made of heavy boards on which there was an inscription in black letters: "Handle with care. N. R. and Co." The sill of the square window was flush with the boy's shoulder. Against the wall there were several narrow shelves, on which cigarette and match-boxes were piled. Next to the box in which the boy sat there was another one, covered with yellow paper, which apparently served as a table. His funny pitiful hands behind his neck, the boy was looking up at the dark windowpanes.

Having undressed the woman, I threw her wet clothes on the stove. I washed my hands in the earthenware washbasin in the corner, and wiping them on a handkerchief, I said to the child:

"Well, now, good-by."

He looked at me, and, speaking with a slight lisp, asked:

"Now shall I put out the lamp?"

"If you like."

LULLABY

"And you—are you going away? Aren't you going to bed?"

With his little hand he pointed to his mother: "With her."

"What for?" I asked stupidly, surprised.

"You know, yourself," he said with terrible simplicity, and, stretching himself, added:

"They all do it."

Abashed, I looked about me. To the right, there was the mouth of an ugly stove, on the hearth were dirty dishes, in the corner behind the box—pieces of tarred rope and a pile of picked oakum, logs of firewood, kindling, and a yoke for carrying pails of water. At my feet stretched a snoring yellow form.

"May I sit with you awhile?" I asked the boy.

He looked at me from under his brows.

"But she won't wake up till morning."

"But I don't need her."

Squatting beside his box, I told him how I had come across his mother, trying to present the matter in a comic light:

"She was sitting in the mud, paddling with her hands and singing. . . ."

He nodded his head, smiling a pale smile and scratching his narrow chest.

"She was drunk, that's why. Even when she's sober, she likes to carry on. Just like a child. . . ."

Now I was able to see his eyes clearly. His eyelashes were astonishingly long, and his eyelids too were thickly covered with beautifully curved little hairs. The blueish shadows under his eyes added to the pallor of his bloodless skin; his high forehead with a wrinkle above the nose was surmounted by a shock of curly reddish hair. The expression of his eyes, which were both attentive and calm, was indescribable, and it was with difficulty that I bore this strange inhuman gaze.

"Your legs—what's wrong with them?"

He fumbled with the rags, disengaging a withered leg which looked like a cabbage-stalk, lifted it with his hand and placed it on the edge of the box.

"That's the sort they are. Both of them. Since I was born. They won't walk, they're not alive—that's how it is."

"And what's in these boxes?"

"A menagerie," he answered, lifted his leg in his hand as though it were a stick, stuck it into the rags on the bottom of the box, and with a serene, friendly smile, offered:

"Shall I show it to you? Well, make yourself comfortable. You've never seen anything like it."

Maneuvering adroitly with his extraordinarily long, thin arms, he hoisted himself up, and began to remove boxes from the shelves, handing them to me one after another.

"Take care, don't open them, or they'll run away. Put one to your ear and listen. Well?"

"Something's moving."

"Aha, a spider's sitting there, the scoundrel! His name is Drummer. He's a smart fellow!"

The boy's marvelous eyes grew lively and tender. A smile was playing over his livid face. With rapid movements of his nimble hands he was removing boxes from the shelves, putting them first to his ear, then to mine, and talking to me animatedly.

"And here is Anisim the cockroach, a show-off like a soldier. And this is a fly, an inspector's wife, a bad lot, the worst ever! She buzzes all day long, scolds everybody, she even pulled Mammy by the hair. Not a fly, but an inspector's wife, and her rooms have windows on the street. She only looks like a fly. And this is a black cockroach, a huge one: Master. He's all right. Only he's a drunk and has no shame. He'll get tight and crawl around the court-yard naked and as shaggy as a black dog. And here's a bug: Uncle Nikodim. I caught him in the court-yard. He is a pilgrim, one of the crooks—makes believe he collects for the Church. Mammy calls him 'Cheat.' He is her lover too. She has more lovers than you can count, thick as flies, even if she has no nose."

"She doesn't beat you?"

"She? You're crazy. She can't live without me. She has a good heart, only she drinks. But on our street everybody drinks. She's pretty, and jolly too. . . . Only she drinks, the slut. I tell her: 'Stop swilling vodka, you fool, then you'll get rich,' and she laughs at me. A woman—foolish, of course. But she's a good egg. Well, she'll sleep it off and you'll see for yourself."

He was smiling so enchantingly that you wanted to howl with unbearable burning pity for him, to cry out so that the whole town would hear you. His beautiful little head swayed on its thin neck like a strange flower, and his eyes blazed with growing animation, attracting me with irresistible power.

As I listened to his childish but terrible chatter, for a moment I forgot where I was sitting. Then suddenly I saw again the small prison window, spattered on the outside with mud, the black mouth of the stove, the heap of oakum in the corner and near the door on a pile of rags the body of the woman, the mother, yellow as butter.

"A good menagerie?" the boy asked proudly.

"Very good."

"But I haven't one butterfly, nor any moths, either."

"What's your name?"

"Lenka."

"You're my name-sake."

"Really? And you—what kind of a man are you?"

"No kind."

"Oh, you're lying. Everybody's something. I know that. You're a good chap."

"Perhaps."

"Oh, I can see. You're a 'fraidy-cat, too."

"What makes you say that?"

"Oh, I know." He smiled slyly and even winked at me.

"Why do you think so?"

"Well, you sit here with me, that means you're afraid to go home at night."

"But it's already daybreak."

"So you're going?"

"I'll come back."

He wouldn't believe me. He covered his dear shaggy eyes with his lashes and, after a pause, said:

"What for?"

"Why, just to see you. You're an interesting fellow. May I come?"

"Sure. Everybody comes here." With a sigh, he added: "You're fooling me."

"I swear I'll come."

"Do come. And come to see me, not Mammy, deuce take her. Let's you and I be friends, eh?"

"All right."

"Very well. It doesn't matter that you're big. How old are you?"

"Twenty."

"And I'm eleven. I haven't any chums. Only Katka, the water-carrier's daughter. Her mother beats her because she comes to see me. . . . Are you a thief?"

"No. Why a thief?"

"Your mug, it's terrible. Skinny. And you have a nose like a thief's. A couple of thieves come here. One, Sashka, is a fool and nasty. The other, Vanichka, he's kind, he's kind as a dog. Have you got any little boxes?"

"I'll bring you some."

"Do. I won't tell Mammy that you're coming."

"Why not?"

"I just won't. She's always glad when men come. Why, she loves men, the bitch. It's simply awful. She's a funny girl, my Mammy. At fifteen she managed to have me, she herself doesn't know how it happened. When will you come?"

"Tomorrow evening."

"In the evening? Then she'll be drunk. And what do you do, if you're not a thief?"

"I sell Bavarian kvass."

"Yes? Bring me a bottle, will you?"

"Sure. I'll bring one. Well, I must be going."

"Run along. Will you come?"

"Positively."

He stretched both his long hands out towards me, and I pressed and shook those thin chilly bones, and without looking back, I climbed out into the yard like one drunk.

Dawn was breaking. Over the damp pile of half dilapidated buildings Venus was trembling as it faded away. From the dirty pit under the wall of the house the panes of the cellar window stared at me with their square eyes, murky and stained like the eyes of a drunkard. In a cart by the gate a red-faced peasant was asleep with his huge bare feet flung wide apart. His thick rough beard stuck up towards the sky, and white teeth glistened in it. It looked as though the peasant were laughing sarcastically with his eyes closed. An old dog with a bald spot on its back, apparently the result of a scald, ambled over to me, sniffed at my leg and howled gently and hungrily, filling my heart with futile pity for it. The morning sky, pale and pink, was reflected in the placid puddles, and these reflections lent the filthy puddles an unnecessary, insulting beauty which debauched the soul.

. . . .

The following day I asked the boys on my block to catch some bugs and butterflies. I bought pretty little boxes at the apothecary's, and I went to see Lenka, taking along two bottles of kvass, some gingerbread, candy, and sweet rolls. Lenka received my gifts with vast amazement, opening his darling eyes wide. By daylight they were even more marvelous.

"Oh, oh, oh!" he cried out, in a low unchildlike voice. "All the things you've brought! Are you rich? How's that —rich, but badly dressed, and you say you're not a thief! And the little boxes! Oh, oh, oh! It's a shame to touch them. My hands aren't clean. Who's in here? Aha, a bug! Looks like copper, green, even. Oh, you devil! And will they run out and fly away? Goodness me!"

And suddenly he shouted gaily:

"Mom! Climb down and wash my hands. And look, you goose, what he has brought me! It's the same fellow, the one who dragged you here last night, like a policeman, it's the same one. His name is Lenka, too."

"You must thank him," I heard a strange low voice behind me.

The boy nodded his head rapidly.

"Thank you. Thank you."

A thick cloud of fibrous dust was floating through the cellar, and with difficulty I distinguished on the stove the disheveled head, the disfigured face of the woman, the gleam of her teeth, the involuntary, indestructible smile.

"How do you do?"

"How do you do?" the woman repeated. Her nasal voice sounded muffled but jaunty, almost cheerful. She looked at me squinting and mockingly, as it were.

Lenka, oblivious of me, munched the gingerbread and hummed, as he carefully opened the boxes. His eyelashes cast a shadow on his cheeks, emphasizing the rings under his eyes. The sun, dull, like the face of an old man, peered through the dirty windowpanes, and a mild light fell upon the boy's reddish hair. His shirt was unbuttoned, showing his chest, and I saw how the heart was beating behind the thin bones, lifting the skin and the barely perceptible nipple.

His mother climbed down from the stove, moistened a towel in the wash-basin, and coming over to Lenka took his left hand.

"He's run away! Stop him! He's run away!" he shouted. And with his whole body he began to thresh about in the box, throwing the smelly rags around, baring his blue inert legs. The woman burst out laughing, fumbling among the rags, and shouted too:

"Catch him!"

Having caught the bug, she placed him on her palm, examined him with her lively eyes, the color of a cornflower, and said to me in the tone of an old acquaintance:

"There are lots of those."

"Don't you crush it!" her son warned her sternly. "Once when she was drunk she sat on my menagerie—and crushed a lot of them!"

"Try and forget it, darling."

"I had to do a lot of burying. . . ."

"But I caught some others for you afterwards."

"Others! The ones you crushed were trained ones, sillybilly! The ones that croaked I buried under the stove; I'd crawl out and bury them—I have a cemetery there. You know, I once had a spider, Minka, he looked just like one of Mammy's lovers, the one who's in prison, the fat jolly one. . . ."

"Oh, my precious darling," said the woman, stroking her son's curls with a small, dark stumpy-fingered hand. Then, nudging me with her elbow, she asked, her eyes smiling:

"He's pretty, my little son? Look at those eyes, eh?"

"You can have one of my eyes, but give me legs," suggested Lenka, smiling and examining a bug. "He's an . . . iron one! So fat! Mom, he looks like the monk, the one for whom you made the ladder—remember?"

"Sure I do."

And laughingly she told me this:

"You see, a monk barged in here once, a bulky man, and says: 'See here, you're an oakum-picker, can you make me a rope ladder?' And I, I'd never heard of such ladders. 'No,' says I, 'I can't.' 'Then I'll teach you,' says he. He opened his cassock and there was a long strong thinnish rope all round his belly He taught me. I twist it and twist it and think to myself: what does he want it for? Perhaps he wants to rob a church."

She laughed aloud, hugging her son's shoulders, stroking him all the while.

"Oh, these cunning fellows! He came when he said he would, and I said to him: 'Here, if this is to steal with, I won't have anything to do with it.' And he laughs slyly. 'No,' he says, 'that's for climbing over a wall. We have a great high wall, and we're sinful folk, and the sin is on the other side of the wall—understand?' Well, I understood. He needed it to go to women at night. He and I had a laugh together over it."

"You certainly like to laugh," the boy said, in the tone of an older person. "You'd better heat the samovar."

"But we haven't any sugar."

"Go buy some."

"But we haven't any money."

"All because you're such a guzzler. Get some from him."

He turned to me.

"Got money?"

I gave the woman some money. She jumped to her feet, took from the stove a little battered tarnished samovar and disappeared behind the door, humming through her nose.

LULLABY

"Mom!" her son shouted after her. "Wash the window. I can't see anything! A smart little baggage, I'm telling you," he continued, carefully placing the boxes of insects on the shelves. They were of cardboard and suspended on strings from nails driven into the cracks between the bricks of the damp wall. "A worker . . . When once she starts picking oakum, she raises such a dust that you almost choke. I shout: 'Mammy, carry me out into the court-yard or I'll choke here.' But she says: 'Have patience. I'll be lonesome without you.' She loves me, and that's all there is to it. She picks and sings. She knows a thousand songs."

Full of eagerness, his marvelous eyes flashing, he raised his thick eyebrows and sang in a hoarse alto:

> Arina lay on a featherbed . . .

I listened for a while, then I said:
"A very dirty song."
"They're all like that," Lenka declared with assurance. Suddenly he started. "Listen! There's the music! Quick, lift me up!"

I lifted his light little bones in their bag of thin gray skin. Eagerly he stuck his head out of the open window, and grew still, while his withered legs swung impotently, scraping against the wall. In the court-yard a barrel-organ squeaked irritatedly, spitting out shreds of melody. A deep-voiced child cried merrily, and a dog howled. Lenka listened to this music and hummed gently through his teeth in time with it.

The dust in the cellar settled, and the place grew lighter. A cheap clock hung over his mother's bed; the pendulum, the size of a copper coin, crawled limpingly. The dishes on the hearth were dirty, a thick layer of dust rested on everything, particularly in the corners, where the cobwebs hung in dirty shreds. Lenka's home resembled a garbage pit, and the ugliness of poverty stared from every inch of it, wounding the senses.

The samovar began to drone gloomily, a hoarse voice roared: "Get out!" and the barrel-organ suddenly grew silent.

"Take me back," said Lenka with a sigh, "they have chased them off. . . ."

I seated him in the box, and frowning and rubbing his chest with his hands, he coughed cautiously.

"My chest hurts me, it isn't good for me to breathe real air for long. Listen, have you ever seen devils?"

"No."

"I haven't either. At night I keep looking under the stove—maybe one will show up. But they don't. There are devils in cemeteries, aren't there?"

"What do you want them for?"

"It's interesting. And what if one of them turns out to be kind? Katka, the water-carrier's girl, once saw a little devil in a cellar—only she got frightened. Me, I'm not afraid of scary things."

He wrapped his legs up in the rags and continued pertly:

"I even like scary dreams, I do really. Once in my dream I saw a tree growing upside down: the leaves were on the ground, and the roots stuck up into the sky. I got into a sweat, and woke up from fright. And once I saw Mammy: there she lies naked, and a dog is gnawing at her belly; the dog takes a bite, and spits it out, takes a bite, and spits it out. And once, our house suddenly shook itself and started to move down the street; it glided along banging the doors and windows, and behind it ran the cat of the Inspector's wife. . . ."

He hunched his sharp little shoulders as if he were chilly, took a candy, unfolded the colored paper wrapper and carefully smoothing it out, placed it on the window-sill.

"I'll make something with these wrappers, something

nice. Or I'll give them to Katka. She likes nice things too: pieces of glass, bits of crockery, paper, and things like that. And listen: if you kept on feeding a cockroach, would it grow to be the size of a horse?"

It was clear that he believed this to be true, so I said:
"If you feed it well, it will."

"Of course!" he cried out joyfully. "But Mammy, the silly, laughs at me."

And he added a bawdy word, insulting to a woman.

"She's foolish! And as for a cat, you can feed it up so it gets to be the size of a horse in no time—isn't that so?"

"Why, yes, that's possible."

"It's a pity, I haven't enough feed! That would be great!"

He fairly shook with excitement, pressing his hand to his chest.

"There would be flies the size of a dog! And cockroaches could be used to cart bricks—if it's the size of a horse, it must be strong, eh?"

"But you see they have whiskers."

"There's nothing wrong with whiskers—they'd be like reins, the whiskers. Or else, you'd have a spider, as enormous as what? A spider the size of a kitten, even that would be frightful. If only I had legs! I'd work real hard, and I'd feed up my whole menagerie. I'd go into business, and I'd buy a house for Mammy in the green fields. Have you ever been in the green fields?"

"Sure."

"Tell me about it, will you?"

I began to tell him about fields and meadows. He listened eagerly without interrupting, his eyelashes dropped over his eyes and his little mouth opened slowly as though he were falling asleep. Seeing this, I began to speak more quietly. But his mother came in with the boiling samovar in her hands, a paper bag under her arm, and a bottle of vodka tucked in her breast.

"Here I am."

"I liked that," sighed the boy, opening his eyes wide. "An empty place—just nothing but grass and flowers. Mammy, why don't you get a carriage and take me to the green fields? This way I'll croak, and I'll never see them. My word, Mammy, but you're a bitch," he concluded, in a sad abused tone.

His mother chided him tenderly:

"Don't you swear, you mustn't. You're still little. . . ."

" 'Don't swear!' It's all very well for you: you go where you please, just like a dog. You're a lucky one. Listen—" he turned to me—"did God make the green fields?"

"Certainly."

"Well, what for?"

"So people can go out on a jaunt."

"Green fields," said the boy, smiling pensively and sighing. "I would take my menagerie there, and I would let them all loose—run along, brothers! Listen: where do they make God—at the poor-house?" *

His mother shrieked and was literally bowled over with laughter. She fell upon the bed and shouted, kicking her legs.

"Good Lord! What a . . . Darling! Why, the icon-painters. . . . It's side-splitting! He's the limit!"

Lenka looked at her with a smile, and swore at her tenderly in filthy language.

"She carries on like a child. Doesn't she love to laugh!"

And he repeated the dirty word.

"Let her laugh," I said. "You don't mind."

"No, I don't," Lenka agreed. "I'm only angry at her when she doesn't wash the window. I beg her and beg her: clean the window, I can't see God's light. But she keeps on forgetting."

* The Russian word for poor-house contains a pun which might suggest this idea to an imaginative child.

The woman, chuckling now and then, washed the tea-things, winked at me with her light blue eyes, and said:

"Haven't I a pretty darling? If it weren't for him, I'd have drowned myself long ago, I swear. I'd have strangled myself."

She said this with a smile.

Suddenly Lenka asked me:

"Are you a fool?"

"I don't know. Why?"

"Mammy says you're a fool."

"But why do I say it?" the woman exclaimed, undaunted. "He brings a drunken woman in from the street, puts her to bed, and goes off, there you have it. I didn't mean any harm. And you, you have to tell on me. Oh, you're mean!"

She too spoke like a child. Her manner of speech was that of a girl in her teens. And her eyes too had a girlish purity, which made her face, with its stump of a nose, its drawn lip and bared teeth, look all the more hideous. Her face showed a constant nightmarish sneer, but it was a jolly sneer.

"Well, let's have tea," she offered solemnly.

The samovar stood on a box beside Lenka. A roguish jet of steam coming out from under the battered lid touched his shoulder. He put his little hand against it and when his palm grew moist, wiped it on his hair, screwing up his eyes dreamily.

"When I grow up," he said, "Mammy will make me a carriage. I'll crawl in the streets and beg alms. When they've given me enough, I'll crawl out into the green fields."

"Ho-ho!" sighed his mother, and directly after, laughed gently. "The country's paradise to him, the darling. But what do you find in the country? Camps, and beastly soldiers, and drunken peasants."

"You're lying," Lenka stopped her, frowning. "Ask him what the country's like: he's seen it."

"And I—haven't I seen it?"

"Yes, when you were drunk."

They began to argue just like children, with as much heat and lack of logic. Meanwhile the warm evening had invaded the court-yard, a thick, dove-colored cloud hung motionless in the reddened sky. It was getting dark in the cellar.

The boy drank a cup of tea, began to perspire, looked at me and at his mother, and said:

"I've eaten, I've drunk, now, by God, I'm sleepy."

"Go to sleep," his mother advised him.

"And he—he'll go. Will you go?"

"Don't worry, I won't let him go," the woman said, nudging me with her knee.

"Don't you go," Lenka begged, closed his eyes, and, stretching cozily, sank into the box. Then suddenly he lifted his head and said to his mother reproachfully:

"Why don't you marry him? And have a wedding like other women? This way you take up with all sorts . . . they only beat you. . . . But he—he's good."

"Hush, go to sleep," the woman said quietly, bending over her cup of tea.

"He's rich."

For a while the woman sat silent, sipping her tea from the saucer with clumsy lips. Then she turned to me as to an old acquaintance.

"That's the way we live, quietly, he and I, and nobody else. In the court-yard they scold me, call me a loose woman. Well, I'm not ashamed before anybody. Besides, you see what a mess I am, everyone sees right away what I'm good for. Yes. Sonny is asleep, the darling. I have a good child, eh?"

"Yes, very."

LULLABY

"I can't look at him enough. And what a head he has!"

"Yes, he's a clever boy."

"That's true. His father was a gentleman, an old man. He was a—what-do-you-call-'em? They have offices— God, I can't think . . . they're busy with papers. . . ."

"You mean a notary public?"

"Yes, that's right! He was a dear old man. So kind. He loved me. I was a servant in the house."

She covered her son's bare legs with the rags, straightened the dingy pillow under his head, and continued casually:

"And then he died suddenly. It was at night. I had just left him when he dropped to the floor, and that was the end of him. You sell kvass?"

"Yes."

"In business for yourself?"

"No. I work for someone."

She moved closer to me, saying:

"Don't turn up your nose at me, young man. You can't catch it from me any more. Ask anybody in the street. They all know."

"I'm not turning up my nose at you."

Placing on my knee her little hand, the skin of the fingers work-worn and the nails broken, she continued affectionately:

"I'm so grateful to you on Lenka's account. He's had a holiday today. It was good of you."

"I have to go," I said.

"Where to?" she asked in surprise.

"I've something to attend to."

"Stay."

"I can't."

She looked at her son, at the window, at the sky, and said softly:

"Do stay. I'll cover my mug with a kerchief. . . . I do

so want to thank you on my son's account. I'll cover up, eh?"

She spoke persuasively, humanly, so affectionately, with such warm feeling. And her eyes, a child's eyes in a hideous face, shone with the smile not of a beggar, but of a person of wealth who can show gratitude in a substantial way.

"Mom," the boy cried suddenly, starting, and hitching himself up. "They're crawling! Mom, come!"

"He's dreaming," she said to me, bending over him.

I went out into the court-yard, and stood there, thinking. A nasal voice was pouring from the open window of the cellar singing a song with a jolly tune. The mother was singing a strange lullaby to her son, uttering the words distinctly:

> The passions will come, and bring
> Every unhappy thing,
> Troubles that turn the wits
> And tear the heart to bits,
> Troubles and grief and care!
> Where shall we hide, ah, where?

I walked quickly out of the court-yard, gritting my teeth so as not to bawl.

1917.

THE HERMIT

THE forest ravine slopes gently down to the yellow waters of the Oka; a brook rushes along its bottom, hiding in the grass; above the ravine, unnoticed by day and tremulous by night, flows the blue river of the sky—the stars play in it like golden minnows. Rank, tangled underbrush grows on the southeastern bank of the ravine. Under the steep side of it, in the thicket, a cave is dug out, closed by a door made of branches, ingeniously tied together; before the door is an earthen platform about seven feet square, buttressed by cobbles. From it, heavy boulders descend in a stairway towards the brook. Three young trees grow in front of the cave: a lime, a birch, and a maple.

Everything around the cave is made sturdily and with care, as though it were fashioned to last a life-time. The interior has the same air of sturdiness: the sides and the vault are covered with mats made of willow withies; the mats are plastered with clay mixed with the silt of the brook; a small stove rises to the left of the entrance; in the corner is an altar, covered by heavy matting which does for brocade; on the altar, in an iron sconce, is an oil-burner; its bluish flame flickers in the dusk and is hardly visible.

Three black icons stand behind the altar; bundles of new bast shoes hang on the walls; strips of bast lie about on the floor. The cave is permeated with the sweet smell of dry herbs.

The owner of this abode is an old man of middle height, thick-set, but crumpled and misshapen. His face, red as a brick, is hideous. A deep scar runs across the left cheek from ear to chin, giving a twist to his mouth and lending it an expression of painful scorn. The dark eyes are ravaged by trachoma; they are without lashes and have red scars instead of lids; the hair on the head has fallen out in tufts and there are two bald patches on the bumpy skull, a small one on the crown, and another which has laid bare the left ear. In spite of all this the old man is spry and nimble as a polecat; his naked, disfigured eyes have a kindly look; when he laughs, the blemishes of his face almost vanish in the soft abundance of his wrinkles. He wears a good shirt of unbleached linen, blue calico trousers and slippers made of cord. His legs are wrapped in hareskins instead of leggings.

I came to him on a bright May day and we made friends at once. He had me stay the night, and on my second visit told me the story of his life.

"I was a sawyer," he said, lying under an elder-bush, having pulled off his shirt to warm his chest, muscular as a youngster's, in the sun. "For seventeen years I sawed logs; see the mess a saw made of my face! That's what they called me, Savel the Sawyer. Sawing is no light job, my friend—you stand there, waving your hands about in the sky, a net over your face, logs over your head and the sawdust so thick you can't see, ugh! I was a gay lad, a playful one, and I lived like a tumbler. There is, you know, a certain type of pigeon: they soar as high up as they can into the sky, into the utmost depth and there they fold their wings, tuck their heads under them—and bang! down they come! Some get killed that way, hitting the roofs, or the ground. Well, that's what I was like. Gay and harmless, a blessed one; women, girls were as fond of me as of sugar, 'pon my word! What a life it was! It does one good to remember it. . . ."

And rolling from side to side he laughed the clear laughter of youth, except for a slight rattle in the throat, and the brook echoed his laugh. The wind breathed warmly, golden reflections glided on the velvety surface of the spring foliage.

"Well, let's have a go at it, friend," Savel suggested. "Bring it on!"

I went to the brook, where a bottle of vodka had been put to cool and we each had a glass, following it up with pretzels and fish. The old man chuckled with rapture.

"A fine invention that, drink!" And passing his tongue over his gray, tousled mustache: "A fine thing! Can't do with a lot of it, but in small quantities it's great! They say the devil was first to make vodka. Well, I'll say thanks even to the devil for a good thing."

He half-closed his eyes, remained silent for a moment and then exclaimed, indignantly:

"Yes, they did hurt me to the core, all the same, they did. Ah, friend, how people have grown into the habit of hurting one another, it's a shame! Conscience lives among us like a homeless pup, it does! It isn't welcome anywhere. Well, never mind, I'll go on with my story. I married and all was as it should be; the wife was called Natalia, a beautiful, soft creature. I got on with her all right; she was a bit of a philanderer, but I'm not all too virtuous myself, not exactly a stay at home, and when there is a nicer, kinder woman about, to her I go. That is all only too human, there's no running away from it, and in one's lusty years, what better can one do? At times when I returned home bringing some money or other goods with me, people would laugh! 'Savel, you should tie your wife's skirts before you leave your house!' Jeering, they were. Well, for decency's sake, I'd beat her a bit and then give her a present to make up for it and just scold her gently: 'You fool,' I'd say, 'why do you make people laugh at me? Am I not your pal, instead of your enemy?' She'd cry, of course, and say they were lying. I know, too, that people are fond of lies, but you can't fool me, all the same: the night gives away the truth about a woman—you can feel it, at night, if she's been in another man's arms or not."

Something rustled in the bushes behind him.

"Ps-sh!" the old man shook a branch of the elder. "A hedgehog lives right here, I pricked my foot on it the other day as I went to wash in the brook; I did not see it in the grass and the needle went straight into my toe."

He smiled as he looked at the bush and then, straightening himself out, went on.

"Yes, friend. So I was saying how deeply they had hurt me, yes, how deeply. I had a daughter, Tasha, Tatyana. I may say in a word, without boasting, she was a joy to the whole world, that daughter. A star. I used to dress her up in fine clothes—a heavenly beauty she was when she came out on a holiday. Her gait, her bearing, her eyes . . . Our teacher Kuzmin—Trunk was his nickname, for he was a clumsy-looking chap—called her by some whimsical name, and when he got drunk he would weep and beg me to take care of her. So I did. But luck had always favored me—and that never makes one popular with other men, it just breeds envy. So the rumor was spread, that Tasha and I . . ."

He fidgeted uneasily on the grass, took his shirt from the bush, put it on and carefully buttoned up the collar. His face twitched nervously, he pressed his lips together and the sparse bristles of his gray brows descended on the naked eyes.

Twilight was setting in. There was a freshness in the air. A quail was crying shrilly close by: "Pit-pit . . . wet my lip . . ." The old man was peering down into the ravine.

"Well, so that set the ball rolling. Kuzmin, the priest, the clerk, some of the men and most of the women began wagging their tongues, hissing and hooting and hauling a man over the coals. It is always a treat for us to bait a

THE HERMIT

man; we love it. Tasha sat weeping, unable to leave the house, for fear of the jeering of street urchins—everybody was having the time of their lives. So I said to Tasha: 'Come, let us leave.'"

"And your wife?"

"The wife?" the old man repeated with astonishment. "But she was dead by then. She just gave a sigh and died one night. Yes—yes. That was long before all this happened. Tasha was only twelve. . . . She was my enemy, a bad woman, unfaithful."

"But you were praising her a moment ago," I reminded him. This did not embarrass him at all. He scratched his neck, lifted his beard with his palm and gazing at it, said calmly:

"Well, what if I did praise her? No one remains bad all his life, and even a bad person is often worthy of praise. A human being is not a stone and even a stone changes with time. Do not, however, get any wrong ideas into your head—she died a natural death, all right. It must have been her heart, her heart played tricks on her. Sometimes at night we would be having a bit of fun and she would suddenly go off in a dead faint. Quite terrible it was!"

His soft husky voice had a melodious sound; it mingled tirelessly and intimately in the warm evening air with the smell of grass, the sighs of the wind, the rustle of leaves, the soft patter of the brook on the pebbles. Had he kept still, the night would not have been so complete, so beautiful, so sweet to the soul.

Savel spoke with a remarkable ease, showing no effort in finding the right words, dressing up his thoughts lovingly, as a little girl does her dolls. I had listened to many a Russian talker, men who, intoxicated with flowery words, often, almost always, lose the fine thread of truth in the intricate web of speech. This one spun his yarn with such convincing simplicity, with such limpid sincerity, that I feared to interrupt him with questions. Watching the play of his words, I realized that the old man was the possessor of living gems, able to conceal all filthy and criminal lies with their bewitching power; I realized all that and nevertheless yielded to the magic of his speech.

"The whole dirty business began then, my friend: a doctor was summoned, he examined Tasha thoroughly with his shameless eyes, and he had another fop with him, a baldish man with gold buttons—an investigator, I suppose, asking questions: as to who and when? She just kept silent, she was so ashamed. They arrested me and took me to the district prison. There I sat. The bald one says to me: 'Confess and you'll get off lightly!' So I reply obligingly: 'Let me go to Kiev, Your Honor, to the holy relics, and pray for the forgiveness of my sins!' 'Ah,' he said, 'now you've confessed all right!' Believing he'd caught me, the bald cat! I hadn't confessed anything, of course, just dropped the words from sheer boredom. I was very bored in jail, uncomfortable, too, what with the thieves and murderers and other foul people around; besides, I couldn't help wondering what they were doing to Tasha. The whole blasted business lasted over a year before the trial came. And then, behold, Tasha appeared at it, with gloves and smart little boots and all—very unusual! A blue frock like a cloud—her soul shining through it. All the jury staring at her and the crowd and all of it just like a dream, my friend. At Tanya's side—Madame Antzyferova, our lady of the manor, a woman sharp as a pike, sly as a fox. Hm, I thought to myself—this one will put me to the rack and worry me to death."

He laughed with great good humor.

"She had a son, Matvey Alexevich—I always believed him to be a bit wrong in the head—a dull youth. Not a drop of blood in his face, a pair of spectacles on his nose, hair down to his shoulders, no beard to speak of, and all he ever did was to write down songs and fairy-tales in a little book. A heart of gold—he'd give you anything you asked for. The peasants around all made use of it: one would ask for a scythe, the other for some timber, the third for bread, taking anything going whether they wanted it or not. I would say to him: 'Why do you give everything away, Alexevich? Your fathers and grandfathers piled it all up, grew rich, stripped people to the skin regardless of sin, and you give it all away without rhyme or reason. Aren't you wasting human labor?'—'I feel I must do it!' he said. Not a very clever lad, but gentle natured, anyway. Later on the Deputy Governor packed him off to China—he was rude to the Governor, so to China he had to go.

"Well—then came the trial. My counsel spoke for two hours, waving his hands about. Tasha stuck up for me, too."

"But was there ever actually anything between you two?"

He thought for a moment as though trying to remember, then said, unconcernedly watching the flight of a hawk with his naked eyes:

"That happens sometimes—between fathers and daughters. There was even a saint once who lived with two of them, and the prophets Abraham and Isaac were born to them. I will not say I did so myself. I played about with her, that is true, in the long, dreary, winter nights. Dreary they are indeed, all the more so for one who is used to tramping around the world—going here and there and everywhere, as was my case. I used to make up stories for her—I know hundreds of fairy-tales. Well, you know, a tale is a thing of fancy. And it warms up the blood. And Tasha . . ." He shut his eyes and sighed, shaking his head.

"An extraordinary beauty she was! And I was extraordinary with women, mad about them, I was."

The old man became excited and went on with pride and rapture, choking over his words:

"See, friend: I'm now a man of sixty-seven and still I can get all the pleasure I want out of any woman, that's the truth! About five years after all this happened how many a wench would beg me: 'Savel, dear, do let me go, I'm quite played out.' I'd take pity on her and do so and she would come back again in a few days. 'Well, so here you are again, are you?' I would say. A female, my friend, is a great thing, the whole world raves about her—the beast and the bird and the tiny moth—all just live for her alone. What else is there to live for?"

"What, anyway, did your daughter say at the trial?"

"Tasha? She made up a story—or perhaps it was the Antzyferova woman who suggested it to her (I'd once done her a service of sorts)—that she had brought the injury upon herself and that I was not to blame. Well, I was let off. It's all a put-up job with them, a thing of no account, just to show what a watch they keep on the laws. It's all a fraud, all these laws, orders and papers; it's all unnecessary. Let everyone live as he pleases, that would be cheaper and pleasanter. Here am I, living and not getting into anyone's way and not pushing forward."

"And what about murderers?"

"They should be killed," Savel decided. "The man who kills should be done away with on the spot with no nonsense about it! A man is not a mosquito or a fly, he is no worse than you, you scum. . . ."

"And—thieves?"

"That's an odd idea! Why should there be any thieves, if there is nothing to steal? Now, what would you take from me? I haven't any too much, so there is no envy, no greed. Why should there be any thieves? There are thieves where there is a surplus of things; when he sees plenty he just grabs a bit. . . ."

THE HERMIT

It was dark by now, night had poured into the ravine. An owl hooted three times. The old man hearkened to its eerie cries and said with a smile:

"It lives close by in a hollow tree. Sometimes it gets caught by the sun, can't hide in time, and just stays out in the light. I pass by and stick out my tongue at it. It can't see a thing, just sits quite still. Lucky if the smaller birds don't catch sight of it."

I asked how he had come to be a hermit.

"Just like that: wandered and wandered around and then stopped short. All because of Tasha. The Antzyferova woman played me a trick there—did not let me see Tasha after the trial. 'I know the whole truth,' she said, 'and you should be grateful to me for escaping hard labor, but I won't give you back your daughter.' A fool she was, of course. I hovered around for a time, but no, there was nothing doing! So off I went—to Kiev and Siberia, earned a lot of money there and came home. The Antzyferova woman had been run over and killed by a train, and as for Tasha, she had been married off to a surgeon's assistant in Kursk. To Kursk I went, but the surgeon's assistant had left for Persia, for Uzun. I pushed on to Tzaritzyn, from there by ship to Uzun—but Tasha had died. I saw the man—a red-haired, red-nosed cheerful lad. A drunkard, he turned out to be. 'Are you her father, maybe?' he asked.—'No,' I said, 'nothing like that, but I'd seen her father in Siberia.' I did not wish to confide in a stranger. Well, so then I went to New Mt. Athos, almost stayed there—a fine place! But after a while—I decided I did not like it. The sea roars and rolls the stones about, the Abkhazians come and go, the ground is uneven, mountains all around, and the nights as black as though you'd been drowned in pitch. And the heat! So I came here and here I've been for nine years and they haven't been wasted. I've built all this, planted a birch the first year, after three years a maple, then a lime—see them? And I'm a great consoler to the people round here, my friend—you come and watch me on Sunday!"

He hardly ever mentioned God's name—while as a rule it is always on the lips of people of his kind. I asked whether he prayed a lot.

"No, not too much," he said thoughtfully, shutting his naked eyes. "I did so at first, a lot; for hours would I kneel down and keep on crossing myself. My arms were used to a saw, and so they didn't get tired, or my back either. I can bow down a thousand times without a murmur, but the bones in my knees can't stand it: they ache. And then I thought to myself: what am I praying for, and why? I've got all I want, people respect me—why bother God? He's got His own job to do, why trouble Him? Human rubbish should be kept away from Him. He takes care of us and do we take care of Him? No. And also: He is there for people of importance; where will He get time for small fry like me? So now I just come out of the cave on sleepless nights, sit down somewhere or other, and, gazing into God's heaven, wonder to myself: 'And how is He getting along, up there?' This, friend, is a pleasant occupation; I can't tell you how fine; it's like dreaming awake. And one doesn't grow weary as at prayer. I don't ask Him for anything and I never advise others to do so, but when I see they need it, I tell them: 'Have pity on God!' You come along and see how helpful I can be to Him and to people. . . ."

He did not boast, but spoke with the calm assurance of a craftsman confident of his skill. His naked eyes smiled gaily, toning down the ugliness of his disfigured face.

"How I live in winter? It's all right, my cave is warm even in winter. It's only that in wintertime people find it hard to come because of the snow; sometimes for two or three days I have to go without bread. Once it so happened that I hadn't had a crumb in my mouth for over eight days. I felt so weak that even my memory went. Then a young girl came and helped me out. She was a novice in a convent, but she has got married to a teacher since. It was I who advised her to do so; I said: 'What are you fooling about like this for, Lenka? What good is it to you?'—'I'm an orphan,' she said.—'Well, go and get married and that will be the end of the orphan.' And to the teacher, Pevtzov, a good, kind man, I said: 'Have a good look at that girl, Misha.' Yes. So very soon they got together. And they're getting along fine. Well, in wintertime, I also go to the Sarov or Optina or the Diveyev monastery—there are many of them hereabouts. But the monks don't like me, they all urge me to take the hood— it would be a profit for them, of course, and serve as bait to people, but I have no wish for that. I'm alive, it does not suit me. As though I were a saint! I'm just a quiet man, friend."

Laughing and rubbing his thighs with his hands, he said with exultation:

"But with nuns, I'm always welcome. They just love me, they certainly do! That is no boast, it's the truth. I know women through and through, friend, any sort, whether a lady or a merchant's wife, and as for a peasant woman, she's as clear to me as my own soul. I just look into her eyes and I know everything, all that troubles her. I could tell you such tales about them. . . ."

And again he invited persuasively: "Come and see how I talk to them. And now, let's have another little go."

He drank. Closing his eyes tightly and shaking his head, he said with fresh rapture:

"It does one good, that drink!"

The short spring night was visibly melting away; the air grew cool. I suggested that we light a fire.

"No, what for? Are you cold? I, an old man, don't feel

the cold, and you do? That's too bad. Go to the cave, then, and lie down there. You see, friend, if we light a fire, all sorts of small living things will come flying here and will get burnt in the flames. And I don't like that. Fire to them is like a trap, leading them to their death. The sun—the father to all fire, kills no one, but why should we, for the sake of our bones, burn up these little folk? No, no. . . ."

I agreed with him, and went into the cave, while he remained outside fussing about for some time; he went off somewhere, splashed about in the brook, and I could hear his gentle voice:

"Phuit . . . don't be afraid, you little fool. . . . Phue-eet. . . ."

Then he broke into a soft tremulous song, as though lulling someone to sleep.

When I woke up and walked out of the cave, Savel, crouching on the ground, was deftly weaving a bast shoe and saying to a chaffinch singing vehemently in the bushes:

"That's it, go on, buzz on, the day is yours! Slept well, friend? Go and have a wash, I've put the kettle to boil for tea and I'm waiting for you."

"Haven't you had any sleep yourself?"

"I'll have time to sleep when I die, friend."

A blue May sky shone over the ravine.

. . . .

I came to see him again about three weeks later, on a Saturday evening, and was welcomed as an old, close friend.

"I'd been thinking already: why, the man has forgotten all about me! Ah, and you've brought some of that good drink as well. Thanks, many thanks! And some wheat bread? So fresh, too. What a kind lad indeed! People must surely like you; they love kind folk; they know what's good for them! Sausage? No, I have no liking for that, that's dog's food, you can keep it for yourself if you wish;

THE HERMIT

but fish I love. This fish, it's a sweet fish, comes from the Caspian Sea, I know all about it. Why, you must have brought food for more than a ruble, you queer fellow! Well, never mind, many thanks!"

He seemed to me still more alive, more cordially radiant—all burdens seemed to fall away from me; I felt light-hearted and gay, and I thought to myself:

"Devil take it, I believe I actually am in the presence of a happy man!"

Nimble and gentle, he performed little domestic duties, storing away my gifts, while he scattered like sparks those endearing, bewitching Russian words, which act like wine on the soul.

The movements of his sturdy body, swift as the movements of an adder, harmonized beautifully with the precision of his speech. In spite of the mutilated face, the eyes without lashes—torn apart as though on purpose to enable him to see more widely and more boldly—he seemed almost handsome, with the beauty of a life whose confusion was multi-colored and intricate. And his outward disfigurement gave a particular emphasis to that beauty.

Again, almost the whole night through, his gray little beard fluttered and the meager mustache bristled as he burst into uncontrollable laughter, opening wide the crooked mouth, in which gleamed the sharp white teeth of a polecat. At the bottom of the ravine it was still; the wind was stirring above; the tops of the pinetrees rocked; the harsh foliage of the oaks rustled; the blue river of the skies seemed violently disturbed—covered by a gray foam of clouds.

"Sh . . ." he exclaimed, softly raising his hand in warning. I hearkened—all was quiet.

"A fox is prowling about—it has a hole here. Many hunting people have asked me: is there a fox near by, grandfather? And I lie to them! Foxes? What should foxes be doing here? I have no liking for hunters, to the dickens with them!"

I had noticed by then that the old man often wanted to break out into real foul language, but realizing that it was out of character for him to do so, he resorted to milder expressions.

After a glass of cowslip vodka, he said, half-closing his lacerated eyes:

"What tasty fish this is—thank you kindly for it—I do love everything tasty. . . ."

His attitude toward God was not very clear to me and cautiously I tried to broach the subject. At first he answered with the hackneyed words of pilgrims, cloister habitués and professional holy-men, but I felt that this manner was in fact irksome to him, and I was not mistaken. Drawing closer to me and lowering his voice, he suddenly began to talk with more animation:

"I'll tell you this, friend, about a little Frenchie, a French priest—a little man, black as a starling, with a spot shaved bare on his head, golden spectacles on his nose, tiny little hands, like a little girl's, and all of him like a toy of God's. I met him at the Pochaev monastery; that is a long way off, over there!"

He waved his hand towards the East, in the direction of India, stretched out his legs more comfortably, and continued, propping his back against some stones:

"Polish people living all around—a foreign soil, not our own. I was palavering with a monk one day, who thought people should get punished more often; so I just smiled and said that if one was to begin punishing rightly, all men would have to go through it, and then there would be time for nothing else, no other work done but just flaying one another. The monk got quite angry with me, called me a fool, and walked away. Then the little priest, who had been sitting in the corner, nestled up to me and started

THE HERMIT

telling me, oh, great things. I tell you, friend, he seemed to me like a kind of John the Baptist. He wasn't quite easy in his speech, for not all our words can be put into a foreign tongue, but his big soul shone through all right. 'I see you do not agree with that monk,' he said, so polite-like, 'and you are right. God is not a fiend; He is a dear friend to people; but this is what has happened, owing to His kindness: He's melted in our tearful life like sugar in water, and the water is filthy and full of dregs, so that we do not feel Him any more; we do not get the taste of Him in our lives. Nevertheless, He is spread over the whole world and lives in every soul as the purest spark; we should seek Him in man, collect Him into a single ball, and when the divine spark of all these living souls is gathered into this powerful whole—the Devil will come and say to the Lord: 'Thou art great, my God, and Thy might is measureless—I didn't know this before, so pray forgive me! I won't struggle with Thee any more now—please take me into Thy service.'"

The old man spoke with emphasis, and his dilated pupils gleamed strangely in his dark face.

"And then the end will come to all evil and wickedness and human strife, and people will return to their God, like rivers flowing into the ocean."

He choked over his words, slapped his knees, and continued joyfully, with a hoarse little laugh:

"All this came as such balm to my heart; it struck a light in my soul—I didn't know how to say it to the Frenchie. 'Might I be allowed to embrace you, you image of Christ?' I said. So we embraced one another and started crying, both of us. And how we cried! Like small children, finding their parents after a long parting. We were both quite old, you know; the bristle round his shaven spot was gray, too. So I told him then and there: 'You're like John the Baptist to me, Christ's image.' Christ's image is what I called him; funny, isn't it, when I told you he resembled a starling! The monk, Vitaly, kept abusing him and saying: 'A nail, that's what you are.' And true it was indeed, he was like a nail, as sharp as one. Of course, friend, you do not understand this sweet joy of mine; you can read and write; you know all about everything; but I, at that time, went about as one blind—I was able to see all right, but just couldn't make out: where *is* God? And all of a sudden this man comes and reveals it all to me—just think, what that meant to me! I told you only a little of what he said to me—we talked until dawn; he went on and on; but I can recall only the kernel of it, I've lost all the shell. . . ."

He stopped speaking and sniffed the air like an animal: "Guess it's going to rain, eh?"

He sniffed again, and then decided contentedly:

"No, it won't rain, it's just the night's dampness. I'll tell you, friend, all these Frenchmen and inhabitants of other lands, they are people of high intelligence. In the province of Kharkov—or was it Poltava—an Englishman, who managed the estate of a great lord, kept watching me; then he called me into the room one day and said: 'Here's a secret parcel, old man; will you take it to such and such a place, and hand it over to such and such a person—can you do it?' Well—why not? It did not matter to me where I went, and it was about sixty miles to the place indicated. I took the parcel, tied it up with a string, thrust it in my bosom and—off I went. On getting to the place, I begged to be allowed to see the landowner. Of course, they gave it to me in the neck—they beat me up and chased me away. 'Curse you,' I thought to myself, 'may you blow up and burst!' Well, the wrapper of the parcel must have got damp from my sweat, and came apart—and what do you think I saw peeping through it—money! Big money! Maybe three hundred rubles. I got scared;

THE HERMIT

someone might notice it and steal it at night. What was I to do? There I was, sitting in the field, on the road, under a tree—when a carriage comes up with a gentleman sitting in it. Maybe that's the man I want—I thought. So I stood on the road waving my staff. The coachman lashed out at me with the whip, but the gentleman told him to stop and even scolded him a bit. Yes, he was the right man. 'Here is a secret parcel for you,' I said. 'Right,' he replied. 'Sit down next to me and we'll drive back.' He brought me into a luxurious room and asked whether I knew the contents of the parcel. So I told him I thought it was money, as I'd seen it peep through the sweaty paper. 'And who gave it to you?' he asked. I couldn't tell, that would have been against orders. He started shouting and threatening to send me to prison. 'Well,' I said, 'do so, if you think you must.' He went on threatening, but it did not work. I would not be frightened. Suddenly the door opened—and there on the threshold stood the Englishman roaring with laughter! Now, what did that mean? He'd arrived by rail earlier in the day and had sat waiting: would I come or would I not? They both knew all along when I arrived and saw the servants chase me away; they'd given them the orders to do so, not to beat me, but just to throw me out. It was a joke, don't you see, to test whether I would deliver the money or not. Well—they seemed pleased that I'd brought it, told me to go and wash, gave me clean clothes and asked me to come and eat with them. . . . Yes, friend . . . I must say, we did have a meal! The wine too—you just take a sip of it and you can't close your mouth afterwards. It burns all your insides—and has such a flavor, too. They gave me so much of it that I parted with it. The next day again I ate with them, and I told them things that surprised them very much. The Englishman got tight, and tried to prove that the Russian people were the most remarkable in the world and that nobody knew what they'd be up to next. He banged his fist on the table, so excited he got. That money they just handed over to me and I took it, although I've never been greedy for money—it has no interest for me, that's all. But I'm fond of buying things, it's true. One day, for instance, I bought a doll. I was walking along a street and saw a doll in the window: just like a live child, even rolling its eyes, it was. So I bought it. Dragged it about with me for four days—would sit down on the road somewhere, take it out of my sack and look at it. Later on I gave it to a little girl in the village. Her father asked: 'Did you steal it?' 'Yes,' I said —I was ashamed to own I'd bought it. . . ."

"Well, and what about the Englishman?"

"They just let me go, that's all. Shook me by the hand and said they were sorry about the joke, and so on. . . .

"I must go and sleep now, friend, I've got a hard day before me tomorrow. . . ."

Settling down to sleep, he said:

"An odd bird I was. . . . Suddenly joy would seize me, it would flood my innards, my whole heart—I would be ready to dance. And I would dance—much to everybody's amusement. Well—why not? I've got no children —nobody to be ashamed of me. . . .

"That means the soul is at play, friend"—he went on thoughtfully and softly. "A capricious thing, the soul, one never knows what might attract it all of a sudden, something quite funny at times, and just make you cling to it. For instance—just like that doll—one day a little girl bewitched me. I once came across a little girl in a country house. There she was, a child about nine years of age, sitting beside a pond, stirring the water with a twig and shedding tears—her little muzzle bathed in them, like a flower in dew, tears dropping down her breast like pearls. I sat by her side, of course, and asked why she was crying like that on a merry day? An angry little thing she turned out to be, tried to send me away. But I was stubborn, made her speak; so she said to me: 'Don't you come wandering around here; my daddy has a dreadful temper; and so has mammy and also my little brother!' I laughed to myself, but pretended I was really frightened, taking her at her word. Then she buried her little muzzle in my shoulder and just sobbed and sobbed, fairly shook with sobs. Her sorrow proved to be not a very heavy one: her parents had gone to a party near by and had punished her by not taking her, as she'd been naughty and refused to wear the right frock. I played up to her, of course, and soothed her, and said what bad people these parents were. So she begged me to take her away from them; she didn't want to live with them any longer. Take her away with me? Why, of course I would, no trouble about that! So off we went. And I took her to where her parents were having a party—she had a little friend there, Kolya, a curly-headed little sprig—that was the real reason for her sorrow. Well, they all laughed at her, of course, and she stood there blushing worse than a poppy. Her father gave me half a ruble, and I went off. And what do you think, friend? My soul had clung to that little girl, I couldn't tear myself away from the place. I hovered around for a week, waiting to see her, to talk to her; funny, isn't it? I just couldn't help it. She had been taken away to the seaside; she had a weak chest; and there I was roaming about like a lost dog. That's how things happen at times. Yes . . . the soul is a capricious bird—who knows where it may go when it takes its flight?"

The old man paused and yawned as he spoke, as though he were half asleep, or in a trance; then suddenly he brightened up again as though splashed by a cold rain.

"Last autumn a lady from town came to me. She was not very comely, rather weedy and dried-up, I'd say, but when I glanced into her eyes—God Almighty, if only I could have her, if only for one night, I said to myself. After that—cut me to pieces, let horses tear me asunder—I don't care, I'll take any death. So I told her straight away: 'Go. Please go, or I may hurt you, go! I can't talk to you, d'you hear? I beg of you, go!' I don't know if she guessed, or what, but she hurried away, anyhow. How many nights did I not lay awake thinking of her, seeing those eyes in front of me—a real torture. And me an old man, too. . . . Old, yes . . . The soul knows no laws, it takes no account of years. . . ."

He stretched himself out on the ground, twitched the red, scar-like eye-lids, then said, smacking his lips:

"Well, I'm off to sleep now. . . ." And wrapping his head in his cloak he remained still.

He awakened at dawn, looked into the cloudy sky, and hastily ran to the brook where he stripped himself naked, grunting, washed his strong brown body from head to toe, and shouted out to me:

"Hi, friend, hand me over my shirt and trousers; they're in the cave."

Pulling on a long shirt that reached to his knees, and blue trousers, he combed out his wet hair with a wooden comb and, almost handsome, faintly reminding one of an icon, he said:

"I always wash with particular care before receiving people."

While we had our tea he refused vodka:

"No, none of that today. I won't eat anything either, just have a little tea. Nothing should go to one's head; one should keep it light. One needs great lightness of soul in this business. . . ."

People started coming after midday; until then the old man remained silent and dull. His merry, lively eyes had a concentrated look; a grave poise marked all his movements. He looked frequently at the sky and hearkened to the light rustle of the wind. His face was drawn; it seemed more disfigured, and the twitching of the mouth more poignant.

"Someone is coming," he said softly.

I heard nothing.

"Yes. Women. Look here, friend, don't speak to anyone and keep out of the way—or you'll scare them. Sit quietly somewhere nearby."

Two women crawled noiselessly out of the bushes: one, plump, middle-aged, with the meek eyes of a horse; the other, a young woman with a gray, consumptive face; they both stared at me in fear.

I walked away along the slope of the ravine, and heard the old man saying:

"He does not matter; he's not in our way. He's a bit touched in the head; he does not care, does not bother about us. . . ."

The younger woman started to speak in a cracked voice, in hurried and hurt tones, coughing and wheezing, her companion interrupting her speech with short, low, deep notes, while Savel, in a voice that sounded like a stranger's, exclaimed, full of sympathy:

"So—so—so! What people, eh?"

The woman began to whimper plaintively—then the old man drawled melodiously:

"Dear—wait a bit; stop that; listen . . ."

It seemed to me that his voice had lost its hoarseness, sounded more clear and high; and the melody of his words reminded me curiously of the artless song of a goldfinch. I could see, through the net of branches, that he was bending towards the woman, speaking straight into her face; while she, sitting awkwardly at his side, opened her eyes wide and pressed her hands to her breast. Her friend, holding her head on one side, rocked it to and fro.

"They've hurt you; that means they've hurt God!" the old man said loudly and the brisk, almost cheerful sound of his words was strikingly out of keeping with their meaning. "God—where is He? In your soul, behind your breasts, lives the Holy Ghost; and these witless brothers of yours have injured Him by their foolishness. You should take pity on the fools—they've done the wrong. To hurt God is like hurting a small child of yours. . . ."

And once more he drawled:

"Dee-ear . . ."

I started: never before had I heard this familiar, trivial little word spoken with such triumphant tenderness. Now the old man was talking in a quick whisper; his hand on the woman's shoulder, he pushed her gently, and the woman rocked as though half-asleep. The older woman sat down on the stones at the old man's feet, methodically spreading the hem of her blue skirt around her.

"A pig, a dog, a horse—every beast trusts in human reason; and your brothers are human beings, remember this! And tell the elder one to come to me on Sunday."

"He won't," said the big woman.

"He will!" the old man exclaimed confidently.

Somebody else was descending into the ravine; clots of earth were rolling down; the branches of the bushes rustled.

"He will come," repeated Savel. "Now, go with God's blessing. All will be well."

The consumptive woman rose silently and bowed low to the old man. He raised her head with the palm of his hand and said:

"Remember, you carry God in your soul."

She bowed again and handed him a small bundle.

"May Christ keep you . . ."

"Thanks, friend. . . . And now, go." And he made the sign of the cross over her.

Out of the bushes came a broad-shouldered, black-bearded peasant, in a new pink shirt, that had not yet been washed; it bulged out in stiff folds, protruding from the belt. He was hatless; his disheveled shock of grayish hair stuck out on all sides in unruly locks; his small, bear-like eyes peered sullenly from under frowning brows.

Making way for the women, he followed them with a glance, coughed loudly, and scratched his chest.

"How do, Olesha," said the old man with a smile. "What is it?"

"Here I am," said Olesha dully; "want to sit awhile with you."

"Good, let's do so."

They sat for a moment in silence, earnestly gazing at each other, then started talking simultaneously.

"Working?"

"Father, I'm fed up . . ."

"You're a big peasant, Olesha."

"If only I had your kind heart. . . ."

"You're a strong man."

"What good is my strength to me? It's your soul I want. . . ."

"Well, when your house burned down, another, like an ass, would have lost courage."

"And I?"

"You—no! You've started all over again. . . ."

"My heart is bitter," the man said loudly, and cursed his heart in foul language, while Savel went on with quiet assurance:

"Your heart's just a common, human, anxious heart; it does not want trouble; it longs for peace. . . ."

"It's true, father. . . ."

They went on like that for about half an hour—the peasant telling of a fierce wicked man, whose life was burdened by many failures; while Savel spoke of another man, a strong one, who worked stubbornly, a man who would let nothing slip away from him, nothing escape him, a man with a fine soul.

With a broad smile on his face, the peasant said:

"I've made it up with Peter."

"So I've heard."

"Yes. Made it up. We had a drink together. I said to him: 'What are you up to, you devil? . . .' And he said: 'Well, what about you?' Yes. A fine man, damn his soul. . . ."

"You're both the children of one God."

"A fine man. And clever, too. Father—what about my getting married?"

"Of course. She's the one for you to marry."

"Anfisa?"

"Why, yes. She's a good housewife. What a beauty she is, too, and what strength she has. She's a widow; her first husband was an old man, and she had a bad time with him; but you two will get on well together, take my word for it. . . ."

"I will get married . . . really."

"So you should."

Then the peasant proceeded to relate something unintelligible about a dog, about letting cider out of a barrel; he went on with his stories, guffawing like a wood-sprite. His sullen, brigand's scowl had become completely transformed, and he now had the silly, good-natured look of a domesticated animal.

"Well, Olesha, move on, here's someone else coming."

"More sufferers? All right . . ."

Olesha descended to the brook, drank some water out of the palm of his hand, then sat down for a few moments motionless as a stone, threw himself back on the ground, folded his arms under his head and apparently went to sleep at once. Then there came a crippled girl, in a motley frock, a thick brown plait down her back, and with big blue eyes. Her face was striking and like a picture; but her skirt was annoyingly vivid, covered with green and yellow spots, and there were scarlet spots, the color of blood, on her white blouse.

The old man welcomed her with joy, and tenderly bade her sit down. Then a tall, black old woman, looking like a nun, appeared, and with her a large-headed, tow-haired lad with a congealed smile on his fat face.

Savel hastily led the girl away into the cave, and concealing her there, closed the door—I could hear the wooden hinges screech.

He sat on a stone between the old woman and the boy, his head bent down, and listened to her murmur in silence for a long time.

"Enough!" he suddenly pronounced, sternly and loudly. "So he does not listen to you, you say?"

"No, he doesn't. I tell him this and that . . ."

"Wait. So you don't do as she tells you, lad?"

The lad remained silent, smiling vacantly.

"Well, that's right, don't listen to her.—Understand? And you, woman, you've started a bad job. I tell you frankly; it's against the law. And there couldn't be anything worse than that. Go, there's nothing for us to talk about.—She's out to do you in, lad. . . ."

The lad, with a sneer, said in a high falsetto:

"Oh, I know that, I do-o. . . ."

"Well, go," Savel said, with a disgusted gesture of dismissal. "Go! You will have no success, woman. None!"

Downcast, they bowed to him in silence and went upwards through the thicket, along a hidden path; I could see that having walked up about a hundred feet, they both started talking, standing close together, facing one another; then they sat down at the foot of a pine, waving their arms about, and a quarrelsome drone reached one's ears. Meanwhile from the cave came pouring out an indescribably moving exclamation:

"Dee-ear . . ."

God alone knows how that disfigured old man contrived to put into this word so much enchanting tenderness, so much exultant love.

"It's too early for you to think of it," he said, as though he were uttering an incantation, leading the lame girl out of the cave. He held her by the hand as though she were a child who still walked uncertainly. She staggered as she walked, pushing him with her shoulder, wiping the tears from her eyes, with the movements of a cat—her hands were small and white.

The old man made her sit on the stone by his side, talking uninterruptedly, clearly and melodiously—as though telling a fairy-tale:

"Don't you see you are a flower on earth? God nurtured you to give joy; you can give great happiness; the clear light of your eyes alone is a feast to the soul—dea-ear! . . ."

The capacity of this word was inexhaustible, and truly it seemed to me that it contained in its depth the key to all the mysteries of life, the solution of all the painful muddle of human relationships. Through its fascination it was able to bewitch not only peasant women, but all men, all living things. Savel uttered it in infinitely various ways —with emotion, with solemnity, with a kind of touching sadness. It sounded at times reproachful, at times tender, or else it poured out in a radiant music of joy; and I always felt, whatever the way in which it was said, that its source was a limitless, an inexhaustible love, a love which knows nothing but itself and marvels at itself, seeing in itself alone the meaning and aim of existence, all the beauty of life, capable of enveloping the world in its power.

At that time I had already taught myself to doubt; but in these hours, on this cloudy day, all my unbelief fled

THE HERMIT 353

like shadows before the sun at the sound of the familiar word, worn threadbare by long usage.

The lame girl gasped happily as she went away, nodding her head to the old man:

"Thank you, grandfather, thank you, dear."

"That's all right. Go, friend, go. And remember—you're going towards joy, towards happiness, towards a great task —towards joy! Go!"

She retreated sideways, never tearing her eyes away from Savel's radiant face. Black-haired Olesha, waking up, stood by the brook, shaking his still more disheveled head, and watched the girl with a smile. Suddenly he pushed two fingers into his mouth and gave a shrill whistle. The girl staggered and dived like a fish into the dense waves of the thicket.

"You're crazy, Olesha!" the old man reproved him.

Olesha, playing the buffoon, crouched on the ground, pulled a bottle out of the brook, and brandishing it in the air, suggested:

"Shall we have a drink, father?"

"Have one if you like. I can't, not until tonight."

"Well, I'll wait till evening, too. . . . Ah, father—" and strong curses followed like an avalanche of bricks—"a sorcerer, that's what you are—but a saint, too, 'pon my word! You play with the soul—the human soul, just as a child would. I lay here and thought to myself . . ."

"Don't bawl, Olesha. . . ."

The old woman with the lad came back, and talked to Savel in a low and contrite tone. He shook his head distrustfully, and led them away into the cave, while Olesha, catching sight of me in the thicket, clumsily made his way across to me, breaking the branches as he came.

"A town bird, are you?"

He was in a cheerful and talkative mood, gently quarrelsome, and kept singing Savel's praises:

"A great consoler, Savel. Take me, for instance, I simply live on his soul; my own is overgrown with malice, as with hair. I'm a desperate man, brother. . . ."

He painted himself for a long time in the most sinister colors, but I did not believe him.

The old woman emerged from the cave, and, with a deep bow to Savel, said:

"Don't you be angry with me, father. . . ."

"Very well, friend . . ."

"You yourself know . . ."

"Yes, I know that everybody is afraid of poverty. A pauper is never liked by anyone, I know. But all the same: one should avoid offending God in oneself as well as in others. If we were to keep God in mind always, there would be no poverty in the world. So it is, friend. Now go, with God's blessing. . . ."

The lad kept sniveling, glancing fearfully at the old man, and hiding behind his stepmother. Then a beautiful woman arrived, a woman from the town, to judge by her appearance; she wore a lavender-colored frock and a blue kerchief, from under which gleamed two large gray-blue eyes angrily and suspiciously.

And again the enchanting word resounded:

"Dee-ear . . ."

Olesha kept on talking, preventing me from hearing what the old man was saying:

"He can melt every soul like tin. . . . A great help he is to me. If it were not for him, Hell alone knows what I'd have done by now. . . . Siberia . . ."

Savel's words rose from below:

"Every man should be a source of happiness to you, my beauty, and here you are saying all these malicious things. Chase anger away, dear. It is goodness we glorify, isn't it, when we glorify our saints on feast days, not malice. What is it you mistrust? It's yourself you mistrust, your womanly power, your beauty—and what is it that is hidden in beauty? God's spirit, that's what it is . . . Dee-ear. . . ."

Deeply moved, I was on the verge of weeping for joy, so great is the magic force of a word vivified by love.

. . . .

Before the ravine had filled with the dense darkness of a cloudy night, about thirty people came to see Savel—dignified, old villagers carrying staffs, distressed people overcome with grief; more than half of the visitors were women. I did not listen any more to their uniform complaints, I only waited impatiently for *the* word to come from Savel. When night came, he allowed Olesha and me to build a bonfire on the stone platform. We got tea and food ready while he sat by the flames, chasing away with his cloak all the "living things" attracted by the fire.

"Another day gone in the service of the soul," he murmured, thoughtfully and wearily.

Olesha gave him some practical advice: "A pity you don't take money from people. . . ."

"It's not suitable for me. . . ."

"Well, you can take from one and give to another. Me, for instance. I'd buy a horse. . . ."

"You tell the children to come tomorrow, Olesha; I've got some gifts for them. The women brought a lot of stuff today."

Olesha went over to the brook to wash his hands, and I said to Savel:

"You speak to people so well, grandfather. . . ."

"Ye-es," he agreed calmly. "I told you I did! And people have respect for me. I tell them each the truth they need. That's what it is."

He smiled merrily and went on, with less weariness:

"It's the women I talk best to, isn't it? It just so happens, friend, that when I see a woman, or a girl, who is at all beautiful—my soul soars up and seems to blossom out. I feel a kind of gratitude to them: at the sight of one, I recall all those I have ever known and they are numberless."

Olesha came back, saying:

"Father Savel, will you stand surety for me in the matter of the sixty rubles I'm borrowing from Shakh? . . ."

"Very well."

"Tomorrow, eh?"

"Yes . . ."

"See?" Olesha turned to me triumphantly, stepping on my toe as he did so. "Shakh, my boy, is the kind of man who has only to look at you from a distance and your shirt crawls down of itself from your back, right into his hands. But if Father Savel comes to see him—Shakh squirms before him like a little pup. Look at all the timber he gave to the victims of the fire, for instance." Olesha fussed about noisily and did not allow the old man to relax. One could see that Savel was very tired. He sat wearily by the fire, all crumpled up, his arm waving over the flames, the skirt of his coat reminding one of a broken wing. But nothing could subdue Olesha; he had had two glasses of vodka and had become still more exuberantly cheerful. The old man also had some vodka, ate a baked egg with bread after it; and suddenly he said, quite softly:

"Now go home, Olesha!"

The great black beast rose, made the sign of the cross, and glanced into the black sky.

"Keep well, father, and many thanks!" he said. Then he pushed his hard, heavy paw into my hand and obediently crawled into the thicket, where a narrow path was concealed.

"A good man?" I asked.

"Yes, but he has to be watched carefully; his is a violent nature! He beat his wife so hard that she could not bear any children, kept having miscarriages, and went mad in the end. I would ask him: why do you beat her?—and he would say: I don't know, just want to, that's all. . . ."

He remained silent, let his arm drop, and sat motionless, peering into the flames of the bonfire, his gray eyebrows raised. His face, lit up by the fire, seemed red-hot and became terrible to look at: the dark pupils of the naked, lacerated eyes had changed their shape—it was hard to tell whether they were narrower or more dilated—the whites had grown larger and he seemed to have suddenly become blind.

He moved his lips; the scanty hair of his mustache stirred and bristled—as though he wanted to say something and could not. But when he started to speak again, he did so calmly, thoughtfully, in a peculiar manner:

"It happens to many a man, this, friend; that you suddenly want to beat up a woman, without any fault of her own and—at what a moment, too! You've just been kissing her, marveling at her beauty; and suddenly, at that very moment, the desire overcomes you to beat her! Yes, yes, friend, it happens . . . I can tell you; I am a quiet, gentle man and did love women so much, sometimes to the point of wanting to get deep inside the woman, right to her very heart and hide in it, as a dove does in the sky —that's how wonderful it was. And then, suddenly, would come the desire to hit her, pinch her as hard as one could; and I would do so, yes! She would shriek and cry: what's the matter? And there is no answer—what answer could there be?"

I looked at him in amazement, unable, too, to say anything or ask any question—this strange confession astonished me. After a pause, he went on about Olesha.

"After his wife went mad, Olesha became still more ill-tempered—a fierce mood would come over him, he'd believe himself damned, and beat everyone up. A short while ago the peasants brought him to me tied up; they'd almost thrashed him to death. He was all swollen, covered with blood like bread with crust. 'Tame him, father Savel,' they said, 'or we'll kill him, there's no living with the beast!' Yes, friend. I spent about five days bringing him back to life. I can doctor a bit, too, you know. . . . Yes, it isn't easy for people to live, friend, it isn't. Not always is life sweet, my dear clear-eyed friend. . . . So I try to console people, I do. . . ."

He gave a piteous smile, and his face grew more hideous and terrible.

"Some of them I have to deceive a little; there are, you see, some people who have no comfort left to them at all but deceit. There are some like that, I tell you. . . ."

There were many questions I wanted to put to him, but he had eaten nothing the whole day; fatigue and the glass of vodka were obviously telling on him. He dozed, rocking to and fro, and his red eyelids dropped more frequently over the naked eyes. I could not help asking all the same:

"Grandfather, is there such a thing as hell, do you think?"

He raised his head and said sternly and reproachfully:

"Hell? How can that be? How can you? God—and hell? Is that possible? The two don't go together, friend. It's a fraud. You people who can read invented this to frighten folk, it's all priests' nonsense. Why one should want to frighten people, I cannot see. Besides, no one is really afraid of that hell of yours. . . ."

"And what about the devil? Where does he live, in that case?"

"Don't you joke about that. . . ."

"I'm not joking. . . ."

"Well—well . . ."

He waved the skirts of his coat once more over the fire, and said softly:

"Don't sneer at him. To everyone his own burden. The

little Frenchie might have been right about the devil bowing down to the Lord in due time. A priest told me the story of the prodigal son from the Scriptures one day—I can remember it well. It seems to me that it is the story of the devil himself. It's he, no other but he, that is the prodigal son. . . ."

He swayed over the fire.

"Hadn't you better go to sleep?" I suggested.

The old man agreed:

"Yes, it's time . . ."

He readily turned on his side, curled himself up, pulled the coat over his head—and was silent. The branches cracked and hissed on the coals, the smoke rose in fanciful streamers into the darkness of the night.

I watched the old man and thought to myself:

"Is he a saint, owning the treasure of limitless love for the world?"

I remembered the lame girl with the sorrowful eyes, in the motley frock, and life itself appeared to me in the image of that girl: she was standing in front of a hideous little god and he, who knew only how to love, put all the enchanting power of that love into one word of consolation:

"Dee-ear. . . ."

1923.

KARAMORA

You know I am capable of heroic deeds. Well, I could say the same about mean, low behavior—sometimes one just longs to play a dirty trick on someone—even on one's closest friend.—THE WORDS OF ZAKHAR MIKHAILOV, THE AGENT PROVOCATEUR, ADDRESSED TO THE COMMISSION OF INQUIRY IN 1917; SEE ARTICLE BY N. OSSIPOVSKY IN "BYLOYE," 1922, VOL. VI.

At times, for no rhyme or reason—mean, evil thoughts flash across one's mind . . .—N. I. PIROGOV.

. . . Allow me to behave like a cad!—ONE OF OSTROVSKY'S HEROES.

A mean action requires sometimes as much self-denial as an act of heroism.—FROM A LETTER BY LEONID ANDREYEV.

One does not learn anything about a man through his deliberate behavior, it is his headlong acts which reveal his real self.—N. LESKOV IN A LETTER TO PILAYEV.

A Russian wears his brain tilted to one side.—I. TURGENEV.

MY father was a locksmith. A large man, so very kind, and so merry. He looked out for something to laugh at in everyone. He was fond of me and called me Karamora—distributing nicknames all around was his chief amusement. There is a big mosquito, rather like a spider, commonly called Karamora. I was a long and lanky boy; my favorite pastime was bird-snaring. I was lucky at games and quick in a fight.

KARAMORA

I have been given reams of paper: to write down how it all happened. But why should I write? They will kill me anyway.

Rain is falling. Actually tumbling down, columns, stripes of rain moving over the fields to the town, and nothing can be seen through the wet veil. Thunder and other noises rumble outside the window, the prison has grown silent, it shudders, the rain and the wind push it about, it seems as though the old building glides on a soapy surface, rolls down the slope towards the town. And as for me, I feel like a fish in a net. . . .

It's growing dark. What shall I write? Two men lived inside me and the one didn't stick to the other. That is all.

Perhaps that is not so. Whatever it is, I will not write. I do not want to. What is more I do not know how. And it is too dark to write. No, Karamora, better stretch ourselves out, have a smoke and think a bit about things.

Let them do their killing.

. . . . . .

I haven't slept the whole night. The air is stifling. After the rain the sun has scorched the earth so severely that a moist heat, as from a steam bath, pours through the window of the cell from the fields. In the sky the quarter-moon shines like a sickle, reminding me of Popov's red mustache. All night I kept looking back on my life. What else is there to do? It is like peering into a chink and behind the chink is a mirror in which my past is congealed, reflected. I remembered Leopold, my first teacher. A small hungry Jewish schoolboy. I was nineteen at the time and he was two or three years younger. Consumptive, short-sighted, with a sallow little mask of a face, a crooked nose, all purple and bloated from the heavy spectacles. He seemed to me a comic character and as frightened as a mouse.

All the more remarkable was it to watch how boldly and

cleverly he tore down the veils of falsehood, how he gnawed at the external links that tie people together, revealing the bitter truth of innumerable treacheries between one man and another.

He was of those who are born wise and he was full of unbridled passion in his indictment of social lies. He trembled from head to foot with anger, disclosing life to us—like the victim of a burglar who after capturing the criminal goes through his pockets.

I was a jolly youth and did not like listening to his talk. I was reasonably satisfied with life, not envious, not acquisitive, earned a decent living, and saw the path in front of me running like a clear stream. And suddenly this Jewish boy came and troubled my waters. It vexed me that I, a healthy Russian lad, should prove to be sillier than this contemptible little foreigner who instructed and irritated me as though rubbing salt into my skin. I could not contradict him, besides it was clear that what Leopold said was true. And yet I wanted to argue against him very much. But how is one to speak?

"All this is true. But I have no need for that sort of truth. I've got my own kind."

Now I understand: had I told him that—all my life would have taken another course. I made a mistake, I did not. Maybe the reason why I kept back my words was precisely because it was too annoying to see four fine sturdy lads sitting around, all of them sillier than such a puny little jackdaw.

Almost all the trade in our town was in the hands of the Jews and therefore they were not at all popular. I had no reason to feel more kindly to him than everybody else did. When Leopold left, I began to jeer at my friends' choice of a teacher. But Zotov, the saddler, who had started the whole business, shut me up angrily and so did the other boys. It was not the first time they had been listening to Leopold and there was a close bond between them.

Having thought things over I resolved to surrender to the propagandist, but my secret aim was to humiliate Leopold in some way in the eyes of the others—that was not only because he was a Jew, but because it was hard for me to get reconciled to the idea that truth should live in such a frail little body. That was not aestheticism but the organic mistrust of a healthy creature who fears contamination.

This was the game in which I got entangled and lost. After two or three talks the truth of socialism became as clear and near to me as though I had myself discovered it. Now, looking back, I believe that in my youthful enthusiasm I overlooked a subtle and dangerous point. It has been proved by the theories on the essence of reason that thoughts are born from facts. With my reason I accepted the socialistic idea as a truth, but the facts which had given birth to that thought, did not arouse any emotion in me and inequality seemed a natural and legitimate factor. I thought of myself as being better than Leopold, cleverer than my other friends. Already as a child I had been used to command; it was an easy job for me to make others obey and altogether I lacked an attribute indispensable to a socialist—what should one call it?—love for mankind, or what? I don't know. To put it simply—socialism did not fit me—it was narrow in some places—wide in others. I have seen many a socialist like that, to whom socialism is something quite alien. They are like adding machines—they don't care what figures they add up, the total is always correct, but there is no soul in them, it's just bare arithmetic. By "soul" I mean an idea sublimated to insanity, so to say a believing idea, which is forever and inextricably linked with the will. I expect that what was wrong in my life was that I had no soul like that and was not aware of it.

I was brighter than the other boys, found my way better among the various pamphlets, questioned Leopold oftener than they did. My hostility to him helped me a lot: in my desire to find him out, to reveal that his knowledge did not cover all the ground and was wrong at times, I wanted to learn more than he knew. This ambition enabled me to advance so rapidly that very soon I became the chief person in our group and could see that Leopold was proud of me as a creature of his brain. I would be almost willing to say that he was fond of me.

"You are a real, a profound revolutionary, Peter," he would say to me.

There was nothing that the boy had not read, he had such a remarkable brain, too. He suffered from a chronic cold and cough. Lean and dark as a burning log, he emitted corrosive smoke, shot out words glittering as sparks. Zotov used to say: "He doesn't live, he just smolders. One can't help feeling that at any moment he might flare up—and vanish."

I listened to Leopold greedily, with great intensity, but liked to hurt him. For instance I would say: "You keep talking of European capitalists—and seem to have forgotten the Jewish ones?"

He would shrink, the poor beggar, blink his sharp little eyes, and say that although capitalism was international, people like Lassalle and Marx were more characteristic of the Jews than capitalists.

When we were alone he would reproach me for being anti-Jewish, but I countered by saying that his reticence about Jews had been noticed by the others as well. That was true.

Eight months after starting his talks with us he was arrested, together with some other members of the intelligentsia, kept over a year in prison, then sent off to the north, where he died. He was one of those men who live like the blind, their eyes wide open but seeing nothing but what they believe in. They've got an easy life. With such an asset I would have made just as good a job of it as they do.

. . . .

They've brought a soldier to the prison—remarkably like my father the year he died: just as bald and bearded, the eyes just as deeply sunk in their sockets and the same embarrassed little laugh which my father had before he died. "Peter," he asked me, "what if a crowd of devils come and welcome you after you're dead?"

It was almost comical how desperately he clung to life, he consulted three doctors at the same time: the famous Dr. Turkin, some woman-quack in the settlement, and the local priest who treated all diseases with a concoction of ephedra vulgaris, a shrub known as "Kuzmich's herb." Also he was anxious about me. He would say:

"Do give up that game, Peter. It isn't your fault that people's lives are not what they ought to be—why should it be your duty to put them right? It is about the same as looking after other people's geese and neglecting one's own."

There's a good deal of truth in blunt thoughts. Yes, people are linked together by the chain of economics. Economic materialism is a clear teaching and allows for no imagination. The external link between people is superficial, automatic, forced upon them. I stand it so long as I profit by it. When that goes—I start on my own—so long, boys! I am not greedy—I don't need much for my share of life.

Among the comrades there were several poets of sorts, lyrical-minded creatures, preachers of love of mankind. They were good, naïve lads, I admired them, but I well knew that their love of mankind was pure imagination and not of a very fine quality. Of course, for those who hang in the air without a definite place in life, for these men the preaching of love of mankind is a matter of necessity—this is very well proved by the naïve teaching of Christ. But fundamentally—solicitude for people does not come from love for them but from the need to surround oneself by them in order to establish one's ideas, one's position, one's ambition, with their help, their support. I know that some intellectuals are actually physically attracted by the people in their youth and take it to be love. But it is not love—it is mere mechanics—gravitation towards the masses. When they reach maturity these same people become the dullest of artisans, just common stokers on the train of life. Solicitude for people destroys the love for them, revealing the simplest of social mechanisms.

There is some shooting going on at night in the town. At dawn today in the cell above me somebody moaned and wailed and stamped. A woman, I believe.

· · · · · · ·

In the morning comrade Basov came with a message from them, asking whether I was writing. Yes, I am.

He was again overcome with horror as at my first questioning, kept gesticulating and muttering: "It is impossible to believe that it could be you, an old party member, the organizer of a revolt, one of our most energetic comrades. . . ." He has an unpleasant manner of speaking, as though chewing his words; they stick to his teeth and his tongue has some difficulty in tearing them away. He is altogether a clumsy, ungainly creature—another "stoker" in a word. His ungainliness has often landed him in prison. A dullard, that's what he is. He has the face of an innocent victim, sentenced for life to be ill-treated. Among the intellectuals there are many men like that with signposts of suffering and grievance on their faces. They became particularly frequent after 1905—stalking the earth with an air, as though the universe owed them sixpence and would not pay it back.

They believe, most probably, that the thought of death will drive fear into my heart and that, miserable scoundrel that I am, I will pour out confessions, like a water-pipe on a rainy day. The odd creatures.

Yes, I am writing. Not in order to draw out for another few days my stay in prison—but—at the wish of a third party. I have already said that two men live inside me and the one does not get on with the other—but there is a third one as well. He keeps an eye on both, watches their conflicts and—I cannot make it out:—does he try to egg them on, set the one against the other—or does he just want to understand: why? how has this quarrel arisen?

It is he who makes me write. Perhaps he is the real me who wants to grasp the meaning of everything or at least of something. And what if the third should be my most cruel enemy? This already sounds like the suspicion of a fourth. Two people live in every man: the one is only aware of himself—the other is drawn towards other people. But I believe that no less than four individuals live in me and they are all on bad terms with one another, they all think differently. Whatever should occur to one, the other disputes and then the third inquires:

"What are you squabbling for? What will be the outcome of your squabble?" Yes, I daresay there is yet a fourth who has concealed himself even more deeply than the third, and watches stealthily, like a wild beast, biding his time. He may keep at bay all through my life, just indifferently observe all this muddle from afar.

I believe that in his youth, while his moral character is being shaped, a man should stifle all the embryos of personalities hidden in him except the one, the best one.

But what if it is just this best one that he stifles? Who on earth is to know which is the best one?

It is all right for the intelligentsia, school does the job for them, kills the useless, the evil seed, but for us, when the insatiable thirst to know all, to try everything, to go through every fire, overcomes us—it is a hard struggle. At twenty I felt I was not a man, but a pack of hounds, tearing and dashing in all directions, on every track, ready to follow all scents, catch all the hares, satisfy all desires, and as to desires there was no end of them.

Reason did not prompt me, did not point out: this is good, this bad. It appears, altogether, not to consider this to be its job. My reason is as curious as a youngster and obviously quite indifferent to good and evil—whether this indifference is contemptible or not, I do not know. This is exactly what I do not know. It is appropriate here to quote Tassya's funny remark: "When a man is very clever, there is something improper about it."

So I am writing at the wish of the third party. Not for *their* sake, but merely for myself and because I am bored. And there is a curious fascination in telling oneself the story of one's life. One looks at oneself as at a stranger and it is fun to catch one's thoughts in their attempts to conceal and lie to the fourth, escape from his vigilant watch. This game is not only worth the candle, it's worth a whole bonfire. Nothing remains of it but ashes? Well. . . . It is unlikely that they should see and read these notes, I'll manage to destroy them in time or pass them on into other hands.

There are three thieves in the cell next to mine, three cheerful lads. The eldest is but a boy, not more than twenty, a student at a naval school. He's a great one for singing ditties, like:

> I was born desperate
> And will die the same;
> If my head is blown off
> I'll put a log in its place.

A bold youngster. I was just like him at his age. Loved danger as much as comrade Tassya loves chocolates. A man always feels at his best in a difficulty. When an ice-floe with fishermen was torn off by a gust of wind and carried away into the sea I jumped in to help them, was torn off in my turn, and floated on alone on a small ice-block with a pole in my hand. It became clear to me at once that the game was up, so clear that for a moment I got all frozen inside. The waves beat against the ice under my feet, one more minute and I would have sunk. The fishermen from the solid ice by the shore threw me a rope—this meant my salvation. And at once as though someone very agile and wicked had jumped into my skin, I shouted to them to throw more ropes while I hurled the one in my hands to the fishermen who were howling in a frenzy of fear some thirty feet away from me. They managed to catch the rope with a pole and pulled me down into the water. But I had had time to seize the second rope flung from the steady block of ice, had tied them together, when there came another one, and the whole lot of men was slowly dragged back to the shore. Of the nine people only one old man was drowned, just pushed into the water accidentally in the bustle. While the ice-floe was being dragged back, the rope almost ate into my body, it had wound itself around me and I was tossed about in the water like a log. Always, when I was faced with danger, as though acting against itself, it multiplied my strength, filled me with cold-blooded assurance, sharpened my wits and allowed me to overcome it. I was impudently reckless and particularly pleased with myself when my life hung on a thread.

There was one funny episode: during an escape from prison which I had organized for a few comrades, the old guard, trying to hold us up, fired his revolver at me four times. After the second shot I stopped. To run seemed a little humiliating and comical. Catching up with me, he fired again, the bullet hitting my boot and scratching my leg. He fired once more straight at my chest—the gun did not go off. I knocked the revolver out of his hand, saying:

"No luck, eh, old man?"

Panting for breath, his voice rattling, he muttered: "You devil, what are you waiting for, why don't you run, man?"

I believe I was really frightened only once, in a dream, when I was living in exile in a little provincial town in Siberia. It was all a series of coincidences: I had read several books on astronomy, had just got over typhoid and was dragging myself feebly along the earth, when a peculiar little man appeared and started preaching about "Him who was crucified for us by Pontius Pilate." He hardly ever said Christ, but always "He who was crucified." He was a pathetic creature, probably not quite in his right mind and obviously not a common pilgrim feeding on the slops in rich women's kitchens, but of the intellectual class, long and lanky, with a scanty little beard, and gray hair on his temples, although he could not have been more than thirty-five. His eyes were the redeeming, rejuvenating feature, they were starry like those of a young girl in love. The blue irises seemed to thaw away and stream upon the large protruding whites of the eye. I was sitting on a bench outside the gate, basking in the sun, snoozing, when suddenly this man appeared at my side, talking of "Him who was crucified." He spoke remarkably well, with a childish directness and as though he had himself lived through the whole adventure of Christ—adventure is an expression of comrade Basov, a specialist on atheism.

I started to argue, of course. He asked for something to eat and I took him to my room, where our argument became still more heated. On the whole he did not really argue with me, he just read poetry from the Scriptures and smiled pathetically. Until late into the night I tried to convince him that every man able to think knows very well that there is no God. Christ is but naïve poetry, lyrics, a phantasy, a fallacy, in one word. One believes in God out of ignorance, fear, habit, stubbornness, some people do because of a devastating emptiness in the soul which has to be filled up with the cotton of religion. Others, maybe, feel towards Christ as they do towards a woman who they know has betrayed them, played them false, but they are used to her—insensible to others and cannot give her up. Anyhow—there is no God. Had there been one—would people be as they are? Although I certainly didn't say these last words to him, I believe it is the first time that I have ever uttered them. They, too, are naïve and clumsy. No, I can't write.

I was talking not so much to him as examining my own self, scrutinizing my opinions on God, religion and all this sentiment of the poor in spirit. He sat on a bench by the window, watching me, leaning against the table, now and then laughing with the inoffensive laughter of an innocent. So we sat until we finally fell asleep, I on the bed, he on the floor.

I woke up in the night and found him standing in the middle of the room, so tall that he almost reached the ceiling, muttering as he glanced out of the window and pointed to me:

"Help him, you *must* help him!" He murmured this sternly, as though issuing a command, as though conscious of his power over someone—this little performance was somehow not to my taste, but I said nothing to the queer creature and went back to sleep again. And then I had a dream. I was walking along the horizon on the edge of a flat circle, covered by the vault of a grayish sky, feeling something cold and hard under my fingers—that was the edge of the sky. It had grown into, stuck to a soundless earth as harsh as iron—my own steps did not echo on it. As a dim mirror the sky reflected my body, hideously distorted, my face grimacing, my hands trembling and my reflection stretched out these trembling hands to me, with curiously stiff, unbending fingers. I had already gone several times round the empty circle, moving more and more rapidly along the horizon—but I could not make out what it was I was searching for and I could not stop. I felt utterly miserable and distressed: I could remember that there was life on earth, people living on it—where was it all? In an unbreakable silence, a complete lifelessness, my movement round the circle grew more and more rapid, now it was like the flight of a swallow and side by side flew my gesticulating reflection, and it was there, wherever I turned. The circle drew in, grew smaller, the vault of the sky descended on me, I ran, I suffocated, I screamed. . . .

The man woke me up and I, in my terror, was so glad to be awake that I seized him by the hands, and jumped about, laughing. I behaved very foolishly, in fact. But I can remember nothing more terrible than that dream. By the way—it is wrong to say that only the unfathomable is terrible. Astronomy, for instance, is quite simple, but is it any less terrible?

Noise and shooting go on in the town. I have no cigarettes—that is sad.

• • • • • • •

I worked with enthusiasm, lived in a state of elation. I liked to have people under my orders probably more than most people like it, particularly intellectuals, who are fond of ordering about but do not know how to do it. No matter what anyone may say, power over men gives one a great satisfaction. To compel a man to think and behave as you want does not at all mean to hide behind him, no, it has a value in itself, as the expression of your own personal ascendance, your own importance. It inspires admiration. . . . And had I not loved power, I would not have been considered as a remarkable organizer.

When I was arrested for the first time, I felt like a hero and went to face the questioning as one goes to fight a bear singlehanded. I am not an expert in suffering and have never gone through much of it in prisons, barring, of course, the usual discomforts of prison life. No freedom? Prison gave me the freedom to read and learn. Apart from that, prison gives a revolutionary something equal to a general's rank, surrounds him with a halo, and one should know how to avail oneself of this when one has to do with people whom one is pushing against their will towards freedom.

The servant of my class enemies, the colonel of the gendarmerie, turned out to be a good-natured, red-nosed, corpulent man, probably a drunkard. He welcomed me with a smile and words which I did not expect, indeed, from an enemy.

"Peter Karazin, alias Karamora? Oho, you're a fine fellow. You'd make an excellent dragoon."

I had been prepared to talk to him sternly and contemptuously, but very soon realized that this would have been ridiculous. Not that he made me relent in any way, but I suddenly became aware that I was facing a sparrow on whom only an idiot or a coward would have opened fire from a gun. When I declared to him calmly and politely that I refused to give any evidence, he wrinkled up his nose and grunted: "Of course, of course. That's what you all do, nowadays. Well—it means a little stay in prison. Hm . . . youngsters that you are . . ."

It almost seemed that the colonel was pleased with my irrevocable decision. It did not occur to me that he might be wanting to hurry off to his dinner and that this was the reason why all had been settled so smoothly and briskly between us. It is possible that it would have been better for me if I had come across another type of man, a regular beast in uniform, a person of determined opinion, in one word, not an official, but an enemy. Life is so queerly arranged that a man's best teacher is his enemy.

However, although since 1905 I have been in prison three times and have been questioned about ten times, I never happened to encounter a man who succeeded in rousing in me a feeling of hostility and hatred. They were all the commonest of officials, some of them quite decent people, too. I say that not in order to irritate my orthodox friends, but to state a fact, perhaps an accidental one. Thin, sallow Colonel Ossipov, dying of cancer, said as he announced my verdict to me:

"You are lucky—your verdict is a light one. You deserve greater punishment, for you are a very dangerous man."

These words sounded to me like praise, although he was uttering them with regret and astonishment.

He was a man of intelligence, with a good understanding of human nature, and one day he embarrassed me with a remark which he need not have made: at the last interrogation he said, watching me through his glasses:

"In my opinion, Karazin, you are either playing the fool or simply have made a mistake and are doing the wrong job."

This offended me greatly. Here I lost my temper and became impudent, but he stopped me short:

"I had no desire to hurt you at all, I was just giving you my opinion, as man to man. You are playing a dangerous game and it seems to me that you are not violent enough for a revolutionary and—forgive me!—too clever."

I believe that Ossipov was an honorable man, besides, all the men who had been in his hands testified to this.

One day the son of my landlady, a schoolboy and a pupil of mine, was arrested together with me. I gave my word of honor to Ossipov that he was in no way involved in my activities, begged that he be released and not expelled from school.

"Very well, I will do it," said Ossipov, and gave the order for his release then and there. When I thanked him for it, he explained:

"But, my good man, it is in our interest to diminish, not to increase the number of rebels such as you are, whereas it would have been in your interest to leave the boy in prison, thoroughly embitter him and so on. . . ." With these words he seemed to teach me a lesson of revolutionary behavior. So I said to him: "Thank you for the lesson."

Probably he, too, had a dual personality. People are divided, of course, into those who work and those who live on the work of others—the proletariat and the bourgeoisie. But that is an external division, internally in all classes they are divided into people with whole and split personalities. The first always remind one of oxen—one can't help being bored by them. I believe that being of one piece is the result of self-limitation for the sake of self-defense. Darwin is of that opinion too, apparently. A man lands in a situation in which some characteristics of his ego are not only superfluous but dangerous for him—his internal or external enemies might take advantage of them. So the man consciously squashes, destroys in himself the superfluous, and thus acquires the "wholeness." For instance: why in the world does a revolutionary want compassion, lyrics, sentimentality, romanticism and all that? All a revolutionary needs is enthusiasm and belief in himself. All interest in the variety of life is definitely a danger to him. It is as easy to get entangled in it as for a child to get lost in a thicket of brambles.

The life of a split person resembles the flight of a swallow. No doubt the man of one piece is from a practical point of view a more useful one—but the second type is more sympathetic to me. A complex man is more interesting. Life is ornamented by useless objects. I have never yet met the idiots who would want to decorate their houses with hammers, screws or bicycles. Although I did know one rich corn merchant who had collected more than five hundred locks and hung them about in two large rooms on red cloth shields. But his locks were so ingenious that I as an hereditary locksmith took great pleasure in examining them. And they were all useless, of course. I am fond of technical tricks, whatever shape they take, as much as I am fond of every play of the human mind.

. . . . . .

One talks so much about "Christian culture." Why lie? How the deuce is it Christian? Where is the simplicity in this culture of ours? There is no evangelical simplicity anywhere. People have bred cunning, evil thoughts and scattered them over the world like a pack of mad dogs. The fools.

. . . . . .

Towards 1908 the strongest men in the revolution had been destroyed. Some of the workmen had gone to Siberia, others, with fear in their hearts, adorned themselves in the pelt of indifference. With time these pelts grew on to their bodies. Others in the desire to "live pleasurably" turned into bandits; "living pleasurably" is always linked directly or indirectly with banditry. Particular dexterity and speed in avoiding the retribution dealt out by the victors was shown by our comrades of the intelligentsia. A filthy time it was indeed. Even people who had proved to be made of the stuff of heroes turned to meanness.

But it is better not to write or think of these times. I do not wish to seem to be hinting: the times were such that . . .

No, I do not want to find excuses. I have my own line, my own aim. A Tartar friend of mine used to say:

"*Min din min—*"—I am I. Whatever I may be—I am I.

The conditions of the time played a large part in my life but only in that it placed me face to face with myself. I used to live, arming, so to say, for battle, and this engaged my strength to such a degree that I had no time to think: who am I? I used to be linked with others by the consciousness of mutual interests, political and economic, by party solidarity, discipline. Now I suddenly felt that these questions did not engross me altogether. I noticed that the solidarity of interests was a matter of doubt and that the laws of party discipline were not always written in the same print. . . . And at the same time I came up with a shock against the question: why were people so unstable, so shaky, why did they betray their cause and their faith with such ease? All this sounds as an excuse all the same. That is a foul trick. I believe it would be more truthful and honest to say simply: I used to work with love, exhilaration, self-denial, now I began to loiter about with my hands in my pockets, whistling, conscious of a reluctance to do any work at all. Not that I was tired and unable to go on—no, I just did not want to. I was bored. And not bored because it had become necessary once more to grab people by the scruff of their necks and drag them towards freedom on to a path abundantly sprinkled with blood—no, not because of that. I performed all these acts, grabbed and dragged and led, but more out of stubbornness, from a desire to prove something to someone, altogether out of other motives, not the old ones, but new ones, which were not clear even to myself. And unstable ones at that.

I was particularly sharply aware of this instability of purpose in my revolutionary work. The ideas were still there, but the energy that stimulated them seemed to demand other outlets. It is difficult to explain this state of quiet, but stubborn rebellion, which produced a slackness of thought and feelings and an obstinate desire for some new experience.

Maybe it was the revolt of the adventurer, the man accustomed to conspiracies, danger, the unknown. Maybe.

But to put it more simply, the fact was that previously I used to speak to people with words borrowed from books, and deafened by their sound I could not listen to the voice within me. Now I became aware that there lived inside me an unwelcome and unpleasant guest who followed my words closely and watched me with doubt and suspicion. I began to notice what had escaped my attention before, namely, that comrade Sasha, a doctor, specializing in children's diseases, was a very nice woman. She was small, plump, gay, her trim little figure had been circling about me for almost a year, her shapely legs flitting about in their blue stockings. She was particularly fond of blue: her blouses, ribbons, sunshades, the little boxes about the room, the pictures on the wall—all was blue. Even the whites of her eyes were blue, but the irises very dark, melting away in tender smiles.

She did not have a very sound grasp of politics, fiction formed most of her reading, she was not fond of serious books, in spite of a very fine native intelligence.

In 1906 when the uprising had been squashed and the gendarmes were destroying our organization and sending people to prison by dozens, Sasha astonished me by her calm attitude to the events. She arranged for me to hide in the house of her uncle, an officer, and as she left me there, shaking my hand in good-by, she said:

"Why do you neglect your nails so? And you have some dry soap in your ears."

I liked that. Afterwards I fell in love with her but kept silent about it. But she soon noticed it and came to my help—it all happened very simply, maybe even somewhat unashamedly. One evening I stopped to have tea with her and all of a sudden she asked me, almost angrily:

"Well, when are you going to make up your mind to tell me that you find me attractive?"

That was all. I had expected something different. It seemed to me that real love, like faith, must be naïve. In Sasha's simplicity I scented no naïveté. I remember that she did not even turn away from me as she undressed, and said boastfully as she stood naked in front of me:

"Don't you think I look nice?"

And thus we started an "affair," with immense pleasure but without joy. A business-like love-affair, so to say, and because one "cannot get on without it."

Comrade Popov—a new figure in the town—kept fussing round Sasha. Clean and well-fed, pink-cheeked and pug-nosed, with a red mustache, he peered into people's eyes with the glance of a devoted dog, stressing his readiness to serve, run and fetch. I was conscious in him of the curiosity of a puppy, rushing around unaware of danger, because of his youth. This curiosity roused courage in him, although he seemed to me to be a coward at heart. He had a talent for telling Jewish anecdotes, could recite a quantity of humorous verse and looked much more like a cabaret-singer or like a swindler, than like a serious revolutionary. There was, however, something charming in him, something brilliant, too. Bright sparks in his words, sharp little needles in his thoughts. I very soon noticed that Popov brought sweets to Sasha too often, bought books for her and, in one word, spent a lot of money in paying court to her. I asked her what she thought about that. She told me that he had a rich brother in Rostov—but this did not allay my apprehensions. Maybe I was slightly jealous, knowing that my wife's sexual curiosity as regards men was very highly developed. As to myself I was easily suspicious, lacked confidence in people, I lived in the period of "agents provocateurs." It began to dawn upon me that the gendarmes had grown better informed, since Popov had appeared in the town. I found him out in a very simple way: first in persuading one of the sympathizers among the intelligentsia of the town to submit to the unpleasantness of a house-search, then Popov was carefully informed that in the flat of the sympathizer, in the sofa of his study, was concealed something of great interest for the police. An hour later the police came to search the flat of the sympathizer, and, going through it in a cursory way, cut up and turned out the sofa very thoroughly. They found nothing, of course.

I was almost alone in the town apart from a small group of young workmen and a mentally unbalanced comrade who lived twenty kilometers away, on the farm of a Cossack friend of ours. I decided to settle with him immediately and single-handed.

Popov lived in the outskirts, in the attic of a house owned by a fruit-grower. He seemed depressed, one was aware of an inner disarray in him; he knew, of course, of the result of the search and probably realized that he was caught. He showed no pleasure in seeing me and declared he had been invited to some celebration at his landlord's —true, from below came the sound of the accordion, shouts and stamping.

In that attic of Popov's I spent the worst three or four hours of my life.

I asked him:

"How long have you been working for the police?"

Popov swayed, dropped some cigarettes, bent down under the table to pick them up, and from there said, stammering in a strange voice:

"S-silly k-kind of joke. . . ." But glancing up at me he slid from the chair to the floor and kneeling on one knee laughed hysterically, sniffling like a woman:

"Leave that. . . . Stop it. . . ." he muttered, watching the revolver in my hand. His mustache bristled, his face twitched, his eyes blinked, the one remained half closed, the other was motionless like a blind man's. I lifted him by his hair, made him sit down, and suggested that he tell the story of his exploits. And I saw opposite me a man who literally had no face left: the face was replaced by a gray mass of jelly and in that jelly trembled two horribly staring eyes. The underlip hung like a bloodless piece of flesh, the chin twitched, wrinkles ran up the cheeks— it seemed that the whole head was decomposing, rotting and about to pour down the chest in a stream of gray mud. And as if to strengthen this impression Popov pressed his hands to his temples, shut his ears.

He told a rather common tale. He had been in the party since 1903, twice in prison, participated in an armed revolt in 1908, had been arrested in the street. He hiccoughed as he went on with the story:

"I really participated, I even fired, killed somebody, I swear it. I am certain of it, he fell. I was threatened with the gallows. But—one wants to live, doesn't one? We're there—to live, a man is there to live, isn't he? Think of it only: life is there for me—not I for life—isn't that so?"

He whispered all this very convincingly, whispered, and asked:

"Yes, yes, isn't that so?"

With one hand he kept scratching his knee, with the other crumpling a bit of paper. I snatched it away from him and read my own name on it, Sasha's and the following sentence: "It would be premature to liquidate Karazin, more useful and convenient to do it in Ekaterinoslav, where he will soon be going."

I was aware that Popov's story did not shock me, what shocked me was his philosophy. And the devil himself seemed to prompt him to absurd words which instantly hardened my heart.

"Did your conscience never disturb you?" I asked.

"Oh, yes, it did," he sighed deeply. "It is terrifying at first. One feels everyone is suspecting the truth. Then, gradually, one gets used to it. Maybe you think the police's job is an easy one? Not so," said Popov; "there, too, one needs to be heroic. They've got their heroes as well, oh, yes! In a struggle there should be heroes on both sides!"

And lowering his voice, with a mean, cunning smile he added:

"It is quite thrilling, working there, perhaps even more so than with us. There are more of us, fewer of them. . . ."

I could see that his fear was fading away, vanishing. He got quite excited as he went on, telling his story very vividly with a number of anecdotes, sometimes quite amusing ones. I believe that quite often I had to conquer the desire to smile, and thought that this calf turned into a police-dog could have written interesting stories.

There was something naïve in his cynicism and I remember that it was this naïveté which rendered me most fierce—rendered me fierce and frightened me at the same time. I experienced a curious feeling of being a stranger to myself. Finally the moment came when I, egging myself on to an unexpected decision, became uneasy.

"Well, Popov, write a note saying that no one is to blame for your death."

He was more astonished than frightened, and frowning, asked:

"What do you mean? Why? What death?"

I explained to him: if he did not write the note—I'd shoot him, if he did—he must hang himself at once in front of me. The first thing he said in reply was unexpected and absurd:

"Suicide? No one will believe that I committed suicide, no one! They'll know at once over there that I've been killed. And of course it will be you. You. Who else but you? They know over there that you are almost alone here . . . And—what right have you to judge, to punish, alone as you are?"

He dragged himself on the floor, catching at my feet, cried and moaned, and I had to press my hand to his horrid slavering mouth.

"No," he cried, imploringly, in a whisper, "you must judge me. Try me, I must have a trial."

This fuss went on for a long time, I was expecting the people downstairs to hear the noise and come to find out what it was. But the accordion became more and more lively, and more and more fierce the shouting and stamping. Popov hanged himself on the stove—I held his hands while he kicked about with his legs and loudly let out wind.

I'll stop writing. What on earth is it for? What on earth?

. . . .

No, writing is an entrancing occupation. As one writes, one feels that one is not alone in the world, that there is someone who is fond of one, towards whom one has never been guilty of anything, who understands one well and sympathizes without humiliating. One feels as one writes how much cleverer and better one becomes. It is an intoxicating job. It makes one understand Dostoevsky. He was a writer particularly inclined to intoxicate himself with the mad, stormy, irrational game of his imagination, a game played within himself. I used to read him with mistrust:

it seemed to me that he exaggerated, terrifying people by the darkness of a human soul, then, in order that they should admit the necessity of God, that they should submit humbly to His unaccountable devices, His unfathomable will: "Surrender, be meek, proud man!"—he said. If this meekness was necessary to Dostoevsky—it was so only among other things and not primarily. He was first and foremost preoccupied with himself—*min din min*. He knew how to let himself be consumed, how to press out the burning, scorching juice from his soul to the last drop. Has a writer ever been known to die at his desk, over a page of unwritten paper? I should have thought so. Having written, exhausted himself to the very end, to the last spark of life—he vanishes. Pity I never tried that intoxicating job before.

. . . .

Well, I will now go on writing about the things that puzzled me.

I walked out of the town, the night was clear and cold, the road was framed by a line of dark trees. I sat down under a tree in the shade and remained there until dawn, until one could hear the creaking of peasants' carts. I felt ill, there was a dumb emptiness in my heart, a vague flatness in my whole body. I was waiting for something to flare up and glow within me. When Popov died—my indignation died as well. A voice whispered to me—you have killed a man. But I realized that this was a mere dry statement, it did not disturb me. The man had been a traitor. I did not feel like a criminal.

But then, from some depths, a disturbing question suddenly faced me: why, actually, had I forced Popov to strangle himself, so unexpectedly to myself, so hurriedly, as though something had frightened me—not in him, but in myself? As though I were destroying not a criminal, but a witness dangerous to me and not because he was a traitor, but for some other reason? His words kept turning over in my brain: "If there is a struggle—there should be heroes on both sides." All his cynical little thoughts went on haunting me, queerly familiar, as though I had known and heard of them long ago.

Like flies a number of questions pestered me: how did Popov behave with the police? Did he entertain them with funny anecdotes and ditties? Maybe he even laughed with them at my expense? But what preoccupied me mostly was the hurriedness, the headlong speed with which I had acted, forcing Popov to kill himself.

In this state of estrangement towards myself, in a semi-dream, I was arrested the next day.

The head of the Police Department Simonov said to me in a husky voice, in a pompous and offended tone:

"Look here, Karazin, although Popenko declares that no one is guilty of his death, he was found actually in so unseemly a condition and the wrists of his hands bear such strange marks that it is obvious that he has been hanged and did not hang himself. On the night of his death you stayed with him until after midnight, this has been established. And it coincides perfectly with the moment of Popenko's death. Furthermore: dactyloscopic investigation will confirm that the fingerprints on the glass ashtray were yours. I understand very well of course what it was that you found out about Popenko, he himself had guessed as much. He has been a useful man to us. You will have to pay for his death in the same manner. Besides—there is some foundation for charging you with murder in a fit of jealousy; Alexandra Varvarina will have to be brought into this—do you see?"

I listened in silence. I will not say that I was frightened, but the threat of prosecution on a non-political charge was, of course, unpleasant. Sasha, implicated in a crime of passion? No. That was absurd enough to be almost funny.

Simonov, standing amidst clouds of smoke, went on in a business-like manner: "I suggest that you take Popenko's place. If you agree to this—you will immediately point out to us a number of people whom it would be useful for us to get rid of. It will then appear that Popenko betrayed his friends and committed suicide out of remorse, whereas you will escape death, not to mention that you might lay the foundation for a fine career. Now I will leave you alone for an hour or two to think it all over. I don't advise you to linger too long."

Leaving me and shutting the door of the small cell, Simonov added:

"You have no other way out."

I remember well that the noose flung around my neck did not terrify me, although I knew that the game had been lost irretrievably. I believe that I did not waste a minute in hesitating as to which decision to make. I had made it the moment I heard Simonov say: "Take the place of Popenko." I recollect well that I was myself surprised at the ease and speed with which this resolution was taken—it occurred as naturally and simply as arises the desire to sleep, to take a walk, to get a drink of water. I sat in the dark little room, listened to the rain pattering at the window and hearkened to a voice within me that should have protested against my decision. Nothing protested.

"What did it mean? Where did this calmness come from, what did it signify? Why do I not feel the same repugnance towards myself as I felt yesterday towards Popenko? I repeated mentally all the words which are used to describe traitors, remembered all that had been said in print and otherwise about them, nothing seemed to touch or perturb me. It looked as though the man who had only yesterday forced a fellow-creature to commit suicide and today resolved to destroy many other lives, had hidden somewhere, while the other one, puzzled, waited to hear him say something, wanted to learn something about him, was searching for the criminal—and did not find him. There was no criminal. Then shadows of thoughts motivated by curiosity stirred lazily in the brain and queried:

"Am I really going to work for the police and betray my friends to policemen?"

No answer came to that, while the curiosity became sharper and more pressing. I clearly recollect that the prevalent feeling in me in these hours was the feeling of curiosity and astonishment that I felt nothing but that. In this state of mind, that of a man puzzled and curious about himself, I confronted Simonov.

"A wise decision," he said, having listened to me, and then started to explain with a certain preoccupation, how futile it had been on my part to have caused so much fuss about that clown Popenko.

"The criminal police has got involved in it. Well, well, we'll arrange all that. According to the rules you'll have to sign this little paper."

Unexpectedly to myself I asked: "What do you think—that I just funked it?"

Simonov did not reply at once, he first lit a cigarette from the end of the old one.

"No, *that* I do not think. You can believe me. But this isn't the moment to talk of it."

In spite of that we talked for a long time, about an hour or more, standing in front of each other. I gathered such a queer impression from that talk: with some sharp angle of my brain I understood that Simonov was surprised at the ease and rapidity of my resolution no less than I was myself, that he did not trust me, that my calmness annoyed him, puzzled him just as it did me; also I felt that he wanted to frighten me in some way, but understood that nothing was able to frighten me. It seemed to me that all he said was to no purpose. Also without any purpose he suddenly informed me that Colonel Ossipov had always expressed admiration of my sharp and independent intelligence. I asked: "Is he alive?"

"No, he died. He was a fine man."

"Yes," I agreed.

Simonov waved away the smoke from his face with a sharp gesture of the hand and added firmly:

"A dreamer, he was. What one calls—a romanticist."

"Yes, yes," I agreed again, and said that Popenko had actually hanged himself with his own hands, although at my instigation, of course. Simonov shrugged his shoulders:

"Let it be so."

All this was unbelievable, and at the same time it was actually happening, I clearly realized with my brain that it was all true. But my brain, watching it all at a distance, kept silent, prompting nothing, just giving way to curiosity. "So, Karamora," I said to myself, "right about face!"

I was still expecting, I think, that someone would cry out:

"Stop. Where are you going?"

But no one raised a voice.

. . . .

In the beginning—the first month or two—Simonov alone stood out among all the improbable facts as the one firm reality.

He was a man in the fifties, of middle height and stocky build. His gray hair was cut short. He had an indefinitely shaped "Russian" nose, soft, slightly reddish, a small inconspicuous mustache, light eyes, glancing at the world calmly, even a trifle sleepily. There are many people of that appearance. One meets them often, they are to be found in every profession, working in innumerable institutions, living on every street, in every town. I used to look upon them as the commonest of types. And it was precisely this commonness of his appearance which lent Simonov in my eyes the peculiar character of reality in all the improbable atmosphere in which I lived and in the midst of the unusual work which I performed. All that he said revealed the attitude of the official already familiar to me, the official to whom the fundamental and final aims of his work are either incomprehensible or alien. Badly informed in questions of history and politics, he was completely indifferent to the interests of the monarchy, of the Czar, to all that he was called to protect, and he indicted the bourgeoisie with particular gusto.

I asked him why he had undertaken so troublesome a job.

"Obviously, because of the pleasure it causes me," he said in his low, husky voice, tapping his cigarette-holder against the lid of his cigarette case, and smiling with a lazy, slightly forced smile, he continued:

"You are a revolutionary for your own pleasure. I—for mine—enter into a combat with you, try to catch you, succeed in doing so. And then I suggest: let's hunt together! That's all to the good. I find my work still more interesting because of it."

For the first time on that occasion I vaguely felt that there was something wrong, something treacherous in him, and soon I became convinced that under a common appearance this man concealed thoughts of an unusual character, or, maybe, they were the usual thoughts of the man-in-the-street, in an extreme form.

I tried to talk to him of all the inequality existing in the world; this, it is affirmed, is the main source of all the miseries of life. In answer he shrugged his shoulders, blew out clouds of smoke, and replied calmly:

"What have *I* to do with it? *I* didn't arrange the world

that way and I don't care. Neither should you care. You've been messed about with by the intelligentsia. You read the wrong books. You ought to read Brehm's *Life of Animals.*"

A cigarette always stuck between his teeth, his face buried in a cloud of smoke, he half closed his eyes, stared at the ceiling and said with a drawl:

"There's no greater joy than to make a fool of a person, get the better of him. Remember your games as a child and follow them up through your life: rounders and aunt Sally, then the games with the girls, games of cards—all one's life is a game. Among you fellows there are also quite a number who play a game with yourselves."

With these words he reminded me of the party struggle, the joy I experienced when I was able to "outwit" my comrades.

"Playing a game and hunting—these are the ideal occupations! If I had had money, I would have gone to Siberia, into the *taiga,* bear-killing. Or to Africa, perhaps. A great thing, hunting. And the fun is not in the killing, it's in the tracking, keeping the animal at the end of your gun and feeling in these moments your human power over it. One kills only out of need, nobody kills for pleasure, only maniacs, or people in a state of fury, but then fury is mania again. That's why murder is mean, because it's never quite disinterested."

I did not believe him much as I listened to him, but I thought to myself:

"Well, if life is controlled by gamblers and hunters—what is there to prevent me from gambling with them and with myself?"

There was in Simonov's mind a dark stain, a mental dislocation, a hardened spot, a callus.

"Games-and-hunting," he said, bringing all his life down to these occupations, but I did not believe him any more, knowing how well people build up barricades to protect themselves from life, in order to explain their reluctance to work for it.

One night we were sitting in a secret lodging, drinking wine and Simonov said:

"I once came across an intellectual—you know, one of those who wander about like ghosts—and he preached to me that man is a beast, gone mad, who had risen on his hind legs and that this started things going as they do in the world, at present. Of course—the man was a madman himself, but it isn't a bad idea. 'History,' he said, 'is the medical treatment of the wild beast.' You know, I have thought a lot about that—it's an idea worthy of consideration. I can't even help believing that if it were possible all honest and decent people would definitely refuse to participate in the history of mankind. But how to refuse? Where to escape? Even hermits and monks get unavoidably involved in all this general round-about."

Simonov considered himself to be a "decent" man, although, in a shady job, he obviously played a shady part. But to remind him of it, to point it out, was wasting time.

"But why—that is childish of you, my dear fellow," he would say. And then add:

"My God, what a mess the intelligentsia have made of you."

There was something in his attitude to me which won me over. It was the interest in a man taken as a whole, in his entirety, a pure interest, so to say. It existed outside the official and calculating attitude, was quite separate and independent, as an interest in a man in general. Simonov did not treat me as a chief treats his subaltern, but as an elder man a younger one. He did not command, did not issue orders, but suggested and even advised:

"What do you think, should we make away with this one?"

And if I considered that this was premature, he agreed with me without further argument.

He felt for me something which I would define as a certain solicitude. Perhaps it was the same feeling of love and care which the hunter feels for a good dog. I say it without irony or bitterness, I know the clever proverb:

> The loveliest girl can only give what she has.

This proverb silences very effectively the cry of the soul.

. . . . . .

It so happened that I had not a single friend among the crowd of comrades. Not a man with whom I would have been able to talk of the most essential subject—myself. I often tried to broach it, of course, but these conversations were not a success. They did not satisfy me somehow. Not all the gaps in the soul can be stopped up with a book, besides there are books which widen and deepen these gaps very viciously. The people who are able to see that everything in this world has its shadow and that all truths and ideas are also not deprived of this appendage—a useless one, indeed—these people, alas, are rare. The shadows rouse doubts as to the purity of the truths, and doubts, although they are not exactly forbidden, are considered shameful, unreliable so to say. A man in doubt always arouses suspicion—this I would consider as the only truth without a shadow. Among the comrades I had the reputation of a man of unsteady ideology, capricious and—worst of all—inclined to romanticism, "metaphysics," as Basov called it—this was the man of whom I saw more than of the rest.

"A revolutionary has to be a materialist—materialism is an expression of will—completely purified from everything unreasonable, irrational," Basov said, rolling his r's. I knew he was right, but out of hostility to him I did not agree.

Simonov was a man with whom one could talk of everything. He listened with attention and was never embarrassed to admit that he did not understand this, did not know the other; sometimes he even frankly announced:

"There is no need for me to know this."

To my astonishment one of the things he did not need to know was God. I say to my astonishment, because I had believed him to be religious.

"Strange that you should ask me about it," he said, shrugging his shoulders. "What can one feel about God when we each have fourteen meters of guts in our bellies? Also—if there is a God, the camel, the perch and the pig should be aware of it too—don't you see? A man is an animal as well. A reasonable one? Well, there are plenty of reasonable animals except man, besides it has been proved that reason has nothing to do with it—God is not grasped by reason. So what about it?—You really ought to read Brehm."

He was surprised:

"What a mess the intellectuals have made of you."

"Well, and if they had not, what do you think would have become of me?"

He glanced at me significantly and said:

"I—I wonder. An inventor of some kind, maybe? I don't know. You're a very queer person."

On the whole Simonov was a man devoid of vitality, disconnected somehow and probably very lonely. Although talkative, he was sparing of gesture, his arms moved slowly, he laughed rarely, and one felt he was indifferent both to life and to people. Also he was lazy, possibly because of a great weariness. I very soon became convinced that all that he said of the joys of hunting, of gambling, was invented for his own use, and based on hearsay, and repeated as a subterfuge. The hunt after human beings did not exhilarate him. He had assistants in the shape of agents provocateurs; this satisfied him completely and he hardly ever showed any personal initiative in his work. Had I actually wanted it, I need never have done anything, just gone on telling Simonov anecdotes from party life, from the life of revolutionaries. The anecdotal side of the revolution interested him, I should say, more than the essence of it. He always listened attentively to anecdotes, and the sillier the anecdote the wider the smile it produced on the depressingly colorless face of Simonov. One day he remarked with a sigh:

"Popenko told these stories in a funnier way than you do. He spoke like Brehm."

"Like Brehm" was the highest praise on his lips. He was always reading the *Life of Animals*, as a German Mennonite *The Bible*.

One day I asked him:

"Why do you call Popov—Popenko?"

"That is how I see him," he replied. "Each man sees differently. Popov should be taller—and his arms longer too."

Simonov had one trait or habit that aroused an unpleasant and suspicious feeling in me: at times, in the middle of a discussion, he suddenly seemed to drop into an abyss and this was very puzzling indeed. On his characterless face appeared a pompous but stupid grimace, the pupils of his eyes grew absurdly dilated, he looked at me with stern concentration, like a hypnotizer, but I felt he saw something else, something almost terrifying. At the same time he hid his hands under the table and moved them about there, giving me the impression that he was getting hold of a revolver to shoot me. These sudden fits of dumb meditation, disappearances into the unknown and unfathomable, were very frequent with him and I always felt uneasy when they happened.

Afterwards I began to think that something considerable, mysterious, was concealed in Simonov, so human that he was afraid of it. I waited for him to reveal it to me and my interest in him became tense and expectant.

There are various theories of goodness: the Scriptures, the Koran, the Talmud, various other books. There must also be a theory of meanness, of evil. There surely *must* be such a theory. Everything *must* be explained, everything, otherwise—how can one live?

. . . .

Yesterday I wrote:
"Had I wanted it, I need not have done anything," that is, that I need not have given away any of my friends. More than that. I might have easily been doing something useful for them. I did do so, but having done it, I felt that I had no need for it and that it changed nothing within me.

I gave them away. Why? I put that question to myself from the first day of my work with the police but I could find no answer. I was waiting all the time for a protest to stir within me, for my "conscience to speak," but it remained silent. Only my curiosity was astir, it kept querying: "Well, what is going to happen next?"

I whipped myself up, trying to awaken a guilty reaction, which would declare resolutely: "You are a criminal."

I realized with my brain that I was behaving in a low manner, but this realization was not confirmed by an appropriate feeling of self-chastisement, repugnance, remorse, nor even fear. No, I felt nothing of all that, nothing except curiosity, this curiosity became more and more corrosive and almost restless, bringing forward questions like: "Why is the passage from heroic gestures to meanness so easy?"

Was that little cad Popov right when he said: "If there is to be a struggle there should be heroes on both sides." I had been a "hero" in the past, now I was merely a man forced, compelled, to solve a dark problem: why, in acting meanly, do I feel nothing repulsive about it? I put this question to myself from every possible angle.

Then it occurred to me: what if Simonov were right and life were just a matter concerning a wild beast, everything in it but a game, and I have been played havoc with by intellectuals, books? What if all these "teachers of life," socialists, humanists, moralists, are lying, and there is no such thing as a social conscience, the link between people is a mere fallacy, and nothing exists but men trying to live at each other's expense. And this will go on forever?

There is nothing else, everything is imagination and lies, and I am called to disclose these lies, I must announce to mankind that it is being betrayed, that life is a naked struggle of beasts and there is no point in controlling, besides there is nothing with which to control, this struggle. I am the first to discover that a man is powerless to protest against the meanness in himself and there is no reason that he should do so—for it is a legitimate and effective weapon in this mutual struggle.

There exists a wicked fairy-tale: a crowd of people are unanimously admiring the beauty and richness of their emperor's attire, when an urchin cries out:

"Why, the emperor is naked!"

And then they all see: yes, indeed, the emperor is naked and hideous.

Am I to play the part of the penetrating urchin?

These thoughts obsessed me particularly in the year 1914 when the infamous war broke out and everything human dropped from men like the scales from rotten fish.

. . . .

Reading over all that I have written, I see that it is not what it should be, the story is not told correctly. I have pictured myself as a man who has got entangled in thoughts, sprained his soul with philosophy, destroyed in it the human element, all that is considered as being kind and good. No, that is not the case, it is not so.

Thoughts, in spite of their abundance, never confused my mind or lured me. They appear to me as bubbles on the boiling surface of feelings—the bubbles come up, burst, vanish, others come in their place. Only such thoughts are vital and effective as are loaded with feeling; when they are that, I become physically aware of them, they act like fingers, seizing, picking up and transplanting facts, molding, and building up, then, fertilized by more feelings, they in their turn give birth to new ones. Without this fertilization, thought plays about with man like a prostitute, unable to change anything in him. Of course one can also love a prostitute quite sincerely, but it is more natural to treat her with a certain caution—she might rob or contaminate one.

For nineteen years I lived among people of uniform ways of thinking, in an atmosphere of uniform-colored ideas. Their particular shade did not satisfy me, seemed dull and joyless like a gray autumn day.

But I well saw that these people were so strongly pulled up by their beloved idea precisely because it filled all their being, penetrated into their flesh and blood. It was not a bubble but a closely pressed fist, relying on its strength.

In the years 1907 and 1914, observing how easily people gave up their beliefs, I became aware that something was lacking in them, something which they had always lacked. What was it? A physical fastidiousness in regard to something that their mind repudiated? Or the habit of living honestly?

Here, it seems to me, I have struck upon something true: the habit of living honestly is something which people lack. My comrades lacked it, too. Their life contradicted their convictions, principles—the dogmas of faith. This contradiction was particularly strongly revealed in the methods of party life, in the struggle with people of the same faith, but of different tactics. Here the most shameful type of Jesuitry took place, crooked tricks were admitted, even the mean little methods of gamblers, exhilarated by the game to the limit of consciousness, playing only for the sake of the game.

Yes, yes, that is so—men lack the habit of living honestly. I know, of course, that most of them did not have and still have not got the chance of developing this habit. But those whose aim is to rebuild life, re-educate mankind, are mistaken if they believe that all means are allowed in a struggle. No, with a dogma like that one will not succeed in teaching people to live honestly.

· · · · · ·

Maybe, on the other hand, the time has come to commit all the meannesses, all the crimes, make use of all the evil in the world in order that one should have one's fill of it, at last, and turn away from it in horror and disgust. It is curious that I cannot help linking myself up with something or someone, men or events. I cannot help it and therefore all I say looks like an attempt to plead innocent, an attempt which I conceal but clumsily.

Nevertheless I know I have not the least desire to find excuses for myself. This is not out of pride, or out of the despair of a man who has irrevocably messed up his life. Nor is it because I should like to cry out: yes, I am a criminal, but so are you, only that you are stronger, so go on and do your killing. I feel no urge to cry out, there is nobody to cry out to. I have no need of people, no feeling for them. All these unconscious attempts of justification prevent me from discovering the chief thing I am searching for: why was it that there was no sound, no cry, no shriek in my soul, nothing that stopped me on the way to treason? And why am I unable to condemn myself? Why, although I label myself a criminal, consider myself as being one, I do not, in truth, feel the burden of the crime?

If my notes have any purpose it is only this one—to solve the question: what is it that has split me in two so finally and irretrievably? I have already said how mercilessly I strained myself to find an answer. I betrayed to the police and sent to hard labor one of my best friends, a man of rare moral integrity. I had a great respect for his character, his indefatigable spirit, his energy, his good-humor and his merry disposition. He had just escaped from prison and gone into hiding for the third time. I betrayed him and waited for something to stir in my soul.

Nothing did.

. . . .

Simonov treated me to a claret of a remarkable flavor and bouquet, and talked.

"Would you like to be transferred to Moscow or Petersburg? These waters here are becoming too shallow for you. I, too, will probably soon be transferred to one of these cities.

"Piotr Filippovich," I asked, "how do you explain to yourself that I am trying so hard to do my work well?"

As usual he did not answer at once, glanced attentively first at me, then at the ceiling, and shrugged his shoulders: "I don't know. You're not greedy for money—I cannot see much ambition in you. Out of a sense of revenge? Doesn't look like it. You've got a soft heart on the whole, you know." He smiled and continued, weighing his words well: "It isn't the first time you ask me about it and I have already told you—you are a queer fish. Are you a bit crazy, by any chance? Doesn't look like it, either. What about yourself—do you know your own reasons?"

I then tried to tell him briefly about myself. He listened to me attentively, listened and smoked one cigarette after the other. When I had finished, Simonov said calmly:

"Well, you know, this is almost dangerous. Faugh, how this bloody intelligentsia has mauled you about!" And lighting a fresh cigarette, he sighed: "If you go on like that you might even try and shoot me. What else is there left for you to do? Only one thing: kill someone. *That* might stir you up and make you shout."

He got up, poured some wine into a glass and lifted it to the light, his back turned to me. An annoyingly plain man he seemed at that moment, more so than ever before. He stood like that for a long time before I guessed that he was having one of his usual fits, the disappearances into the unknown.

"What is the matter?" I asked.

He turned round slowly, sat down, sipped at the wine, sighed and lit another cigarette:

"You've made it all up, my dear fellow, all this mental stuff," he said. "Made it all up, yes! Just for the fun of it. I know it, I do it myself. I go to bed and if I can't sleep, I picture myself at times as a desperate scoundrel, at other times as a saint. It's quite funny. And oftener still as a conjurer, a remarkable, eccentric conjurer." And suddenly, leaning on the table, more animated than I had ever seen him before, Simonov went on with his story in his hoarse little voice: "As a remarkable conjurer I see myself, I do. First I come out on the stage in tights—do you see? Like an acrobat. No pockets." He smiled the smile of a happy man, gave me an absurd wink: "Suddenly there is a duck in my hands. I put it down on the floor, it walks about the stage, quacks and lays eggs. D'you see? It lays an egg and a sucking pig comes out of it, it lays another and it is a hare, another—an owl and so on, ten eggs. You can imagine the reaction of the audience, eh? They all stand up in their seats, rub their eyes, peer through their glasses—general amazement! They all feel like fools, the deputy governor especially—and do you think it's any fun for the deputy governor to feel like a fool in front of all the others? Then suddenly—I grow a second head! I light a cigar—instantly there are two of them—but they let out no smoke, the smoke comes from under my toes— see? Meanwhile the hare jumps about, so does the pig, the owl stares at the audience with wide open eyes, dazzled by the footlights, the other animals dash about, they grow in number all the time—what a circus!" And opening wide his colorless eyes, the head of the Police Department, Piotr Filippovich Simonov, fighter against the revolution, said with deep conviction, almost with relish: "By Jove, how one can take in people! By Jove, one can."

Listening to his absurd divagations, I felt like an idiot. He was not drunk; he drank a good deal, but was never intoxicated.

I asked him:

"So this is what you think of, when you seem to drop off to sleep amidst a discussion, as though vanishing somewhere?"

"Yes," he said with a nod. "It comes upon me quite suddenly. One day while making a report in the Police Department it suddenly occurred to me that I could write my name in characters of fire in the air. And what do you think? I began to write and it came off. Letters of fire burning in front of the Head of the Department: Simonov, Simonov. . . . I stared at him and wondered: couldn't he see them? And then he asked me: 'What is the matter? Are you ill?' Frightened, of course, he was."

Mild insanity shone in Simonov's eyes and his face acquired from that an importance, a significance. With a vague hope in my heart, I asked:

"Is that all you have to say?"

He asked me in return: "What do you mean?"

He died in a curious manner: we had been sitting talking for two hours, in the night, he was feeling perfectly well, and at four o'clock in the afternoon he died in a hammock in the garden.

· · · · · · ·

Comrade Basov has been here and he brought with him a red-haired man with his head bandaged up. "You don't recognize me, Karamora?" he asked. He proved to be one of the three men whose escape from prison I had organized. I did not remember him.

Basov asked whether I had been already serving in the police when I organized that escape? A stupid question. By the Police documents he should have known that I had been. They talked with me for half an hour in the tone of righteous judges—as one might have expected them to do—and went.

Possibly they will let me live. It is interesting to know what I shall do with my life. That is another question: is life given into a man's power or is man given up to be consumed by life?—And whose idea is it anyway—life? A bad idea, on the whole.

Yes, working for the police I allowed myself the luxury of planning little pleasures for my comrades: escapes from prison, from exile, organizing printing offices and arranging for the storage of propaganda literature. But I played this double game not in order to give them up to the police after establishing myself in their confidence; no, it was just for the sake of variety. I often helped out of a feeling of friendship, but chiefly out of curiosity—what now?

· · · · · · ·

It has been said that there is a certain crystal in the eye and that it is that crystal which actually regulates the sight. One ought to insert such a crystal into the soul of a man. But it is lacking there. It is lacking, that is what is wrong about it all.

· · · · · · ·

The habit of living honestly? It is the habit of feeling truthfully, and that is possible only on condition that there be complete freedom to reveal such feelings, but this freedom in its turn makes a scoundrel or a beast out of a man, if he has not arranged before to be born a saint. Or with a blind soul. Maybe blindness is saintliness itself?

. . . .

I have not written everything and what I have written is not all it should be. But I do not want to write any more.

The prisoners are singing the "Internationale," the guard in the passage is humming the tune softly in accompaniment. We used to have a propagandist in the committee, comrade Tassya Mironova, a remarkable girl. What a tender and at the same time what a resolute heart she had. I would not say that she was beautiful, but I have never seen anyone sweeter. Why did I suddenly remember her? I never gave *her* away to the police. The stream of thought. The uninterrupted stream of thought.

. . . .

And what if I really am that urchin, alone capable of seeing the truth?

The emperor is naked—can't you see it?

There they come again. I'm fed up with them.

1924.

NOTE ON THE TRANSLATIONS

THE versions of "Chelkash," and of "Twenty-Six Men and a Girl" are by Emily Jakowleff and Dora B. Montefiore, and first appeared in a collection of short stories under the imprint of Duckworth & Co., London, 1902. The translation of "Cain and Artyom" by A. S. Rappoport was first published in a volume entitled *The Individualists* (London, Maclaren & Co.). "Creatures That Once Were Men," "The Hermit," and "Karamora" have been translated by Baroness Moura Budberg. Much of the text has been revised by Avrahm Yarmolinsky, who is also responsible for the translation of the remaining pieces. So far as is known, "Red," "Evil-Doers," "Going Home," "Lullaby," "Karamora" and "The Hermit" have never been done into English before.

The Russian text followed throughout is that revised by Gorki for the edition of his collected works, which was issued simultaneously in Moscow and Berlin in the nineteen-twenties.

The year given after each story is the date of its first publication in the original.

Thanks are given here to Messrs. Duckworth & Company, of London, for permission to use their translations of "Chelkash" and of "Twenty-Six Men and a Girl."

THE PUBLISHERS.